INSIDE THE LABYRINTH

A BO LANDRY THRILLER

A NOVEL

BY

BOBBY DELAUGHTER

Cover design by Brandi Doane McCann, www.ebook-coverdesigns.com
Cover images licensed from Can Stock Photo, Inc./Zhuzhu;
Shutterstock.com/Kotin, Kuznechik, Tibor
Edited by Kate Stewart, www.EbookEditingServices.com
Formatted by IRONHORSE Formatting

ISBN: 1496119428
ISBN-13: 978-1496119421

To Peggy Ann, with all my love;
forever and under all circumstances.

Justice has but one form, evil has many.

Moses Ben Jacob Meir Ibn Ezra,
Spanish-Hebrew poet and philosopher, *c.1070-1130*

There are three all-powerful evils:
lust, anger, and greed.

Goswami Tulsidas, Hindu poet, *1532-1623*

AUTHOR'S NOTE/READER ADVISORY

Hell is said to be where Heaven isn't; yet wherever God has His church, the Devil will have his chapel, and recognizing the face of evil is not as easy as it may seem. Malevolence lurks behind many deceptive visages. Ted Bundy was charming, John Wayne Gacy a clown, and Dennis Rader an unassuming family man of America's heartland. All of them, however, were sexual predators, serial killers, modern-day Jack-the-Rippers. Although this book is a story of good as well as evil, of love as well as heartache, and is not without occasional humor, it also delves into the mind and atrocities of a vicious sexual predator; thus the reader is forewarned of the story's graphic violent and sexual content.

I have drawn extensively upon two primary guides on this journey into darkness. One is the collective non-fiction work of John E. Douglas, the former FBI profiler who probed the minds of Bundy, Gacy, Rader, and others like them. Additionally, I have drawn upon my own experience spanning decades in the criminal justice system. As a defense attorney, prosecutor, judge, and even as a prisoner, I too, have looked into evil's soulless eyes, heard its callous, taunting confessions, felt its icy chill. Welcome to a world of darkness that somehow flourishes in the plain sight of light.

PROLOGUE

Although eighteen years had passed since emerging from his mother's womb, he was not born in any meaningful way until tonight. Spring Break, South Padre Island, Texas. He had followed the young couple throughout the day, and was now watching them in the dark. He was waiting ever so patiently behind one of the dunes of the nude beach on the north end of the island. They were going at it something fierce - it should have been him with her instead of that clumsy oaf.

The voyeur first crossed paths with them that afternoon while walking along that same stretch of beach. The guy wore those little Speedo swim trunks, the girl a bikini, sans the top. She carried it in her hand, gleefully raising it to the breeze, transforming the cups into fluttering twin triangular pennants. Her long, auburn hair was carried, by a southerly gulf gale, across the face of the moron at her side. Beautiful legs, long and graceful, carried a goddess. Even her medium-sized, well-shaped breasts were evenly tanned.

As the voyeur drew closer, he fixed, not on her naked chest, but her eyes—green as emeralds and as sparkling as diamonds. Her hair again blew into her companion's face, but this time the visage that was revealed, as she brushed the stray tress aside, was not that of the moron, but rather, that of the voyeur. Cerebral neurons shifted into fantasy overdrive. It was him with her, on her, licking the salty ocean mist from almond areolas. The surreal experience of plunging into the depths of those incredible, liquid eyes was as blissful as her sweet moistness.

This vision, however, was shattered as the voyeur detected something quite disconcerting emanating from the captivating orbs. Mockery? The realization that she, and the moron, were actually laughing at him snapped the voyeur fully awake. Only then did he become aware of the

1

visible evidence of his arousal. Even after they passed, the couple kept turning, pointing, and giggling. Unforgivable.

It was not the first time he was the subject of ridicule, and the wages of such sin were always death. In the past, it was usually some poor animal that paid the price for the voyeur's tormentors. However, if he could not find a convenient, sacrificial beast, retribution could be extracted through a fiery blaze. He felt so much power watching the flames, feeling the heat, and blinding the world to his dark desires.

Neither creature nor conflagration would suffice this night. The monster within him had matured; it could be pent up no longer. Although the voyeur could not put a label on it, he sensed an intensified, rising presence of the beast within from the first sounds of the couple's obnoxious merriment. Thus, operating more from some raw, primal instinct, than a cognitive analysis, he had followed them at a safe distance.

Amid the dunes, near the bitch and moron, was a cache of scuba-diving paraphernalia and a cooler. "What do we do with all the gear?" the bitch asked, putting on her top.

"We'll come back this evening for a night dive, so just leave everything," the moron replied. "Except, of course, this," he added, picking up the cooler.

They drove away in a Jeep parked close by. Some time was lost walking to his own vehicle, but the voyeur easily picked up their trail. The Jeep was burnt-orange, with a Texas Longhorns bumper sticker. "Hook 'em Horns!" it read. *I'll hook you all right, moron.* They never noticed him; the bitch was preoccupied smiling and waving to all of the other idiots crowding the main drag, and the moron concentrated on the bottle of Lone Star beer he was nursing.

Driving to the south end of the island, they pulled into the Sheraton Resort parking lot. Walking to the building, they shouted to some other numskulls that they would meet them at Brady's at nine. Since the pub was on the opposite end of the island, near their hiding place, the voyeur guessed that it would be their last stop of the night before their planned dive. *Alcohol before diving? Definitely imbeciles.* Consequently, instead of following them the entire time, the voyeur decided to just be at Brady's before nine o'clock. Waiting for them at the dunes would have been even simpler, but the voyeur wanted to observe and study them.

Once at Brady's, he was tempted to have a Guinness, but it was important that all of his faculties and instincts remained razor-sharp so he opted for an O'Doul's. The voyeur had even shunned booze at Tequila Joe's, where he had spent the earlier part of the night watching all the drenching, bouncing cleavage at a wet T-shirt contest.

The bitch and her moron arrived at Brady's shortly after nine. *Punctual cretins.* Like any woman, she went straight to the can. By the time she returned, Prince Charming was holding a Lone Star with one hand, and groping a waitress's tush with the other. *Jeez, he was a moron with a capital M, who else drinks Lone Star in an Irish pub?*

"You're a real bastard, Dewayne! You know that?" After giving him the obligatory slap in the face, the bitch turned to leave.

"Where you going?" Dewayne asked.

"Out!"

Dewayne laughed. "Where? You don't have any wheels."

She gave him the finger as she made her exit.

"Colleen, get your ass back here. Nobody walks out on me!"

Colleen. Such a pretty Irish name, and although a bitch, I must admit that you are indeed a fine physical specimen. The voyeur made his way through the crowd outside to the deck, and spotted her walking north, along the beach, sandals in hand. Curious to see if ole Dewayne would go running after her, the voyeur did not immediately follow.

Instead, he re-entered the pub just in time to see Lover Boy pulling a wad of cash from his pants pocket to pay the waitress he had fondled. Dewayne did not realize that his Jeep key had come out with the cash and fallen to the floor, as the sound was muffled by the blaring music and partying patrons. He was holding a bottle of cheap wine in his other hand.

Just as the voyeur predicted, Dewayne scampered up the beach after Colleen like a dog in heat. The voyeur followed only long enough to satisfy himself that the lovers had made up. They continued their walk to the dunes for the night dive so immersed in reconciliation, they gave no apparent thought to the fact that they were leaving their vehicle behind.

Back in the parking lot at Brady's, the voyeur made sure that no one was around to notice before jumping behind the wheel of the Jeep. He turned the ignition with the key that he had retrieved from the pub floor. *Time to hook 'em horns! Well, almost.* Allowing them to make their dive had given him time to park the Jeep and, under cover of darkness, hunker down, undetected, in a spot very close to the couple's hideaway. He was there now, watching while he patiently waited.

After the dive, the couple stripped and passed the wine bottle back and forth, kissing and giggling between her sips and his gulps. Before long, the make-up sex was in full swing. As the voyeur ogled the scene, his senses escalated to full alert. The southerly breeze coming off the gulf did nothing to cool his raging heat. The emerald and sapphire waters of the day were now a pewter glaze under the moon. He was not only mesmerized by the rhythmic carnal frolicking, but also, the surge and ebb of the sea—mercurial, power in motion. That's how it was with the monster within him, except tonight it was all surge, no ebb.

The beast's concentration on the two silhouettes was only periodically pierced by the distant sound of some band in a beach bar banging out Jimmy Buffet's "Why Don't We Get Drunk and Screw?" While Dewayne succeeded in the former, he failed miserably in the latter. Colleen got louder, but her entreaties went unrequited, her partner still and silent.

"Dewayne?"

But Dewayne was in no condition to move or speak. Disgusted and frustrated, Colleen managed to roll her comatose Casanova off of her, and stormed off into the water, cooling down with a swim.

The voyeur took advantage of the opportunity. Moving quickly but noiselessly, he approached Colleen's beach towel and grabbed both parts of her swimsuit. Crouched again in his nearby lair while Colleen swam, the voyeur gently nuzzled her thong, taking in her scent and fantasizing every move he would make. It was all so clear and vivid, pre-ordained. His reverie was broken by the sounds of Colleen's unsuccessful attempts to rouse Dewayne. Finally, she gave up and lay down.

The beast was frantic to get out of its cage. In a blitz attack, he was on her. He would no longer be a simple watcher. He was a doer. With lightning speed, Colleen's thong was stuffed into her mouth, and her top whipped around her neck.

Her eyes no longer flashed at him in amusement; they were now wide with horror. The beast wasn't sure what color terror came in, but he found what he saw in her eyes quite pleasing, and her strong, lithe body thrashing beneath him, arousing.

Twisting the top tighter and still tighter, the thought that his face would be the last visage that she would ever behold almost caused him to lose control of the surge in his groin. As her body at last went limp, he quickly lowered his shorts and gushed onto her un-mocking, silent face. After all was said and done, it really wasn't about sex. It was all about his power, and her degradation.

Zipping up, the beast's keen eyes were riveted on the dive knife lying among the scuba gear. He visualized the crimson masterpiece that he could paint with such an instrument. The strokes would be so well placed. Such a perfect body, such a perfect canvas. Although his brain was warning him of the mess such carnage would leave, his barbarous urge was overwhelming. The beast at least needed a souvenir of this high-water mark in his life.

Tear it up! Those were the words the bitch had earlier screamed to her lover. "So be it, honey," the beast now whispered, and the stainless-steel blade glistened but twice in the moonlight, before yielding the soft blood-soaked memento. Despite a strict religious upbringing, the beast was not sure of an afterlife; but even if there were one, he had made sure that orgasmic pleasure would not be among the heavenly joys this bitch would experience.

Alive. He thought it odd how that had worked. Her demise was his birth, his glory. The breath of life infused and enlivened his soul of stone. However, he had second thoughts about keeping his trophy, as desire and logic engaged in an internal war. Without the memento, however, what would he do if the memories dimmed over time to the point of becoming impotent? The answer, of course, was he would just have to keep doing it. So the beast arose, calmly walked to the shoreline, and flung the telltale tissue into the gulf. Maybe Poseidon would gift it to a favored Oceanid—with two of them she could enjoy double the pleasure, so to speak.

Off to the south, toward Brady's Irish Pub, lightning flashes streaked the ebony sky, followed seconds later by the roll of thunder rumbling across the gulf. The beast carried Colleen's body to the water's edge. There, he cleansed her before reuniting her with Prince Charming. It wasn't a ritual steeped in symbolism. It simply would have been stupid not to do so. The beast had succumbed to the inner fury, and knew that he would do so again and again in order to relish the feelings that he was so much enjoying. But that would be impossible if he were caught and locked in some cell. He had read about trace evidence, and would not risk leaving any. *He* was no moron.

So, although the beast knew this was only the beginning of his true power, he resolved that his rage would be unleashed only in a cold, calculating, and controlled manner. During the interim he would come and go like anyone else on this dull planet. After all, the FBI profiler he had seen on a television special about serial killers said that predators come in many forms and guises. *Is that what I am, a serial killer in infancy?* Assimilation would be quite a challenge for someone who enjoyed the rush of the raw power and control, such as he was experiencing on that secluded stretch of beach. He would become an expert in human nature, a cunning manipulator of the situation at hand.

Ah, the manipulation could be as intoxicating as the power. This revelation came to the beast as he realized that, by leaving Dewayne unharmed, he would eventually awaken, clutching his bloody dive knife. The moron's arrest, trial, and conviction would fall like dominos. Nobody would believe his pathetic pleas of innocence. *Officer, I swear I was passed out, drunk. I don't know what happened!*

It was such a thrill for the beast to be the one to tip off the cops, bright and early the next morning, telling what he had chanced upon while taking an early jog. The moron was still passed out, blood-caked blade in hand, when the beast led the authorities to the location. Eight months later, he was on the witness stand, relating to a jury the ghastly discovery, and the fact that he had been among the patrons at Brady's to witness the couple's argument and Dewayne's parting words: "Nobody walks away from me!" Dewayne soon became a resident at Huntsville, but not for long. Texas empties death row quite often.

Over the ensuing years, the beast raped, tortured, murdered, and moved on, honing his skills along the way. Now, on the twenty-seventh anniversary of that Spring Break, he was stirring again.

PART I: MADNESS IN MISSISSIPPI

CHAPTER 1

Todd Murphy was livid. He had just finished the "perp walk". Fingerprints and mug shots taken, he now sat on the cold, steel bench in a holding cell. Unlike the kind generally seen on television shows, there was no cot or bed of any kind. Todd was still clad in his grey suit, and the handcuffs pinched his coat sleeves, causing a good four inches on the cuffs of his white dress shirt to mushroom beyond. Lowering his head in disgust, he saw that the lower parts of his pants were similarly distorted by the shackles.

Just who does that Judge Davis think he is, anyway? The very idea of thwarting the will of the people was repugnant enough, but treating Todd as a non-entity was unforgivable. When Todd had tried to speak during the court proceedings, the judge told him that he had no standing. *No standing? If the President of the Southern Voice had no standing to speak out in defense of our honored state flag, assailed by niggers, latter-day carpetbaggers, and scalawags, then who the hell did?*

Mississippi's flag incorporates the Confederate battle flag, and in recent years several bills had been filed, at the NAACP's urging, to change it. The bills met a quiet demise each session, always failing to make it out of committee. However, once the business community and a coalition of ministers united and flexed their combined political muscle, legislative resistance somewhat softened. The solons were not about to cast a "yea" or "nay" roll-call vote on such a volatile issue, especially in an election year. Instead, they opted for a less courageous path. Drawing inspiration from the most shameful example of leadership in the history of mankind, the representatives elected by and supposedly for the people, like modern-day Pontius Pilates, ceremoniously washed their hands of the controversy. In effect, they were telling the rabble, "You decide."

They churned out a resolution putting the issue to a statewide popular vote. Cognizant that the odds were heavily stacked against them, but believing that there are some rights beyond majority rule, several prominent African-Americans filed suit, asking the court to enjoin the vote and declare the current flag unconstitutional.

Todd and his brotherhood organized rallies from one end of the state to the other, galvanizing the rednecks and Sons of Confederate Veterans into a unique and formidable alliance. The most recent poll foretold a landslide victory for them. So, as far as Todd was concerned, everything was in place until Judge Thomas Jefferson Davis III entered the fray. Subsequent to the attorneys' arguments, the judge took the matter under advisement, and Todd had a bad, sinking feeling. He had sensed doom from the moment he first learned that the case was assigned to Davis, Charles Summerville's persecutor. That's when he went to visit Sonny Clark.

Todd felt that the State's position was a strong one. After all, Mississippi's constitution provided that the people have the inherent, sole, and exclusive right to regulate the internal government, and that the right to petition the sovereignty concerning any subject was never to be impaired. Surely, Todd reasoned, that included the right for the majority to select a flag.

He was pleased with the young lawyer from the state attorney general's office who performed admirably in framing the issue for His Honor. The judge's retort, however, had left the lawyer speechless, "Well, Mr. Williams, what do you have to say about Section Seven of the Mississippi Constitution?" Observing that the lawyer was at a loss, Judge Davis put on his reading glasses and opened one of several legal tomes stacked on his bench and continued, "It provides, 'No law shall be passed in derogation of the paramount allegiance of the citizens of this state to the government of the United States.'"

Silence.

"What I am asking, counselor, is whether or not you agree that a resolution authorizing the people to vote on whether to fly, as our official state flag—one that incorporates the battle flag of the Confederate States of America—is somewhat in derogation of allegiance to the government of the United States."

"No sir, Your Honor, I do not agree," the young barrister replied, but offered nothing in support of his feigned confidence.

"Your grandfather and my father fought side-by-side in World War II, Mr. Williams," the judge said affably. "In all honesty, would you be defending the flag if it incorporated the Swastika or Rising Sun?"

"Absolutely not, Your Honor, but..."

9

"So how is this different?" the judge interjected. Removing his glasses and pointing them at the lawyer to emphasize the import, he continued, "Correct me if I'm wrong, but wasn't the CSA just as much of a wartime enemy of the USA as were Germany and Japan?"

"Yes, Your Honor."

"And was not the major interest of the CSA in that war the perpetuation of slavery?"

Todd had been observing the exchange from the gallery, and before the lawyer could respond, leapt to his feet, bellowing, "That's a Yankee lie perpetuated by the liberal media!"

When the judge threatened to hold him in contempt, Todd reminded the court that he, too, was a licensed attorney. "Then you should know better," Judge Davis explained, and proceeded to inform Todd that he did not, in any event, have standing to speak in the case.

"I represent hundreds of thousands of true Mississippians and sons of the South..." Todd continued, or at least attempted to do so. At a nod from the judge, two bailiffs began escorting him out of the courtroom. Todd offered no physical resistance, but he would not be silenced. "...and we hold *you* in contempt!" he shouted at the judge as the heavy, wood door closed and muffled the tirade.

Now sitting in a holding cell in the Hinds County Detention Center, adjacent to the courthouse in Jackson, Mississippi, Todd Murphy closed his eyes, attempting to will his fury under control. He wondered whether he was just experiencing another one of his episodes and whether, when he blinked his eyes open again, everything would have passed. It was to this end, eyes still closed, that Todd focused all of his cerebral energy. He was convinced that there was nothing he could not accomplish with his mighty mind. As hard as he tried though, the continued yelling and cursing from other inmates, as well as the overwhelming smell of pine-scented disinfectant, emphasized the disappointing assurance of reality. Todd's eyes sprang wide open at the sound of the cell door clanging open.

"Put these on," a burly guard growled, lobbing a garbage bag to the floor at Todd's feet. Bending over and opening the bag, Todd saw that it contained orange coveralls and matching flip-flops. "Everything you have on goes in there," the jailer instructed. "I'll be back in a few minutes to pick them up. Hold out your hands and I'll get those irons off."

Todd stood and extended his arms. Once the handcuffs and shackles released their grip, he could feel a tingling in his extremities as the circulation gradually returned. He instinctively flexed his long fingers, and as the guard turned to leave, Todd's immediate thought was to wrap them around the jailer's neck. It was thick as a stump and the man clearly out-sized him, but people always underestimated Todd. Although confident of his superior prowess, Todd quickly subdued his initial urge and politely asked, "Sir, while the door is open, would you please show me where the restroom is located?"

"Sure," the guard replied, and with a smirk, he nodded in the direction behind Todd.

Todd turned his head and, for the first time, he noticed the stainless-steel toilet in the rear of the cubicle. He looked back at the guard, who roared with laughter as he slammed the door and turned the key. Todd glared at the man, regretting his decision to override impulse with reason. Once his tormentor was out of sight, Todd approached the head and began to relieve himself. As the urine swirled around the inside of the stainless-steel bowl, the object of his feral focus shifted. "Well, piss on you, Judge motherfucking Davis," Todd muttered.

By the time he was undressed and donned in jailhouse attire, Todd had decided on Plan B: he would not let Sonny Clark exact vengeance for him. Manipulation had its thrill, and Sonny was as easy as a puppet on a string, but this called for a personal hands-on solution. He just had to get out of jail quickly and beat Sonny to it, for Plan A was already in motion. Todd's bad feeling began to feel so, so good.

CHAPTER 2

As he drove through the night, Judge Thomas Jefferson Davis III was as mixed up as his name, philosophically torn, emotionally spent, and alone in so many ways. He had been down this road before, and had prayed that he would never have to travel it again. Yet he was there—not the concrete pavement of Highway 18, which connected the county's two seats of government, but rather on a far bumpier path on which his career had again placed him.

Fifteen years ago, while serving as district attorney of Hinds County, Mississippi, Davis's principles required his vigorous investigation and prosecution of one Charles Summerville, a former Ku Klux Klan hit man, for the assassination of a black civil rights activist two decades earlier. Although he was repeatedly warned that the past was best left there, Davis had won a conviction. There were enough good people with clear heads and understanding hearts to keep him in office for another term, and eventually put him on the circuit court bench. It was hard though, ignoring the threatening letters, harassing phone calls, and even a bomb threat. The case destroyed his marriage. Sarah had left him in the middle of it all. He assured her that it was only a small, but vocal group responsible for the backlash, but it fell on deaf ears. The last he had heard, she was in Savannah.

There were no promising prospects for a new love in the judge's life, but that was just as well; the law really was a jealous mistress. Bouts of despondency occasionally afflicted him, though, at the contemplation that he constituted the end of the family line, still childless. Davis knew that whenever his time came, his grave would be tended by a stranger, if anyone.

Things had been going well for Davis on the bench. More than the proverbial new lease on life, it had been nothing short of rejuvenation. He relished the freedom of no longer having to carry the burden of an advocate. He could research and apply the law simply for what it was, and he loved it. Even the attorneys on the losing sides of his rulings respected him, and the dark days of the Summerville case had passed, leaving no sign of further retribution. But he was now very much aware that was about to change.

A storm was brewing; the judge had sensed it for several weeks now. Normally a social drinker, he had been imbibing more frequently, developing a recent taste for Chivas Regal, straight on the rocks. In fact, he probably had one too many of those at the Walthall lounge with Judge Stillwell before making the drive home. The last thing that Judge Davis needed was a DUI charge, but he needed those drinks. It had been rough lately.

The negative fallout started to resurface with Mississippi's first automobile manufacturing plant. The governor, legislature, and business leaders had enticed the automaker to build a sprawling facility off Interstate 10, in rural Warren County, thirty miles west of Jackson. The state agreed to buy the large tracts of needed land through a shell corporation and subsequently signed a lease-purchase agreement on terms extremely beneficial to the automaker.

Most of the landowners were more than happy to sell. They made a healthy profit while doing what they considered to be their part in bringing more jobs and income to the region. What took some by surprise, however, was that a single black family refused to sell for any price. The land, which sat at the center of the proposed development, had been in the Dennis family for generations, going back to an ex-slave's forty acres. It accommodated the interred earthly remains of their ancestors. When the family would not sever such dear ties, the State of Mississippi embarked upon the diabolical course of taking it—in a court of law, no less.

Understandably, none of the Warren County judges wanted to touch the case and recused themselves for various reasons, asking the state supreme court to appoint a judge from another county to hear it. Davis was tapped and his much-awaited decision was released just before he left the courthouse in Jackson and headed over to the lounge at the Walthall, a historic downtown hotel. It would make the television news tonight and tomorrow's newspapers. He had ruled in favor of the Dennis family, holding that the state's awesome power of eminent domain was to be limited to those instances where the public necessity was for the state's actual possession and use of the land. He simply could not condone any government, much less one of which he was a part, seizing someone's land only to turn around and lease or sell it to a private enterprise, no matter how beneficial that business might prove to be to others.

However, Mississippi elects its judges, and campaigns require financial backing. The decision would not only infuriate the rednecks who had condemned him for prosecuting Summerville and were now hoping for work at the plant, but Davis was going against big-money people, many of whom had helped keep him in office.

As if all of that was not enough, the auto giant's general counsel, Jim Blackwell, was a classmate and fraternity brother with the judge at Ole Miss. The two were like brothers for years, before Jim moved away and Davis lost track of him. He had not known of Jim's professional position until Jim paid him a recent visit, and it hurt Davis to know that his ruling would adversely affect someone so close to him. By then, the decision had been made, just not known—Davis had not even mentioned it to Jim during their brief reunion. Although he was not about to change his ruling, it still weighed heavily on Davis's mind.

The most recent cause of the judge's emotional turmoil, however, centered on—of all things—a piece of cloth. *That damned flag.* Davis wished that cup had been passed on to his protégé. Judge J. Alexander Stillwell was a decade younger than Davis and possessed a steel-trap legal mind that could more easily navigate the murky waters ahead than Davis's tired brain.

Thomas Jefferson Davis III, or Tom, as his friends called him, was not a descendant of either President Jefferson or Davis. His grandfather, however, had instilled in him a great appreciation of Thomas Jefferson's great libertarian mind. And like Jefferson Davis, Tom's roots ran long and deep in Mississippi. Those roots began with George Lamar, who in 1819, at nineteen years of age, was among the first freshmen to enter the University of Virginia. It was there that the family's love and respect for Jefferson, the school's founder, first germinated. Lamar studied and practiced law briefly in Richmond, until the vast and untamed lands of the west beckoned.

He settled on a picturesque tract just outside of Raymond, Mississippi, which had just been established in 1829 as the new governmental seat of Hinds County. Not far from the Natchez Trace, the town quickly became a bustling hub, where merchants plied their trade and lawyers, physicians, and prostitutes practiced their professions. George Lamar parlayed his earnings from the east several times over, and in 1845, oversaw construction of a palatial home which he christened Lamar Hall. The estate was so peaceful that it was spared from Yankee torches, eighteen years later, by one of Grant's subordinate officers. It was George and Ann Lamar's daughter, Olivia, who married Tom's great-grandfather, Patrick Henry Davis, also a lawyer.

Grandfather, great-grandfather, and great-great-grandfather had all been lawyers and judges. Only Tom's father, TJ, broke the chain, making his fortune running bootleg whiskey, whores, and numbers during Prohibition and well past its repeal, (Mississippi remained "dry" for decades). Only once did Tom question the reason for this lapse in the family profession, and the explanation of his father, a man of many thoughts but few words, was simple, "Thought it was time somebody restored some respect in the family."

Driving toward the home that had been in his family for over 150 years, Tom could not keep from chortling at his memory of the remark. He supposed there had been lawyer jokes as long as there had been lawyers, and was pleased at his realization that not all of his humor had been extinguished by the enveloping turmoil.

CHAPTER 3

Sonny Clark watched and waited. He had clearly visualized in his mind's eye, over the past months, everything that he would do to the son-of-a-bitch who gave him thirty years for possessing some cocaine. It was not, by any means, his first offense, but the judge had not known that. Sonny's crimes had thus far gone undetected, committed in darkness in more ways than one. With no prior record, Sonny's court-appointed lawyer had assured him that if he pled guilty he would come out of it with a suspended sentence and probation. However, the fact that the contraband had been found in Sonny's eighteen-wheeler was enough for that prick-in-a-robe Davis to sentence Sonny for transportation, rather than for mere possession, slamming him with the max—thirty damn years.

Probation alone would have put a crimp in Sonny's lifestyle, but he knew that he could have eventually conned the probation officer. Prison however, was totally out of the question for Sonny Clark. Didn't the judge see that? *You'll soon see it. And oh, so much more.*

Sonny did not understand why having a personal stash of coke was a crime, any more than he understood as a boy, why peeping through the bedroom windows of the young neighborhood ladies ignited his mother's ire. *All I wanted to do was watch.* After he was eventually spotted by one of the shapely beauties, his mother carped that he was fortunate that the woman had phoned her instead of the police. *Fortunate? The bitch beat the shit out of me.* Sonny would have preferred taking his chances with the cops—at least if they had been the ones to work him over, he would have had some legal recourse. Not so, with respect to the woman who spawned him.

Sonny's father had deserted them long before Sonny grew up; but

Sonny could not imagine his old man, even if his sorry, drunken ass had still been around, packing a bigger punch than that which he suffered on a regular basis at the hands of his mother. Sonny supposed one reason that it was difficult for him to see any distinction between what other people saw as right and wrong was because his every action drew the same violent reaction from his mother. The bitch.

In retrospect, Sonny saw one benefit from his abusive childhood: it forced him to contemplate his every move before daring to make it. He tried to blend into his surroundings, being as inconspicuous as possible wherever he was, particularly outside the houses where he continued to peek as often as he could. Gradually he could not resist the urge to go inside the dwellings of his subjects, to get up close and personal.

Moving from place to place, and regularly changing occupations, were tactics that prolonged Sonny's survival. Working the oil rigs off the Texas and Louisiana coasts proved the most profitable as far as money was concerned; but driving his own tractor-trailer rig through the cities, towns, and hamlets of America had afforded him the best means of putting his slash-and-burn technique to work. Now the semi was gone, forfeited to the state, at the order of Judge Davis. *That's okay. What goes around comes around. Soon, Your Honor, it will be you who forfeits something—no, everything.*

Another skill that Sonny mastered was the ability to choose places with easy escape routes, even where none existed to other eyes. The thought that this talent had even worked in Sonny's prison escape brought a wry smile to his face.

Sonny had one bit of luck when he was assigned by the Department of Corrections to a small, privately operated satellite unit in the east-central part of the state, rather than to the sprawling, infamous Parchman Penitentiary in the Mississippi Delta. It seemed that overcrowding had its perks. Classified as a non-violent first offender, Sonny managed to secure an assignment working in the twenty-acre garden outside the fence of the minimum-security facility. In no time, Sonny bamboozled his way to being designated the trustee in charge of the detail. It was hard work—hoeing and picking peas, beans, corn, and every other vegetable known to man in the stifling, humid Mississippi air with no refuge from the sun. *And the goddamned snakes; shit, I hate snakes.*

A damn horse; who would have believed it? Sonny smiled again at the memory. It had been dusk, that time which belongs to neither day nor night, when nothing has any particular shape or hue, just indiscernible blends of gray. Sonny feigned ignorance of the horse grazing near the far end of the garden, just feet from the edge of the thick, piney woods of the Bienville National Forest. He knew it was there though, because Todd

Murphy, the white-supremacist lawyer who volunteered to work on Sonny's appeal in exchange for a favor, had put it there for him. When it was time for the crew to call it a day, Sonny turned in that direction. "Y'all hear something?" he asked the group.

The others likewise turned and strained their eyes, finally discerning the faint image of a saddled, but riderless, bay. The reins were slowly dragged along the grass as the horse grazed from one spot to another. Mario, the smallest, but most outspoken of the bunch, offered his assessment, "Looks like some fool riding d'em forest trails done got his ass throwed."

"I believe you're right," Sonny replied. "I'll go tie him up. I reckon Bronco Billy will come dragging his busted ass over here sooner or later."

"Man, you do what the fuck you want, but we s'pose to be inside as we speak," Oscar protested. The others agreed and started walking toward the compound gate, Oscar bringing up the rear. Mario, however, lingered.

"Go on," Sonny ordered. "I don't expect you to get in trouble because of me, but..." Sonny paused and added with a gleam in his eyes, "I sure would appreciate it if you'd walk slow, real slow." He smiled.

Recognition flashed in Mario's eyes. "You crazy white motherfucker."

"Mario, come on and leave that dumb cracker alone," Oscar hissed, some twenty feet down the path.

"You all go on," Mario directed. "I got a rock in my shoe I got to get out. It's hurt'n like a bitch." Mario sat down, removed his right shoe, and looked up at Sonny. They were concealed behind cornstalks, tall that time of year, and Sonny appeared to be re-adjusting the bandana protecting his hairless head from the sun. "Get outta here, motherfucker," Mario said. "You ain't got long 'til I get this rock out. Then I'm gonna start screaming like a motherfucking banshee that yo lily-white ass is gone."

Sonny neither delayed, nor expressed any gratitude. Nonchalantly, he slid the shank he had concealed, back under the rim of his bandana. He had been ready to use it if necessary, on Mario. Then Sonny made his equine escape.

It had taken several weeks for Sonny to get where he was now. He had negotiated wooded trails on horseback, thickets on foot, and had stolen a car in Jackson. He made it and, instead of a crudely formed shank, it was an old-fashion barber's straightedge razor he had found that he now caressed, waiting. Many pairs of bestial eyes shone through the blackness of the woods surrounding the homestead, all searching for prey of one kind or another, but only one pair lasered in on Judge Thomas Jefferson Davis III.

There would be no witnesses. Mario was alive only because the kill would have been an unnecessary risk. The guards would have soon determined, in any event, that Sonny was on the lam. He just needed time, and Mario agreeably provided it. Nor would there be any signs of forced entry or trace evidence—not one hair. For years, Sonny had been totally bald. A tattoo of an eagle, wings spread over the tops of Sonny's ears, spanned his entire head. In a nearby creek, Sonny had shaved every inch of the rest of his body with the straightedge. Just in case a hair or two had not washed off, Sonny wore a full-body dive skin and heavy-duty latex gloves. Todd Murphy had put them in the saddlebags on the horse just as Sonny had specified.

Once Sonny's score was settled with the judge, he would turn his attention toward Serena Raven, the court-appointed bitch who had misguidedly advised him to plead guilty although there was no agreement in place with the prosecutor. It was on her advice that Sonny had thrown himself on the mercy of the court. As it turned out, he had hoisted himself on a petard.

Yes, the roles would indeed soon be reversed. The judge and lawyer would both be at Sonny's mercy, and he had none. The cacophony of the crickets, owls, and other creatures of the night would soon be displaced by agonizing screams. Those of his male victims were not as continuous as the females, but they were just as piercing.

CHAPTER 4

Judge Thomas Davis continued his drive along Highway 18. It was roughly laid out along the same route that General John Gregg of Texas had followed in leading his already fatigued Confederate brigade of two-thousand on another forced march the morning of May 11, 1863. They had finished a trek of two-hundred miles from Port Hudson, Louisiana to Jackson, Mississippi, only the previous day. Those who were not resting around the camp, set up about a mile north of the capital city, were enjoying a cool plunge in the water of the nearby Pearl River. A bugle blast sounding the assembly brought the respite to a halt. The Johnnies were heading twenty-one miles southwest to Raymond, with orders to quickly rout what a scouting party had reported as a Yankee brigade on a marauding excursion. The federal forces awaiting Gregg and his troops, however, were not the skirmishers of a cavalry brigade, but rather Grant's entire 17th Corps, twelve-thousand strong, under Major General James McPherson. Military intelligence was evidently as much an oxymoron in the nineteenth century as it is today.

Prosecuting Charles Summerville had been a long, emotionally exhausting journey for Tom Davis. Although his reprieve spanned fifteen years, the flag case brought on a renewed weariness. He felt that he too, was on a forced march of sorts. His call to duty was not by bugle blast, but by who and what he was. It was brought to bear, not by an invading army, but by the filing of a lawsuit.

During Mississippi's Reconstruction period, the legislature divided Hinds County into two judicial districts, each with a courthouse and offices of the same elected county officials, such as the sheriff and supervisors. Thus Raymond, formerly the sole county seat, accommodated what became the Second Judicial District of the county, and Jackson, long serving as the state capital, assumed an additional role in county government, as the new First Judicial District. The dividing line ran north and south, crossing Highway 18 just west of the Springridge Road intersection, where the red traffic light caused Tom to stop.

As Tom waited, he reflected on the legal arguments of the day. Todd Murphy had gone rabid when Tom posed a few probing questions to the state's attorney. The inquiries were by no means indicative of Tom's decision. He truly did not yet know which way he would rule. The soundness of litigants' cases, and not the performance of their lawyers, should be the basis of judges' decisions. But human nature, being what it is, invariably makes the task more difficult than it seems. Serena Raven, the lead attorney for the plaintiffs in the flag case, had performed well. Tom had found her always well prepared.

"Thomas Jefferson, whom I know you admire," she began her argument, "made it abundantly clear that no generation has the right to bind another with laws or constitutions. We submit that you can add flags to the list. The fact that this flag has flown for over a century does not make it sacrosanct; if anything, it means that it is time for a change."

"So is it not the ballot box that is the best means of ascertaining what flag the current generation of Mississippians desire?" Tom asked.

"Some rights are beyond the ballot box, Your Honor. Section Fifteen of the Mississippi Constitution of 1890 states that, 'there shall be neither slavery nor involuntary servitude in this state.'"

"Come now, Ms. Raven, surely you are not suggesting that slavery or involuntary servitude still exists here, are you?"

"Not by chains or shackles, Your Honor; but…"

"You admit then," Tom interrupted, "that we have made tremendous strides in this state concerning equal rights and race relations? I believe that I read that we have the highest percentage of minority public officials of any state in the Union, Ms. Raven. You can't exactly call that disenfranchisement, can you?"

"No, Your Honor, but that was not brought about because of the willingness of most Mississippians. It was the result of federal legislation, intervention, and oversight. I think it is somewhat noteworthy that while Mississippi has a due process clause in its constitution mirroring its federal counterpart, *to this day* there is no state provision that guarantees equal protection under the law to all citizens, as does the Fourteenth Amendment of the federal Constitution. I just find it curious that Mississippi adopted due process for everyone after the Civil War, but not equal protection."

"As to race relations, Ms. Raven, you must admit that we haven't had any major problems here in over thirty or forty years. Places like New York, Philadelphia, Boston, and Los Angeles can't say that, can they?"

"We have indeed, come a long way in that regard, Your Honor. But the fact that we are taking our grievances to the tribunals of justice, instead of the streets, does not make those grievances any less real, or lessen their merit."

"Let's explore that merit for minute," Tom replied. "With all of this progress, aren't you putting more into symbolism and shoving substance to the side?"

"Mr. Jefferson wrote that the hope of government lies in an enlightened, really free people. We are not contesting the right of individuals, or private enterprises, to exercise their First Amendment rights of free speech, flying whatever flag they desire. It *is*, however, our steadfast position that when *the state* flies a banner which unquestionably symbolizes the willingness and determination to perpetuate slavery, then the hundreds of thousands of black Mississippians, many of whom are direct descendants of slaves, cannot be said to be really free."

"I appreciate the Jefferson references, Ms. Raven. But the opinions of one man, no matter how profound, do not carry the weight of law, now do they?"

"Your Honor, we do not rest our prayer for relief based solely on those sentiments. Indeed, we have cited several constitutional provisions to Your Honor, federal and state. The State's brief makes much ado about numbers, about majority rule; but I respectfully submit, Your Honor, that one, plus the law, is a majority. Furthermore, legal scholars have frequently observed that while the Constitution forms the framework of our law, it is the Declaration of Independence that embodies its soul. So, I respectfully ask you, Your Honor, what better authority exists to explore that soul than its author?"

"Proceed." She was sharp.

"So, how then, Your Honor," Serena continued, "can African-Americans pursue their right to happiness under an official flag incorporating a banner that figuratively, but quite effectively, proclaims slavery forever?"

"But we have a situation here that pits some people's rights not to be offended against other people's rights to honor their heritage," Tom noted. "So, what do we do when the pursuit of happiness of one interferes with that of another?"

Before replying, Serena Raven flashed one of the loveliest smiles Tom Davis had ever seen. "We bring the conflict into a court of law, to the attention of a well-reasoned and good-hearted judge." With that, she sat down. *Talk about putting the pressure on.*

It was during the state attorney's argument that Todd Murphy had exploded over Tom's comment that slavery was the underlying issue of the Civil War. *A Yankee lie?* Tom was still reflecting on the outburst when the light changed to green, and his Mercury Grand Marquis accelerated past Mississippi Springs, where defeated Confederate troops had encamped along their retreat from Raymond to Jackson.

True, the North resisted secession to preserve the Union, and protect its economic reliance on southern agriculture. There was no official agenda of the federal government to abolish slavery until Lincoln's Emancipation Proclamation in 1862, over a year into the war. Even that action only freed the slaves in the states remaining in rebellion. It was perfectly legal to own a slave in federally occupied New Orleans, Baltimore, and even Washington, D.C. Perhaps such Yankee hypocrisy clouded southern views of the intrinsically evil nature of slavery, and later segregation; but it was no lie to say that slavery was *the* core reason for Mississippi's rebellion. The delegates to the state's secession convention were very explicit about that; "Our position is thoroughly identified with the institution of slavery—the greatest material interest of the world," read the convention's declaration.

Tom's ancestor, Judge George Lamar, sixty years old at the time, was one of the elder statesmen to sign that document. That he had done so perplexed Tom for years, considering that Lamar was a Unionist in the Whig party. Tom later found a journal kept by the old judge, which provided some answers. Maybe it would likewise share some useful insight regarding the dilemma at hand.

Tom and three other judges served the circuit court of the county. While the other three judges worked exclusively in Jackson, Tom served both judicial districts. Although he kept an office in the "newer" Jackson courthouse, built in the 1930s, he also maintained one behind the courtroom of the antebellum courthouse in Raymond, finished in 1859. Holding court there was special to Tom, infusing him with a greater appreciation of place and time. It was there that he kept Lamar's journal, among the material he enjoyed perusing while waiting on juries to reach their verdicts. Tom decided to retrieve it before repairing to the house, and returned his thoughts to Serena Raven. She had also been the lead attorney for the Dennis family. By now she would know that she had won that case. Serena was something special in more ways than one. It had pleased Tom that he was able to rule in her favor. He thought a lot of her as a person, as well as a lawyer, but he was as torn about her escalating relationship with Bo, as he was about her flag case.

Bo was a friend. No, he was more like the son Tom had imagined he and Sarah would have raised, and Tom was concerned about him. It would not be easy for someone like Bo to have an acceptable, open affinity with someone like Serena. Things had not changed *that* much here, or anywhere else for that matter, in Tom's opinion.

He picked up his cell phone and tried to call Bo, but was immediately directed to Bo's voice mail, which usually meant that Bo was working undercover. Tom would try again later. He was approaching the town of Raymond.

CHAPTER 5

Stakeouts sucked, at least as far as Bo Landry was concerned. They required a lot of something that he did not possess—patience. He liked action, and the more of it the better. Bo wished that he was doing anything tonight other than sitting and waiting, at the edge of the Delta National Forest, with a dozen or so other camouflaged agents of the Mississippi Bureau of Narcotics. According to a confidential informant, a cocaine-laden Cessna was due to land in the adjacent clearing in a few hours. Not knowing how far in advance the retrieving crew would be on the scene to await the cargo's arrival, Bo and the other agents were there early, forced to maintain absolute silence, not moving a muscle.

It seemed to Bo that he was the target for every mosquito in the Mississippi Delta. Clothing-covered areas weren't so bad, but the bloodsucking pests were feasting on his neck, face, and ears. Bo hoped to God that he would be able to see the Cessna land in the dark field, unable to rely on his hearing since every buzzing mosquito around him sounded like a B-52 bomber.

Trying to avoid going stark raving mad, Bo focused on something else. Serena Raven was something else all right, and Bo thought back to that July day of the previous year when they first met. He had been coaxed by Tom to join him at the Mississippi Bar Convention in Destin, Florida. Bo left the district attorney's office in June. However, due to some bureaucratic snafu, he could not start his new job with the MBN until August. Scuba diving and beautiful women were plentiful along the Emerald Coast in July, and Tom knew that Bo had an appreciation of both.

Nursing an O'Doul's, as he sat alone at the only vacant table near the Sandestin beach cabana, Bo could not help staring when Serena drew near, a drink in one hand and a book in the other, in search of a place to sit. Tom had spoken of her, but Bo had never seen her. She rivaled any Greek goddess. Although draped in a long, floral-print sarong tied at her waist, the sunlight filtered through and revealed the silhouette of beautifully shaped legs. As Bo's eyes gradually worked their way up, he noticed just how tall, yet graceful and well proportioned, she was. And her smooth, unblemished, caramel skin was especially pleasing to the eye. An aqua tube top completely encased her breasts, but left little to the imagination. Long, thick curls of dark-brown hair cascaded over comely nutmeg shoulders, and high, finely sculpted cheekbones accentuated a radiant, regal face.

When Bo offered to share his table, Serena flashed a smile that could confiscate the stoutest male heart and ensnare any man's soul. It was hard deciding which was brightest—her sparkling white teeth or luminous, green orbs. If one's eyes really were the portals of the soul, Serena's emerald gateways bespoke a sensual, yet innocent, spirit beyond. There was an instant mutual affinity.

Although Serena was born in Christiansted, on the Caribbean island of St. Croix, the home of her Creole mother, most of her life was spent in New Orleans. Serena remembered her mother, Victoria, as very beautiful and loving. Her parents had met while her father, Sam Raven, was stationed at the United States Naval Base in San Juan, Puerto Rico, where Victoria was visiting relatives. Their paths crossed during a night on the town, and romance soon followed. After Sam's military service was done he and Victoria taught school on St. Croix, encouraging their daughter to be studious—not only in schoolwork, but also in developing a love for all sorts of knowledge and adventure.

But that created some problems, Serena confessed to Bo, beginning around her fourteenth birthday. Becoming bored in school, she routinely played hooky and took a small boat offshore in search of a dolphin friend she had happened upon. They would gently nuzzle against each other, and the dolphin, allowing the young maiden to grasp its dorsal fin, would propel them through the warm Caribbean waters.

It seemed to Serena that, even as a teenager, she always had a book on hand. On the days that she could not find the dolphin, Serena would let the boat drift while she read, fantasizing about a true, pure lover arising from the sea, lifting her from the boat, and taking her away to live happily ever after together.

"And did that one true, pure lover ever arise from the sea?" Bo asked.

"I once *thought* that he had. But, as you can see, I'm still hanging around the water waiting." Bo gave an understanding nod. Seagulls were all about. As some squawked overhead and others poked at the sand for various morsels, Serena continued her story. Her mother died of cancer when Serena was sixteen. Serena and her father stayed on St. Croix long enough for her to finish high school, but after graduation, Sam withdrew his retirement benefits, and they moved to New Orleans, his hometown.

Sam was a mix of African-American and Native-American descent, and had grown up on Piety Street, in the Bywater district of the Crescent City; but he was always fascinated with the historic and bohemian character of the French Quarter. So upon his return, Sam rented a cozy two-bedroom apartment on the 1000 block of St. Peter Street, between Rampart and Burgundy. Serena too, was quickly enchanted by the Quarter's unique culture, and especially charmed by its many eccentric denizens. She loved to people-watch, and in the Vieux Carré, she struck a gold mine of diverse humanity.

For over three centuries, New Orleans' French Quarter had accommodated thousands of people in search of a new life. Sam Raven, himself such a pilgrim, did not yet know what he would do to earn a living, but he did know that he did not want to continue teaching. A new beginning warranted a new vocation. There was no hurry in deciding however, as Serena and he could live on his pension for a while—Sam guessed six months or so.

One of Sam's favorite haunts was an Irish pub located at the corner of Toulouse and Burgundy Streets, only a few blocks from their apartment. A few tourists occasionally wandered in, but mostly it was a hangout for locals. Sam never had more than one or two drinks, but it was not spirits of alcohol that enticed him, rather, it was the spirit of camaraderie—both with the other patrons and Luke, the owner. The place was invariably crowded on weekends, both day and night, much to Luke's delight. But Sam preferred the less hectic weeknights, which were more conducive to conversation.

One such evening, the wall-mounted televisions in each corner showed an LSU baseball game, and two of the regulars—Barry, and a guy Sam knew only by the initials LB—played pool beneath a low-hanging light which had a handwritten sign advising, "Do not set your drinks or asses on the table." Sam sat at the dimly lit bar beside Luke, and the two pontificated the meaning of life and its unforeseen twists and turns. Sam was quite surprised when Luke confided that he was seriously considering selling out and travelling. But he was even more taken aback at the owner's inquiry whether Sam would be interested in buying the place.

"Me, own a pub?" Sam asked. Convinced the proprietor was pulling his leg, Sam laughed. "Do I look Irish to you?"

"You think I am?" Luke replied, also laughing. "Actually my name is

Luka—German."

Sam considered the name of the pub. "Your last name isn't McCormick?"

"Hell no. It's Smith, or rather Schmidt. I bought the place from an Italian named Luigi. And no telling who he got it from. So why not a Sam?"

"Because *this* Sam knows what real estate runs in the Quarter," Sam observed, "and there's no way that he can afford this," he continued, gesturing to the surroundings.

"I just rent the building," Luke explained. "Same with the pool tables and poker machines. Aside from the booze on hand, you'd only have to pay me for the good will and name of the business." Luke could see the wheels turning in Sam's head. "Sam, did you know that McCormick is a more modernized Irish form of the ancient Gaelic name of Cormac?"

"Can't say that I did," Sam replied.

"So I assume you are also unaware of what it means," Luke continued, as he glanced up at the nearest overhead television to catch up on the score.

"Your assumption would be correct," Sam replied and took another sip of his gin and tonic.

Luke leaned in close to Sam and, for added effect, whispered, "It means *raven*, my friend."

Ancestors on both sides of Sam Raven's lineage believed strongly in omens. They were something to be taken very seriously. How could he dismiss one of this magnitude? As billiard balls caromed and clattered in the background, Sam gave it some thought and tossed back what remained of his drink. Turning to Luke, he asked, "What do we need to do?"

Luke instructed Lauryn to bring them a pen, some paper, and another round. That it was Lauryn, Sam's favorite of Luke's mixologists, who delivered the instruments with which the deal was worked out, was yet another favorable portent. Sam was able to make the down payment from his savings and borrow the balance.

McCormick's continued to do well under Sam's proprietorship, but not nearly well enough to generate the funds needed to put his daughter through college. However, with Serena's intellect and multi-faceted minority status, she was awarded a sizeable scholarship at Tulane University—large enough that Sam's earnings easily made up the difference. Serena attended classes in the mornings, studied in the afternoons, and helped Sam behind the bar at night. She finished Tulane with a degree in philosophy.

"Go straight to law school?" Bo inquired.

"No, that came a few years later."

"Knock around for a time?"

For the first time during their conversation, Serena looked saddened. "You might say that." She paused, studying her frozen daiquiri, then continued, "I developed a rather severe crush on a photographer who hung around the pub. I thought he was Mr. Right. I let him take pictures of me—you know, the rather risqué kind. Believe me, it didn't take long for me to realize how stupid that was. One night, soon after that, he was gone. I didn't see him for about a year, and that was in court."

Bo looked puzzled. "Court?"

"The bastard sold the photos to one of those magazines, forging my signature on the release. My father tracked him down and wanted to scalp him—literally. I talked him into letting some lawyers do it instead with a pen and calculator. He relented only after he realized that the suffering would last longer that way. The whole matter broke his heart, but the settlement put me through law school, and paid off the loan for Dad's bar."

"Is he still living?"

"Yes, indeed. He's in that bar every day, and calls me every night, bless his heart."

By all appearances, Sam and Victoria Raven had genetically engineered a fascinating and very intelligent daughter, nurturing in her a confident, yet unpretentious, independence.

"Now," Serena stated to Bo, "your turn."

It was the damnedest conversation in which James Wayne Landry had ever engaged with someone he had just met. He found himself telling Serena things that he had never felt comfortable discussing with anyone. He even brought up his alcoholism and how Judge Tom Davis had taken him under his wing. Tom was like a father. There was no other family. Bo, an only child, was Mississippi-born. After finishing high school, he had enlisted in the Navy, eventually joining the elite Seals. While he was away, his parents became missionaries in Africa and were among those slaughtered in one of the continent's endless bloody revolutions. Extended family was long gone.

Upon his discharge, Bo returned to Mississippi, married Debra, his high school sweetheart, and went to work at the Jackson Police Department. He worked his way from patrol beats to various detective squads, ending with a stint in the homicide division. His favorite assignments though, were those as a member of the SWAT team.

Tragedy soon struck however, when Debra was killed by a drunken driver. Bo sought solace in the bottom of a bottle, and it made no difference what was in it; whiskey, gin, rum, or tequila—as long as it numbed the pain. Tom, the district attorney back then, had taken a liking to the young, but thorough, homicide detective. Unwilling to sit back and witness such a waste, Tom put Bo in rehab, but Bo's position at the police department was not waiting for him when he got out. So, when Tom offered to hire him as an investigator at the district attorney's office, Bo gladly accepted. He stayed on there after Tom left for the bench, but when another D.A. had taken office it was soon evident to Bo that it was time to move on.

Bo told Serena that he had stayed *dry* since his rehab. Remembering Debra, he had successfully fought the urge and remained on the wagon. But as he also explained, it was for the same reason that he had avoided any meaningful relationship with a woman. Debra was never far from his thoughts. The frivolous dalliances over the years were really too numerous and trivial to mention, but Bo realized at that beachside table that Serena Raven had him talking in a way that had vanished after Debra's death.

Bo still got a thrill out of knocking heads, but nothing ever quite stirred his blood and moved his soul like Serena Raven—not even Debra, may she rest in peace.

By the time the droning of the plane pierced the uproar of the forest nightlife, Bo Landry was stirring in so many ways.

CHAPTER 6

It was after eleven o'clock by the time Serena Raven finally turned her red Jaguar through the gates of Rose's Bluff, an exurb overlooking the Ross Barnett Reservoir. Once Judge Davis's decision in the Dennis eminent domain case was made public, reporters had converged in droves on her office. The interviews had taken some time, but were fun. They always are when you win. Although she had telephoned her clients with the good news before speaking with the reporters, Serena felt obliged to make a personal visit as well. With neighbors and other well-wishers also on hand, the attorney-client conference had evolved into a full-blown victory party.

Although it was a typical muggy Mississippi summer night, Serena made the drive home in the convertible with the top down. The warm wind blowing through her hair felt wonderful. She felt so alive. Once inside the kitchen, she poured herself a glass of pinot noir, grabbed the mail from the table where Edna, the housekeeper, always left it for her, and proceeded upstairs.

Serena lost no time peeling off her business attire, which the humidity had caused to cling to her like Saran wrap, and stepped into her shower, the extravagance of the house she most enjoyed. Jet-stream nozzles protruded from the sides as well as from above, and Serena luxuriated in the sensation of the stinging spray pricking at her silky skin. The water pulsating on her from all angles was pure ecstasy.

Dripping, Serena stepped out onto the ceramic-tile floor and realized that, in her haste, she had forgotten to retrieve a towel from the cabinet by the door. With a palm, she swept away the condensation from the steam-soaked, full-length mirror on the wall beside her vanity. She surveyed the reflection of her entire body—a ritual Serena performed to satisfy herself that there were no new pimples, no signs of crow's feet, no flab on her hips, and that her breasts were as full and perky as ever.

After drying off with a thick, thirsty towel, Serena tied a bright sarong around her hips, and glided perfectly pedicured feet into soft rubber thongs. She picked up the mail and turned off all of the lights, except bedside lamp. Opening the French doors, Serena stepped out onto the deck, lit a citronella candle, and stretched out on one of the chaise lounges. The flickering taper and soft glow of the bedroom lamp cast just enough illumination to read, but not enough to make her partial bareness conspicuous.

The mail would have to wait a few minutes. Eyes shut, Serena inhaled deeply and slowly let it out. The adrenaline had been pumping in overdrive, but now she could unwind and relax. Bo was working tonight, and she worried about him. Although Serena missed his company, she really needed this time to herself. Subconsciously, her breathing adjusted to the rhythm of the reservoir waters gently lapping against the pilings beneath her pier. Her heartbeat, that cadence of life, soon followed suit.

Opening her eyes, Serena gazed up at the star-studded heavens; everything was clear, calm, and peaceful. She embraced the solitude and, as the temperate breeze tenderly caressed her bare upper body, she closed her eyes again. The air felt so sensuous. Warmed by the sultriness of the night, every molecule of the soft air currents gingerly fondling her bareness felt like the gentle strokes of millions of tiny, probing fingers. The magical moment was shattered, as she realized that her telephone was ringing. Almost immediately after the sound pierced her dreamy musing, it fell silent.

Whoever had called left a message on the answering machine; it was her father, "Hi, Sweetie, I was just checking on you, and wanted to see if the clipping that I mailed to you had gotten there yet. Anyway, I love you, bye...Oh, yeah, this is Dad."

Clipping? Serena located the envelope bearing her father's return address, and opened it. A short note was included with the article.

In the spring of 1890, while monuments were being erected across the nation marking the twenty-fifth anniversary of Appomattox, *Harper's* magazine ran a piece that included interviews of some former slaves. Part of that story had recently appeared in the program her father purchased while touring an exhibit on the history of race relations at one of the facilities of the Louisiana State Museum in New Orleans. The portion Sam cut out and sent to his daughter contained the recollections of a recalcitrant Virginia slave sold and uprooted to the west. Part of it read:

Due to my refusal to give ritualistic respect to every white person simply because they were white, my Virginia master sold me to a slave trader. Eventually I was taken to the lucrative New Orleans slave market, placed on the auction block, and sold to Judge George Lamar of Raymond, Mississippi, for $1,000. It was in this manner that I came to Lamar Hall and became one of 217,329 slaves imported into Mississippi from 1830 to 1860.

My God, Serena thought, his new master was an ancestor of Judge Davis. She read on.

Love is no small matter for any man, but for a slave it represented a major crisis in life. During the trip to the judge's plantation, I told him that it was only fair that he know that I had vowed never to marry, nor would I again face separation from loved ones. Since my outspoken nature was responsible for my plight at that time, I thought it prudent to quickly add that if he ever forced me to marry I hoped it would be with a woman from another plantation because I just could not bear to see her mistreated.

The judge informed me that he was not a brutal man nor would I be forced to marry. He was true to his word in both respects, an exception to the other masters I had been around or heard of. He never once resorted to the lash, and even broke the law by teaching me to read, write, and keep his ledgers.

I knew the judge put a lot of faith in me, not just as a slave, but as a man. Thus, when he needed me most, entrusting me with a special mission involving one of the young misses, his granddaughter Emma, I considered it a sign of honor, trust, and respect. Thus, he did not have to bribe me with the promise of freedom to enlist my aid. I was already in the wagon with Miss Emma, loaded and ready to embark upon our journey, when he handed me the paper and told me that it was my freedom. "Lucas," he said, "today I'm finally making good on the original promise of this country."

That was the day I took on the name of the man whom I learned from the judge had once written that "all men are created equal, endowed by their Creator with certain inalienable rights," among which is freedom. Thus, I was no longer merely "Lucas." I became Lucas Jefferson.

According to the article, Lucas Jefferson continued his pursuit of knowledge after coming to New Orleans in 1863, and eventually became a respected student and teacher at Southern Agricultural and Mechanical College, founded in 1880, in Baton Rouge. He married and raised six children. The article contained more excerpts from his memoirs donated to the school, but Serena had read enough.

All of the legal arguments had been made, and it was never easy letting go of a case. Inevitably, there was a point which later came to mind that Serena wished had earlier surfaced in her thoughts when it would have counted for something. Normally she might have just suffocated in her own frustration, but Serena was determined to get a copy of the article in Judge Davis's hands. In short, but powerful prose, Lucas Jefferson's words conveyed the debilitating effects caused by the symbols of white supremacy, constant reminders ravaging the human spirit. Yet, it also equally conveyed how one person can make a difference in enabling another person to reach their full potential by exhibiting signs of respect and trust instead of oppression,

Abraham Lincoln once observed, "In giving freedom to the slave, we assure freedom to the free—honorable alike in what we give and what we preserve." To Serena, no Mississippian, black or white, could really be free to reach their full, honorable potential as a human being until that flag, a symbol of oppression and disrespect in her mind, was furled and replaced with something symbolizing unity in freedom, mutual respect, and trust. She thought how ironic it was that fate had made Judge Thomas Jefferson Davis III, direct descendant of Master George Lamar, the one person who could make it a reality, thereby making good the same original promise of this country for the descendants of a slave once merely named Lucas.

It may be the Thomas Jeffersons of the world who pen inspiring words, Serena thought, but it is the George Lamars and Tom Davises who are called upon to put them into action. The article spoke volumes. Serena would elaborate only by citing a single Bible verse on a yellow Post-it affixed to the judge's copy—James 1:22: *But be ye doers of the word, and not hearers only, deceiving your own selves.*

Before she turned off the lamp, Serena phoned her father; she wanted to thank him. No, there was much more in her heart that she needed to say.

CHAPTER 7

The otherwise sleepy town of Raymond found itself the stage of sheer drama in 1863. Spring comes early in Mississippi, and it was already bright, hot, and humid the morning of May 12 that year, as General John Gregg's brigade marched through the town to take on the advancing federal marauders. Tom Davis's Mercury was now traveling along the same street that had been lined with jubilant women, children, and old men. The belles and children cheered loudly, waving the Bonnie Blue Flag. In reply, the troops, duty to the South manifest in each face, gave the all familiar Rebel yell, a battle cry which many Yankees described as a demonic scream straight from the bowels of hell, but thought by Stonewall Jackson to be the sweetest music to ever touch one's ears.

Never entertaining the notion that their gallant defenders might lose, the women had spread a lavish picnic for their champions to enjoy after vanquishing the invaders. Six-year-old Estelle Trichnell's mother had Estelle gather flowers early that morning to toss at the passing soldiers. Yet, Estelle wrote years later, bashfulness overcame her when the moment arrived. Beginning with the first boom of the cannons, and rattle of rifle fire, and for years thereafter, the girl's conscience was tormented by her failure to act as she knew she should.

Tom Davis knew all too well that there is no acquittal in the tribunal of one's own conscience, and he pondered the possible casualties of his own inner conflict. He truly did not wish to rule against the banner of the state he loved. But would such a decision doom him to the suffering of a never-healing wound to his psyche, perpetually inflicted by conscience?

Grossly outnumbered, by the time the sun settled below the western horizon, what Confederates were not lying dead or wounded, along Fourteen Mile Creek and the nearby cotton fields, were in full retreat toward Jackson, and the federals began pouring into town. All the ladies of Raymond could do was watch in dismay as the victory vittles, prepared by them for the troops in gray and butternut, were quickly devoured by men in blue.

The courthouse, only four-years-old at the time, became the center of activity. Tunes, such as "The Union Forever," filled the air, and Old Glory was raised atop the courthouse cupola for the first time in two years. Tom Davis was approaching that building now. Floodlights on the front lawn illuminated the Stars and Stripes, and Tom felt himself being sucked back to that inauspicious time more than a century ago.

He parked on Main Street, below a giant live oak, and strode across the grounds where the Yankees had stacked their arms and encamped. Throughout the night, the townsfolk heard fifes, drums, and jubilant shouting, periodically interrupted by the racket of trespassing miscreants shooting a cow or tearing down a fence for their cooking pots. However, due to the number of wounded federal soldiers, an estimated 340, none of the buildings were burned. The Union wounded were placed in the town's churches and many of the homes. The Confederate wounded were taken to the courthouse.

Tom fumbled through his pockets and found his key. As he unlocked the door and stepped inside, he again experienced the eerie sensation that he was crossing a threshold of time. Shaking off the feeling, Tom plodded up the staircase to the second floor, twenty-four steps in all. Victor, the maintenance man, routinely turned off the air conditioner at 5:30 p.m., making the upper floor especially hot within a few hours.

Tom refrained from turning on any lights as he entered the courtroom as the floodlights from the front lawn cast a sufficient glow through the tall, undraped windows. Also, Tom did not want to cause unnecessary alarm to any townsfolk at that late hour and he knew exactly where the journal was located.

Proceeding toward his chambers, Tom absently drummed his fingers on one of the long, antique wood tables. It was one of two still used by lawyers during trials. One of similar construction, but much longer, was in the jury room. Bloodstains on the underside of all three bore witness to the horrors of a Civil War surgeon's scalpel. Tom himself had used the table he now unconsciously touched, numerous times over his career, but tonight the contact sparked something that sent a brief, but potent, chill up the back of his neck.

He quickly retrieved the journal, its leather binding old and rotting, the pages browned and brittle. Tom knew that he needed to take measures to preserve it, but never got around to doing anything about it. *Was the flag also a piece of history that needed to be preserved?* The thought was catapulted into oblivion when everything suddenly went black. The exterior lights no longer shone, and the heavy, wood door to his chambers slammed shut. Tom jerked at the startling resonation. There was no draft that could have possibly blown the portal closed.

Tom groped for the light switch in his chambers, but to no avail. Reaching to turn the doorknob, he found it ice cold, causing him to reflexively draw back. He reached again, forced the uncomfortably frigid knob, and stepped into a terrifying, grisly panorama of mayhem, gore, and misery. It was a mass of suffering humanity such as he had never beheld, even in his worst nightmare. Passing before their shocked and horrified spectator were scenes of the courtroom from the night of May 12, 1863!

Mangled bodies were strewn everywhere. Tom did not have to count them; he knew the number by heart—252 Confederate wounded. Flies swarmed about the room and crawled on the helpless men, relentlessly feeding on the blood that flowed, soaked, and eventually crusted. Most of the wretched beings were not men at all, but rather pitiful boys of sixteen or seventeen, and they were suffering. Oh, how those boys were suffering.

Minie balls were cylindrical bullets made with hollow bases to expand upon impact. If bone in a limb was struck, it was not just broken, but completely shattered, leaving nothing to be reset or mended. In such cases, amputation was certain. While chloroform existed, it was in short supply two years into the war. There was never enough on hand. Death even lurked for many with less serious injuries. Antiseptics were not yet dreamed of, so even a small wound to the hand or foot was susceptible to gangrene, and an ensuing slow demise.

Tom witnessed some of the lads screaming in agony at the torture of having an arm or leg sawed away. Others moaned or pleaded for water. Those who foresaw their end begged the women attempting to ease their misery, to write mothers or sweethearts, conveying love and letting them know where their bodies might be found. Then all, every last one of them, turned their faces to Tom, and cried out, "Don't! Don't!"

It was all that Tom Davis could bear. He tried seeking sanctuary in his chambers, but the door had again closed, and this time it was locked. He shut his eyes, tears trickling, and backed against the wall. He inched his way to the rear of the courtroom, found the door, and flung it open. He sprinted the short distance to the stairs, but just as he was turning to descend, a shocking sight outside froze him in place.

Tiny St. Mark's Episcopal Church, built in 1854, was just across the side street west of the courthouse. On the rear lawn of the church was a great pile of severed legs and arms. As Tom stared in disbelief, a woman in a long dress and bonnet appeared, her back to him, walking from the courthouse to the churchyard. She was carrying a metal washtub.

Approaching the ghastly mound, the woman turned, revealing her profile to Tom. Although most of her face and head were concealed, he thought there was something vaguely familiar about her. Tom could clearly see that the tub contained more human limbs; those on top protruded above its edge, and some even hung over the side. Legs were hooked on the rim at the knees, and arms were caught at the elbow.

The woman dumped the carnage atop the rest. Head down, she walked several steps back toward the courthouse. For no reason apparent to Tom, she stopped. After stooping to set the empty container on the ground, the woman slowly raised her head until she was gazing, through the second-floor window, directly at Tom, and pushed back her bonnet. *Merciful God!* Recognizing Olivia Lamar from family photographs, Tom felt tipsy. *Had he drank that much?*

Then it happened: ever so gradually, Olivia Lamar raised her right arm and pointed her finger at Tom. Her hellish scream, "Don't!" rattled the window glass, instinctively causing Tom to step backward. Downward the judge plunged, and blackness fell upon him.

CHAPTER 8

The rich aroma of freshly ground coffee brewing wafted through Lamar Hall. It momentarily diverted Tom Davis's attention from his soreness, which would only get worse, and a splitting headache that could not get any worse. He knew that he should go to the hospital to make sure nothing was broken and that he had not suffered a concussion. Nevertheless, after pouring a cup of the steaming java, Tom padded down the hall to his study.

Raising the window by a large, overstuffed leather chair, Tom was immediately greeted by the strong, sweet fragrance of the gardenias below, which thrived in the warm humidity. Easing himself into the soft chair, he pondered the strange phenomena of the previous night. Tom didn't know for sure how long he had been knocked out by the fall or exactly how many of the two dozen steps he actually hit. That he had lost track of time—by a hundred years or so—was an understatement.

Victor, the maintenance man, had found him at the base of the staircase when he arrived for work at 7:30 a.m. It was all so peculiar. What, if anything, was Tom to divine from the unanimous, distressed warnings of the specters? *Don't!* Don't what? It made no sense. Then again, as Tom once heard his grandfather say, "If the world was a logical place, it would be men who rode sidesaddle."

It was 8:15 a.m. now; the morning sun was rapidly rising over the high treetops of Lamar Hall's east woods, and Tom detected the faint scent of honeysuckle riding on the breeze from that direction. He normally savored some leisurely reading by the sunlight coming through the window while sipping his whole-bean roast, but today the glare was exacerbating his headache. He eased out of his chair to pull the drapes. Hundreds of books lined the room's shelves, but the one that captured

Tom's attention, as he resumed his seat, was the journal, in disarray, on the desk. It had come apart during its own tumble down the courthouse stairs, and Victor had helped him gather the pages, which were now, for the most part, randomly stuck between the fragile leather covers.

Tom perused the first of the loose, out-of-order pages, and the top line, penned in George Lamar's exquisite handwriting, sprang from the parchment. The first word was short and simple; yet Tom was almost as stupefied seeing it now as he had been hearing its apparitional directive the previous night—*don't*. The sentence actually began on the previous page, and once Tom starting reading, he could not stop.

I pray that we don't ever again succumb to the forces of extremists. One need only look to my own poor example at the Secession Convention to understand this lesson. It was in the futile hope of maintaining unity and, I am ashamed to now admit, out of fear of losing all influence in public life, if we persisted in our resistance that I and other Unionist delegates ultimately bowed to the will of the majority. We had made our fortunes and had much to risk in a war whose outcome to worldly men was clear before the first cannon fired on Sumter. We were vastly outnumbered by younger, brasher, ambitious men recklessly bent on acquiring slaves and broad acres. In the end, emotion outweighed reason.

Mr. Jefferson believed that if self-government was not to deteriorate into a general populace, it must be restrained by prudent and courageous statesmen. We failed—I failed—miserably. Almost a century ago, Mr. Jefferson recognized that in a democratic republic the exercise of one man's rights would occasionally interfere with those of another. His writings urged us to bridge the chasm between "rights" and what is right.

This sacrifice of my personal convictions and my participation in the madness that plunged our state into destitution and ruin will eternally grieve me. Newton was not entirely correct: every action does not cause an equal reaction. The counteraction can be much more severe. Our actions led to war and all of its horrifying realities and destruction. And if that were not sufficient penance, we are presently suffering the indignities of Reconstruction. The pendulum has, indeed, swung with greater force on its return.

We have given little heed to Mr. Jefferson's teachings this past century. Perhaps that will change by the end of the next hundred years. God willing, by the 1960s, we will have more fully appreciated the concept that our "pursuit of happiness" is not rooted exclusively in selfish ambition, but also in genuine benevolence. Jefferson believed that a benevolent Creator endowed us with a moral sense and has so arranged our nature that we receive pleasure from doing good to others. Consequently, the exercise of benevolence is our own interest, for our happiness depends on the happiness of others. It may be that the dream of a new and more benevolent society will become reality, and my descendants will no longer have to bear the burden of my weakness. It seems, however, that although the battle is long over, no one knows it.

Is that what Olivia Lamar attempted to imprint on Tom's very soul when she unleashed that horrible scream? *Don't!* Don't capitulate to extremists like Todd Murphy. Their path leads to destruction—if not of body, at least of spirit? And what of the frightful chorus of all the dying and maimed? *Don't!* Don't be misguided by the demagoguery of politicians?

Look at us. Behold our suffering and consider the reason. Yes, in the end we defended our homes, but the madness was set in motion by one issue—slavery. You see, hardly any of us came from slave-owning families. Our wounds came from the blast of gunfire, but our death warrants came with the echo of the gavel's fall adjourning that infamous convention. You've seen the document; the politicians proudly and defiantly committed their reason to paper. We were made to believe that our whole way of life would be erased. We were duped. Will you be, as well? Don't!

Tom knew in his heart what he had to do, but could he bring himself to really do it? He picked up the phone and punched in the number to the chambers of Judge J. Alexander Stillwell. Although he told his protégé about his fall, Tom dared not mention his vision, hallucination, or whatever the hell it was.

"My God, Tom! Are you okay?" the younger jurist asked.

"Yes, yes. Just the price of getting old or clumsy—or both," Tom replied.

"Fifty-five is hardly old."

"Which narrows it down to being a klutz." When Stillwell didn't respond, "No argument, Alex?"

"Be it beyond me to ever argue with the senior judge."

"Such patronizing bullshit will get you everywhere." After a pause, "But seriously, in addition to letting you know that I will not be in today, I need a favor."

"Consider it done."

"I think I've made my point with Murphy. If I keep him locked up any longer, I'm afraid I'll make a martyr out of him."

"You want me to sign an order letting him out?"

"I'd appreciate it, but put something in there that will get the point across that similar misconduct in the future will carry much harsher penalties."

"No problem," Stillwell replied. "Just between us, have you decided what you're going to do with the flag?" Tom told him what he was contemplating. "Jeez Tom, you stand for election next year."

"You're right. So why don't I exercise my prerogative as senior judge and reassign the case to you?"

"Why don't we just forget I even asked?"

Tom laughed. "Anyway, if you need me for anything, I'll be here at the house relaxing and drafting the ...damn."

"What is it?"

"I don't have a computer here, and I left my laptop at the office."

"In Jackson?"

"Yeah."

"If it will keep you from reassigning the case from hell to me, I'll bring it to you."

"I thought you had a trial today."

"Settled. Got the call last night. I've got a sentencing in a few minutes, then I'll come on over."

Tom thanked Stillwell, and asked him to let Kay know what was going on. Tom was not up to repeating the details of his fall to his court administrator. He had other things on his mind. While talking with Stillwell, he had not heard a car drive up, but as Tom hung up, he was certain that he heard footsteps on the veranda.

CHAPTER 9

Tom Davis was stunned by the presence of the large-framed man ascending the veranda steps. Although they had spoken sporadically over the phone, Tom had not personally visited with his college roommate in years. Now, the Republican senator from Mississippi—the President *Pro Tem* no less, third in the line of constitutional succession to the most powerful position on Earth—was making an unexpected house call. Even as United States Senator Robert Devereaux smiled, and the beefy paw that had shaken a million hands wrapped around Tom's, the judge knew that something was afoot. The news left him dumbfounded.

"Of course I'm flattered, Bob. I don't know what to say. I'm speechless."

"That'll be the day," the senator quipped.

"But it's been decades since I set foot in federal court. I'm afraid I'd be lost."

The senator had anticipated Tom's reticence, but Devereaux had mastered the talent of reading people, evaluating their strengths and weaknesses as deftly as he had read those of opposing quarterbacks as Ole Miss's All-American middle linebacker. The senator also knew through his sources that Tom had been seeking sanctuary in a bottle, and Devereaux was determined to provide a safer, loftier haven, one that he knew his friend had privately longed for, even while advocating others for similar positions; and the senator had the political juice to bestow it— a federal judgeship on the Fifth Circuit Court of Appeals.

"Lost? Who are you kidding? All you have to do is read, for crying out loud. And that's all you do anyway, ole buddy. Besides, you'll have a damn army of law clerks at your beck and call. So what do you say?" Tom's ensuing hesitation caused Devereaux to wonder whether his roommate was being coy or seriously considering declining. "I understand your concern, Tom. I really do. But *you* have to understand that everything is changing in Washington, and I mean *everything*. The Democrats are filibustering every damn one of the President's judicial nominees."

"I'm aware of that. We do have televisions out here. So why should I be an exception? The last thing I want is to go down a dead-end confirmation process, only to get Borked. It seems to me the President cannot afford that kind of long and bloody battle."

"You're right, he can't; which is the very reason he asked me about you."

"The President?"

"Let me tell you something about politics: perception is *everything* and you're not exactly unknown outside of Raymond, you know. Whatever sons-a-bitches in the country haven't seen the movie about your stand in the Summerville case, have heard about it. Just last night, every major network was carrying the news of your latest crusade for that poor, struggling black family against one of the corporate giants of the auto world." Devereaux said it with more than a touch of sarcasm.

"I'm no crusader, and the Dennis family is neither poor nor struggling. I simply ruled in favor of their right not to have the government pirate their property. Any other spin on it is sensationalism. Capitalizing on it just doesn't seem right."

"I repeat, perception is everything, and at this crucial moment, like it or not, you're perceived as a damn hero. Even to the Democrats. No, correct that. *Especially* to the Democrats. With the President nominating you, capped with a few well-timed news conferences by me and other Republican stalwarts, you'll be confirmed in no time."

"But how can you be sure I'll be nominated? Isn't some lawyer on the coast supposed to have the inside track through Bishop?"

"I'm not getting through to you, am I?" the senator rhetorically asked, shaking his head in frustration. "First, while he and I try to agree on a name to submit to the President, George Bishop is the *junior* senator from Mississippi. You're looking at *senior*. Second, I was sent here by the President. We met last night. The President of the United-fucking-States directed me to get my big ass down here immediately to tell you that he would consider it a personal favor to be able to submit your name to the Senate. I'm to deliver your answer to his face, in the Oval Office, this afternoon. So what's your answer to the President, Tom?"

Tom Davis did not consider himself a hero of any sort. He certainly had his flaws, and nobody was more cognizant of that than he was himself. Need, greed, job security, sense of civic duty—whatever the reason, the fact was he did covet the life appointment. No more pandering for votes. The angst of how his decisions would be perceived by a fickle electorate gone forever. "Okay," he said. "If you think it will work."

"Dammit, Tom, I'm telling you that it's a cinch."

"You know as well as I do how everything is dug up. It could be anything."

"Not with you. You're the most boring person I know."

Tom was far from mollified, worried about what skeleton might be discovered in some closet of his past and yanked into the light. His increased drinking and the lapse in judgment years ago that led to a regretful indiscretion in Reno were but two instantly coming to mind. Wishing neither the President, nor his friend, to be blindsided, Tom laid the cards on the table.

"Ease up on yourself. It'll be okay," the senator assured him. "It's not a big deal. If she hasn't come forward by now, after the movie and all that publicity, it's history. Leave the past in the past. Speaking of which, please tell me that you're not thinking about ruling on this flag crap anytime soon?"

"I'm still mulling it over. I keep bouncing back and forth. I don't know what I'm going to do."

"Mull all you want, but no decision until after confirmation. You've got the perfect alliance right now, but it's fragile. If you rule against the flag, you will lose your base of Republican support. On the other hand, if you rule for the flag, you can kiss all of your backing from the Democrat side of the aisle good-bye. Any decision at all would be screwing yourself, so just stay pat. Understand?"

CHAPTER 10

It was good to be home, but he did not yet feel released. Although it was only one night that Todd Murphy had been confined, he could empathize with the thing inside him, in a cage of sorts and craving liberation. It had to be accomplished tonight.

The phone was ringing as he stepped into his apartment shortly before noon. The machine picked up the call before he could answer.

"I don't know where you are, mother..."

Recognizing Sonny Clark's voice, Murphy yanked up the receiver. "I told you to never call me here. I was going to call you from a pay phone."

"Shut the fuck up and listen."

"I'll call back within the hour. We need to talk, but not on this line."

"This child didn't just arrive in town on the back of a watermelon truck, asshole. You're dodging. So you go ahead and hang up if you choose. But if you do, I'll eventually find you and slit your throat from ear to ear." Todd was seething, trying to restrain his anger, but Sonny misinterpreted the hesitation for fear. "That's better," Sonny continued, "I'm in no mood for bullshit. I sat in the damn woods all night and the son-of-a-bitch never came home. He's still among the living."

"I know."

"Where the fuck you been? I've been calling all morning."

Todd could see on the digital display that eight messages had been left since he was last home. He filled Sonny in on the events leading to his overnight stay in jail, which Sonny found quite humorous. "Well, that explains that, but what the fuck you mean, you know?"

"Know what?"

"When I told you the man was still alive and kicking, you said- I know. How's that? What kind of shit you trying to pull on me, man?"

"It was Davis who called Judge Stillwell this morning to get me out. It's as simple as that. I'm not pulling anything." *Not yet anyway. I so look forward to pulling a blade across your arrogant throat.*

"I'm going to get me some sleep, but I'll be back out there tonight."

It was then that a brainstorm struck Todd. With some finesse, he could kill two birds, so to speak. No loose ends. And that was what Sonny Clark had become. "That's the spirit, my man," Todd replied. "But, just to make sure that one of us gets him, I'll be out there too."

"I ain't your damn *man*, asshole, and the motherfucker is mine. You got it?"

"Sure." Todd felt himself growing more enraged at the insolence. *Control. I've played Sonny well up to now. Stay calm and think.* He decided to tweak Sonny a little. In one respect, Todd thought the other man was like a woman—hell-bent on doing whatever was forbade. "The more I think about it, there is no way that you can go out again, Sonny. You're forgetting who the escapee is. Your damn face is plastered all over the news. There's too much of a chance you'd be spotted. The best place for you is right where you are."

Midway through an explosion of expletives, Sonny noticed what was airing on the television in his room in one of the fleabag motels on Highway 49. His lips twisted into a sardonic smile. "Hey, asshole."

"What?"

"I'm not the only one on the fucking news. Check out channel three."

Todd glanced around the room for the remote and clicked on the television just in time to see himself being led through the tunnel connecting the Jackson courthouse to the jail. Footage showed Todd screaming and hollering every step of the way. An interview with Serena Raven followed. She was praising Davis's ruling in the Dennis case, and expressing confidence in a favorable decision regarding the state flag. "It is time that people in other parts of the world realize that Mississippians are not insensitive, backward, bigots in sheep's clothing. The few like Todd Murphy do not represent the vast majority of the people of this state. It is true that I was not born here, but neither was Mr. Murphy. I understand that he is actually a transplant from New York."

Now it was Todd Murphy who blew up. "That cunt!" he screamed into the phone still in his hand.

Sonny had the last laugh, and hung up. He would get some sleep like he said, and be back in the woods after nightfall. The die was cast; Judge Thomas Davis, Todd Murphy, and Sonny Clark had a rendezvous with destiny. With that thought in mind, Sonny slept like a baby.

CHAPTER 11

The sound of tires grinding against macadam alerted Tom Davis that another visitor was coming up the road to Lamar Hall. Tom was stepping out onto the porch as a black Lincoln Town Car ground to an abrupt halt. The hissing beneath the car's hood was apparently not the only thing running hot. Jim Blackwell was boiling over.

Tom had been dreading this inevitable encounter, and attempted to allay his trepidation, and his fraternity brother's pugnacity, with a little humor. "Nice car, but it doesn't say much for your faith in your own product," Tom remarked, after Jim slammed the door shut.

"It's a rental, asshole. And don't you dare talk to me about faith. Your decision doesn't say much about faith in friendship, brotherhood, and loyalty, does it?"

"Come on in, Jim, and let's talk about it." Tom turned and led the way inside to the study. He settled back in the easy chair and offered the high-backed one behind the desk to his irate guest. "Coffee?" Tom offered.

"No, I don't want any damn coffee!" Blackwell caustically snapped. "What I want," he threatened, leaning forward in the chair and resting his forearms atop the desk, "is to break your neck. We had an understanding."

"The only thing I promised you was that I would give every consideration to your company's position. Anything that you understood beyond that was evidently what you wanted to hear."

"Don't split legal hairs with me, Tom. I came to you, in private, as a brother in need. I confided in you. You knew my future hung in the balance with us getting that property. Forget the benefits to the company. Hell, even setting aside the economic boon it would have been to the

48

state, and the hundreds of jobs to the locals, you turned your back on me *personally* when I needed you most. And for what? A handful of niggers."

Now it was Tom whose ire was raised. "Let me tell you something, Jim. It was only out of friendship and brotherhood that I didn't have your racist ass tossed right out of my chambers to begin with and report the matter to the bar. It was an *ex parte* communication and totally out of line. A true friend would not have put me in that position. As to loyalty, if you don't know that my foremost allegiance is to the law, then you don't know me at all."

"You could have ruled either way. There was enough gray area in the law."

"Bullshit."

"So why did I have to hear it on the news, Tom? Didn't I at least deserve the courtesy of hearing it directly from you?"

"No, you did not. You haven't understood a word I've said. You're a selfish rat scurrying around in a little corporate maze looking for one thing—your damn cheese. Blind to everything around, you run into a wall. Then, instead of reasoning things out, you get pissed off and run headlong in the opposite direction until you collide into another wall."

"We're not talking about *cheese,* damn it. I lost my fucking *job!*"

"What?"

"I promised the board of directors. I laid my job on the line."

"I'm sorry," Tom replied. "All I can say is that you put yourself, as well as me, in a helluva position."

"You self-righteous prick!" Jim bellowed, bounding up from the chair.

"Coffee's ready." Alex Stillwell was standing in the doorway, holding a silver tray with a carafe and two china cups. "Don't mind me," he said, looking at Blackwell, who quietly returned to his chair.

The only sound in the room was that of Stillwell setting the tray on the desk and pouring coffee. Passing a cup to Davis, he said, "Tom, I forgot to tell you earlier that Serena Raven sent something to you. It's in that envelope on the tray." Noting the confusion on Tom's face, Stillwell explained that Serena had dropped by to see Tom at the courthouse, and took up his administrator's offer to send the envelope with the laptop, via Stillwell.

Tom nodded his understanding. "Jim, I'm a little stiff today," he confessed to Blackwell. "Would you save me the trouble of getting up and hand me that letter opener? There, in front of you, on the desk." Blackwell, who had calmed somewhat in the younger judge's presence, obliged.

As Tom slit open the envelope, Stillwell was filling Blackwell's cup and could not resist a barb. "Mr. Blackwell, from what just I heard, I assume you do not prefer yours black." He stopped pouring and met the other man's eyes. "Cream? It's white and rich."

Blackwell stormed out of the house and made a quick retreat from the estate, slinging gravel and leaving a billowing cloud of dust.

Tom appreciated his young colleague more than words could express, especially his congratulatory encouragement earlier when Tom confided in Alex the details of Senator Devereaux's unexpected visit. Tom enjoyed the company of his protégé, and hated that he, too, had to leave.

"Alex, why don't you come back out tonight? I'd really like to pick your brain about this flag case."

CHAPTER 12

Tom Davis was delighting in the camaraderie. He had spent the better part of the day reading George Lamar's journal. Now, as the long shadows of dusk engulfed Lamar Hall, he was taking a swig of the Chivas Regal his visitor had poured for him. Alex Stillwell was sipping Jewel of Russia on the rocks.

The men talked more of Tom's eminent appointment to the federal bench, and the senator's request that no decision be made concerning the state flag until after the confirmation vote. Even if Tom honored the request, he saw no harm in discussing the merits of the case with his protégé. The conversation segued from the arguments, to the lawyers who had delivered them.

"Speaking of Serena Raven, do you mind if I ask what urgent message I delivered for her this morning?" Stillwell asked.

"You know, after the hubbub with Jim, I completely forgot about it. It's still on the desk, in front of you. Read it to me."

After Stillwell finished, Tom's only comment was, "Well I'll be damned."

"What was the special mission regarding Emma?"

"Bits and pieces of the story have been passed along over the years. There's a lot of history in this land, Alex, even in this house. I've never given you the grand tour, have I?"

Alex shook his head. "No, and I would love to hear all about it."

"Come along then, my young friend, and I'll reveal what I know. Oh my, if these walls could speak." After a pause, he chuckled, "Perhaps they will, once we refresh our libations."

After several refills during the course of the tour, Tom was feeling no pain and soon under-the-table plowed. Alex was thankful they had

51

already made their way to the second floor and he did not have to worry about getting Tom up a flight of stairs to his bedroom. Alex half-guided, half-carried his mentor to the bed, momentarily balanced him on the edge, and let him fall into the down comforter. As Alex swung the older man's feet onto the mattress, he was startled by the sound of someone pounding on a door downstairs.

Bo Landry was wired, scared, and confused. "Where's Tom? I need to talk to him?"

"He's upstairs, Bo. What's the matter?" By the time he finished his question, Bo was halfway to the second floor. "Bo?"

"Tom!"

"Bo!"

Alex entered the bedroom behind Bo, who found Tom, mouth agape, motionless on the bed.

"How long have you been here?" Bo demanded. "Tell me what happened, goddammit!"

Tom remained oblivious. "We had a few drinks," Stillwell replied, "or rather in Tom's case, several too many. He's soused."

"What?"

"Smashed, canned, tanked, stewed, passed-fucking-out. Other than that, he's fine." As if on cue, Tom started snoring. "Why don't we go downstairs and leave Sleeping Beauty alone?" Alex suggested.

Once they were in the kitchen, Bo asked, "What the hell were y'all celebrating?"

"He wanted some company. The next thing I knew, he was giving me what he called the grand tour of the house," Alex explained.

Bo was calmer. "I'm glad that he finally found someone who was interested."

"You mean you've never been on it?"

"Not by a long shot. This old place has always given me the creeps."

"And you are giving *me* the creeps. What's wrong with you tonight?"

Bo spent the next thirty minutes telling Alex about the drug bust of the previous night. One of the ground crew members they had apprehended sang like a canary and agreed to turn state's evidence. The man he worked for was none other than Todd Murphy. "Seems that he was funding his flag campaign with a little Colombian snort," Bo explained.

"Jeez Bo, I'm sorry. I signed an order for Tom this morning releasing him from jail. Tom had him in for contempt."

"I know," Bo replied between chuckles. I nabbed him pretty much right after he got home. Asshole was calling somebody a cunt over the phone as we entered."

"So what's any of this have to do with Tom?"

"Murphy is scared shitless of prison and wanted to deal. I told him I wasn't interested and that nothing would please me more than him becoming the belle-of-the-ball at Parchman. Then he asked if my pleasure was worth Tom's life. Son-of-a-bitch actually smiled when he said it."

Now it was Alex who expressed concern. "Go on."

"The lowlife wanted to trade the details for a deal. It was all that I could do to keep from breaking his neck, but I played along. He said that he had it on good information that Sonny Clark, who escaped from prison a few weeks ago..."

"I know who he is."

"...was planning a hit on Tom." Bo let it linger a moment. "Tonight."

"My God."

"I was afraid Clark had gotten to Tom before I could get here."

"So what's your plan?"

"These woods will soon be crawling with deputies. In the meantime, I'll hang around outside and keep watch."

"What kind of deal did you have to make with Murphy?" Stillwell asked.

"Only bail."

"You let him out! What if he skips?"

"I will personally track his sorry ass to the far ends of the planet."

"Don't underestimate him."

"I don't underestimate anyone."

"How soon before the Cavalry arrives?"

"Shouldn't be more than thirty minutes."

"Want me to stick around until then?"

"Not hardly. If I come across the bastard, the last person I want as a witness is a judge." There was no doubt in Alex's mind of the seriousness beneath the words.

"Then I guess I'll be on my way."

Driving down the road, Alex passed a caravan of police cars speeding toward Lamar Hall, and felt better, much better.

*****

Sonny Clark scrutinized the increasing activity on the Lamar Hall grounds with acute concentration. Cops, and lots of them, were dispersing in all directions. Sonny was confident that he could handle his own against a lesser force, but sticking around this hornet's nest would be insane. He had mastered patience. There would be other more opportune nights.

Sonny's decision to leave was his last. He never saw anyone, nor heard or felt a thing—not even the single stroke of the razor-sharp edge of honed, stainless steel. Yet, for a second or two that seemingly lasted eons, he was keenly aware that his head was nearly severed from the rest of his body. Then mercifully, his oxygen-starved brain shut down and Sonny Clark was no more. The tattoo on his falling, bald head was a curious sight in the weeds. The eagle had landed.

CHAPTER 13

Several hours had passed since the sun had made its daily descent. A full moon now presided over the clear, starlit firmament surmounting Lamar Hall, casting an umbra against the forest encircling the lawn. Smaller, more defined shadows stirred on the periphery of Judge Tom Davis's house, shaped by deputies slowly pacing the four galleries. Inside, as Bo Landry hung up the phone, the 18th century grandfather clock, which the judge's ancestor and first lord of the manor had transported from Virginia, was striking the hour. It was eleven o'clock, and Bo had called Serena Raven to explain his ongoing MIA status. Although it had been but two nights, it seemed ten times that.

Their lapse in companionship was equally disappointing to Serena, but the letdown took a backseat to concern for the judge's safety. Before exchanging "Goodnights," Serena said that she would leave her backdoor unlocked, a ray of hope that the danger would quickly pass and Bo would steal his way into her lonely bed.

"We'll see," was all Bo could say. Ending the call, he joined the deputies on the front veranda. The hoots of two owls communicating to each other, and the typical refrain of the other woodland life forms offered assurance that nothing was amiss.

Returning inside, Bo proceeded to the kitchen and put on a fresh pot of coffee. He had never developed a taste for it, but thought it might be appreciated by his comrades. Once the brew started dripping, Bo crossed the foyer into the study, and took a seat at Tom's desk. Everything had been so hectic the past forty-eight hours. Now that he was forced to cool his heels, he would make the most of the lull by catching up on his reports.

Bo was sure Tom wouldn't mind him using the laptop that was

already open and turned on. At Bo's touch, the screensaver disappeared, revealing the text of a document. From the menu, he brought up the "Save As" dialog box. To get some inkling of what to type, Bo scanned the page. Reading something about the Confederate flag, he surmised that it was about Serena's case, and curiosity got the best of him. He scrolled to the top of the page.

An estimated 25,000 American troops died in the Revolutionary War, it read; *20,000 in the War of 1812; 13,283 in the Mexican War; and 2,446 in the Spanish-American War.* Wondering what these casualties had to do with Mississippi's flag, Bo continued his perusal.

World War I resulted in 116,516 deaths of American soldiers and World War II was fought at a cost of 405,399. We lost 36,516 in the Korean War and 58,209 in Vietnam. The Persian Gulf War resulted in 299 American deaths; and, to date, a little over 4,000 American soldiers died in Afghanistan and Iraq.

Bo was still at a loss regarding the relevance, and was confounded by the absence of any reference to Civil War casualties. Tom soon, however, began tying it together.

These fatalities total a whopping 620,939. Yet, this figure—the sum total of American casualties in all major wars in the history of this country, save that of the Civil War—is less than the 625,000 who perished in that single conflict.

As a former Navy Seal, Bo Landry could appreciate the willingness of men and women to lay down their lives for their country; but this information was rather staggering. He read on.

There is much merit in the plaintiffs' arguments concerning any officially sanctioned vestige of the underlying, explicit reason for the government of this state to secede and join ten other seceding states to form the government of the Confederate States of America, a wartime enemy of the United States of America. Undeniably, the reason for such governmental action was slavery.

Serena would be thrilled. The thought of her prevailing in such a passionate cause brought a smile to Bo's face. Then he saw the "but."

But, it must be remembered that what is loosely referred to as the "Confederate" flag was actually never the official flag of the Confederate States of America. Thus, it cannot be logically said to be representative of the reason for any state's secession and participation in the formation of the ensuing government, i.e. slavery. General P.G.T. Beauregard designed the banner which is the subject of the lawsuit before this Court. He did so in distinction of the Confederate soldiers, not their government; and most of those soldiers came from non-slaving-holding families. Thus, they fought for reasons aside from slavery, and it

*would be the greatest negligence to blame the soldier in any war for the
actions and motives of the politicians who brought it about.*

Tom followed this reasoning with a quote from the commentaries of
Carlton McCarthy, a teenager who joined the Confederate army: *If the
peace of this country can only be preserved by forgetting the
Confederate soldier's deeds and his claims upon the South, the blessing
is too dearly bought... When we fill up, hurriedly, the bloody chasm
opened by the war, we should be careful that we do not bury therein
many noble deeds, some tender memories, some grand examples, and
some hearty promises washed with tears.*

There was more, but Bo's heart sank for Serena, and the clock in the
foyer chimed once, indicating that thirty minutes had passed. The coffee
was more than ready, and welcomed by the deputies. Tired as he was, Bo
was determined to maintain an alert vigil. He simply could not do any
less than what was expected of the others dutifully on hand.

Thus, returning the empty pot to the kitchen, Bo pulled a Coke from
the fridge and popped open the tab. As he took in the caffeine-loaded
beverage, his mind wandered back to Serena. Everything seemed
peaceful, and the men outside were some of the sheriff's best. Besides,
Bo reasoned, he was not entirely sure Todd Murphy had not fabricated
the entire story about Sonny Clark, in an effort to gain some leniency on
his dope charge. Bo could not mention to Serena anything of what he had
just read, but a little cuddling and pampering before she received the
news would not hurt. Thus, he decided to take her up on her invitation to
come over.

Setting his can on the countertop, Bo padded up the stairs to check on
Tom. He eased the bedroom door open and saw the measured rise and
fall of the judge's breathing beneath the covers. Satisfied that his charge
was safe and sound, Bo quietly closed the door and returned downstairs.
Just as he entered the kitchen, he felt the vibration of his cell phone.

"What the hell do you mean Todd Murphy is out?" Bo hissed.

"I dropped by the jail to see if I could squeeze some information out
of him about his supplier," explained Dennis Phillips, another agent with
the Mississippi Bureau of Narcotics. "When I asked for him, I was told
he had been released."

"How? Why?"

"According to the desk sergeant, the son-of-a-bitch produced a copy
of a release order signed by Judge Stillwell."

"That was to release him for contempt, goddammit; not the dope
charge."

"Hey, don't shoot the messenger."

Dennis had already issued an APB, or "All Points Bulletin", for

Murphy; the only thing they could do was wait. It seemed to Bo that's all he ever did these days. Angry and frustrated, he walked outside and stood on the front veranda trying to collect his thoughts. The Choctaws who once inhabited the land believed owls to be harbingers of death, and damned if they weren't kicking up a ruckus now.

Was Sonny Clark really out there watching and waiting? The sole evidence pointing toward him was Todd Murphy; but even if Murphy had lied, it could have been only a partial falsehood. Bo had conducted enough interrogations to know that the best prevarications were those laced with a tinge of truth. Did any fallaciousness in Todd Murphy's statement lie in his accusation that anyone was coming to murder Tom, or in fingering Sonny Clark as the would-be killer? For all Bo knew, it could even be the liar himself.

Before speculation spiraled out of control, Bo focused on the one thing of which he was certain: that he could not—would not—under any circumstance, leave Tom. Piercing his heart was the dagger of guilt that he had come so close to defecting for personal desire.

Bo considered calling Serena to tell her to go ahead and lock up; that it was certain he would not be coming. However, it was after midnight and she would be asleep. Bo did not want to wake her. He grabbed his soda and returned to the study as there were reports still requiring his attention.

CHAPTER 14

Soon after Bo's call, Serena went through her ritual, making her nest in the satin sheets and pillows. She paid no attention to her bedside clock as the minute digit advanced, displaying "11:42" as the time. Nor was she cognizant that the pons area of her brain, situated at the organ's base, was transmitting signals to the thalamus region, which relayed them to the cerebral cortex. Although unaware of the physiological cause, Serena would shortly be fully conscious of its effect, for she was entering that phase of sleep known as REM, or rapid eye movement, the stage during which the strange, illogical experiences we call dreams proliferate.

Researchers candidly confess they do not know much about why we undergo such visions—Freud believed them to be "safety valves" for unconscious desires; but whether or not we are able to recall the experience, most of us spend in excess of two hours each night dreaming. The cerebral cortex is the outer layer of the brain and serves as the center for our learning, reasoning, and informational organization. Thus, some scientists theorize that dreams are the cortex's attempt to find meaning, or some rationalization, in the random signals it receives from the thalamus, creating a story out of the fragments. When the story results in inescapable terror, fear, or extreme anxiety, we know it as a nightmare, which tends inexplicably to be more common in females.

Tonight, the story authored by Serena's cortex had a rather benign beginning. In fact, it was quite serene. She was stretched out in the small boat of her childhood, gently rocking, like a baby in a cradle, by the soft tide of the Caribbean. A book of Greek myths rested, opened, across her stomach. Although Serena's eyes were shut, she was not asleep, but rather wistfully musing on the story she had just finished: "The Myth of the Minotaur," a creature with the body of a man and head of a bull, the byproduct of a queen's lust for a beautiful white bull.

Just as many people today are all too quick to bargain with the Almighty, making grand promises in exchange for some miracle, King Minos offered a prayer to Poseidon. If the god of the sea would bestow Minos with the grandest of creatures, the king would return the gesture as the worthiest of sacrifices. But, in prayer, as in most things, one should exercise caution in what is beseeched.

Minos had no sooner made his petition when, miraculously, a splendid snowy-white bull emerged from the ocean depths and swam ashore. Although his supplication was granted, the king's life was soon thrown into turmoil by allowing his covetousness to overwhelm his moral obligation, deciding to keep the tribute for himself, and sacrifice to his god a less sterling substitute.

Enraged by the insult, Poseidon caused the king's wife to fall madly in love with the beast. Overwhelmed by this unnatural passion, Queen Pasiphae enlisted the assistance of Daedalus, a renowned craftsman, who constructed a hollow, wooden cow, and covered it with hide. Together, they wheeled it into the pasture where the magnificent bull was kept. After helping the queen inside the structure, through a door he had fashioned, Daedalus withdrew, and let the queen's perverse desires run their course. The progeny of that lust was the hideous, flesh-eating Minotaur.

Desperately wanting to hide this living evidence of the royal family's shame, the king sought the guidance of the oracle at Delphi. As a result of the insight he gained, the king commissioned Daedalus for another project: the design and construction of the Labyrinth, an enormous maze in which the Minotaur was penned, but the beast was not alone. Young men and women were also shut into the maze, as sacrifices, by the king. Hopelessly lost, they wandered about, panic-stricken, until invariably caught and devoured by the Minotaur.

These were the thoughts that filled Serena's mind as the ocean's tender oscillations brought on a gradual slumber as effectively as a mother's lullaby. A dream within a dream began to take shape: of a sublime, caring suitor. At first, the visage of the figure walking atop the calm sea toward Serena was nebulous, shrouded by the fog that had set in. It was a recurring dream, but her lover had a different face in each one, and he was never someone Serena knew. *What would her paramour look like this time? Would she finally recognize him? It would surely be an encouraging omen if it were Bo.* Their relationship felt promising enough; or was it all a fairy tale? As Serena pondered these questions, the nearing figure steadily emerged from the haze. This was no romantic tale, however; it was a living nightmare! The countenance which Serena beheld was of no man at all, but rather a bull. It was the Minotaur, and with mighty vaporous snorts, it was coming for her!

CHAPTER 15

Most mammals and birds show signs of REM sleep, making it possible to think that they, too, dream. Cold-bloodied animals are a different story. For them, dreams are impossible. One such beast slowly made its way along the reservoir water, progressing with fixed determination toward its prey. Although the beast could not recall ever experiencing a dream, he was not without his sexual fantasies. Whether or not they admit it, everyone has them, and the beast was no different in that respect. Nor was the beast a unique breed by feeling anger and, at times, even outright rage. Most Homo sapiens however, come into this world with a kind of internal cage, in which they keep the hobgoblins of their minds under restraint.

It wasn't that the beast was born without such a cage, for he could exercise restraint if he willed it enough. The beast merely chose to unlock his door more often than most. When those opportunities arose, the demons indeed roamed at will, but there was a method, an order, to the havoc. In fact, the most chilling aspect of the beast, like that of many other serial killers, was his ability to remain very rational and calculating.

One down, more to go. Sonny Clark had simply been an impediment to a goal. And although that particular objective had not yet been attained, the beast was not concerned. It was only a matter of time, and he could adapt. He was very adept at that. Consequently, the beast had decided to simply alter the order of items on his agenda, and he was glad that he had. Sonny Clark had been a necessity, but this was going to be blissful.

Helping himself to a bass boat, which he found farther up the Ross Barnett Reservoir, the beast leisurely made his way along the shoreline.

When the moonlight revealed the rear of Serena Raven's house, he killed the Evinrude and traveled the rest of the way by the silent, electric, trolling motor, concealing the craft among the trees at the water's edge. Eight-foot-high brick walls extended from the shore, along the north and south boundaries of the backyard. The beast crept toward the house, between the one on the north side and tall shrubbery.

None of the house lights were on, inside or out. However, those radiating a faint, aqua luster from beneath the swimming pool's surface, and the luminosity of the full moon, warranted precaution. Since disconnecting the phone line would be futile against the use of a cell phone, the beast would not waste the time or effort. The alarm system though, was a different matter. He was considering the most efficient means of disabling it as he neared the corner of the house. This train of thought was suddenly broken however, by the sound of the sliding-glass door being pulled open.

Startled fully awake by her nightmare, and unable to go back to sleep, Serena thought some aerobic exercise would help. Rising from bed, she had pulled on a terrycloth robe and went out to the pool for a swim.

Although it would be unusual for anyone to be on the water at this hour, Serena nevertheless scanned the environs. Detecting no potential invasion of her privacy, she loosened the belt and let her covering fall on the patio pavers.

It was a long time and many victims ago, since South Padre Island when, with bated breath, he had first loitered and watched. On that occasion, the beast's breathing had been rapid with excitement. Now however, the inhalation and exhalation were as unvarying and mechanical, as if he were on a respirator. In retrospect, that initial foray had been somewhat sophomoric, but over time, his senses had become as finely tuned as the most exquisite Stradivarius.

The beast hungrily took in the welcome display of his victim's nakedness, as she took three slow, smooth strides with long, shapely legs, and momentarily paused at the pool's edge. She brought her arms together, straight over her head, slightly flexed her knees, and sprang. It might have technically been a dive, but to the beast it seemed more like she effortlessly glided—first in air, then the water. Serena flowed along the surface by strokes of arms as graceful as the bard described the oars of Cleopatra's royal vessel. Back and forth she swam, and with each lap the beast's appetite became more ravenous.

Finally, she stopped, stood, and slicked back her wet, glistening hair. As she ascended the steps in a corner of the pool, the beast considered how appropriately she had been named: Serena—goddess of the hunt, nature, and the moon. The droplets trickling down her nude figure shimmered in the moonlight. Although the gossamer breeze warmed the air, the water must have been cool, the first fruits of which were the pair of hard, unripe berries now protruding in profile from Serena's naked breasts. As far as the beast was concerned, she was the pure essence of nature in the raw, and he was the quintessential hunter. The death of such a she-god at his hands would surely infuse him with infinite dominion and power.

Attired again in the terrycloth, Serena returned inside. The beast listened carefully; what struck him was what he did *not* hear—any click of the lock on the glass door. Just in case she recalled the oversight and returned, the beast remained in his hiding place. Besides, what he had in mind would go more smoothly if she were afforded time to go to sleep. A half hour had passed when the beast emerged and headed for the unsecured entrance.

CHAPTER 16

The swim proved to be a panacea, and Serena Raven was asleep in no time. Again, random signals emanated through her brain; but this time the scene formed by the cerebral cortex was a tranquil one. She was floating, supine and nude, on the water, eyes closed. Her arms and legs were outstretched, but she was unable to move them. Indeed, signals sent by the pons during REM sleep can shut off neurons in the spinal cord, actually causing temporary paralysis of limb muscles, but Serena did not find this inability alarming. In fact, she found her state of suspension very pleasing. Something was nudging her natant, unveiled form, but it was gentle, much like the dolphin friend of her childhood. *Could it be?* Possibly, she thought at first; but it had never touched these places. Tender caresses, beginning on her breasts, moved downward and lingered at her abdomen before continuing their journey. This was the unmistakable fondling of a lover.

Interestingly, researchers have discovered that, although there are some differences between the male and female brain when it comes to sexual pleasure, there are not many. In both genders, the brain's lateral orbitofrontal cortex, located just behind the left eye and believed to be the center of reason and behavioral restraint, shuts down. In this respect, the human brain during orgasm, whether of a man or a woman, is much like that of one on heroin. It becomes a repository of utter pleasure and the person cannot get enough of it.

For both sexes, the most erogenous zone of the body is the mind, but the path by which a woman reaches her plateau is significantly different than the route most appealing to a man. Men make love with their eyes, more readily aroused by literal erotic images. This is not to say that women cannot be similarly titillated. Indeed, they are stimulated by a wider variety of erotica and are more flexible in their carnal interests than men. An orgasmic mind is a terrible thing to waste, and so a woman uses much more than her eyes. She is stimulated by all of her senses; what she tastes, smells, hears, touches, and how she is touched. Nor is her sight limited to what is actually registered on the retina and transmitted by the optic nerve to the brain. She explores the realm of imagination and fantasy, and so it was with Serena. *Had Bo silently slipped in after all, or was this yet another fantasy lover?* Either was fine with Serena. In dreams and in love, all things are possible, and the pleasure the same.

Thus, as lips left a path of leisurely kisses along the inside of her calf, hesitating to leave a couple behind her knee, Serena was at ease. She felt safe with her dream lover, whoever he was. He was so tender, caring, and attentive. Serena was still adrift, and soft music played in the background. Her heart rate and blood pressure increased, causing her chest, neck, face, and ears to flush.

Because all forms of erotic pleasure are transmitted through the skin, its entire surface has been referred to as the body's largest sex organ. Thus, as the lips made their way up the inside of one thigh, stopping just short of the trimmed pubic area where Serena was most moist, she felt a heightened sensitivity rippling throughout her entire body on a sensual journey.

Serena felt aflame as her heart rate and blood pressure spiked. The amorphous portal to her womb instinctively expanded, and she periodically sensed the now engorged folds draping the entryway being sucked between the lips of her lover. Her already ample breasts grew even larger, her nipples stood erect, and her breathing became heavy. When a tenacious tongue, as animated as an excited serpent, began rapidly flicking across the tissue housing more than 8,000 nerve endings, every muscle in Serena's body tensed. Her back arched in debauched arousal, reflexively driving her hips upward, in anticipation of the rapture to come. *Like a person on heroin.*

Abruptly, her lover stopped and retreated, letting all hedonistic promise momentarily hang before evaporating. Serena was frustrated and confused. *Did I do something wrong or offensive? Or maybe I failed to do something that he desired?* If she could only touch him, embrace him, stroke him, reciprocating the passion he had dispensed to her, then they would finish together what her lover had initiated. Still however, Serena's limbs felt useless.

"Now, now," he said. "You can't exactly say that I've been selfish, can you?"

What? As if a blindfold had been yanked from her face, Serena was suddenly aware that her eyes were open. The room was dark, but she could make out her enigmatic lover's silhouette against the moon's incandescence through the balcony's French doors. He was standing between the foot of the bed and the doorway to the hall, his right arm extending to his right. *Was he pointing at something?* Two sconces gradually illuminated the room to a soft glow. *He is turning the dimmer on the switch. But why now?* As her lover's face was revealed, recognition replaced bewilderment. Serena no longer liked this dream, not at all. Determined to end it, she tried to roll over and turn on the lamp, but she could not move.

Consciousness was coming in small doses. If this was reality, it was a worse venue than the realm of Serena's dreams. Her paralysis had not been the result of mind-play during sleep, but rather the pantyhose she now saw binding her wrists and ankles to the four posts of her tester bed. Panic-stricken, Serena craned her head upward and to her right to see if there were any sign of give in the restraint while she pulled with everything she could muster, but it held tight. As she redirected her strength to the stricture abrading her left wrist, she felt her assailant's hands grasping her legs, followed by his body weight settling between them and on the mattress.

Revulsion coursed through Serena's body as she saw him kneeling between her spread-eagle legs. There was no doubt he would continue to have his way with her, but it would not be in a way she had ever fantasized. Worse still, there was nothing she could do. *Oh God, at least use a condom.* She tilted her head forward to see, and laid it back down with a miniscule degree of relief.

As if the rapist had read her mind, he actually giggled in amusement. Serena closed her eyes. *Just get it over with.*

In seconds—only five staccato, primal thrusts—Serena felt him withdraw. It had been brief and robotic, no frenzied finish. Serena was almost certain he had not even ejaculated, and was confounded as to the purpose of her defilement if it was not for his sexual satisfaction. She could not bring herself to look at him. *Was he gone?* Tears welled in her shut eyes at the thought of Edna, her cleaning lady, arriving at 8:00 a.m., and finding her in such an embarrassing position. She would have to recount the sordid experience with her, as well as with the police. *Oh God, what would Bo think of her? What would she say to her father?*

Angry with herself for the illogical, self-inflicted guilt, Serena furiously writhed and tugged at the restraints. Singing, over the sound of running water in her shower, stopped her cold. *Son-of-a-bitch.* That the bastard was enjoying himself was infuriating. But the fact that it was in some non-sexual yet perverse way, leaving other possible motives, sent an unnerving shiver up her spine.

The beast returned to the bedroom wearing only a towel wrapped about his waist, and walked to the near side of the bed. Leaning in close, he observed Serena's tear-streaked face and angry eyes. "Oh, dear, have I still not brought you to the erotic heights of your dreams?" he asked.

Serena spat in his face. For a moment, the beast froze in place. He stood erect and wiped off the spittle with the towel. "Well," he harshly began, and stopped. Naked, the beast walked to the chair, on which his clothes were neatly folded, and rummaged through his pants pockets. After replacing his trousers on the chair, he pulled on a pair of thin latex gloves and approached the foot of the bed. Leaning toward Serena's genitalia, still fully exposed by her widely splayed legs, the beast snarled, "Let's see if we can find that G-spot." The last thing Serena saw, before passing out, was a glistening blade.

CHAPTER 17

Serena blinked open her eyes, staring into those of the beast mere inches away. "That's it, time to wake up," he said. "I want to ask you something, and it's very important." Daring not to utter a word, Serena felt the bare mattress beneath her. The sheets were gone. Something soft began to constrict around her throat. "What does it feel like," the beast asked, drawing the ligature tighter, "to know you are going to die?"

The band pressed harder into Serena's neck. She couldn't breathe. But just at the point of respiratory standstill, the constriction relented, followed by a sharp slap across her face. "I asked you a question, Serena. How does it feel to know you are going to die?"

Serena tried to speak, to say something, anything, but her lungs' desperate labor for breath left her voice box stranded. She was still gasping to fill her lungs with as much precious air as possible when the strangling strap squeezed once more. Serena, barely conscious when it ceased, was almost oblivious to the next slap. Her eyes spasmodically fluttered, and she vaguely deciphered the beast's cruel utterance, "I didn't hear you, Serena. What, not in the mood to talk?" *Just get it over with.*

There was no retreat the next time. The subnormal oxygen level in Serena's blood supply to her brain brought on rapid and irrevocable unconsciousness. As brutally effective as it was, the pressure exerted by the instrumentality's soft texture was insufficient to occlude both the carotid artery and jugular vein. Only the vein, nearer than the artery to the skin's surface, was closed, causing blood carried to the head to become trapped. The excessive engorgement of theses blood vessels caused scattered pinpoint hemorrhages, called petechiae, in Serena's eyelids and the mucous membranes connecting the inner eyelid and eyeball. This congestion also caused Serena's luscious green eyes to become firmer than usual and bulge.

The beast examined these signs in confirmation of a job well done. Placing a hand on Serena's chest, he detected an erratic heartbeat, a phenomena which he had found not so unusual. It was a stubborn organ, continuing at times for several minutes after the lungs had "given up the ghost." During those few fragile minutes, resuscitation was possible. When unattended however, the heart's last-ditch effort was fruitless. It was only a matter of time.

Meanwhile, the beast dressed and then methodically inspected everything. The sheets were in a trash bag he had found in a kitchen cabinet. Two pint-sized Ziploc bags sat on the dresser—in one was the fleshy sacrifice; the other contained the surgical blade which had made the excision. Satisfied that nothing would link him to the scene, it was time to make his exit. *Two down, more to go.*

Before leaving however, the beast re-checked for a heartbeat. Finding none, he stood back and took a final look at Serena. "Sigh no more, my beauty," he whispered in reverent awe. "Nothing in your life became you like the leaving of it." Almost instantaneously, it came to him what he could take as the perfect memento. He would need another garbage bag.

The beast stuffed both Ziploc bags in his pocket, grasped a garbage bag in each hand, and left. Once at the boat, he removed the gloves and put them in the garbage bag with the sheets. After loading both of the larger containers, he untied the mooring and once again employing the electric motor, he quietly slipped away.

Some distance from the house, the beast killed the motor and drifted, gazing up at the star-studded night firmament. A few minutes passed before he removed the Ziplocs from his pocket, and picked out the one he wanted. The beast opened it, and lobbed the contents, followed by the container, into the water. As he motored off, he sang.

A snapping turtle surfaced in the wake, quickly devoured the floating flesh, and submerged. The plastic bag bobbed to the tempo of the fading refrain.

CHAPTER 18

It had been ages since officers of the Jackson Police Department patrolled their beats with partners. Safety had surrendered to economics. Funding was down and not surprisingly, crime was up. Officer Melvin Spann was not complaining, however. Only two years out of the academy, he considered himself fortunate. Although he had not been able to avoid the midnight shift, his beat was in one of the statistically safer areas of the city. And besides, he had his Kevlar vest. Since he had not yet wed and started a family of his own, the hours were not all that disruptive.

Just as the law had proven a jealous mistress for Tom Davis, Officer Spann might as well have been married to the police force. He was a legacy of sorts: his father had been one of the first African-American officers in the department, and the first to attain the lofty title, "Chief of Police." Both older brothers preceded Melvin in the blue ranks. Consequently, Spann felt that he had a lot to live up to, and was still green enough to embrace the opportunities with enthusiasm.

He had become aware at roll call, of the APB for Todd Murphy, whom Spann knew to live on his beat. The sergeant had not made too big a deal about it, though, mentioning it in a singsong voice amid other tidbits to the men and women of Precinct One. After all, it wasn't like the guy was wanted for murder, just dope. But to an eager-beaver like Spann, a collar was a collar, not to mention the extra satisfaction he would derive in arresting a lawyer on the lam—and a racist one to boot. The son-of-a-bitch had to know that returning to his house was risky, but there was always a chance that Murphy might be foolish or desperate enough to take it.

So, as Spann made his routine rounds up and down the streets of the neighborhood, just north of Lakeland Drive, and east of the vacant baseball stadium that was once home to a minor league team, he made a point of keeping an eye on Todd Murphy's house. It was located near the end of the westernmost street, across from a wooded park that separated the residential area from the deserted sports complex. Officer Spann had already made numerous passes, and was slowly coming up on the Murphy residence again when a figure stumbled from behind a large pin oak, on Spann's left, and into the left front fender of the cruiser. "Shit!" Spann exclaimed, braking and throwing the gearshift in park. He exited the car, motor still running.

A body was curled in a semi-fetal position on the edge of the pavement and facing away from the vehicle. Whoever it was, Spann guessed some drunken bum straggling around the park, was barely stirring but moaning. As the officer approached, the hard soles of his smartly polished, black shoes crunched on the pebbles of the street's shoulder. When he stooped to get a closer look, the disheveled form whirled on its side, viciously slashing with something in the left hand, and several times catching Spann's unprotected right, upper arm. Instinctively, the startled and injured officer recoiled, and in the process awkwardly toppling backward, against the idling car. His right hand had just found the revolver on his hip when the beast was on him, forcing Spann atop the hood. Blood draining from the officer's sliced arm sizzled on the hot surface, as the point of a knife came to his stomach.

Recognition shown in Spann's eyes as he looked into the face of the beast that asked, "Tell me, officer; how does it feel to know you are going to die?" Officer Melvin Spann's firearm withdrew only inches before the blade sank into his abdomen and savagely twisted. Excruciating pain froze him in place. His life of twenty-three years was flashing before him when the knife withdrew. Momentarily suspended above his face, held in a gloved hand, it plunged through Spann's chest and into his heart. Then everything went dark.

The beast quickly pulled the body off the hood, heaved it into the passenger side of the cruiser, and walked around to the driver's side to get behind the wheel. Along the way, he spotted the officer's hat in the street. After retrieving it, the beast drove the short distance to the house and backed into the driveway. Spann's body was tugged into position behind the wheel and the seatbelt secured to hold it in place. As a final touch, the beast placed the hat on the officer's head and tilted it to where it covered his upper face. Stepping away from the vehicle, the beast was satisfied that, from a distance, it looked like an officer, while staking out the house, had dozed off. Finally, he could get inside and change his clothes. He knew there would not be a lot of time before Spann was missed and other cops were dispatched to the scene, so he would have to hurry.

CHAPTER 19

Detective Charley Matthews had been in the homicide squad way too long. He had seen so many dead bodies that cynicism had set in, producing a gruff, crusty persona. Yet, as he pulled up to this particular scene, he was shaken. A cigarette flickered in his trembling, nicotine-stained fingers. This time, it was one of Jackson's finest who lay lifeless, and the word had spread like wildfire throughout the brotherhood. The sun had not yet risen, yet men and women in blue already crowded the area. Most stood in shocked silence while a few were giving an officer, positioned between them and cordon of yellow tape, a hard time for having the audacity to impede their way.

"Christ," Matthews muttered to himself. He knew they would be on edge, wanting to immediately jump in and take action to avenge the killing of one of their own. Charley Matthews knew this because it was how *he* felt. But he also realized, from the time of arriving at his first murder scene years ago, how complex a homicide investigation could be. He was the detective in charge of this one and as such, it was imperative, from the moment he exited his unmarked car, he employed methodical procedure, resisting impulses arising out of a sense of urgency.

"Boys," Matthews began, as he walked nearer, "I understand how you feel, but if any of you fuck up my crime scene.... Well, you just don't want to do that." As the detective-in-charge, he would be the key man in the investigation, from start to finish. On his shoulders fell the responsibility of coordinating all of the forces the State of Mississippi would bring to bear in putting Officer Spann's killer on death row, including the rest of the detective squad, the coroner and medical examiner, the lab technicians, and even the district attorney. To properly utilize these available resources of the criminal justice system, the head investigator must be knowledgeable of each component's potential and what action those components must take.

Thus, amid the grumbling of the dispersing, well-meaning assemblage, Matthews turned to the vigilant officer and glanced at the nameplate above the shirt pocket. "Officer Moore, you the first on the scene?"

"Yes, sir."

"What do we have?"

Officer Henry Moore recounted that, after receiving the dispatch, he arrived at 2:35 a.m. Approaching Spann's car, he noticed what appeared to be dried blood smeared across the hood. Spann was behind the wheel, unresponsive. Opening the door, the officer saw dark stains on the vest and felt Spann's neck for a pulse. There was none. By that time, other units arrived. While Moore called it in, other officers secured the residence. When their commands went unanswered, they kicked open the front door. Finding no one inside, they returned outside and roped off the area. Nobody had since been inside the residence.

Detective Matthews nodded his approval, "Good job, Moore. Where's the body now?"

"After the coroner and Mobile Crime Lab unit got here and took their photos, it was taken out of the vehicle for the coroner to get a better look. He's over there," he said, pointing toward the area behind Spann's vehicle.

On the way over, Matthews paused on the driveway at Spann's police cruiser, seeing for himself the stains on the hood that Moore had mentioned. They were no longer red, but dark brown and crusted. Blood dries faster on smooth and non-absorbent surfaces, such as that of the car, and is further accelerated by heat. The detective placed a hand on the surface, which he found still warm from the engine.

On the other side of the hood, a technician with the Mobile Crime Lab unit (MCL) was rubbing a portion of the stain with a cotton swab, which Matthews knew would have been first moistened in a saline solution, then a drop each of phenolphthalein reagent and three percent hydrogen peroxide. Within fifteen seconds, the swab turned pink—a positive reaction, indicating the presence of blood.

It was only a field test. The blood could have been from an animal. Even if human, it could be the killer's blood, if wounded in the attack. Blood would be drawn from Spann's body and compared with the crusted samples the MCL technician was now scraping into a vial. The car would be towed to the lab, the interior processed for blood, as well as trace evidence, such as hairs and fibers. Matthews moved on to see what light the coroner might shed on the situation.

Any resident at least twenty-one years of age with a high school diploma in their pocket is considered by the State of Mississippi as qualified to run for the position of county coroner. If elected however, before allowed to take the oath of office, the person must successfully complete Mississippi Crime Laboratory and State Medical Examiner Death Investigation Training School. Even after being sworn into office, the individual is required to maintain a minimum of twenty-four hours per year of continuing education, prescribed and certified by the State Medical Examiner, and re-tested at least once every four years.

Linda Clark-Harvey, now in her third term as Hinds County's coroner and chief medical investigator, went far beyond these minimum obligations. As an RN in the University of Mississippi Medical Center ER for over a decade, there was little she had not seen concerning physical evidence of the barbarity with which some of our species dealt with their fellow man. George Elliot wrote, in *Adam Bede,* that our deeds determine us, as much as we determine our deeds. As far as Clark-Harvey was concerned, a being which exhibits little or no humanity could hardly be considered human.

She took her job seriously, believing there was no greater trust. Souls, which once occupied the lifeless shells she was called upon to examine, depended on her to voice the words they could no longer utter: "This is what happened to me." Deciphering, from the body's clues, the cause and manner of death frequently led to the perpetrator's identity.

The forty-three-year-old was one of a handful of Mississippi's eighty-two coroners who were African-Americans, and no non-physician coroner, of any race, in the state possessed as much specialized training and education. County coffers paid only the expenses for the statutory minimum continuing education, but sharing a checking account with her cardiologist husband, Dr. Gregory Harvey, enabled Linda, two or three times a year, to attend seminars and schools conducted by the nation's most renown medical examiners.

Affability, or at least its façade, is a necessary ingredient for anyone to get elected to public office, and rarely does the electorate permit an asshole to stay in office. Even though Clark-Harvey's geniality was genuine, she had learned from years of dealing with prima donna doctors, including her husband, to walk the fine line between amiability and submissiveness. The skinny-as-a-rail black woman allowed no one to push her around.

Clark-Harvey had carefully removed Officer Spann's uniform protective vest, uniform shirt, and undershirt, which were at his side awaiting retrieval by the MCL. As Detective Matthews approached, trailed by Officer Moore, the coroner appeared to be taping a wound with

Scotch tape. "Little late for that, ain't it, Lin?" the detective teased.

"Kiss my skinny, black ass Matthews," she replied, not even looking up at him.

The detective chuckled, but Officer Moore was confused by her task and had a bona fide desire to learn. "Seriously, what's she doing?" he whispered to Matthews. The detective only shook his head, giving the officer a look that conveyed the message it was best not to ask.

The coroner looked up at Moore and stared a moment. Satisfied that the question was posed in earnest, she beckoned him to take a knee and observe. Pointing to an open Y-shaped cut in Spann's abdomen, she explained, "The edges of the wound are sharp and un-abraded, which tells us they were caused by a knife, as opposed to something duller, like a screwdriver or scissors. Matthews here, would naturally like to know something about the blade he's looking for, but measuring the length of a gaping stab wound that we know was caused by a knife is pointless. Why? Because they are rarely inflicted without some cutting taking place at the same time, since the knife is usually either pulled upward or downward during the thrust in or withdrawal. So the slit is almost always longer than the widest part of the blade that made it. The only way to get a reasonable idea of the width of the blade is to manipulate the skin to its original position, hold it together with transparent adhesive tape, then measure and photograph it."

"What do you make of the Y-shape?" Moore asked.

"Could mean two separate stabbings in the same area, just at different angles. Or it may be one stabbing and, following the thrust, Spann either fell, causing the blade to incidentally twist, or the assailant may have intentionally twisted it; in either case, making the other cut during withdrawal. Since stabbing someone is a process involving considerable, relative movement between the victim and perp, there are all kinds of possibilities."

Moore gave an understanding nod, but was still puzzled by one thing. "But he had his vest on."

"It's a *bulletproof* vest," Clark-Harvey pointed out. "It's designed to stop bullets, not knives. Vests like this are made from multiple layers of super-strong fabric. When a bullet passes through each of the outer layers, it slows and deforms, spreading the pressure over a wider area until it finally stops. Of course, a blade doesn't deform or slow down. If anything, as the assailant continues to push it, the pressure increases on a very narrow point of concentration, and passes *between* the fibers. They do make stab-proof vests, with chain-metal or ceramic plating, but low-level gear like this one, and the one you have on...all those normally issued to police officers, are completely useless against anything other than a few pistol rounds."

"Damn," Moore responded, subconsciously bringing his right hand, which had been resting on a knee, to his stomach. His thoughts lingered briefly on a false sense of security until he noticed Clark-Harvey stand and tell Matthews, "Of course, the chest wound will tell us more." She explained to Moore, now also on his feet, "Due to its rigidity, bone maintains the dimensions and shape of a stab wound a lot better than skin or other soft tissue; but that will have to be determined by the medical examiner at the autopsy."

"How long would you say the blade was?" Moore inquired.

"That too, will have to be determined at the post-mortem. I don't do any probing."

"Yeah, Lin here is a real tease," Matthews interrupted. "Fondling is allowed, but never penetration."

Other than rolling her eyes, the woman ignored the comment. "What I *can* tell you," she said to Moore, "is that the depth of the wound doesn't just depend on the length of the blade. In fact, the depth usually exceeds the blade's length." Walking up close to Matthews, she jutted a bony finger into his substantial paunch and pushed hard. "You see?" she said to Officer Moore, "During the thrust the body, particularly the abdomen, gives under the force of the fist holding the knife. I've seen stab wounds determined by the M.E. to be six to seven inches deep, but inflicted by a four-inch pocketknife."

Matthews and Moore watched the coroner continue with her measurements and photographs. Afterward, she ungloved and repacked her equipment. "All I can tell you right now," she told Matthews, "is that you're looking for a knife with a blade about twelve millimeters, just under a half-inch, at its widest point."

"Okay, Officer Moore," the detective said. "Time to get some of these guys and search the house. Wait for sunup to do the grounds."

Moore followed Matthews for a few steps, then turned around toward Clark-Harvey. "Thanks for the lesson."

"You bet," she replied to the officer, then called out to the detective, who was now at the front steps of the house, "Hey, Matthews! The lab will want to take a close look at his clothes, particularly the cuts in the vest and both shirts!" He waved to her in silent acknowledgement. "And," she added, "be sure the MCL guys bag them separately—paper bags, not plastic!"

"Yeah, yeah, yeah, got it," Matthews mumbled. He was all too familiar with the fact that airtight containers, such as Ziploc bags, increase the putrefying rate of blood, rendering it useless for analysis. *She's a bossy little thing. And my gut still hurts.* As he reached to turn the doorknob, he heard Clark-Harvey yell to the two EMTs, who had been on hand with an ambulance, waiting for her to release the body for transportation to the morgue, "You can get my body now. It's all yours, guys!"

Grasping the doorknob, Matthews turned his head and started to speak. After pausing for a couple of seconds, he said to no one in particular, "Naw, I ain't going there." He turned the knob and stepped inside with Officer Moore on his heels, grinning.

Inside, Matthews oversaw the systematic search of the premises, every nook and cranny, and was disgusted with the unfavorable results.

More important than training and knowledge, the better homicide investigators bring to the table the invaluable ingredients of good judgment and imagination. As Detective Matthews stood in the book-lined den and looked around again, he noticed that, by far, most of Murphy's belongings were books, all on floor-to-ceiling, wood shelving and meticulously arranged so the spine of each was flush with the shelf edging. They were obviously possessions Murphy prized.

"The books," Matthews said. "Search behind and inside every damned one of them."

Officers began pulling editions off the shelves and thumbing the pages. After twenty minutes of such rummaging, Matthews heard one of the men say, "Detective." Matthews glanced up from the hardback he had been going through. "You need to take a look at this," the officer advised.

The detective strode across piles of texts strewn on the floor and, standing by the officer, gazed at the discovery lodged between the open pages. "What the hell?" It was not a knife, but rather some sort of small razor blade. Matthews had never seen one quite like it, but knew from its obvious dimensions, that it had not inflicted Officer Spann's wounds. Yet, it appeared to be covered with blood, which had smeared the two pages when hidden in the closed tome of Shakespeare's works. The detective noticed, on the left page, three words of Lady Macbeth highlighted in yellow, *unsex me here*.

"I don't know what the hell we have," he said, and motioned for one of the MCL technicians to come over and retrieve it. "Get the lab to process the blood on the blade and pages, for type," he instructed. "Preserve enough for DNA for any future comparison. No reason to process the book for prints, only natural for Murphy's to be on it, but see if any are on the blade. Speaking of which, let me know what the damned thing is. I'll need to run a cross-check on cases involving injuries consistent with it." The technician nodded his understanding and assumed custody of the find. "Keep looking!" Matthews barked to the others.

When none of the other books in the den revealed any further secrets, the officers moved to the kitchen and quickly scanned behind and through a few cookbooks. Still, nothing relevant surfaced. Before wrapping things up, Matthews made one more pass through each room. In the master bedroom, a rather large Bible sat on a nightstand. The detective picked it up and flipped through the pages. A section had been crudely hollowed out and, in the hidden cavity was a closed switchblade knife. The hole began in the Book of Proverbs. The twenty-fifth chapter was on the last full page preceding the opening, and the second verse was highlighted: *It is the glory of God to conceal things, but the glory of kings is to search things out.*

Matthews shouted, "Moore!"

"Sir?" the officer, now standing in the bedroom doorway, asked.

"Get that lab guy back in here, if he hasn't left."

CHAPTER 20

"Hey, Sleeping Beauty! You alive?"

Bo Landry managed to partially open an eye, and saw a large, blurry form in a doorway. Rising vapors obscured the apparition. A pleasing aroma filled the surroundings, but Bo was having trouble identifying it. Once he blinked his orbs into focus, he was able to see Randy Jordan's copious frame holding a cup of steaming coffee. "Podna, you okay?" the deputy called.

As Bo gradually lifted his head, it felt unusually heavy and something inside of it was pounding like a jackhammer, eliciting a groan. He leaned its weight back, only then cognizant that he was in the high-backed chair in Tom's study. He had been asleep, his head resting on the desk. Bo took in a deep breath and forced his eyes to open wide. Slowly letting the breath go, he finally replied to the deputy's question: "Yeah,...gesso; but...head...killin...."

Squinting at him, Jordan took a sip of his coffee and pondered whether to speak his mind. "Bo, you ain't off the wagon, are you?"

All Bo could do was slightly rock his head against the back of the chair. "Feels like...dun think so."

The deputy gave him a hard look. The two lawmen had known each other a long time, and Jordan didn't mince his words. "What kind of bullshit answer is that? You either did or you didn't."

But that was the problem; Bo couldn't recall, for certain, one way or the other. He merely rocked his head again, saying, "Dunno. Why you ass?"

"Well, Podna, it's like this," Jordan began, and proceeded to count off each evidentiary item with fingers nearly as thick as hoe handles, "One, you got a history with the hooch; two, you say you got a bitch of a headache; three, your speech is all slurred; four, a blind man can see you're not thinking straight—hell, you can't even remember if you took a drink or not; it's like you got fucking amnesia or something." He paused, shaking his head. "I'm your friend, Podna, but this just ain't right. Not at a time like this, for chrissakes. Know what I mean?"

Bo didn't know what he meant. Randy was right about his condition, but it just didn't *feel* right. He couldn't put it all together. "Time ligh whah? he asked.

"Time like a damned lunatic on the loose with his sights set on Judge Tom!" the deputy roared, pointing upward.

"Oh yeah," Bo replied. Making an unsteady effort to stand, he asked, "Evthing awright?"

"Everything but you. Sit your ass back down I'll get you some coffee. Christ." Jordan was gone before Bo could decline. When the deputy returned with the mug, Bo asked him what time it was. "Seven-thirty. I'm heading up the new shift. Been here 'bout a half hour."

"Tom up?" Bo inquired.

"Ain't heard a peep."

"I need…look in…him," Bo said.

"You stay put. I'll do it."

Bo heard the boards of the stairway creak, succumbing to Randy's bulk. Within minutes, it sounded like an elephant descending them. "Sheriff, this is Jordan," Bo heard the big man, out of breath, saying between labored breaths. "Hate to bother you so early, but we got a problem, a big fucking problem." Bo was standing up to see what was going on, when Randy stepped into the doorway and closed his cell phone. "You better sit back down, Podna."

CHAPTER 21

In the United States, cuttings and stabbings are second only to gunfire as a cause of homicidal death. But instances where the knife or other weapon is left in the victim are few and far between. As improbable and implausible as it seemed, Bo Landry would forever be haunted by the macabre sight of the letter-opener protruding from Judge Tom Davis's throat. Of course, Bo had not heeded Deputy Jordan's advice to take a seat and patiently await the sheriff's arrival. Hearing Jordan's shocking announcement that the judge was dead, Bo had immediately raced up the stairs to see for himself. The confrontation had sobered his speech and cleared his thought processes, but left him afflicted by grief and guilt.

Now crowded into Davis's bedroom were the sheriff, coroner, and technicians from the State Crime Lab. Digital cameras steadily clicked, graphically recording the gruesome tableau. The photographers had finished with the body and were concentrating on the various patterns the arterial spray of the judge's punctured carotid had left on the bed coverings and floor. The weapon had been photographed, then carefully removed and collected as evidence and Clark-Harvey was now cleaning blood from the wound. Unlike the ones she had observed only hours earlier on Officer Spann, the edges of this one were abraded, consistent with the scraping of a relatively dull and thick object used as a weapon, such as the recovered letter-opener.

"That's odd," Clark-Harvey commented to Sheriff Wilbur Johnson, at her side.

"What is?" he asked.

"Should be some bruising in close proximity to the wound, caused by the impact of the fist that thrust the weapon, but I don't see any."

"Maybe it's subcutaneous and the M.E. will pick it up?" the sheriff suggested.

"Could be," the coroner agreed. "If so, the area will give you an idea of the size of the assailant's fist."

"Any defense wounds?" Johnson inquired.

Clark-Harvey meticulously examined the hands and arms. "None," she answered.

"I didn't think so. I don't see any sign of a struggle around here," the sheriff observed, looking again about the bed.

"And there was just the one wound to the neck," the coroner added. "If there was any resistance, I would have at least expected a couple of superficial marks left by the attacker's struggle to get the weapon in place."

"Thanks. If you need me, I'll be downstairs with Bo." As the sheriff exited the room, Clark-Harvey heard him rhetorically exclaim, "Goddam, how did this happen!"

Bo Landry did not have an answer to that question, either for the sheriff or for Judge Alex Stillwell, who had arrived while the sheriff was upstairs with the coroner. Bo was empty and numb, in shock, nauseated.

"I imagine any judge makes a lot of enemies over the years," the sheriff noted, "but either one of you guys know of anyone in particular who'd have a grudge against Tom to do something like this?" Bo related what he knew about Todd Murphy, and Judge Stillwell told the sheriff about Jim Blackwell accosting Davis the previous day, but added that he found it difficult to believe that Blackwell would actually do anything violent. All bark no bite.

"You never know," the sheriff replied. "I'm sure in your position, Judge, you know that more so than most folks." Stillwell had to agree. "Anyway," the sheriff continued, "one of the few things not covered in blood up there was the handle of the letter-opener, shielded by the killer's hand wrapped around it, and the lab guys found a useable print on it. We'll have to exclude Tom first, since we're relatively certain the letter-opener was his. If we don't get a match, I'll have a comparison run with Murphy's prints, which we have on file. If those don't match, I'll get this Blackwell fellow in. And if we strike out there, all I can do is run it through AFIS and hope for a hit." He referred to the Automated Fingerprint Identification System, a database maintained by the FBI and accessed by law enforcement agencies nationwide.

Bo gave the matter some thought. "I just don't understand; how the hell did anybody get past your men outside?"

"I don't know," the sheriff conceded. "I've grilled every damned one of them pretty good, and they swear they never dozed off nor saw or heard anything unusual. But *somebody* evidently got by them...." Bo, angry not only at whoever had unmercifully slain Tom in his bed, but also at himself for failing in his watch, was taken aback to hear the sheriff, now staring at him, add, "or maybe nobody did."

"What the hell are you talking about?" Bo asked.

"Well son, the only person we know was in the house is you, and you got guilt written all over your face."

"Wilbur, have you lost your fucking mind?" Stillwell asked. "Tom and Bo were like father and son, for crying out loud."

"Now don't go getting your panties in a wad, Judge. I'm not accusing Bo of anything. But it is rather curious, don't you think? Especially since he says he doesn't remember much?"

In the deafening silence that followed, the coroner stepped into the study and relayed news she had just received from her colleague in Madison County, that attorney Serena Raven had been found murdered in her house. After a dazed moment, Bo dashed outside to the veranda, and vomited into the gardenias.

CHAPTER 22

Within a twenty-four-hour period, a police officer, a lawyer, and a judge had been slain. Each murder was investigated by a different law enforcement agency. While there was not yet any physical evidence connecting the three cases, it was too coincidental to be coincidence. The sheriffs of Hinds and Madison counties vowed cooperation between each other, as well as with the Jackson Police Department. The result of this collaboration was the formation of a task force headed by Detective Charley Matthews. Even though his department had its own crime lab, physical evidence in all three cases was analyzed at the State Crime Lab in Jackson. Notwithstanding its backlog, the cases were given priority status.

In the weeks that followed, it was determined that there were no fingerprints on the bloody razor blade found in the Shakespeare book, in Todd Murphy's den. The blade was a rib-back, carbon-steel, surgical blade manufactured by Bard-Parker. The blood on it was that of Serena Raven. Similarly, no prints were located on the switchblade, an Italian-made stiletto, also found in Murphy's house. However, blood on the blade was confirmed as that of Officer Melvin Spann. His blood was also detected on some of the cut edges of the cavity in the Bible, where the knife was secreted. The hiding place had been fashioned with the same blade, after being used on Spann.

Matthews opined that Murphy killed the attorney who was trying to turn his 19th century Southern world upside down. Afterward, he returned to his residence for something, maybe just to change his clothes, and while there, hid the two blades. Whatever the reason, Spann had gotten in the way.

If Matthews was correct in his theory, it would also make perfect sense that Murphy somehow slipped past the guarding deputies, and killed the judge assigned the flag case. However, the print on the letter-opener belonged neither to Tom Davis nor Todd Murphy. Rather, it was that of the right, index finger of Jim Blackwell, whom Judge Stillwell said blamed Davis for the loss of his job. What were the odds that the judge and an attorney in the flag controversy were murdered within hours of one another by different people having no connection? Although the coincidence stretched credulity, Charley Matthews was trained to follow the evidence; and to him, physical evidence did not lie.

The grand jury agreed, indicting Blackwell for the capital murder of fraternity brother Tom Davis. The murder of a judge carried a possible death penalty, which in most circumstances justified denial of bail. However, because Blackwell did not fight extradition from Illinois, the judge who was specially appointed to hear the case (due to Stillwell being a prosecution witness, and the other judges stepping aside) was persuaded to set bail, albeit high. Blackwell quickly paid a bonding company the $100,000 necessary to secure an insurance company's surety to stand good for the million dollars set by the court. One of the conditions imposed required Blackwell to surrender his passport.

The death penalty was indeed imposed, not by the State of Mississippi, but instead by Jim Blackwell's own hand. The prosecution refused all attempts by Blackwell's lawyers to plea bargain, and according to his wife, he had become increasingly anxious and depressed, as the trial date approached. Returning home from a quick trip to the grocery store, Mrs. Blackwell found her husband, and his exposed brain matter, in the living room along with the pistol he had stuck in his mouth.

Todd Murphy had wasted no time in driving to Brownsville, Texas. Cruising along US 77, he drove through San Benito, in the Lone Star State. About midway between there and Brownsville, he passed a sign indicating the turnoff to State Highway 100 and South Padre Island.

With a pair of death-penalty murder charges tacked on to the drug charge, one for killing a police officer, and one for killing Serena Raven during the course of sexual battery, Matthews enlisted the assistance of the United States Marshal's Service in tracking Murphy down. Although he had not made any effort to disguise his identity, Murphy had acted swiftly and they were too late. Once in Brownsville, Murphy crossed the border into Matamoros, Mexico. After parking his car outside Mexican customs, he had gone inside the building and first secured a tourist permit. With that in hand, he walked across the lobby to the Banjercito, the Mexican military bank. Upon presenting his driver's license, tourist permit, vehicle registration, passport, and credit card, Murphy was given a temporary importation permit for his vehicle.

The final step in the process was purchasing insurance coverage, which he quickly secured from a vendor conveniently located adjacent to the Banjercito. The whole process had taken less than thirty minutes, and Murphy was on the road to Monterrey, west of Brownsville. According to his credit card records, he stayed overnight in a motel and caught a flight the next morning to Havana. The United States does not have an extradition treaty with Cuba, and as evidenced by his credit card expenditures, Murphy was living a rather good life there.

Bo Landry had remained sober, but was consumed with anger, first and foremost at himself. I could have, I should have, and I wish that I had, figured prominently in his vocabulary, with respect to both Tom and Serena. Tom was buried in Raymond, and Serena was entombed in New Orleans. Although Bo attended memorial services for both, he was not able to look anyone in the eye, especially Serena's father. Yet, his anger was directed at Serena as much as it was at anyone.

It was like a worm continually eating away in his head, and there was only one thing that would kill it, so Bo drove to the nearest liquor store. Soon afterward, he was pulled over and arrested for DUI, but that was only the beginning of a long, downward spiral.

CHAPTER 23

Sooner or later, there comes a time when everyone must suffer grief, the normal response of sorrow, emotion, and confusion that afflicts us, as mere mortals, from losing someone near and dear to us. Grief lasts for however long it takes to accept the loss and to learn that life goes on, which oftentimes depends on the relationship and how prepared one is for the death. Consequently, the length of the process varies from person to person—for some, it may be a few months; for others, like Bo Landry, it takes much longer.

Tom Davis was a father figure and Serena Raven was everything Bo had prayed for in a soul mate and lover. She was what he lived and breathed, as vital to his being as air. For him, her loss was smothering. The sudden and violent manner of both their deaths came as a shock and, in the weeks that followed, they provoked certain physiological changes. Without warning, and for no discernible reason, Bo found himself trembling, nauseated, and having difficulty breathing. Sleep came hard, and what time he slept was riddled with strange dreams and nightmares. Having no appetite, his weight dropped by at least twenty pounds, and he lost all interest in work.

There are a variety of triggering mechanisms that may cause alcoholics to relapse. For Bo, there were several acting in concert, and once unleashed they seemingly fed on themselves, the initial depression and anger of his bereavement, followed by the ennui during his two-week leave from work. Most of the people Bo knew were social drinkers, and he envied their ability to enjoy the euphoric lift, temporarily dulling the ailments and woes attendant to life, then walk away from it. With Bo, however, it was all or nothing and he had gone from nothing to all with time passing in a haze of melancholy.

That is not to say that he was entirely without lucid moments; he was cognizant of his depression and knew that it was partially responsible for his relapse. The irony of turning to alcohol, a depressant, as a cure for depression did not escape him. He just decided to hell with it. It killed the pain, at least for a while, and whenever he felt the hurt insidiously creeping back, all he had to do was grab another bottle. It was a vicious cycle from which there was no escape. Even worse, Bo had no desire to stop the cycle, even if he could.

At first, his supervisors at the bureau were understanding, and insisted that his leave be extended to a full month. Their largesse wavered then evaporated however, when after another fortnight, Bo did not return to his job, nor did he return numerous phone messages left by his superiors. In a way, the telephone itself operated as a trigger. It got to where Bo never answered a call. At each instance he just mumbled, "Fuck it," and took another swallow. Finally, he found his walking papers slipped under the door of his apartment.

Bo rarely made it to his bed before passing out, and the night of November 1 was no exception. He awoke on the den couch. A pizza, still in the delivery box and only a single slice gone, sat to his left. Wedged between his right side and the couch arm was a near-empty bottle of Jim Beam. Something was bursting in his head. Realizing that it was artillery fire in whatever World War II movie was on the television, Bo dug around the cushions and debris until he found the remote and clicked it off. Shuffling to the kitchen sink, he splashed some water on his face. Through the window, he saw that it was night, but could not have cared less as to the actual time. It had become a meaningless measurement of light and darkness.

For no special reason, Bo wanted to get out, to just take a drive. It didn't matter where. Wherever he ended up was fine. Although not sober, Bo felt that he was up to managing the wheel, and cranked up his Pathfinder. On the road, his mind wandered; but as always, his thoughts returned to Serena and Tom. He was looking for a liquor store, but soon realized he was on the Natchez Trace, a federal parkway. *Damn.* The next exit he came upon was the one to Raymond. *Shit.* He was in the part of Hinds County that was still "dry" as far as booze was concerned—none available for miles. "Fuck it," he said, and turned off at the exit. At least he had thought to bring what little was left of the Jim Beam.

Apparently some force, apart from Bo's, was in charge of the steering wheel, rendering him a mere shell of a person in more ways than one. He had no predetermined design to go to the Raymond cemetery, yet that was where he was parking his vehicle. He got out and, bottle in hand, walked over to the wrought-iron fence surrounding the Davis family plot, beneath a massive cedar.

Bo opened the hasp securing the small gate, and sat Indian-style by Tom's grave. Although the dirt was no longer loose, it still formed an elongated mound, just not as high as when Bo last saw it. "Tom," he said, "I am so sorry. So very fucking sorry for everything." Tears welled in his eyes until they could not be contained any further, and trickled down his face. Wiping the rivulets aside, he continued, "I'm sorry this happened to you. I'm sorry I let you down." Bo uncapped the Jim Beam and took a swallow. After the burn passed, he said, "Hell, I'm forgetting my manners. You want a snort? Hell yeah, I know you do." Bo tipped the bottle, drizzling Tom's grave with the whiskey.

After the soil absorbed the last of the flow, Bo wiped his face again and, sighing heavily, looked up to the night sky. It was clear, adorned with an array of stars and the mere sliver of a waning crescent moon, signaling the passing of two weeks' time since it was last full. Bo had missed seeing that one, and realized that it had been six weeks since Serena had been forever taken away from him. Random thoughts buzzed in his head. *Serena, goddess and personification of the moon. The moon still visible, but rapidly fading. The crescent. New Orleans, the Crescent City, and host of Serena's earthly remains.*

Bo stood up and held the bottle as a best man would a glass, in toasting a betrothed couple. "Gotta roll, Tom, but here's to you," he said, and finished off what was left.

Bo walked back to the graveled lane where he had parked, turned the ignition, and pulled the Pathfinder onto Dry Grove Road. He took a left onto Highway 18 and turned south on Midway Road, which eventually meandered under I-55. At the intersection of Highway 51, Bo headed south, parallel to the interstate, until he came to Crystal Springs, turned west on Highway 27, and found a liquor store. Whatever day it was, he knew it wasn't Sunday, and whatever time it was, it was not yet ten o'clock since the store was still open. Bo wheeled into the parking lot.

After making his purchase, Bo drove the short distance to the connection of I-55 South, the artery that would take him most of the three-hour drive to New Orleans and Serena, and set the cruise control at 75. It was a simple act, but like a stone tossed into a pond, it would send out ever-widening ripples until they touched lives theretofore far removed from Bo Landry's. He had no inkling of the chain reaction he had set in motion.

PART II : ANEW IN NEW ORLEANS

CHAPTER 24

Separating Lake Pontchartrain, to the north, and a west-to-east bend in the Mississippi River, to the south, is the strip of land that would become New Orleans. In its natural state, Bayou St. John drained much of the swampy, northern portion into the lake. As evidenced by maps as late as the 19th century, the bayou's tributaries extended as far south toward the river, as what is now the Central Business District, to an area just above the circle on present-day St. Charles Avenue, over which a monument in honor of General Robert E. Lee presides. In the early 1800s, the bayou served as a major backdoor water route, by which the pirate Laffite delivered his smuggled goods into the city, bypassing the customs offices on the river. Later in the century, the area along Bayou St. John reputedly witnessed many rituals of Marie Laveau, the renowned voodoo queen.

On one side of the bayou today, is City Park and, on the opposite side, the fairgrounds. Linking the two is Esplanade Avenue. Near the point where this thoroughfare crosses Bayou St. John is St. Louis Cemetery No. 3. Established in 1854 as Bayou Cemetery, it stands on an old leper colony that was known as Leper's Land, and the body of Serena Raven lay in eternal repose in one of its many aboveground vaults. There is a lengthy waiting list for families wishing to purchase plots in this historic burial ground, but a city councilman who frequented the bar of Sam Raven, Serena's father, had gladly pulled the necessary strings.

Bo Landry did not remember much of his drive, but was able to recall that the cemetery was close to the fairgrounds, where he and Debra had taken in the Jazz Fest the spring before her death. The gates were locked at 4:30 p.m, and the surrounding walls gave the place the appearance of a city within a city, a virtual fortress. Getting inside would be tricky.

Reconnoitering the area, Bo was forced to turn around a few times on dead-end streets. He drove alongside the bayou, on Moss Street, and turned right on Desaix Boulevard, in search of a side street that would put him at the cemetery's rear. Finding what he was looking for at Trafalgar, he turned right and let the vehicle idle while he surveyed his surroundings.

On Bo's right were the backyards of the residences on the south side of Desaix, and on his left were the fairgrounds. Running between the fairgrounds and the residences was a ditch, guarded on each side by eight-foot-high wire fencing. A section of similar fencing also ran parallel to Trafalgar Street, which was obviously intended to keep the neighborhood kids out of the channel.

Bo however, was no child and scaled the barrier easily, slipping the toes of his shoes into the diamonds formed by the chain-link. Dogs in a few of the backyards started barking, so Bo didn't waste any time. After scurrying by the fairgrounds, he released a sigh of relief. The perimeter of that part of the cemetery was not a wall, but fencing similar to what he had only moments earlier negotiated.

Once on the other side, Bo scanned the crests of the tombs in this city of the dead. It took only a few seconds for him to spot the crosses atop the five rounded spires capping the Hellenic Orthodox Community mausoleum. Serena's tomb would be close by.

As he cautiously crept between the crypts, Bo noticed various flower arrangements placed at the base of many of them, the petals of those fashioned with fresh blooms dancing in the cool, autumn breeze. However, walking up to Serena's vault, he saw that hers was uniquely adorned with ears of dried corn and a cedar amulet. Bo did not quite know what to make of it, but surmised that Sam had placed them there, and that they held some significance rooted in his Native American heritage.

Now that he was there, Bo was not sure where to begin. What does one say concerning responsibility for another's death? *Sorry about that, but shit happens? I don't know what I was thinking?* Bo thought again of the first time they had met, and played through his mind all of the joy they had shared, but it was impossible to erase or fast-forward past the scene of Serena in Alex Stillwell's office.

It was the day after his surveillance in the Delta. As he waited in the woods, even while hounded by hordes of mosquitoes, he thought only of Serena. Anxious to see her, Bo had gone by her office in Madison, the next day. When the secretary told him that Serena had gone to the courthouse in Jackson, Bo didn't hesitate in continuing his search for her, even though downtown parking was always a headache.

Bo saw them, through the open door, in the anteroom of Stillwell's chambers. Neither Serena nor Stillwell had seen him approach. *How could they, the way they were looking at each other?* Bo lingered in disbelief, followed by anger, then slipped away before being noticed. He had tried to put it out of his mind, but he just couldn't let it go. When Bo had gone to Tom's house that night and found Stillwell, he wanted to kill him. Serena? Well, she *was* dead, and Bo regretted that he had let his temper get the best of him. However, there was nothing he could do about it now. Nor was there anything more to do at her crypt. He really didn't know why he had come.

The moon had climbed higher, and there was something inexplicably alluring about it; Serena, the moon goddess, beckoned.

Bo retraced his steps to his vehicle and made a U-turn on Trafalgar, back to Desaix. Crossing over Bayou St. John, he turned left on Wisner, again on Esplanade. The night remained quiet as he drove past the front entrance of the cemetery. Discerning no indication that he had been noticed, Bo breathed a little easier and continued on, under the canopy of Esplanade's giant live oaks and past the columned homes, one of which had been the residence of noted artist Edgar Degas.

He knew the avenue would take him to the river, at the northeast corner of the French Quarter, and he found the bohemian playground was in full swing. Bo lucked out, however, in spying a parking space just off Esplanade, on Decatur Street. It was a tight fit for the Pathfinder, and it took some careful maneuvering for Bo to get it in. He placed the bottle of Jim Beam he had purchased in Crystal Springs back in the brown paper bag, remembering that having beverages in glass containers was one of the few taboos in the Vieux Carré, and would quickly draw the attention of unwanted, police attention.

Walking back to the corner at Esplanade, Bo crossed Decatur, continuing past the Old Mint. Constructed in 1835, during the presidency of Andrew Jackson, savior of the city in the War of 1812, it has the distinction of being the only building in America that served as a mint for two different governments—the United, and the Confederate States of America.

At the end of the avenue, Bo veered right, onto Peters Street, and made his way alongside the open-air pavilions of the French Market. They were empty, closed for the night, but the vendors would return early the next morning, setting up their stalls, unpacking their wares, and waiting for the tourists to stream in, hawking every kind of bauble, trinket, and flea-market item known to man. At the end of the second pavilion, Bo spotted a walkway to his left, in all likelihood leading to the river, Bo's intended destination.

Across the trolley-car tracks and atop the embankment of the Mississippi River, Bo found the "Moonwalk", a landscaped, brick walkway named for former New Orleans Mayor Maurice Edwin "Moon" Landrieu. Bo started upriver on the walkway, in search of an empty bench. Five rather grungy males were at the first one—three on the bench and two others sitting on the ground facing them, passing around what Bo recognized as a "blunt." The one in the center of the bench wore a beat-up, black top hat, and mumbled something, causing the others to erupt in laughter. By the way it was dutifully and overly done, Bo guessed that Top Hat was the leader of the cadre. Then too, Bo thought, they may just be so stoned they would think a funeral dirge hysterical. In any event, these punks wouldn't give a rat's ass about a guy drinking some whiskey, and Bo saw that the next bench beyond was unoccupied.

He sat down and pulled the bottle from the bag, just far enough to see how much was left. It was only about two fingers deep, but Bo couldn't have been in any better venue in the world for replenishment. He slid the bottle back inside, twisted open the cap, and drained what remained. The burning in his throat and chest was a welcome respite against the crisp wind blowing over the river.

The lights on the bridge, farther upriver and to Bo's right, were lit up like a Christmas tree, joining the stars as reflections on the dark water below, twinkling on old man river's perpetual ripples. Bo didn't know how long he had been transfixed, for some reason mesmerized, by the sparkling panorama, when he heard someone speaking.

"Dude! Can you spare a few bucks for me to get something to eat?" It was one of the thugs from the nearby bench, evidently experiencing a bad case of the munchies.

"Sorry pal, can't help you," Bo answered.

"He says he's sorry, can't help!" the moocher called to the others, still at their bench. He smiled, and Bo couldn't help but notice that what teeth were there and had not rotted brown, were badly yellowed. Bo also saw the other four rise like vultures from their roost, and amble over in his direction, Top Hat in the rear. Bo crossed his left ankle over his right knee.

"Since you can't spare a few dollars for something to eat, you owe us twenty for the bench rental," Yellow Teeth advised. By that time, his cohorts, with the exception of Top Hat, were standing beside him.

"Fuck off," Bo replied.

"Fuck off? Man, I don't think you understand who we are."

"I don't give a shit who you are. Just leave me the fuck alone; okay?"

"Not okay." It was Top Hat, whom Bo estimated to be about six-four—close to seven feet, if you included the tall, black hat—but could not have weighed more than one-ninety. He wore an open, black coat, which extended nearly to the ground; and although nighttime, round, dark spectacles concealed his eyes. "I am known as Warlock, lord of the night," he said. Sweeping an extended arm around the environs, he advised Bo, "And this is my realm."

Bo's ensuing derisive laugh evoked an indignant air. "Homage is due, which can be done the easy way," the freak explained, rubbing his right thumb up and down his fingertips. "Or," he said after a pause, "another way." He tilted his head toward Yellow Teeth, who brought out a switchblade, springing it open. The other three just stood there, sneering.

During this monologue, Bo had been scratching the calf of his crossed leg with his right hand, which suddenly drew the small semi-automatic from his ankle holster and leveled the weapon at Top Hat's head. "Tell him to drop it, or I'll remove your fucking head from under that ridiculous hat right now." Again, all it took was a slight nod of the head from Top Hat for Yellow Teeth to obey.

"Now let me introduce *myself*," Bo continued. "I am known as Killer, and my domain has no bounds. I don't give a fuck whether it's day or night. I came here to choose a worthy victim, so I had no interest in dip-shits like you. But I'm willing to lower my standards if all of you are not out of my sight by the time I count to ten. One, two...." None of them moved.

"Oh, I know what you're thinking," Bo proclaimed. "There's no way I can shoot all of you. Maybe, maybe not. But it's absolutely, positively certain, *Warlock,* that you will be the first sent straight to the bowels of hell in the next eight seconds. Three, four, five...." The four toadies scampered off. Warlock too, turned and was leaving, but in an unhurried gait, the bottom portion of his coat billowing in the wind.

Bo stood up, maintaining his aim as he continued to call out, "Six, seven." Just as he was about to count off "ten," Warlock reached an opening in the wall separating the Quarter from the tracks, and paused long enough to doff his hat to Bo. "Crazy motherfucker," Bo said to himself before re-holstering the pistol and making his departure, on the hunt for a drink.

Even though the first stop wasn't what Bo had in mind, he said, "Fuck it, booze is booze." While there was some truth in that observation, it came with a price. The same damned, upbeat Key West music went on, and on, and on. It just wasn't suited for Bo's mood, and it wasn't long before he settled his tab and got the hell out.

He crossed Decatur and headed in the direction of Jackson Square, soon passing the year-round Christmas store where he and Debra had bought a few decorations you couldn't find just anywhere, and he reminisced about how bubbly she would get each Yuletide season. His walk took him past retail shops offering a wide assortment of merchandise: souvenirs, pralines, beignet mix, hot sauces, alligator heads, Mardi Gras masks, and wearing apparel. One store even specialized in custom-made capes. Some of the dresses on display were like the ones Serena favored, but Bo refused to think about it, continuing his quest.

The crowd grew larger with each step of the way. People of every age and description packed the sidewalk, and it seemed the whole world was dressed in either purple and gold, or red and blue, thousands of fans having made the hour drive from Baton Rouge after the LSU-Ole Miss football game. Although the revelry slowed Bo's hunt for libation, he actually enjoyed the endless jostling since among the throng were voluptuous, young coeds eagerly throwing all inhibition to the wind.

Delightfully wedging his way through the youthful female bodies, Bo halted in front of a store and stared at two of the T-shirts hanging in the open doorway. "If alcohol kills brain cells, I must be a frick'n genius," read the front of one. Printed on the one hanging above it was a drawing of the devil: "God is busy, may I help you?"

Bo found the inscriptions bothersome. He knew he had to get his act together, and he would; just not tonight. He resumed his walk, soon coming at last to a bar on the corner of Decatur and Madison. He had heard of Tujague's, it had been around a long time and was supposed to have a bar of some historical or architectural significance. In fact, Tujague's was the city's first stand-up saloon, and Bo had no idea how long he stood, falling further from grace, at the tall, mirrored bar that was already a full century old when Guillaume Tujague acquired it from a Paris bistro.

After slinging back shot after shot, Bo eventually stumbled outside and staggered right, singing in a slow and slurred tone, indifferent that he did not have the words quite right, *"I'm walking in New Orleans; I'm walking in New Orleans...."*

Turning the corner at Jackson Square, across from the Café Du Monde, Bo was distracted by some guy completely covered in silver and posing as motionless as a statue. Bo bumped into a middle-aged, rotund woman brandishing a red and blue pompom. Seeing that her equally large husband was sporting a blue Ole Miss cap, Bo slurred, "Hoddy fucking toddy," in a bastardized reference to the school's hallmark cheer.

"Just ignore him," the man instructed his wife. "He's just had too much to drink."

"Wrong," Bo advised. "I haven't had nearly enough. So I'm on my way to Shit Street to get Bourbon faced. Isn't it somewhere around here?"

"Well, I never," the woman huffed.

Looking her up and down, Bo replied, "From what I see, I know that's right." Bo's night on the town drew to an abrupt close when a fist punched his lights out.

Simultaneously, at the Esplanade end of Decatur Street, a tow truck was pulling away with a silver Pathfinder bearing a Mississippi license plate.

CHAPTER 25

New Orleans is one of the few cities in the world readily identified by a single structure. St. Louis Cathedral or, more precisely, The Cathedral-Basilica of St. Louis King of France, dates back to 1716, making it the oldest Catholic cathedral in continued use in the United States. Its triple spires tower majestically over the bronze statue of the gallant, horseback general for whom the public square below is named. To the left, the cathedral is flanked by The Cabildo, constructed 1795-1799, as the seat of the Spanish municipal government. It was there, in 1803, that emissaries from Napoleon's money-strapped France transferred the vast lands of the Louisiana Purchase to a nation still in its infancy, and over the years visited by five American Presidents. To the right of the cathedral stands The Presbytere, so named because it was erected on a site which previously served as a residence for Capuchin monks. Built soon after, and architecturally matching The Cabildo, The Presbytere was used for commercial purposes until becoming a courthouse in 1834. Today both buildings are integral components of the Louisiana State Museum.

The land beneath these historical edifices, as all of Jackson Square, was once owned by the father of Baroness Micaela Almonester de Pontalba, a Creole who married a cousin at the age of fifteen. In 1834, the same year the Presbytere was converted to a hall of justice, the baroness somehow survived several gunshots fired at point-blank range into her chest by her father-in-law, who that night turned the pair of dueling pistols on himself. He however, did not survive, and the baroness's subsequent inheritance made her the wealthiest woman in New Orleans. It was she who built the matching brick row houses, with their distinctive ironwork balconies, that bordered the sides of the square perpendicular to the cathedral.

Jackson Square, nee the Place d'Armes, is the heart of New Orleans, and it was on these grounds, where soldiers once drilled and criminals once hung from gallows, that Bo Landry awoke as someone shook him by the shoulder. "Hey," a woman said. When Bo opened his eyes, at least the one that wasn't swollen shut, she advised, "You better at least sit up. Some of the cops don't take kindly to vagrants here."

Bo pushed himself to a sitting position and saw that he was on a bench in the plaza, between the square's fenced garden and the cathedral. Although he could not see his black left eye, the pain did not elude him. Nor could he see the red streaks, perfectly matching the width of the bench's iron slats, that numbed the right side of his face. In some indecipherable tongue, Bo attempted to express his appreciation to this Good Samaritan, one of the numerous denizens of the square who came early each morning to showcase their artistic works.

She was a petite woman, appearing to be in her late 20s, early 30s at the most, clad in jeans and an unbuttoned, paint-splotched denim shirt. She had the sleeves rolled up to her mid-forearms and wore it un-tucked, as a light jacket, over a white T-shirt. Strawberry-blonde hair was loosely gathered on her head and held in place by a long, slender paintbrush. A few freckles nicely accented an otherwise unadorned, but well sculpted, countenance. The absence of makeup was not at all detractive. Although she was not, by any means stunning, as was Serena, she was in a word, cute.

"Are you okay?" she asked. "You look like hell." Again, she was unable to comprehend Bo's garbled grumbling. "You *sound* like hell, too."

"Thanks!" Bo snapped. "I said, Thanks!" It came out harsher than he intended, but she seemed deaf.

"Well excuse the hell out of me," she replied, and returned to resume her work in setting things up for the day.

I wish someone would excuse the hell out of me, Bo thought. *An exorcism, that's what I need.* He struggled to his feet and, while attempting to get his bearings, something caught his eye. It wasn't a fist this time, but it was just as striking, knocking him for a loop. He drew nearer to a large oil painting that Bo's rather miffed benefactor had propped against the ironwork fence. It was as if his view of the river, stars, and crescent moon the night before had been photographed. The painting's detail and size were attempting to convey some meaning, or message, with an exclamation mark; for included on the bottom left was the rearview of a man sitting on a bench. Standing and facing him were five other men, one of whom was shrouded in a long black coat and donning a top hat and sunglasses.

"Did you do this last night? Were you there last night?"

"No," the artist curtly answered. After a moment's pause, she gave him her best guess as to the approximate period of time she had painted the piece. Bo was not assuaged by what she said. In fact, he became agitated, pressing her for an exact date.

"Think!" he repeatedly urged.

"Then shut up, so that I can!" Although she was becoming increasingly perturbed, it seemed that the quickest way to get rid of this rude pest was to satisfy his curiosity, however odd.

Beth Callahan couldn't recall the date, but she would never forget the event. It was not often that she completed such a painting in a single sitting, but it was one of those times when she was really in her "zone." She had retired to bed early that evening, after a light meal, waking late in the night and beginning the picture. Her brushes seemed to have had a mind of their own and in no time, daylight broke through the skylight of her Madison Street studio apartment. Instead of being exhausted, she was exhilarated. Thinking about it, Beth remembered that the canvas was one of those she had last purchased from the art supply store on Royal Street, out in the Bywater, and used that night. Just this morning while unpacking, she had noticed a few receipts in the plastic tackle-box where she stored her brushes. Rummaging through the container, Beth was relieved to find the one that would have the answer.

As Bo's mind processed the information, a shiver ran up his spine—this woman had painted last night's scene during the very night Serena and Tom were killed. It was in a cold sweat that Bo Landry turned and shuffled off.

CHAPTER 26

According to the Book of Proverbs, the wicked flee when no one pursues. Bo didn't know from what it was, exactly, that he was fleeing, but he was well aware of what he had become. From the day he learned that his parents were martyred in Africa, he had rid himself of the burden suffered by those who believe in an ever-loving God. Guilt requires conviction. Atrocities, such as those suffered by his parents, had exorcised all belief in an omnipotent God of love and mercy. Bo's guilt for Serena and Tom's deaths, and especially that of Serena, was swept away by anger. Even from the grave Serena was tormenting him. Whether or not there was an afterlife, and his soul doomed to the fires of hell, Bo Landry was living in purgatory.

A mother pulled her four-year-old son by the hand from the path of the unshaven man with the bushy, unkempt, brown hair and a hideous, puffed, black and purple eye, aimlessly approaching St. Louis Cathedral.

Ascending the steps, and entering the vestibule through the tall, wood doors on the far left, Bo was confronted by the statue, to his right, of the Virgin Mary, mother of God. She was reaching out to two poor souls in purgatory, who at least knew that the punishment for their un-confessed, venial sins was temporary. Bo's iniquity, however, was mortal. His soul was not merely weakened; it was dead.

A man with a camera hanging on his neck exited the sanctuary and held the door open for a woman who followed him out. Bo grasped the door by the edge before it closed, and looked inside. Seeing that the place was relatively empty and that no service was going on, he eased inside and looked around. It would be a good place to sit and think.

Behind him was a statue of St. Louis, the only French monarch to be canonized, and in whose honor the magnificent place of worship was named. Five splendidly crafted stained-glass windows on both side walls depicted the life of King Louis IX: his early years; his coronation at twelve years of age; his marriage to Marguerite of Provence; as the builder of Sainte Chapelle, his personal chapel within the palace complex in Paris and now the Hall of Justice; embarking on the Seventh Crusade; receiving the key to the conquered Egyptian city of Damietta; his ministry to lepers; his illness and death during his second crusade; the return of his body to France; and finally his canonization by Pope Boniface VIII.

Flags of every nation to rule over New Orleans, from its founding to the present, hung in grandeur from the balconies. Staring upward, as he walked down the nearer of the two center aisles, toward the altar, Bo took in the brightly colored frescos on the ceiling. In the center was Jesus telling Peter: "Feed my sheep"; and further back, above the entrance, Archangel St. Michael was shown defeating Satan, who was portrayed as a dragon. Bo felt like a sheep himself, except he wouldn't, couldn't, be fed. He was more on a path to a slaughter pen, doubting if there was any power capable of slaying his dragons or even having any inclination to make the attempt.

Despite his skepticism, Bo couldn't bring himself to directly confront the altar, choosing instead to take a seat to the side. *But which one?* If the left, a huge painting of Mary would be looking down on him; if the right, one of equal size of St. Francis of Assisi. Although Bo had been raised a protestant, he knew from Debra, something of Catholicism. As with most teenage boys, Bo had done everything he could think of to impress his girl, including occasionally meeting her at mass, much to the chagrin of his Methodist parents. Aware that St. Francis was the patron saint of animals, and questioning whether any prayer Mary might offer for his lifeless soul would extend into the depths of hell, Bo opted to take a seat on a pew to the right. After all, he *was* an animal.

Bo became vaguely aware of a few people coming inside, by their semi-hushed voices and the echoes of their heels striking the marble floor. A priest emerged from the side, giving Bo a close look as he continued to the back. Bo was still lost in his thoughts, staring blankly at the painting of St. Francis, when the priest returned. "Are you all right, my son?" he asked.

Bo turned his head and advised the gray-haired clergyman, "No Father. I'm dead."

"Rumpled, yes. Injured, yes. No doubt disturbed, but also obviously still among the living."

"That's a matter of opinion," Bo informed him.

"I see," the priest replied. Sitting beside Bo, he extended his open right hand and said, "I'm Monsignor Ambrose, the rector here." Bo started to reciprocate the introduction, but was cut short by Ambrose: "You need not tell me your name; it doesn't matter. What matters is what troubles you so."

Returning his gaze to the painting, Bo replied, "I've sinned, Father. Big time."

"All have sinned and fallen short of the glory of God, my son. Would you like for me to take your confession?"

"I'm not Catholic."

"And you consider that a mortal sin?" It reminded Bo of a line in a *Seinfeld* episode he had seen. He turned to face the priest and saw a slight smile and sparkling mischievous, blue eyes. "Sorry; I've been waiting for the opportunity to say that. Seriously though, since you are not of the faith, I can't give you absolution, but I can advise you how to obtain it."

"Okay," Bo said, slightly bobbing his head.

"Are you an adherent of *any* faith?"

"Not anymore. I grew up as a Methodist, but the only faith I've had for years has been in myself. Now that's gone too."

"And what was the cause of this self-imposed excommunication?" Ambrose asked.

Bo told him about the deaths of his parents, and those of Debra, Serena, and Tom; and his alcoholism and relapse. However, he chose not to mention his culpability for any of those deaths nor any of the others by his hand. Since the priest had already explained that he could not provide absolution, Bo wasn't sure how much of his revelations would be considered privileged information.

After patiently listening, the monsignor informed Bo, "The wages of sin is death. So in a way, you were correct in your self-diagnosis: you are suffering from a sentence of death, the spiritual death of separation from God. But, in His infinite mercy and love for us, God has provided everyone who will accept it a free gift of salvation, a pardon from that sentence."

"You don't know what I've done, Father. I don't deserve any such gift."

"That's right, you don't," the priest agreed. "Nor has, nor will, anyone else. It is not by one's own doing that one is given the gift, not by any good works, but by the unearned grace of God. Through the boundless riches of His Son, Jesus Christ, God promises that He not only wishes you to have a life, but to have it in abundance."

Bo tensed and reddened. "You say God wants that for everyone? Is that what you said, Father?"

"It's true," the priest said assuredly.

"Then what about Debra? What about Serena? How about Tom, my mother and father? God evidently didn't want *them* to have a life at all, much less in abundance," he vented.

"A valid question, and perhaps someday an answer which you find satisfying will come to you. But it will remain elusive, I fear, until you realize that your anger is robbing you of all joy." Seeing Bo shaking his head in doubt, the rector asked him what he did for work.

"I *was* a cop," Bo answered.

"Ah, a peacekeeper; 'for they shall be called children of God,'" the priest recited from the Beatitudes. "Then I pray that, according to the riches of His glory, the Lord grant that you be strengthened in your inner being with power through the Holy Spirit. And that you lead a life worthy of the calling to which you have been called, with all humility and patience, making every effort to maintain the unity of the Spirit in the bond of peace. In the name of the Father, the Son, and the Holy Spirit, amen."

Bo thanked him and stood to leave. "Do you have a Bible at home, my son?" Ambrose inquired.

"Yeah, somewhere. Why?"

"I would like for you to find it. If you don't read any other verse, I want you to read and underline Philippians 4:4: *Rejoice in the Lord always. Do not worry about anything; but, in everything, by prayer and supplication with thanksgiving, let your requests be made known to God. And the peace of God, which surpasses all understanding, will guard your heart and your mind in Christ Jesus.*"

"Sure," Bo replied, even though he still didn't believe, and again turned to depart.

"Let me at least help you in a more tangible way," the priest urged, as he rose from the pew. "Why don't you come with me, and let's get you cleaned up some?"

Bo accepted, but explained that he first needed to check on his car. Ambrose asked where it was parked; and when Bo told him, the priest chuckled and took him by the arm. "In that case, you will also need a phone to call a cab, for the City of New Orleans is not as forgiving as the Lord. I'm sure your car has already been towed. Come, and I'll give you the address where they impound them."

CHAPTER 27

Rescuing souls might be the Church's foremost mission, but it does not necessarily come first. Until certain basic physical matters necessary for minimum survival are met, spirituality remains an abstract, ephemeral concept. Until Bo Landry re-attained sobriety and conquered the alcoholism sucking the life out of him as effectively as a vampire, he would not be able to focus on most of what the priest had said, nor begin to face the other demons tormenting him.

Thus, Monsignor Ambrose did much more for Bo than afford him the use of a telephone and tend to his swollen black eye. The priest had offered to contact the Catholic Charities office in Jackson, Mississippi, enlisting assistance in getting Bo into a rehab facility in his hometown.

Bo declined, not daring to tell Ambrose of the strange phenomena drawing him to New Orleans lest the clergyman would be calling someone to put him in a padded cell. The reason proffered by Bo was terse, "There's nothing for me there anymore."

The priest was saddened by the gloomy response, but delighted when Bo asked, "What about here, in the Big Easy?"

"Even less of a problem, if that is what you wish."

"Why not?" Bo rhetorically asked. "Who knows, maybe I'll start spelling my name B-E-A-U-X."

Monsignor Ambrose gladly made the necessary calls and, in no time, Bo was admitted to a rehabilitation facility located near the river bridge. Possessing Bo's power-of-attorney, Ambrose diplomatically tended to the cancellation of Bo's apartment lease, and to the storage of his belongings, including the impounded Pathfinder. The priest paid that cost, as well as the rehab expenses, out of a checking account funded each month by the direct deposits of Bo's retirement benefits. With the rector graciously tying up Bo's worldly loose ends, Bo could concentrate solely on getting himself back together.

Experience has shown that whatever success is achieved in attaining and, more importantly, maintaining sobriety is directly proportional to the amount of time dedicated to rehab. It was close to a year that Bo was in the intensive and highly structured rehab program, residing in a dormitory and progressing through several phases of treatment. The process was slow; but with baby steps, he regained some sense of self-worth and, toward the end of his stay, busied himself with lending a hand on the used-car lot located on the premises, one of the means by which the facility defrayed its expenses.

The ninth of The Twelve Steps of Alcoholics Anonymous requires that direct amends be made to people the alcoholic has harmed. At noon on November 2, Bo, now clean-shaven and his hair cut to neatly trimmed waves just touching the tops of his ears, walked out of the facility, and was picked up by Monsignor Ambrose in the Pathfinder. The priest drove to the intersection of Royal and Orleans, behind St. Louis Cathedral, and pulled to a stop. He patted Bo on the leg, told him to come by later, and got out.

It felt strange, but in a good way, to be behind the wheel again. Bo turned right, onto Orleans, and continued straight ahead for three blocks, to Burgundy. His mind was once again clear, and it was indeed ironic that his first stop after getting out of rehab, would be a bar. Serena had mentioned that her father's pub was on a corner of Burgundy and Toulouse, and that was where Bo was headed. In his mind, he had wronged Sam Raven and it was time, for better or worse, to face him and try to make amends.

All of the narrow streets of the French Quarter are one-way, and Bo realized his mistake when he braked at the stop sign at Burgundy. Toulouse was two blocks to the left, but he couldn't turn in that direction. Instead of trying to solve the maze, he turned right, and parked in the first available spot he came upon. It was by a neighborhood grocery, at Burgundy and Dumaine, with the exterior painted bright yellow. *This should be hard for even me to miss.*

After backtracking on foot for four blocks, Bo pushed through the door of McCormick's Irish Pub, almost tripping over a blonde Labrador retriever stretched out on the floor and sporting a purple kerchief tied around its neck. A U-shaped bar was to the left, but Bo didn't see anyone tending it. Billiard balls clattered about on the pool tables to the right. A game was just underway at the one nearer to Bo. The guy doing the break had his back turned, affording Bo a good look at the words on the back of his baby-blue T-shirt: "We don't have a neighborhood drunk; we all take turns."

Playing on wall-mounted televisions was the LSU-Ole Miss football game. *Déjà vu*. Although the contest was in Oxford, Mississippi, noticing the telecast caused Bo to reflect on how far he had fallen when the teams squared off only a year ago in Baton Rouge and Bo had wandered into a new life in New Orleans. The point was emphasized by a sign taped to one of the two vertical posts extending from the front corners of the bar countertop to the ceiling: "One tequila, two tequila, three tequila, floor! Please drink responsibly." Bo had never developed a fondness for tequila, but he had sure hit the floor in almost every sense of the phrase. Over the past year, he had even taken a liking to coffee.

"Bo!" He turned and saw that it was the proprietor coming from what Bo guessed was a storage room.

"Hi, Sam," Bo sheepishly responded. "Can we talk?"

"Sure, I've got a spot saved for you, right over here." Sam led the way to the far side of the bar. At the end, he pulled out the last stool. A sheet of notebook paper taped to the seat read: "Reserved for Bo Landry." "Sit," Sam directed, after ripping away the paper. Puzzled, Bo complied and noticed a clean, empty coffee mug in front of him on the bar. Before he could say anything, Sam was filling the vessel. "Here you go, just the way you like it—black, but none of that chicory crap."

Bo was completely thrown, unable to say anything that he had rehearsed. "How..." he began, but was interrupted by a man to his left, seated two stools down the bar. He looked to be in his forties, with black, greasy hair combed straight back and a drooping mustache.

"Hey, Sam!" the man bellowed. "Where y'at last night? Ya missed it!"

"All Souls' Day, Homer. I always take off for it."

"What-tever; but, like I say, you miss out on ole Remy here," Homer advised, pointing at the carrot-topped fellow to his right, seated next to Bo and grinning from ear to ear. "Go hed, Remy, tell 'em." Remy, however, just kept smiling. "Okay, d'en, I tell it.

"We was over dare shoot'n da pool, and dis here couple come waltzing in. Musta come over from da hotel, cause dey all gussied up—him in a coat'n tie, she in a fancy dress and all, lemme tell you."

"Well, dey take a sit-down at dat table dare, by where me'n Remy, we shoot'n da pool. Lauryn, she bring 'em dey drinks, and da woman asks, 'What you got to eat?' Lauryn tells her to look around, dis t'aint no café, but she got some Chex Mix. Da woman says she'll take dat, so Lauryn, she bring her a bag.

"Few minutes later, da woman, she starts to having a coughing spell and t'aint stop. Remy, here, he stop shoot'n, walks over to her and asks,

'Can ya swallow?' She shake her head no.

"Remy asks, 'Can ya breathe?' Well, she turn blue in da face and shake her head again. So Remy, here…" Homer was laughing so hard, he had to pause for a moment in his story.

"Remy, here, he walk over, help da woman to her feet, and, afore you can blink an eye, he lift dat woman's dress up over her waist, yank down her drawers, bend hisself down and run his tongue up one o' her arse cheeks.

"Oh, bullshit, Homer," Sam said. "I need to talk to Bo here, about something serious. Can't this wait a minute?"

Homer however, was resolute. "I almost done," he said, "and dis here da best part. Don'tcha see, da woman, she so shocked, she whatcha call spasm all over, and dat Chex Mix, it come flying out her mouth. I tell ya, ya coulda heard a pin drop in dis place. Then Remy, he says to everyone wit dey mouths hung open, 'What da matter, you t'aint never see nobody do da hind-lick mar-nu-var?'"

Homer and Remy were bursting a gut, laughing at themselves and punching each other's shoulder. As they got up and walked toward the pool tables, Homer jubilantly exclaimed, "We sho got Sam, didn't we Remy? He never seed it coming!" Sam shook his head. "Our local comedians," he explained to Bo. "Sorry, what were you saying?"

"Sam, you act like you knew I would be here today."

"That's because I *did* know."

"Did Father Ambrose call you?"

"Who's he?" Sam asked.

"What's going on, Sam? How did you know?"

"From Serena," Sam calmly announced as he methodically placed clean tumblers on the shelves behind the bar.

Now Bo thought it was Sam being the comedian, and Bo didn't see the humor. He had come in earnest and didn't appreciate being jerked around. "What the hell are you talking about, Sam?"

"I'm part Pueblo, you know. My people, as many other tribes of the southwest, celebrate the dead on All Souls' Day, November 1. Like you heard me tell Homer, that's what I did yesterday. It's a day when spirits return, visiting family and friends."

"Come on, Sam, you can't possibly believe that."

"Believe what you will. You're the one who asked how I knew you would be here today. Bo, you and I have barely spoken to each other; yet here you are drinking coffee, and like I knew you prefer it."

Bo's head was spinning, and he recalled the unusual arrangement of dried corn and cedar woodcarving he had seen at Serena's tomb the previous year—the night of November 1, All Souls' Day. Questioning

Sam about it, Bo learned that Pueblo families do such things in preparation of the anticipated visit of their loved ones' spirits.

"She doesn't blame you, you know," Sam announced.

"What?" Bo asked, lost in thought.

"I know from Serena where you've been - getting help. And she knows you're going to need more help, now that you're out. She asked me to help you, and I will. If my baby loves you, how can I feel otherwise? So you don't have to worry about saying any of the things to me that you intended." Grasping Bo's wrists atop the bar, Sam added, "It's okay. We're good."

It was too much for Bo, and he was afraid he would get all misty-eyed in front of the crowd. The dog with the kerchief ambled over, providing a welcome diversion. "This your dog, Sam?"

"Yeah; name's Norton."

"Norton? Funny name for a dog."

"Really?" Sam asked. "You don't think he looks like Ed Norton? You know, on *The Honeymooners?*"

"The what?"

"Never mind, before your time. Anyway, have you given any thought about what you're going to do? You gotta work, keep busy."

"No. I guess I'll start checking the want ads."

"PI work; that's what you need to do. Lot of things in the Big Easy that need investigating, and it's in your blood, my friend. It's your calling."

Calling? A year ago Monsignor Ambrose had mentioned Bo's calling in a prayer; that Bo be empowered to lead a life worthy of his calling. Now, a year later, Sam Raven referred to his calling as an investigator. Bo was sifting through all of the bizarre events, trying to make some sense out of the pieces, when Sam asked, "Know where you'll be staying."

"No, I don't," Bo replied.

"It wasn't a question," Sam said to Bo, then shouted to his right, "Hey, LB! That apartment across from your place still available?"

After his shot, the pool player in the baby-blue T-shirt turned around and replied, "Yeah! Know anyone who wants it?" *I'll be damned,* Bo thought. It was Judge Harper. Things just kept getting weirder and weirder.

CHAPTER 28

Although L. Blake Harper, a former colleague of Tom Davis on the Hinds County, Mississippi Circuit Court, was at least a dozen years older than Tom, he never looked a day older. The source of this fountain of youth was the easygoing manner with which he approached life, both personal and professional. Bo had always felt at ease on the occasions he testified in Harper's court, and knew of Tom's fondness for the man as well.

Although a successful attorney in private practice, and a well respected jurist, there was nothing pretentious about Judge Harper. Very few people knew that his first name was Leonardo, and outside the courtroom, his friends just called him Blake. There was even less formality in the Big Easy, where he was simply known around the Quarter as LB.

Harper and his wife Robin had kept various apartments here and there in the Vieux Carré long before making the one on St. Ann Street their permanent home when he retired. The bohemian atmosphere was the ideal place for them to get away and relax, especially after all the hype during the Summerville trial, which Tom Davis had prosecuted, and over which Blake Harper had presided. Most folks in the neighborhood didn't know or care about Harper's former life. They just knew him as LB, the guy who late each afternoon shot pool at McCormick's while his wife pulled up a stool at one of the video-poker machines. He was the guy with the short-cropped beard who was quick, especially after several gin and tonics, to distribute oral invitations to the other patrons to join he and Robin for dinner that evening, or for breakfast the next morning—his treat.

There was a natural easiness about LB and Robin that made people relax; but the manner in which they teased each other, or playfully spoke of the other to third parties, could take some getting used to. Once around them enough, especially if a third party made the mistake of speaking derisively of one within earshot of the other, it became all too apparent how much, deep down, they adored each other. Beneath the superficial razzing was a comfortable relationship built upon the solid foundation of mutual respect, trust, and admiration.

After LB shared with Bo what he knew of the vacant apartment on St. Ann, Sam asked, as he glanced around the pub, "Where's Robin, LB?"

"She'll be here in a while, but I think she's mad at me."

"What did you do this time?" Sam asked.

"I walked back to the bedroom to see if she was ready to leave. She was at her vanity, putting on makeup, and I told her she didn't need any, and she said, 'It's for you, you know.'"

"Why did that make her mad? You paid her a compliment."

"Well," LB explained, "I pretty much ruined it when I told her that if it was for my benefit, I was going to walk on over and get started; that liquor *in me* made her look better than makeup *on her*."

"LB, LB," Sam mockingly chided. "How she puts up with you, I'll never understand."

Nor did Bo understand when Robin showed up. She was far from the crone Bo had expected. Ten years younger than LB, the auburn-haired woman would be considered attractive at any age. The kiss she planted on her husband's cheek, and his ensuing impish smile, were Bo's final clues that the former jurist had been jerking them around.

"Robin knows more about the place than I do," LB advised Bo. "She's been snooping around over there while the workers have been doing some repairs." Turning to his wife, he continued, "Tell him, Robin. I'm up this game."

As LB strode to a pool table, Sam made the introductions, explaining to Robin, Bo's interest in the apartment. He let them talk while he mixed a dirty vodka martini for Robin.

*****

Liking what he saw, Bo took the apartment on the 900 block of St. Ann, between Burgundy and Dauphine. It was the left side of a charming cottage, a wood-frame duplex or what was referred to in New Orleanean-speak as, one-half of a double. Louvered shutters covered the windows and exterior door. The layout consisted of a den, kitchen, bath, and two bedrooms, one of which Bo intended to use as an office if things worked out with his PI venture. All of the rooms were spacious, with hardwood floors and twelve-foot-high ceilings. Best of all was the rent. Robin had been with Bo when he met the realtor and hearing that it was less than she and LB were paying for their one-bedroom unit across the street, she suggested to Bo that they swap. He was not at all sure it was said in jest.

Bo gave the realtor two checks on the spot—one as a deposit, and the other for the first month's rent. That night, Bo slept on the couch at the Harper's place and drove to Jackson the next morning, leaving LB an extra key to his new apartment. The Entergy serviceman was scheduled to turn on the power and gas that day, and LB agreed to be on hand to let him inside. In Jackson, Bo rented a U-Haul truck and retrieved his belongings from storage.

The return trip to New Orleans was a nightmare. Things went well until Bo reached the southernmost stretch of I-55, which spanned thirty miles of bayous and swamps, and ran into a hellacious thunderstorm. Worse yet was the eastbound traffic backed up on I-10 that he encountered as soon as he exited off I-55 at La Place. Turning on the radio, Bo learned the cause of the bumper-to-bumper congestion. Of all the days to move, he had picked the Saturday of the Bayou Classic, the annual football game between rivals Southern University, in Baton Rouge, and Grambling University, in Ruston. Fans from all over Louisiana were converging on the Superdome and Bo was among them, towing his Pathfinder on a trailer, hitched to the back of the large rental truck, and inching along at a snail's pace in pouring-down rain.

Finally arriving back at his new apartment, LB and Robin braved the elements and pitched in. While Bo and LB began unloading the truck, Robin backed the Pathfinder off the trailer and went off in search of a place to park it. The truck was empty by the time she walked into Bo's apartment. All three looked like drowned rats.

Needing to get the truck and trailer off the street as soon as possible, Bo drove the rig to the nearest U-Haul facility—on Tulane Avenue—and LB followed, but not in his vehicle. Parking in front of his apartment was no mere preference for LB; it was an obsession. Once there, the Harper BMW moved only in the direst of circumstances. Cruising the French Quarter and dodging inattentive drunks in the frustrating quest for a parking spot were endeavors LB loathed. As he explained to Bo, "When you live in the Vieux Carré, you learn to walk, and you don't even have to do that when you live within easy crawling distance of McCormick's." Thus, even though Robin had just parked it, it was in Bo's vehicle that LB followed Bo to the U-Haul place.

CHAPTER 29

Due to his years of investigative experience in law enforcement, Bo was able to obtain an agency, rather than an individual, license from the Louisiana State Board of Private Investigator Examiners. This meant that he did not have to find employment; he was his own agency, free to work for himself or to do contract work for other agencies. He hit a snag however, by being too candid in filling out the application.

Bo was, and always would be, an alcoholic. But he was not a "practicing" one, which would have disqualified him under Louisiana law. Instead of merely verifying that the disqualifier did not pertain to him, Bo gave an explanation about his recovery which was a big mistake. There is a lot of truth in the adage about no good deed going unpunished, especially whenever the government is involved. Bo's honesty only prompted more questions, necessitating a trip to Baton Rouge to be interrogated by a board committee. The notice he received called it an "interview," but the adversarial nature of the discussion didn't come as a surprise, considering the fact that the committee was comprised of PIs who already had their licenses, and thus possessed an economic interest in keeping everyone else out of the profession.

Fortunately, Sam, LB, Monsignor Ambrose, and Milan Fortunato, Bo's AA sponsor, testified on Bo's behalf. He was soon cleared to attend the required forty-hour Basic Private Investigation Prepatory Course, and to take the exam. Once over those hurdles, it was only a matter of forking over $345.25 to the State of Louisiana.

Some of Bo's fellow officers in Mississippi who had retired and taken up PI work had told him that bars were the best sources of business. Recalling that tidbit of information, Bo made the rounds to most of the dives in the French Quarter. Although he limited his libations to Diet

Coke, the bartenders and waitresses eventually warmed up to him, gladly displaying a stack of his cards in their establishments. Bo soon came to be considered the man to call if a spouse needed the goods on a cheating partner, or if someone's lawyer was in need of legwork defending a DWI or dope case. While a narc, Bo knew how to make cases. Conversely, as a PI, he became pretty damn proficient at finding weaknesses to dismantle them. He also dropped in on several of the well-established agencies in the city, letting them know of his expertise, and offering his services in the event their offices became backed up in their labor, or needed an unfamiliar face in the field.

Things were going well for Bo, and his resurrected optimism was not confined to his work. The Christmas season was a great time to be in New Orleans, particularly the French Quarter, which was decked out in 19th century ornamentation. The guided-tour carriage rides operated year round, but for some reason the ones that passed by in December just seemed more special. There was caroling at Jackson Square, a bonfire on the levee, and many of the merchants set out complimentary beverages and hors d'oeuvres on tables outside their shops. At least twice a week, for the entire month, noted jazz musicians, such as pianist Ellis Marsalis and trumpeter Irvin Mayfield, performed free public concerts in St. Louis Cathedral. Each one was standing-room-only, and Bo was there, joining Monsignor Ambrose, who reserved several places on a center pew for Bo and any friends he wished to bring along. LB and Robin came a few times, as did Sam and one or two other pub regulars, including Stan, a nerdy, but likeable, computer techie, and Mark, who worked as an assistant for a veterinary ophthalmologist.

Emerging from the church after the performance one night, Bo was starving, and did not want to take the time or trouble of cooking. Outstanding seafood and Cajun cuisine abounded in the Vieux Carré, but Bo was craving a good ole burger. At the bottom of the steps, he turned right, heading to the next street, St. Peter, and the place that served the best Bo had ever consumed anywhere, bar none.

A little more than halfway up the block, between Royal and Bourbon, Bo walked into Yo Mama's, a dive little known to tourists, but well known among locals for its monstrous burgers, grilled to order, and available with some twenty different dressings. Bo's personal assessment was validated by The City's Best award proudly displayed behind the bar. Hanging beneath the award was a sign boasting "Blazing Fast, Friendly Service." Two frozen concoctions advertised only as "The Pink Shit" or "The Purple Shit", were available to those who dared to heed the notice "Don't ask, just drink."

Bo took a seat near the far end of the bar, opposite a framed print of a prone, nude woman with a large serpent wrapped around her, and ordered his favorite: the Roquefort cheeseburger, fully dressed, and baked potato with all the fixings—butter, sour cream, chives, and cheddar cheese. It was a good thing that the stools on both sides of him were unoccupied; he would need the elbow room.

Finishing the cholesterol-laden feast, Bo paid the tattooed woman behind the bar, and set out for home. The scarcity of parking in the Quarter was actually somewhat beneficial for him. With an overabundance of delectables, but for the exercise Bo received by walking, he would have weighed three hundred pounds.

Since St. Ann was two blocks over, Bo would have to take a right, either at Bourbon or Dauphine; he opted for Dauphine. It was not that Bo was averse to any of Bourbon Street's offerings of debauchery, it just didn't fit the serene mood in which he found himself that night. Consequently, he continued along in the relative quiet of St. Peter. The only other person on this section of the street was a dark-haired woman in her late twenties or early thirties, sitting on the steps of a duplex and wearing a long, pleated, colorful cotton dress. "Want to see my sea urchin?" she asked, when Bo came within earshot.

Not understanding, he stopped. "Your sea urchin?"

"Yeah," she responded, simultaneously hiking the hem of her dress above her knees and spreading them. Bo had not, by any means, led a sheltered life, but he had never been flashed by a woman, and not a bad-looking one at that. She had to be high as a kite, Bo deduced. There was a first time for everything, and it seemed appropriate that the venue for this virgin episode in his life was the French Quarter of New Orleans.

Speechless, Bo stared at the woman's pubis, laid bare in all its glory. After an awkward moment he noticed that she was smirking at him. "I have to admit that it is, indeed, a very nice specimen," he said at last, and walked on.

"Hey, where you going, honey?"

Bo turned his head back toward her, and called out, "Like I said, your sea urchin is nice, but I don't think it can handle my eel. It's a real monster!" Making his turn at the corner, he saw that her knees were still drawn up, but she had lowered the dress over her shins and, with her head tilted upward against the door, was cackling away. *High as a kite.*

Once home, Bo retrieved his mail from the box, and noticed a note taped to the door: "Will be at McC's. Walk over when you can. LB." Bo removed it and unlocked the door.

Inside, he sat down and thumbed through the envelopes: utility bills, junk mail, and something from Michael Dunn, an attorney in Raymond, Mississippi. For the second time that night, Bo was stunned. According to the lawyer evidently handling Tom Davis's estate, Bo had inherited Lamar Hall, free and clear of all encumbrances. Scanning over the enclosed copy of Tom's last will and testament, Bo saw that it was true. He replaced the documents in the envelope, and walked up the street, toward Burgundy.

"Holy shit! Y'all seeing dis?" Homer was shouting above the hubbub as Bo entered McCormick's. Suddenly, the bar got quiet and everyone turned toward Homer, who was pointing at a television. The local news was on, showing video footage of a man, poised on the Huey P. Long Bridge, threatening to jump into the Mississippi River, eighty feet below. According to the on-the-scene report, the man was a schizophrenic, with a history of mental problems and clashes with the police.

Before Bo and the others could hear the outcome, Homer called out, "Hey LB, got a legal question for ya! If someone wit multiple personalities, like dis guy, threaten to kill hisself, is dat considered a hostage sitch-e-a-shun?"

After the collective roar of laughter subsided, LB responded, "Yeah, I guess it is." Then to Bo, "Grab a Coke and come on over."

"So how's business?" Sam inquired, filling a glass with ice.

"Can't complain. Good actually."

"Bet you've met some real interesting people, huh?"

"I guess so. Most are okay, but a few egotistical assholes."

"No different from the folks who wander into here," Sam replied. "But I've learned over the years there's some good in everybody, Bo." After pausing while he poured a Diet Coke over the ice, Sam added, "And there's one good thing about egotists too." Seeing the way Bo arched a questioning eyebrow, Sam continued his observation, pushing the soda across the bar: "They talk so much about themselves they don't have time to talk about anyone else."

"You've been hanging around Homer too long," Bo replied, and joined LB at a table.

"Oh, I've been meaning to get this back to you," LB said, digging in a pocket of his jeans and sliding a key across the table.

"Keep it," Bo instructed. "You never know when I may need you to get inside for me while I'm away or if I lose mine."

As LB nodded and was putting the key back in his pocket, his wife came in and took a seat with them. "You still mad at me?" LB asked her.

"About what?" she asked, obviously dumbfounded.

"You know," LB insisted. Robin and Bo knew that he was setting up some punch line, but played along.

Thus, although his wife didn't know what he was talking about, she patted LB on the hand and cooed, "No, I'm not still pissed. How can I be angry with someone as cute as you?" LB was still beaming when Robin added, "You know me—I don't get mad. I get even." With that, she got up and walked to the bar.

"Okay, LB," Bo said. "I'll bite. Why was she mad at you?"

"We were in bed last night, watching *Who Wants to Be a Millionaire*. After it was over, I started getting amorous, and she said, 'Not tonight; I'm tired.' So I asked her, 'Is that your final answer?' When she said, 'Yes,' and rolled over, I told her, Then I'd like to phone a friend."

The two men were still guffawing so hard that tears were coming out of their eyes when Robin returned with a martini. "LB, you do live on the edge," Bo was finally was able to say. It felt good to once again be able to laugh.

Robin, of course, knew from the comment that she had just been made the subject of some LB-style humor. Believing that a quid pro quo was in order, she informed her husband, "You got a phone call after you left."

She let the information hang, forcing him to ask, "Well, who was it?"

"Your proctologist. He called to tell you that, after looking at your x-rays, he was able to find your head."

"Ouch!" Bo exclaimed amid the laughter. "When she says she gets even, she means it," he added, slapping LB on the back.

After things quieted down again, Bo told the Harpers about Tom bequeathing the house and acreage to him, which they thought was great news. "But I'm just now on my feet down here," Bo lamented. "What would I do with it?"

"Sell it," Robin quickly urged. "Then you can buy a nice condo with a courtyard, a balcony, maybe even a pool." "You just want my apartment," Bo teased.

"And your point is?" she asked.

"Don't get me wrong," Bo said. "That Tom wanted me to have that place means the world to me. I know how ungrateful this sounds, but I just don't want to go through the hassle right now of getting a realtor, putting it on the market, and all of that."

"Sell it to Alex," LB suggested.

"Are you serious?" Bo asked.

"Yeah, I'm serious. He's in the market and hasn't been satisfied with anything he's seen. I know he loves the place."

"Alex Stillwell?" Bo asked, the image of Stillwell and Serena gazing adoringly into each other's eyes clouding his thoughts.

"Look Bo," LB advised. "You know Alex, he'll pay top dollar to get what he's looking for. I'll get Mike Dunn to do everything. He'll arrange for an appraisal and get it to Alex. The worst that can happen is he'll say no. And if it works out Mike can send the paperwork to you; you wouldn't even have to leave New Orleans. All you would have to do is deposit your damned check."

Bo considered it for only a millisecond before replying, "Let's do it."

"Sam, bring the Joos!" LB exclaimed, referring to a special, very potent vodka concoction. "A toast!"

"These are on me," Bo announced and walked to the bar to get another Diet Coke and to tell Sam the news. "You were right, Sam. Even egotists can be beneficial."

CHAPTER 30

"Can an Ethiopian change his skin, or a leopard his spots?" This question rhetorically posed by the God of the Israelites through the prophet Jeremiah was similarly asked by the beast, of himself. Circumstances of the past year had required him to adapt, caging his urges. While he had succeeded, he was what he was, and his arrival in New Orleans could not have been more fortuitous. The beast could now operate in the murder capital of the world.

According to FBI statistics, his previous hunting ground—Jackson, Mississippi—had the fifth most homicides per capita in the nation, but the Big Easy was once again numero uno. More encouraging to the beast was seeing on *The Times-Picayune* op-ed page that the premier ranking was despite the city having one of the largest police departments in the country. And best of all, that only twenty-four percent of felony arrests the past year resulted in convictions. Fortune had once again smiled. The beast was in the country's premier killing ground, and he would do his part to keep it at the top of the charts. January 1 came and went and while the rest of the city celebrated the fresh start of a new year, the beast scoped out his new territory.

Six miles west from the center of New Orleans is the strip of land that Etienne Bore, the city's first mayor, acquired in the late 18th century, stretching from what was then Nayades (now St. Charles) Avenue to the Mississippi River. There, Bore cultivated Louisiana's first sugarcane crop. Later, on the eve of the Battle of New Orleans, the land housed the camps of Andrew Jackson's Tennessee and Kentucky troops; and nearly a half century later, the tents of Civil War soldiers for the South, then the North. Purchased by the city in 1871, the property soon became a park, named in honor of John James Audubon, the famed artist and naturalist who, starting in 1821, lived in the French Quarter, maintaining a studio on the 700 block of Barracks Street, between Royal and Bourbon.

Early in the 20th century, part of the park became home to the Audubon Zoo; and on a cool, but sunny, Saturday morning in January, it was to the zoo that the beast headed. Driving along Magazine Street, dissecting the park, he slowed as he saw the golf course on the right. A little farther down, the beast turned left, into the zoo parking lot.

He spent most of the morning taking in the mix of exotic animals from around the globe. He observed beasts that could not break out of their cages; although billed as engaging in natural habitats, they were still pent up, doomed to permanent confinement. Among those exhibited were unique white alligators and white tigers. The beast too, was an extraordinary predator. And while his repression had lasted only a year, he vowed it would never reoccur. He could not free these other beasts; but he could, and would, avenge the underlying reason for their captivity—the pleasure of the viewing public. Once the beast within him was again set loose, he would give them something to behold that they would never forget.

It was with this resolve that the beast decided to check out some of the other areas of the park. Following the route indicated on the map he had picked up at the zoo, he slowly drove to the Riverview, a section of Audubon Park better known among locals as the Fly. It was a popular gathering spot featuring sports fields and picnic facilities along the Mississippi River. Several soccer fields were covered with scurrying kids, barely school age, swarming in disorganization around a moving black-and-white-checkered ball, much like fire ants on the attack. The beast's focus, however, was not on the playful antics of children. Where there were such youthful soccer players, there had to be soccer *moms* close by. Seeing that he was right, the beast looked for a place to park. A closer inspection was in order.

Miraculously, only a few of the park's centuries-old live oaks fell among hurricane Katrina's victims in 2005, and the beast pulled his vehicle beneath one of the many that had stubbornly defied that storm, as it must have done to countless others before. He approached one of the dads, who also appeared to be a coach, but it was hard to tell for sure since every adult male around was shouting directions to the undulating mass of preschoolers.

The beast had guessed correctly though, confirmed by the man's irritation at the interruption when the beast introduced himself—a fabrication, of course. "Can't you see I'm trying to coach a game?" the coach snapped.

The beast forced a smile and an apology, explaining that he too, was a coach; in search of a soccer field on which his newly formed boys' church team could practice. "How," he inquired, "should I go about reserving one of these?"

"Forget it," the coach answered. "These are taken up every day of the week—games on both days of the weekends, and practices every afternoon, from the time the schools let out until the park closes at dark."

"Every afternoon?" the beast asked.

"That's what I said; unless it's raining. Now, if you'll excuse me?"

"Thanks, pal," the beast replied, and walked off, quite giddy with the assurance that it did not matter what fair afternoon he selected. Any day that he chose for the hunt was guaranteed to provide a bevy of prey— thirty-year-old moms. He need only devise a way to flush one away from the rest of the pack.

Strolling happily to his vehicle, the beast noticed a few joggers trotting along the land's end by the river, and walked over. An older runner, with a blue headband about his gray hair, was slightly bent over, hands resting on thighs, catching his breath. The beast asked him about the route, and learned that it was a 1.8 mile paved track, ringing that area of the park. If unsuccessful in separating one of the women from the soccer fields, he might find one jogging alone on some remote stretch of the track.

Continuing the circular drive, the beast headed back in the direction of Magazine Street. He passed tennis courts on the right, and soon made a sudden stop. Something on his left had caught his alert eye.

According to the ancients, nature reflects the laws of creation, and Labyrinths were considered extensions of man's desire to co-create with nature, their spiraling pathways uniting the walker with his natural habitat. These sacred gateways are said to enable the walker to confirm oneness with the cosmos, awaken vital forces, and elevate consciousness. The serpentine flow of the spirals generates a wealth of subtle, potential energy. As one moves along the pathway, thereby unwinding the coil, this stored energy is released and magnified. If of the proper, meditative mind, the walker is able to harness the exponential energy.

There is no right or wrong direction in walking a Labyrinth where, as in life, one encounters many turns. One simply learns to trust the path. It is a ritual of contemplation, self-discovery, transformation, and renewal. Moving through a Labyrinth alters ordinary avenues of perception, linking the inner-self and outer-being, the right brain and the left brain, by a series of paths representing the realms of the gods. The joy of unveiling the true self, freed of restraint, cannot be surpassed; and the means to that end lay before the beast—not one, but two Labyrinths— convolutions of different-colored brick pavers set in the ground, sometimes called pavement mazes.

The first that he came upon was the smaller of the two, consisting of seven circuits leading to the center, laid out in a pattern dating back to 2,000 B.C. Beyond this was a larger Labyrinth, forty feet in diameter, replicating one built, in 1203 A.D., at the cathedral in Chartres, France; eleven meandering circuits, divided into four quadrants, winding to the center.

Recognizing the importance of the appropriate frame of mind, the beast sat on a nearby bench to momentarily tune out the world. Reverently bowing his head, but before closing his eyes, he noticed a bronze plaque affixed to the concrete slab beneath the bench and between his feet. "It is well with my soul," it read. Once the beast was properly prepared, he took his time walking the circuitous, unbroken paths of both mazes; to the center and back of each one. Thoroughly rejuvenated, he drove away. The beast's sabbatical was at an end.

CHAPTER 31

The beast was relaxing in his quarters, listening to an old Louis Armstrong album he had found in a vintage record shop on Royal Street. As Satchmo rasped his classic "What a Wonderful World", the beast ruminated on things past and those to come. It was as if he were espousing, via mental telepathy, his manifesto to anyone blessed by the gods with the gift of listening in a like manner.

Since it all began that night on South Padre Island, I've killed in many different ways and with no discernible pattern. I've shot, stabbed, and strangled. I've used parks, alleys, hotel rooms, and the homes of the subjects of my masterpieces. I lurk in churches and malls. I prowl the streets as you drop your children at school, and the highways on the scent of lone travelers; yet you have no idea because I blend into normal society. That is what makes me so dangerous.

But only now, having walked the Labyrinth, do I realize just how blinded people are by mazes of their own construction: their preconceptions, greed, hatred, and bigotry. Inside such Labyrinths evil dwells unnoticed and unchecked, enabling me to roam and ravage.

The reign of terror for the Minotaur of myth ended at the hand of Theseus; but I have transcended into the realms of the gods themselves. I am, in Shakespeare's words, "the be all". Yes, there will come a time when my reign of terror, too, will come to an end, but I am also "the end all." I am my own Theseus and master of my fate. My "retirement" will come at a time and in a manner of my own choosing. And oh, what a legacy I will leave.

It was only at the conclusion of these thoughts that the beast refocused on the music, just in time for the last verse. It was about watching babies grow up to know more than we ever will. Through the beast's progeny, chaos would continue to reign long after his time came to an end. For now, mayhem, with a little touch of misdirection, would be the order of the day. After all, this is the city where Yellow taxis are orange, the West Bank is east, and the Mississippi River flows south to north. A land where nothing is as it seems.

CHAPTER 32

Bo was waiting impatiently, always detesting being put on hold, but at least this call had been answered by a living, breathing person instead of a machine. It would have been a sad note in any commentary on what our society had become if he had been forced to navigate through a menu of robotic voices in order to speak with someone at the U.S. Marshal's Service. At last, Jack Parker, the marshal in Jackson, Mississippi, came on the line. "Bo, good to hear from you."

"You're probably going to take that back. I think I saw Todd Murphy today."

"He's holed up in Cuba, Bo."

"Not anymore. As I was walking into a place to grab a bite to eat…"

"Here, in Jackson, I assume?" the marshal interrupted.

"No. I'm living in New Orleans now," Bo explained. "Anyway, as I was about to go in, I could see that a guy, with a to-go order in his hand, was coming out; so I held the door open for him. His hair was different, much longer and lighter. He had a beard and was thinner than I remembered, but it was Murphy, Jack. I'm sure of it."

"Bo, a moment ago you said, 'I *think* I saw him.'"

"We were practically nose to nose, dammit. It was him. Why else would he take off?"

"He ran?"

"Like a jackrabbit. And you just don't throw down a Po-Boy from Domilise's. Hell, that in itself is incriminating down here."

"Yeah, I've heard of that place. Where is it?"

"Goddamned, Jack! I'm calling about Todd Murphy."

"And I need to know exactly, where he was last seen. Besides, you're the one who mentioned the sandwich, not me."

"Sorry; corner of Annunciation and Bellecastle. In the Uptown area."

"I'll look into it, but I can't imagine the guy risking coming back to the States. He had it made where he was."

"I'm telling you, it was him," Bo insisted.

"And I told you that I'd see what I can find out. Give me your number."

After ending the call, Bo headed to the Paradise Beach & Music Club for an appointment with one of the owners. They operated two Bourbon Street bars, very popular with tourists. The original location had recently been badly damaged by a fire, and was shut down pending an investigation into the cause. With the NOPD and an insurance company involved, the owners were savvy enough to take precautionary steps in protecting their interests. It was not that they were under any suspicion; money was being lost with each passing day. The quicker they could cut through bureaucratic red tape the better. They had retained a law firm which, in turn, brought Bo on board, and he was to have his first meeting at the business's other Bourbon Street location.

When he finished an hour and a half later, and was walking home, his cell phone rang. It was Jack Parker.

"Bo, there's been no activity on Murphy's credit cards for several months."

"I knew it."

"Hang on, it doesn't necessarily mean he's not still in Cuba. He may have finally been able to get his identity changed and dumped his old accounts. It's probably not hard to do down there, once you hook up with the right people."

"No, he's here." There was a long silence on Parker's end of the line. "You're not arguing with me. What else did you find out?"

"Murphy was heavily involved with some white supremacy groups, so I checked with agencies that keep tabs on them. According to my contacts, nothing specifically concerning Murphy has popped up on their radar, but they have verified intel that several groups in Louisiana are joining forces, pooling their resources. The epicenter of this activity is on the Pontchartrain north shore, just above New Orleans, and they are targeting blue-collar whites in the city as recruits. But it doesn't make any sense for the guy to stick his neck out on two capital murders just to recruit."

"With some people, a cause can be all-consuming," Bo offered.

"That's true," Parker conceded. "I've alerted the fugitive task force in our office down there, and the intel guys will keep both offices posted. That's all I know to do right now, buddy. But if he's back, we'll find him. It's just a matter of time."

Satisfied that he had been sufficiently convincing, and that the manpower and other resources of the United States government were focused on Todd Murphy, Bo disconnected.

Entering his apartment, Bo discovered a large brown envelope on the coffee table. A typed note was attached with a paperclip: "Saw Alex briefly today. He didn't want to risk anything with the mail. Congrats Mr. Millionaire. LB" Bo opened the envelope and pulled out the contents: his copy of the closing papers for Lamar Hall, and a check drawn on Mike Dunn's trust account for $1.5 million.

Yes, Bo was now a millionaire. He had understood the words the first time he had heard of Alex Stillwell's offer, but the reality of it had not sunk in until now. Even so, more pressing matters occupied Bo's mind. He replaced the check and documents in the envelope as he walked to his office. After hiding it beneath other papers in a desk drawer, he went to his bedroom and was in the process of changing clothes when his phone rang. It was LB.

"I'm heading to McCormick's. Want to walk over with me?"

"Maybe later," Bo said. "But it's such a pretty day, I thought I'd do some jogging."

"Be careful. That shit'll kill ya."

No mention was made of the check. Bo's thoughts were indeed elsewhere.

CHAPTER 33

The last thing Cindy Latour Babineaux had on her mind was her son's soccer practice. It was Monday, and what she had contemplated, hoped for, and done only two nights earlier, monopolized her thoughts. She was thirty-seven, and had always kept herself physically fit and attractive, or at least she had thought so. Lately, it seemed that the harder she tried to please her husband, the farther away he pushed her.

Friday, when Chad came in from the antique shop they owned on Magazine Street, he had not given any indication of noticing the new top she had worn just for him. All he said was that he was going to their fishing camp at Cocodrie for a long weekend, and would not be back until late Monday evening. Claude, the assistant manager, would mind the store. Chad was gone in a matter of minutes, not even inquiring about Ryan's absence, much less attempting to tell his son goodbye. After walking into the dining room and blowing out the candles that had cast a soft illumination on the special dinner she had waiting, Cindy sank into a chair, and a state of gloom.

She wasn't sure how long she had wept, and did not remember going upstairs, but realized she was in their bedroom. She turned on the television, and as she was about to undress, noticed herself in the dresser mirror. What is wrong with me? she wondered. The answer eluded her. For although you couldn't tell it at the moment, with smeared mascara causing her to look like a raccoon, Cindy believed that, while she might not be glamorous, she was pretty. Her five-foot, four-inch frame might not be that of a Playboy Bunny, but her breasts seemed ample enough, and her legs looked great, thanks to her exercise regimen. She considered herself much more desirable than Patty Richards. Yet Chad had made a fool of himself the way he fawned over Patty at the Richards' Christmas party. If the problem wasn't her, then it had to be Chad. *An affair? Have I been that blind?* Whoever was to be blamed, enough was enough. Beginning the next day, Cindy would take steps to determine the problem, starting with herself.

At the Saturday morning soccer game Cindy had asked Jackie Monroe, whose son Jake was a teammate of Ryan's and his best friend, if it would be okay for Ryan to stay over another night. Jackie said that it would be fine, of course, but asked if anything was wrong. Cindy explained that her mother was ill in the hospital in Lafayette and that she needed to be there, but did not think it a good idea to make Ryan tag along. Cindy had picked him up from the Monroe's after she attended Sunday morning mass.

The Babineauxs didn't live far from Audubon Park, and Cindy had walked Ryan to his Monday afternoon practice. In dire need of clearing her head, she had worn her jogging togs, and had her long, chestnut hair pulled into a ponytail. Arriving at the field in the Riverview area of the park, Ryan had scampered off to join the other kids, and Cindy sought out Jackie.

"How's your mom?" Jackie asked.

"Better," Cindy answered. As bad as she hated the lie, it was comparatively nothing to what really laden her soul. Yes, she had confessed to her priest, and all had been set right with God, but Cindy didn't know if she would ever receive absolution from herself. Once a lie is set in motion, it builds in momentum, so Cindy felt trapped into its perpetuation. "But I really have a lot on my mind about it. I never thought about her not being here. You know, mortality and all that. Would you mind watching Ryan while I get in a run and work through some of this? I should be back about the time they finish."

"You go right ahead. Even better, let Ryan come home with Jake."

"You sure?"

"Yes, I'm sure. Go on. But I'm a good listener if you ever want to talk."

"You're the best," Cindy replied appreciatively. She walked over toward the field, waving a hand until finally drawing her son's attention, and motioned for him to come over. When she explained that he was going home again with his best bud to stay the night, Ryan turned and ran back toward the team, yelling, "Hey Jake, guess what?" Cindy couldn't help but smile before hitting the track.

One of the chicks had thus indeed been separated from the rest, and the beast was watching from the blue rental van parked beneath the same live oak where he had conducted his reconnaissance on Saturday. He was sure that it would bring him luck, and he was right.

He had first noticed the brunette in the running attire when she had walked onto the scene with her son. All of the other parents had driven up and parked near the beast. This soccer mom and son, he deduced, must live nearby. While the beast was checking out the other moms, he saw the one with the ponytail briefly speak with another woman, and then her son before running off to the track. It was possible that Ponytail had simply asked the woman to keep an eye on the boy during practice while Ponytail got some exercise, but the beast didn't think it likely. Factoring in the way the kid wearing the number 5 jersey had excitedly run off, shouting "Guess what?" the beast thought it more probable that number 5 would be leaving practice with a friend. That, in turn, meant that Ponytail intended to run the full circuit. Since she had started on a section to the beast's left, she would be finishing from the right.

He exited and locked the van, first making sure he had not left his hip-pouch inside. The beast casually walked around the vehicle, satisfied by a final inspection that the tinted windshield and windows would suit his purposes. He strode over to the stretch of the track that would be the end of the line for Ponytail, which was the portion that ran along the river's edge.

The first spot he chose was closer to the van, but he had not anticipated so much river traffic. Although a little farther from his vehicle than he preferred, the beast soon came to an ideal place where the track was concealed from river pilots by a wall of willows, from ten to thirty feet in height. He turned to see what was behind him, and saw only baseball fields under construction. However, due to universal law that construction workers called it a day no later than four o'clock, no one was around.

According to a scientific study, great white sharks, the fearsome predators of the sea, utilize the same hunting strategy as do human serial killers. Both stalk their victims, hanging back and observing, with the utmost focus, from a not-too-far, not-too-close base. Having determined the place where he would first strike, the beast took a shortcut to the Labyrinth, where he would sit and wait. It was sufficiently close to the track to enable him to easily see Ponytail when she passed by and fall in behind her, yet it was far enough that she would not be paying him any attention. He would be focused on her, and not vice versa.

Cindy hadn't been on the track for long before her pores started exuding perspiration, and she wished that she could, with similar ease, expel the guilt, shame, and anger. Before going to sleep Friday night, she had resolved to put herself to the test. The next day, after speaking with Jackie about Ryan staying a second night, she called her friend Marcia. "Hey, girlfriend, you in town? No? Rats. Chad's away too, and I was hoping we could do something. Oh well, another time."

That evening, Cindy opened a bottle of ice-cold pinot grigio, put on some soft music, and settled into the tub for a long, soothing bubble bath. Cindy knew that she would never do what she intended without first fortifying herself with some liquid backbone, and by the time she rose from the tub, more than half the bottle was gone. It was just the right dose for the desired effect. Toweling herself dry, Cindy detected a heightened sensitivity of her smooth, tan skin to the touch of the terrycloth. The perfumed powder brought on different, more soothing caresses across her body, simultaneously releasing an olfactory stimulation. Relishing the sensations, Cindy opted to do her makeup and hair before putting on any clothes. Before beginning, she examined, from all angles, her nude reflection in the mirror. She just didn't get it. What the hell did Chad see in that bimbo Patty that she didn't have?

When the time came to dress, she shunned pantyhose, slipping on a Jacquard-embroidered, black sheer garter-belt and thong. Sitting on the bed, Cindy slid her shapely legs, one at a time, into black stockings until the tops reached the garters, slightly more than halfway up her thighs. Once they were secured, she stood and walked to her closet.

Stepping into a black skirt, Cindy pulled the waist over her hips, and pulled at the zipper in the back. It was not a miniskirt, as the hem fell a few inches above the knees, but the slit promised to be rather provocative. Next, she slipped on a white three-quarter-sleeve top. It was not low-cut, but sans bra, the tight fit accentuated her 34A breasts. The protruding nipples would be impossible to miss. That was, for anyone but Chad. The outfit was the same one she had briefly worn for him the night before.

Cindy replaced her crucifix with a Byzantine gold necklace, selected some gold hoop earrings to match, and returned to her bathroom vanity. After putting them on, she dabbed a little perfume behind each ear, and touched up her hair, pleased with the way the long, wavy tresses cascaded over her shoulders. Okay, she thought, looking in the mirror. What's missing? *A bracelet.* She would be sure to get one in the bedroom. *Oh, my wedding ring!* Cindy hid it under some other items in her jewelry box when she selected a bracelet. *Are you ready to do this?* Hell yeah, she thought. *You go, girl. Patty Richards doesn't hold a candle against you, and you're going to prove it.*

Downstairs, while rummaging through her everyday purse, in search of her car keys and a few items to transfer to her black clutch, Cindy realized that she had neglected to put on any shoes. She returned upstairs, grabbed the black heels she had in mind, and told herself to settle down. Easier said than done, she walked to the bathroom and refilled her glass.

She continued to sip the wine, descending the stairs, shoes in the other hand. Once shod, Cindy retrieved her black cape from the closet, and turned the goblet up, swallowing what was left before going out the door.

Marcia was single and worked as a sales rep for one of the pharmaceutical companies. She had told Cindy about The Rajah Club, a high-end restaurant and martini bistro tucked away in the French Quarter on Conti Street. It was one of Marcia's favored places when she was not away on business. "Great atmosphere and full of business suits," she had said. It sounded just like the place where Cindy could find out, once and for all, if there was something sexually repugnant about her, with no chance of Marcia being there tonight. Cindy had made sure of that when she called her friend earlier in the day. All systems were go.

The club was just as Cindy had pictured it from Marcia's description. She was standing in the entrance and still taking in the candlelit ambience when the host asked if he could take her wrap. As she undid the cape and handed it to him, she was distracted by immediate, not-too-subtle glances by some of the men nearby, which she took as a promising sign. When she realized that the host was inquiring whether she was there for dinner, she answered, "No, just a couple of drinks." Asked if she preferred a table or the bar, Cindy looked around and did some quick calculating. The men seemed to outnumber the women three to one; and most of them—even the ones without female companions—were seated at the tables. Cindy however, opted for an empty stool at the bar, thinking that her legs would be better noticed there, especially if she chose to cross them.

Although still nervous, she was further encouraged by the attentive bartender. Handing her a leather-bound martini list, he complimented her on how nice she looked. Since the bold effects of the wine were evaporating, she didn't waste any time in ordering the Classic Cosmopolitan, handing him a credit card on which to run a tab. She had chosen well; made with Absolut Citron, a splash of cranberry juice, Rose's lime juice, and triple sec, the cocktail was the best Cindy ever had, and was gone before she knew it. Slow down, a voice inside her head warned.

While the bartender made her another, Cindy looked around. Everything was decadent, but tasteful; decorated in a plush English theme, with overstuffed, leather wingback chairs, rich, dark wood, and oil portraits. A live band was playing some light jazz, but the music was not deafening. She could tell that the people were enjoying their conversations. When the bartender brought Cindy her second drink, he said, "This one is on the gentleman over there," tilting his head in the direction behind her.

Instead of immediately turning to see her benefactor, Cindy took a slow, deliberate sip. In one fluid motion, she turned on the stool, affording a generous view of her crossed legs through the slit of her skirt, and held up the glass, slightly tipping it toward the man as an appreciative gesture. He immediately excused himself from his male companion and walked to an unoccupied stool beside Cindy.

Although she knew that it was a cliché to think in such terms, the guy really was tall, dark, and handsome, and probably ten years younger than her. "May I join you?" he asked in an obvious Italian accent. Oh this is getting better and better, Cindy thought; but play it cool.

"If you tell me my name," she replied.

"Pardon?"

"I don't drink with strangers, even if they buy," she explained.

"But of course. My name is Antonio."

"Well, *Antonio,* that only solves half the problem. What's *my* name?"

"But that is for *you* to say, is it not?"

"I'm not the one asking for anything."

Antonio was about to tell her that he had no time for such an impossible game, and walk away. However, the bartender interrupted, setting another drink for Antonio on the bar. "Enjoy your martini, sir. I think you'll find this one quite satisfying." Antonio turned and saw the bartender, still in possession of Cindy's credit card, staring down at the cocktail. Instinctively, Antonio looked down as well, and noticed handwriting on the napkin, beneath the clear base of the glass: "Cynthia."

Antonio quickly picked up the napkin along with the glass, wadded it in his palm and placed it to the side on the bar. "So," he said to Cindy, "you say you are not asking for anything? I am afraid that I do not believe that…" Seeing that she was about to interrupt, he quickly added, "Cynthia." It caught her off guard, and before she could think of something to say, Antonio theorized, "But you are American, and knowing how much you Yanks are so fond of what you call 'nicknames,' I will venture to say, Cynthia, that your friends call you Cindy." When she did not immediately protest, he told her, "And since *I* have now called you Cindy, I presume that I, too, am your friend, and may join you."

"Well done, Antonio," she replied, tipping her glass as a salute. "Have a seat."

Cindy found chitchat easy with Antonio. He was from Milan and worked in the fashion industry as a broker for several Italian designers. He was in town to see buyers from some of the local high-end retailers. As they talked, laughed, and flirted, Cindy wondered why it could not be this way with her husband, and what he would think if he knew that she was in a bar, seductively teasing a handsome, younger stranger. She even wished, in a way, that Chad was there, seeing firsthand what she needed, and how it should be dispensed.

They eventually moved from the bar to a table in one of the alcoves, affording more intimate, private dining, shielded from other patrons by curtains. Cindy had come here for answers, and could leave now with the knowledge that she had not lost her allure, confirmed by the progression of touches, caresses, and kisses behind the closed curtain that had sent Cindy into a sphere of steaming sultriness. Then the spell was broken.

Antonio had taken Cindy's left hand in both of his and brought it to his lips. He softly kissed, then massaged, her fingers. As he did so, his eyes were fixed on Cindy's face, but she hadn't noticed. What caught her attention, as blatant as Hester Prynne's scarlet "A," was the un-tanned, bare ring of skin formerly shielded from sunlight by her wedding band. The night had unfolded as she initially intended, and her husband would probably never know, but a guilty conscience requires no accuser.

Cindy realized it had been a foolish endeavor in a moment of anger, weakness, and vulnerability; and there were consequences for every choice made. Thus, she grabbed her clutch and aborted the ill-conceived mission. In her hasty exit, she had forgotten the cape she had checked.

The conglomeration of alcohol, her uncharacteristic behavior, and what she had actually contemplated left Cindy's mind reeling as she turned the ignition in her car. Added to these complications was the fact that she had not spent much time in the French Quarter, and became disoriented on the one-way streets.

Even now, on Monday afternoon, as she jogged around the park, there was a gap in her memory from that point until a nice man had tapped on her window, and helped her inside his bar. He had made fresh coffee for her, and kept a watchful eye until satisfied with her ability to drive home. Cindy wished that she could remember his name. She did recall that the bar was on the corner of Toulouse and Burgundy, and she would make it a point to go there tomorrow and thank him. She needed to go to The Rajah Club anyway, to see about getting her cape and credit card, which she should have already done, but had put off, fearing that she would run into the same bartender, waiter, or host. God, she was so embarrassed. And the private investigator—she needed to give him a call, and see if he could find out if Chad was up to anything. She had found some of the PI's business cards on the bar while sobering up, and stuck one in her clutch.

CHAPTER 34

So many things were racing through Cindy Babineaux's brain that she gave little attention to the man who had fallen in behind her on the track, near the Labyrinth. At first he trotted at an even pace with hers, but his steps quickened as she rounded a curve by a pavilion. This was the stretch of the track by the river, the killing zone that the beast had selected.

Drawing nearer and nearer to the bouncing, cinnamon-colored ponytail, accelerating with each stride, the beast was rapidly converging on his human prey, much as a great white shark soars upward from the dark ocean depths, toward an unsuspecting school of fish; except, for this shark, this fish was alone. The closest people were preoccupied on the soccer field, at least the distance of two football fields away.

The beast was breathing hard and rapidly. He was so close now that he could smell her sweat and hair. Whether from the sound of his footfall or heavy respiration, or possibly his own scent, Cindy turned her head, to the right, just as the man sprinted by. Within seconds, he began slowing to a staggered walk, and collapsed onto a bench beside the track. Drawing closer, she saw that he was slumped forward, clutching his left, upper arm. By his grimace, the man was in obvious pain, and she knew how idiotic her words must have sounded as she uttered them, "Are you okay?"

The man was trying to say something, but he was having difficulty breathing. He let go of his arm, and feebly motioned for this Good Samaritan to come closer with his right hand, which then dropped to his lap like a ton of bricks. As Cindy leaned in close, in an attempt to make out what he was weakly gasping, his left hand sprang upward and held her right arm like a vise. Simultaneously, a hard object jabbed into her stomach.

"If you make a sound, one peep, one move to draw attention, I will not only blow you away right now, and fling your body into the river...," he hissed, then paused for effect. Knowing what would be going through her mind in that millisecond, he continued, "I will then cover that field with bullets. I may or may not get them all, but I assure you that number 5 will be laid out among the dead."

Cindy knew from the evil emanating from this monster's eyes that he meant every word, and she regretted allowing Ryan to talk her into letting him wear his game jersey to practice. He was the only kid on the field with one on. While she would willingly jeopardize her own well being by chancing a shout of "rape!" or "fire!" under no circumstance would she leave the safety of her child to fate, whatever the odds. So when this monster, this beast, instructed her to walk quietly with him, the gun now in the small of her back, she nodded in silent assent.

At the rear of the van, the beast retrieved the keys from his hip-pouch with one hand, while continuing to hold the pistol on Cindy with the other, and unlocked the door. When it opened, she saw that the vehicle was recreationally outfitted with two swivel chairs with arms, positioned on opposite sides of a small, round table. The rear windows were darkly tinted, and she suspected those on the side door were as well; but it was hard to tell, because both sides, the floor, and ceiling were covered with milky, plastic sheeting, held in place with gray tape. The same kind of sheeting was also pinned to a curtain at the far end, concealing the cab area. A blanket lay folded lengthwise on one side of the floor.

"Have a seat," the beast ordered, giving her a shove. After Cindy complied, the beast—still standing outside and pointing the gun at her—reached his left hand to a nearby compartment and pulled out a roll of duct tape. He lobbed it on the table and asked Cindy if she was right or left handed.

"Right," she replied.

"Then I want you to take that with your right hand, and tape your left wrist to the arm of your chair," he said, and hopped inside the van.

He was securing the door when he heard her whimper, "No, please." The beast turned and saw her shaking her head, repeating the plea. Keeping his eyes and the weapon on her, he pulled out a scoped rifle that had been hidden beneath the blanket. "With this, even at this distance, I can make sure that your son is the first to go. Tape your fucking arm—now!"

Cindy picked up the tape and, with trembling fingers, pulled a few inches from the spool. She rested her left forearm in position and, with her right hand, guided the loose end of the tape to her wrist. Stopping after the first revolution, the beast said, "Keep going until I tell you to stop."

Several turns later, the beast pulled a small pair of blunt-tipped scissors from his pouch, and laid them on the table. "Cut it with these," he directed. When the freed cylinder dropped to the floor, the beast picked it up, and eased around the table until he was at the right arm of Cindy's chair. He placed the tape on the table and, with his free hand, snatched her right wrist and slammed it down. He laid down his weapon, picked up the tape and lashed her wrist.

Fearing what was coming next, Cindy was somewhat thrown when the man let out a deep exhalation, and said, "Okay, let's talk."

Cindy closed her eyes, shaking her head in bewilderment. She had resigned herself to the vile fact that she was to be the victim of a rapist, another statistic in the city's crime report, and she only wished to grit her teeth and get it over with. As debasing and traumatic as it would be, she would have her son, and that was all that mattered at this point. *So why was he waiting? Why linger?* She assumed that he would want to get his sick jollies and get away as soon as possible. "What do you want?" she asked.

"What everyone wants: respect, acceptance, power."

"Well, this is a helluva way to get it."

"Nicely put," the beast said, "Hell's way. I like that."

"You're going to kill me, aren't you?"

"Whether it is a day of demise or deliverance is entirely up to you. What's your name?"

Cindy gave only her first name, and he seemed content with that. "Well Cindy, tell me about yourself." She remained silent, glaring at him. "That's okay. I already know everything about you."

"You know *nothing* about me."

"No? I know from looking at your pretty self that you're in your mid-to-late thirties, maybe right in the middle... say, thirty-seven?" Judging from the change in her almond eyes and other body language, he knew that he had struck a nerve. Enjoying mind-games, he continued to probe, to taunt.

"Did you happen to know that it is, coincidentally, that same age range when women are at their sexual peak? Sure you do because you're *feeling* it, aren't you?"

Sensing that he was again on the mark, the beast maintained his fire in the same direction. "That could be wonderful, except for one not-so-small thing. Men ascend their plateau between eighteen and twenty-two." He reached out and tapped Cindy's wedding band. "But you also know that all too well. You're married but I doubt it's to someone that young. I mean, how many eighteen-year-olds do you know who possess the savoir faire to entice a woman your age into bed? It takes more than raw sex to arouse a woman like you, and they are much too young and inexperienced to have learned anything about the mystique of a mature woman's passion. Am I right?"

Taking notice that Cindy was reddening in the area of her neck where a small, gold crucifix dangled from a thin chain, the beast laughed. "What a cruel joke your God has played! Just as you're hitting your sensual stride, and hubby has the know-how to spur you on to the finish line, he doesn't because he's lost interest. Tsk, tsk."

Observing Cindy's ire grow, the beast said, "Oh, the two of you still do it occasionally, but it's bland copulation. Probably always in bed, just before going to sleep. No? Tell me then, when was the last time it was fantastic, make-the-earth-move, teeth-clinching, spontaneous fucking?

"That's what I thought. And you know what? Although you miss it, even crave it, what's worse to you is the void of any other intimacy; spooning in bed, a hug every now and then, a pat on the ole tush when you least expect it, holding hands, him draping an arm around you while watching TV on the couch. And communication—forget that, right? Hubby doesn't even try to understand the state of your sensuality, much less make an effort to accommodate your needs, because he's a selfish moron. And that's what you really, I mean *really*, resent—that the bastard is content with it all, totally oblivious! Hell, you feel cheated, and have probably considered doing some cheating. Go ahead. Tell me I'm full of shit."

Cindy Latour Babineaux was scared out of her wits by the uncertainty of her fate, but she was also boiling in anger at the knowledge that this stranger, this beast, had her pegged. "What are you, a shrink or something?"

"Or something," he replied, nodding. "Let's just say that I'm a student of human behavior."

Ryan's soccer practice would be over soon; so Cindy thought whatever was going to happen would also be done by then. This guy would not want to chance doing anything with so many people returning to their cars parked right by the van. Thinking she might luck out of enduring anything worse than being held in this van if she kept him talking, she said, "I've told you my name, what's yours?"

"Cindy, Cindy, don't try toying with me."

"Why not, can't you take it?"

"I take what I want."

"So we're back to my first question: what *do* you want?"

The beast laughed. "Isn't that rather obvious? I want *you*; but I had to first know what I would be taking. Now I know that you're passionate, but controlled; protective, but self doesn't come first; calculating and careful, but spunky. I like that."

"What do you care?"

"We are what we consume, right?" Reading Cindy's mind as terror tore through her like a tidal wave, the beast assured her, "No, no, no. How base would that be?"

Cindy let out a reassured breath, and was even more encouraged when the beast rose, peeked through the curtain, and announced, "We're almost done; practice is over." He began unwrapping her bindings. I did it, she thought, but the exhilaration was short-lived. He completed the release of each upper limb with one hand, gun in the other, and resuming his seat, instructed her to take off her clothes.

"But you said...."

"Oh, I meant that I'm not a cannibal. I never said we weren't going to do the dirty deed. Sorry for the misunderstanding, but do it!"

"But they will be here in a few minutes. What's the point now?" The observation was made and the question posed without any knowledge by Cindy Babineaux concerning scientific comparisons of great white sharks and serial killers, or of a major difference between the two species: motive. Sharks attack for food; not thrills.

The beast responded by taking another peek through the curtain. "My," he said, "number five looks so happy. What a shame." He reached for the rifle.

"Okay, okay," Cindy replied, and stood to undress. When she had finished, the beast took in the acorn-like nipples and the trimmed tawny tuft between her legs But what really excited him was the horror that filled her orbs when he pulled the knife from his pack.

"Did you know that a blade of any kind instills more fear in the average person than a gun?" he asked. "Now sit." The beast stood and undressed with one hand, laying the pouch on the table and tossing his clothes to the side. He sat back down and swiveled the chair away from the table. Waving Cindy over with the knife, the beast asked, "Are you a swallower or spitter?"

The chatter of approaching parents and children could be heard as she knelt, and the excitement sent blood surging to his member. The touch of her hand was nice, but what really caused him to stiffen was the look in her fawn eyes when he put the blade to her throat, and said, "Don't try anything stupid."

To her pleasant surprise, Cindy had barely begun when he told her to stop. "Stand up, and step back," he directed. She obeyed, and the beast reached once more into his bag, pulling out a condom. "For my protection; not yours," he jeered, and swept the pouch off the table. The beast stretched out a hand and pulled the blanket toward him, spreading it over the table. "Can't leave any DNA," he explained.

The beast stood to the side, and ordered Cindy to bend over the table. He maneuvered behind her and unfurled the condom into place. Moving toward his target, he told Cindy to widen her feet.

It was to the laughter of children, parental directives for them to get in the car, and the sounds of doors opening and closing that the beast began rhythmically thrusting. The whirring of motors faded as his cadence grew until the only thing audible in the van was the staccato slapping of flesh. While intercourse itself might have been stimulating enough for most red-blooded males, the beast was losing interest now that the real thrill was gone. The climactic moment was salvaged however, by replacing the knife to Cindy's neck with one hand, jerking her ponytail backward with the other. "Look at me," he growled. And the fright, the humiliation, that he saw reflected in those eyes caused him to spasm and release.

As he dressed, Cindy pushed herself from the defiling altar of this beast and reached for her clothes. "Put those down," he snapped. "I'm far from finished." He sneered as he held up the knife, gently testing the edge with a fingertip.

"But you said it was up to me," she sobbed; "that if I did everything you said, and I *have*."

"Alas, another misunderstanding. I said that it would either be a day of your demise or deliverance. This won't be your demise, dear Cindy, but rather your deliverance—to your savior."

Ashen, she fell into her chair and clasped her crucifix. "Will you at least make it quick?"

"Very brave of you, but no," the beast said, shaking his head. "It would take away from my power; not as much energy generated. The *vitality!*"

"You really don't have to kill me at all, you know. I don't know who you are or anything about you. You've obviously covered your tracks," she added, gesturing around the van. "Even if I wanted to say anything, I don't *know* anything; but I wouldn't. I wouldn't say a word. Just, *please*, let me go."

"No can do, Cindy."

"Hail Mary, full of grace…," she began, still clutching her crucifix, eyes closed, and tears streaming down her cheeks.

"Oh, stop that nonsense. It never works."

"…the Lord is with thee…"

"It's no use, I tell you."

"...blessed art thou among women..."

"Very well," the beast huffed, and took a seat. "See for yourself."

"...and blessed is the fruit of thy womb, Jesus..."

"It's fate, Cindy."

"...Holy Mary, Mother of God..."

"Don't you get it? It's part of *His* plan?"

"...pray for us sinners now..."

"He's answering my prayer; not yours."

"...and at the hour of death."

All was silent in the van, and the beast cocked his head and directed his eyes upward in mock concentration. "Oh, what the hell. But before I let you go, how about another bonk, for old times' sake? Assume the position."

It was odd how everything in life is so relative, Cindy thought. Any other time and place she would have thought herself deranged for welcoming being raped and forced to sodomize; but here, under these circumstances, that is precisely how she took the beast's latest statement. With relative gladness, she stretched herself again across the table.

This time when the beast positioned himself behind her, he had not undressed as before. Cindy surmised that, for time's sake, he would just lower his pants. However, what she heard—and only for a nanosecond— was not the sound of a zipper; but instead that of the first of two .22 caliber bullets entering the back of her head.

"Another misunderstanding," the beast said. "But you have to admit—I'm just a softy at heart. I trust that was quick enough."

The beast pushed her body off the table, and rolled it face up. It was time to excise the spoils and clear out. Finishing the cut, he pulled out a Ziploc bag, and dipped a finger in the blood. After writing what he deemed an appropriate note, the beast used Cindy's top to wipe what remained on his finger. He placed all of her clothing on the table, and bundled them in the blanket.

Opening the rear door just wide enough to stick his head out, the beast glanced around. Neither seeing nor hearing anything in the immediate vicinity, the beast jumped out of the rear, opened the front door and got behind the wheel. After backing out of the parking lot, he drove the short distance to a pier, for an idea struck him what he could do with the body.

After unloading sweet Cindy, the beast exited the park, took a right on Magazine Street, and a quick left into a parking area by the golf course. Activating the map app on his iPhone, he keyed in the address listed on the driver's license of Cynthia L. Babineaux that was in the wallet he found in her fanny-pack, along with a set of keys. It was just as he suspected, the thirty-seven-year-old not only lived close to the park, her house was right on its northern cusp, on Exposition Boulevard near the point where Laurel Street entered the park.

Once again on Magazine, the beast turned the van left, soon slowing and signaling his intent to make a right. Just as he began turning the wheel however, he saw that Exposition was not exactly a boulevard; in fact, it was not a street at all, it was nothing more than a sidewalk. The swerving van on busy Magazine Street prompted a few irritated motorists to lay down on their horns.

The beast turned right at the next cross-street, taking note of the sign in the process, pulled over, and re-examined the map on his phone. He was on Calhoun and could reach his destination, marked by a digital red push-pin, by continuing on a few blocks and taking a right on Laurel.

The van inched along the last stretch of Laurel Street, crossed Exposition, and came to a stop in a small clearing to the right, beneath a canopy of several colossal gnarled live oaks draped in low-hanging Spanish moss, eerily fluttering in the breeze off the nearby river, like wisps of gray cotton candy.

Exiting his vehicle and pushing the door with just enough force to hear it catch, the beast took quick stock of the area. Audubon Park sprawled behind the van, and in the foreground were the spiraling Labyrinths he had earlier walked, siphoning off their exponential energy. The beast could feel the harnessed power pulsate in his loins as he scoped out the row of houses in front of him. Although he couldn't make out the address numbers, he was certain the keys clutched in his hand would unlock one of them.

The beast did not have to walk far before finding the dwelling that had housed the life he had just seized for himself, and was pleased to see no lights on inside. He had neither the time nor inclination to disarm the alarm system appreciatively advertised by the little sign stuck in the flowerbed at the foot of the front steps, and was fully aware that once he opened the door he was now studying on the veranda, he would have only sixty seconds to accomplish his purpose. Thus, after trying several keys on poor naïve Cindy's ring, he struck upon the one that easily turned the deadbolt. Grasping the brass handle with his handkerchief, the beast pushed, opening the ornate portal just wide enough to toss in his delivery. After closing the door, he quickly withdrew the keys and made a hasty retreat to the van. He had just entered Laurel when the alarm blared.

Driving again on Magazine, en route to clean out and return the van, the beast turned on the radio. The previous user had it tuned to what a promo proclaimed to be the city's only classic rock station and it was conducting a hot mom contest. Visit the station's website, the promo urged. View the photos of the hottest moms in the area and vote. The beast didn't give a rat's ass about voting, but considered the website a possible resource. He doubted it would list the contestants' addresses, but you never knew. People acted pretty stupid in what they posted on the Internet. He'd at least check it out.

Not caring for the song that followed the advertisement, the beast turned the radio off and sang his own tune, Sam Cooke's "Bring It On Home To Me".

CHAPTER 35

Later that same Monday night, as Chad Babineaux turned his SUV off Laurel onto the alley that ran behind his house, he was shocked to see flashing blue lights and hear the undulant wail of an alarm. He was even more stunned and confused when he was greeted at his garage by NOPD officers and neighbors, and realized that the ear-piercing alarm was his own.

"Mr. Babineaux?" an officer asked.

"Yes. What's going on? Is my family okay?

"Sir, if you will deactivate the alarm, I'll tell you what we know, which isn't much."

"Certainly," Chad replied. He hurried to his car and hit the garage-door remote, instantly noting the presence of his wife's Camry, and his gut wrenched. He had hoped she was away on some errand. He felt like he was going to throw up. *What has happened to Cindy and Ryan?* With officers in tow, Chad unlocked the door with a shaky hand and keyed in a code on the control pad inside.

Once the alarm was silenced, the same officer who had spoken to him outside introduced himself. "Mr. Babineaux, I'm Officer Jacobi. We responded to a call placed by your security company. When we arrived, no one answered the door or phone. No sign of forced entry, but we did notice that, although the front door was closed, it was unlocked. Not knowing whether anyone was in the house in need of assistance, we came on in. I hope that was all right."

"Sure, sure. But what about my wife and son?"

"Nobody was here, Mr. Babineaux; and since our only purpose for coming inside was to see if there were persons in need, or possibly even perpetrators, once we determined that no one was here, we returned outside to await your arrival. The security company called back and advised that they had reached you."

"They did, but I thought Cindy must have accidentally set off the alarm again. I was on the road, and tried calling her. Should we call missing persons?"

"I don't think so, Mr. Babineaux. I did, however, call another department."

"I don't understand."

"Let *me* explain, Mr. Babineaux." Chad turned to see a mustached man with salt-and-pepper hair, dressed in a cheap coat and tie, walk in. He flashed a badge as he said, "Lieutenant Deschamps, robbery/homicide."

"Cindy and Ryan are dead?"

"I honestly don't know...." The detective started to say.

Chad stumbled into the kitchen and sank to a chair. He saw Jacobi whispering to Deschamps, handing him something. "What is that?" Chad asked. "What aren't you telling me!" he shouted, storming toward the two policemen.

"It's something the officers found on the floor of your front foyer," the detective explained. As Deschamps spoke, he held a Ziploc bag to his side, out of sight, attempting to manipulate the contents such that he could show Babineaux one object, while shielding the other in his hand. Accomplishing the feat, he asked, "Do you recognize this?"

"It looks like my wife's crucifix, but I can't be sure unless you take it out of the bag."

"Can't do that, sir. The lab will have to process it before we touch it."

"Then turn it over, so I can see the back. If it's Cindy's, her initials will be on it."

As Deschamps did so, Chad saw the etched lettering: "C.L.B." But there was something awkward in the manner that the detective had handled the plastic bag; like there was something else inside that he kept concealed. Still clasping the part revealing the crucifix and broken necklace, Chad suddenly jerked it away from Deschamps. "Don't, Mr. Babineaux. For your own peace of mind, don't."

Chad looked quizzically at the clear container, probing with his fingers the unknown, but apparently bloody and squishy contents. "What the hell is it?" he inquired.

"We won't know for certain until a pathologist looks at it," he sighed. "But we think it's body tissue."

Now Chad Babineaux actually vomited.

CHAPTER 36

A riverboat makes runs throughout the day carrying passengers to and from the French Quarter and Audubon Zoo, and six-year-old Billy Randle and his parents were among those picked up behind Jackson Square on Tuesday morning. The low and heavy fog shrouding the river played well into Billy's imagination, and he had always exhibited a rather vivid one. Today, the carrot-topped boy was not really with his mom and dad; he was the youthful red-headed hero in his favorite movie, an oldie on one of the many DVDs in the Randle household. During the upriver excursion, Billy was engrossed in adventure, refusing to respond in any way to his parents unless they called him Huck. He talked incessantly of make-believe villains popping out of the fog, only to be outwitted and vanquished by the valor and savvy of Huckleberry Finn.

The boat finally pulled alongside the pier at the Riverview area of Audubon Park. While the crew secured the moorings and the captain advised the passengers of certain safety precautions on a PA system, Billy raced down the steps from the upper deck, and wormed his way to the front of the line. When the gate opened, he was off like a shot down the pier.

"Billy! Billy Randle!" his mother shouted in vain. She yelled "Huckleberry" once, but to no avail. The looks and snickers the moniker drew from other passengers embarrassed her into not trying it again. "William Randle, you come back here right now!"

"He'll be fine, Gladys," Mr. Randle assured her.

A few minutes later, they too were on the pier, and soon met their son, running full bore toward them. "Mom! Dad!"

"Billy Randle, didn't you hear me calling you?" Mrs. Randle scolded.

"But Mom, listen...."

"No, you're the one who needs to do the listening."

"But Mom, I found a body, just like Huck Finn!"

"That's enough of this foolishness. You stay with your father and me, or he'll take off his belt and tan your hide good." She reached for his hand, but he was quicker, bolting off again down the pier. "Billy!"

The boy stopped only long enough to turn and yell, "Come on! I'll show ya!"

Almost immediately, Mr. and Mrs. Randle heard bloodcurdling screams, and picked up their pace. Park personnel were attempting to usher aside the crowd gathering at the end of the pier and keep everyone calm. "See?" Billy said, pointing to their right. "I told ya."

Lashed with duct tape to a corner post of the pavilion, within ten feet of the pier, was the nude and obviously dead body of a woman. Scrawled diagonally across her torso, seemingly in her own blood, were the words, in French, of what has become the motto of the Big Easy: "Laissez les bon temps roulez!" Let the good times roll.

CHAPTER 37

Tuesday morning, as the Randle family and other zoo visitors disembarked at the Riverview pier, soon to make the grisly discovery of Cindy Babineaux's corpse, Bo Landry awoke thoroughly rejuvenated. It had seemed eons since he had slept so soundly. Showered, shaved, and dressed, Bo sat on the sofa in the front room of his apartment, re-examining the documents that promised financial security for a long time to come. He still could not believe his good fortune. With a few strokes of a pen, Bo would actually be a millionaire.

Bo's eyes lingered on the check, making sure the number of zeros had not been a mirage. He didn't know what he would do with all that money, but was determined not to blow it. Until he had a better idea, he'd just put it in the bank. He checked his watch and saw that it was almost eight o'clock. He had an hour before the bank opened, and he was famished. Sliding the contents back into the brown envelope, he set out for a tasty breakfast.

The Fleur de Lis was a hole-in-the-wall café on Chartres Street, nestled between Conti and Bienville. It was a good walk from Bo's apartment, but well worth it. He usually had the two-egg breakfast—scrambled—with whole-wheat toast, bacon, and hashbrowns which were out of this world, and all for $6.95. Today, however, was special and Bo ordered the Fleur de Lis Omelet: three eggs, pepper jack cheese, jalapenos, onion, and bell pepper. And of course, a heaping side order of the seasoned hashbrowns.

Those of a lesser constitution might consider such a combination first thing in the morning, a gastronomical nightmare. But it was a scrumptious feast for Bo Landry. Washing down the last morsel with a final gulp of black coffee, he picked up the brown envelope and walked three blocks back toward Jackson Square, to the bank.

As it turned out, the one he had used in Mississippi also did business in several southern states, including Louisiana. In fact, there was a branch in the French Quarter. Along the way, the near-deafening horn blast of a cruise ship on the river caused Bo to jump. The source of the start prompted Bo to toy with the idea of using some of his money to take a cruise himself.

At the bank, he explained to the manager that he needed to sign some documents in the presence of a notary and make a deposit. She was all too pleased to accommodate him, especially when he handed her the deposit slip and endorsed check.

Exiting, Bo felt a sense of relief that the check was no longer in his care. Once one more chore was tended to, the sale to Alex Stillwell would be complete—at least on Bo's end. He crossed Toulouse and walked in the direction of Royal Street. About halfway up the block, he stopped in front of a nightclub to see if he had correctly read a couple of posters in the windows. Sure enough, the current attraction was a burlesque revue called The Fleur de Tease; and soon to come was The Dead Celebrity Ball where everyone dressed as their favorite dead celeb.

Only in New Orleans, Bo mused, and continued his walk, crossing Royal and proceeding another block to Bourbon, where he turned right and walked another five blocks to the intersection of St. Philip. He had copies of the notarized documents made at a postal store, and mailed the originals to Mike Dunn. It was up to Dunn, as the closing attorney, to see that the original papers were properly filed. The funds were now rightfully Bo's, but until he really needed the money, Bo wanted to forget it was there. It was time to get back to work and real life.

That a fire originates either intentionally or accidentally is rather axiomatic. Thus, when attorney Philip Moreau had asked Bo if he knew anything about fire investigation, the PI had not outright lied, he just didn't explain that this was the extent of his knowledge. It was odd how he got himself into such situations. Bo didn't like getting into anything over his head, but the opportunity to be a part of the Paradise Isle fire investigation was irresistible.

He had been instrumental in exonerating a medical student on a federal drug charge. The defendant was the son of one of Moreau's partners and the acquittal had salvaged the family name as well as the budding doctor's career. Outside the courthouse after the verdict, the grateful lawyer inquired how, beyond money, he could ever repay the PI for his superb work. Bo asked only that he put in a good word with Moreau, whose name had appeared in the newspaper account of the Paradise Isle fire.

Now that he was in the loop, Bo was in much the same position as a successful car-chasing dog. *Now, what are you going to do with it?* At the conference the day before, Bo had listened quietly while Moreau explained a dual strategy to the clients. The insurance company would want to drag its heels, making sure that the owners did not intentionally set the blaze, before writing a check for the damages. One way that authorities customarily attempted to prove that a fire was intentionally set, was by circumstantial evidence, to systematically eliminate the possibility of an accident.

Thus, to speed up the investigation, Moreau suggested a pro-active, converse approach, seeking first to establish accident by ruling out arson, taking advantage of the legal maxim that every fire is presumed to be accidental unless proven otherwise. At the same time, the private investigation would also gather circumstantial evidence removing any suspicion from the owners, even if arson became suspected. Moreau confidently informed the clients that Bo would stay in touch with them, letting them know the specific information needed. In truth, Bo didn't have a clue what that would be, but he knew someone who did.

Gary Borden and Bo had been Boys Scouts together in South Jackson's Troop 91. Gary was now retired from the Jackson Fire Department's Arson Investigation Division and working for the Mississippi State Fire Marshal. After reaching him on the phone, Bo explained the situation and asked for whatever guidance Gary could offer.

After a productive lengthy conversation with Borden, Bo spent the rest of the morning and early afternoon at his computer, typing the helpful notes he had taken, pulling up online accounts of the Paradise Isle fire, and e-mailing suggestions to Philip Moreau and the clients. He was still at it when his cell phone rang. Word that he was helping another bar's owner must have spread quickly in the Quarter, for it was the manager of another bar. Bo wrote down the address and headed out. The place was located on Dauphine Street, just a little over four blocks from Bo's apartment, within easy walking distance.

The Box Score was a bar known for welcoming drag queens and their paramours. According to the manager, two patrons "got into it" Saturday night, or more accurately, in the wee hours of Sunday morning. They took their business to the sidewalk, just outside the bar, ending with one assaulting the other and consequently hauled off to jail. In the litigious society in which we live, the management was fearful of being sued for failing to protect the injured patron.

"You need to be talking to a lawyer, Mr. Dixon," Bo advised.

"We have a lawyer—Jonas Willoughby. Do you know him?"

"No, can't say that I do. Did he recommend me?"

"No, no. I heard what you're doing for Paradise Isle. But don't worry, I told Jonas I would be calling you and he is okay with it."

"What exactly do you want me to do?"

"Take statements from everyone who was here. I don't know if we are going to be sued, but if we are, I want to have a file ready to show that we did everything we could reasonably do under the circumstances."

"I see," Bo said. "Why don't we start with you? What were the circumstances?"

"Frank Johnson just lost his mind. I don't know what set him off, but once he and Jamie Applewhite were outside, Frank beat poor Jamie unmercifully in the face and on the head."

"With his fists?"

"Heavens no. With a weapon."

"What kind of weapon, a gun?"

"A boot."

"A what?"

"A boot. One of the gold lamé boots Frank was wearing that night."

"And you said the police were called?"

"Yes. They arrested him for aggravated battery and obscenity."

"Obscenity?"

"Yes. It was not a pretty sight. When the police put the cuffs on Frank, he went berserk. They didn't cuff his hands behind his back like you see on TV, and Frank lifted his red dress and began urinating in the direction of one of the officers."

"You're shitting me."

"No pun intended I'm sure, but I kid you not. As they were dragging him away, Frank kept shouting, "You can't touch me! I work with the FBI!"

Bo stared at the man in disbelief.

"Well," Dixon said. "What do you think?"

"I think Frank was telling the truth."

"What on earth do you mean?"

"Sounds just like a Fed to me. If he's not, he could be charged with impersonating a federal officer."

Since the manager appreciated the humor, Bo agreed to do what he could to help and left. *Only in New Orleans.*

Mentally exhausted after his lessons in fire investigation and assault by deadly gold lamé footwear, Bo decided to stop by McCormick's before returning home. He turned off of Dauphine, onto St. Louis. Rounding the corner to the right, at Burgundy, he heard a female voice from above, belting out a horribly off-key tune. He looked up and scanned the balconies, but saw no one. As the racket continued, his line of vision zeroed in on a figure sitting on the roof of a building across the street, and a little farther down the block. Although Bo was not the only pedestrian out and about, no one else gave any apparent attention to this unusual sight and clamor. Once again he thought, only in New Orleans. Evidently such an exhibition was not a rarity at all down here, and Bo wondered what it would take to draw a second look in such a place.

Enthralled with what, at least to him was an oddity, Bo continued his walk, giving frequent glances upward at the wailing siren, until the neurons in his brain made the connection. *Sea Urchin!* He quickly crossed to her side of the street, out of her field of vision.

Once at the end of the block, Bo re-crossed Burgundy and stepped into McCormick's. While LB busied himself at a pool table with Wayne, a local who Bo thought was the spitting image of Peter Lorre, Robin was nursing a gin-and-tonic at the bar. Sam was standing behind the bar opposite her, and the two were gazing at a television. Bo took a seat beside her and asked her what was up. "That poor woman," Robin replied, and gave Bo a recap of the news concerning the brutal murder of an Uptown wife and mother, identified as Cynthia Babineaux. Included in the news report was a photo of the smiling victim.

"She was in here, you know," Sam said.

Robin and Bo spoke over one another, "What?" and "You're kidding?"

"Yeah," Sam assured them. "Saturday night. Nice lady."

Before anything else could be said about it, LB joined them, prompting Sam to announce to Bo, "You know these two are about to celebrate their fortieth wedding anniversary."

"Wow, that's great. Congratulations," Bo offered.

"More like condolences," Robin jokingly corrected, rolling her eyes.

"So that's like a big one," Bo said. "What are you going to do to celebrate?"

"A trip. That's what *I* want to do," Robin advised. "But you know LB—he isn't moving that car for anything."

Robin's mention of travel seemed like news to LB. "A trip?" he sarcastically asked. "Where would you want to go?"

"I don't know. Somewhere I haven't been in a long time."

"The kitchen?" LB guessed, incurring a fast jab to his ribs by his wife's right elbow.

"I swear," Sam said to Robin, "there's a special place reserved for you in heaven for putting up with this guy."

"It's just a matter of learning to enjoy the little things in life. If you get my drift," she replied.

"I would say that I resemble that remark," LB declared, "but I think that would make it even worse." After everyone agreed to this astute observation, he held up a middle finger to Robin, good-naturedly saying, "So I'll just say, enjoy this."

After some chortling all around, including Robin, Bo announced, "I think I'll leave on that one," and made his exit, armed with an idea.

Once home, he logged in on the Internet. A cruise was still on his mind and he ran searches for ones out of New Orleans. Carnival offered several options, the most expensive being a seven-day voyage in the western Caribbean; making stops at Belize, Isla Roatan, and Cozumel. Bo clicked the link for information and prices for the rooms, and saw that the suites were the highest in cost—about two grand per person. At the bottom of the page, he spotted what he had hoped to find. After moving the cursor to "Gift Certificates," he left-clicked the mouse.

The certificates came in $25, $50, $100 and $500 denominations. The priciest cruise, with the most expensive accommodations, would come to about $4,000, and Robin and LB could select exactly what they wanted. Bo however, wanted them to have plenty of spending money, too. Never having been on a cruise, Bo didn't have any idea how much to add, wondering whether he should just double the fixed cost. In the end, he purchased twenty of the $500 certificates in the names of LB and Robin Harper. Best of all, LB wouldn't even have to move his car. If Bo was unable for some reason to drop them off at the terminal, they could catch a cab.

LB was a proud man and Bo knew that he would be reluctant to accept the gift, but Bo had an idea about that too. As he was contemplating the plan, he heard someone banging on his front door. It was a very agitated Chad Babineaux, demanding an explanation why Bo's business card, which Babineaux shoved in his face, was found in his dead wife's purse.

"I don't know," Bo replied, not liking the direction this was heading. But he, too, was concerned about the connection, so he gestured for Chad to take a seat in the upholstered La-Z-Boy. Bo sat in a leather wingback on the other side of the small front room.

"Okay, just calm down," Bo began. "You say you found one of my cards where?"

Chad closed his eyes for a moment, taking in and letting out a deep breath. "My wife, Cindy, was raped and murdered last night."

Nodding, Bo said, "Yeah, I know."

"What do you mean you know?" Chad asked suspiciously.

"It was on the news, Mr. Babineaux. About an hour ago."

"Oh yeah." Chad was silent for a minute, then began sobbing. "I'm sorry. I just can't believe she's gone...what happened...so terrible...makes no sense...looking for answers...."

From his experience as a homicide investigator, Bo knew that it was best not to interrupt. Only when Chad pulled a handkerchief and wiped away his tears, apparently not intending on adding anything else at the present time, did Bo coax him to continue. "I assume the police are looking into it?" Chad nodded. "So tell me about it. You say you found one of my cards?"

Babineaux nodded again and explained. "I've been trying to make funeral arrangements, calling family and friends, things like that. Cindy's 'filing system' was her purses. She kept *everything* in them. But after using one, she wouldn't take everything out and put it in the next one. She'd just take what she needed each time. So to find all of the information I needed: her driver's license, Social Security card, insurance information, pieces of paper she'd write phone numbers on—I had to go through all of the them, and I found this in one," again holding up the card.

"May I see that?" Bo asked, rising from his chair. Chad extended his hand, and once Bo retrieved the card he retook his seat and studied the item. Determining that it was indeed his, he turned it over to see if Cindy Babineaux had written anything on the back. There was nothing.

"She hired you to spy on me, didn't she?" It was more of a declaration than a question by Chad.

"Mr. Babineaux, if she had I wouldn't tell you. But she didn't. What makes you think otherwise?"

"She just seemed so unhappy lately and I don't know why. I actually thought she might be having an affair. One of our friends told me that Cindy had prevailed upon her several times the last few days to keep our son, Ryan, overnight while I was out of town. In fact, that's where Ryan was last night when Cindy was killed."

"So I guess he doesn't know anything."

" Only that his mom walked him to soccer practice, it's at the Riverview part of Audubon Park and we live close by—and called him aside to tell him that he could spend another night with his friend Jake."

"And it was Jake's mother who told you she had kept Ryan for a couple of nights?"

"That's right. Friday and Saturday nights. Her name is Jackie Monroe."

"I'm assuming then, that she was at the practice."

"She was. Afterward, she took the boys to her house."

"So what does she say?"

"That Cindy seemed preoccupied, and asked her to keep an eye on

Ryan while she did some jogging."

"So your wife intended to return to the practice?"

"Not according to Jackie. Cindy was going to get in her run, then leave. Like I said, our house is right by the park."

"Did Ms. Monroe notice anything or anyone suspicious or unusual in the area?"

"No; nothing other than Cindy's preoccupation."

"Who's heading up the investigation?"

"Lieutenant Deschamps, Winston Deschamps."

"In speaking with him, do you know whether anyone saw your wife after she left the soccer field?"

"No. That seems to be the last she was seen."

"Has he talked to the other people there; coaches, other parents, the kids?"

"Most of them, he says, but no one saw anything suspicious."

"Not even a vehicle that seemed out of place?"

"No, not that Lieutenant Deschamps mentioned."

"So they don't have any leads that you know of?"

"None that they've shared."

"No hairs, fibers?"

"Not that I'm aware of."

"That's unusual in a rape case, Mr. Babineaux. How do you know she was raped?"

"They didn't find any semen at the autopsy, but the doctor said that there were other signs of recent sexual activity. The bastard just used a rubber."

"And it could have been consensual," Bo noted. Seeing Chad's puzzled expression, Bo explained. "You yourself suspect that she had a lover. Her murder may not be connected to any sexual activity."

"Her body was not the only thing the doctor examined," Chad declared. "If you knew what they found in a plastic bag in my house...," he began, and broke into tears.

"Tell me," Bo urged. And when Chad Babineaux managed to utter the words, Bo told him that it sounded like a case in Mississippi, and revealed the identity of the killer—Todd Murphy. Bo had to get involved, and thus offered his services to Babineaux.

"How much will that run?" Chad asked.

"Not a dime," Bo answered.

"No, I couldn't let you do that," Chad responded. "Just promise me that you'll tell Lieutenant Deschamps about Murphy and that case in Mississippi."

Chad was not making this easy. "What do you do for a living, Mr.

Babineaux?"

"I have an antique shop on Magazine. Why?"

"I tell you what," Bo proposed, "I may be getting another place in the near future, and I may develop a taste for some antiques. You hire me, tell Deschamps to keep you in the loop through me, and let's see what I can do. If you're not satisfied, you owe me nothing. I just wasted my time. If you're happy with the results, we work a deal, in trade. Fair enough?"

"Sure, but why would you do that?"

"Let's just say it benefits both of us."

After Babineaux went on his way, Bo noticed, on a small glass-top table by the chair where Bo had sat, the business card that had brought the bereaved husband to Bo's door. He picked it up, walked to the spare bedroom, and dropped it in a desk drawer. The adrenaline was flowing, and it was time to get back online.

CHAPTER 38

After leaving the Babineaux house Monday evening, the beast had resolved to check out the website as a possible resource, but other business had delayed his search until now. Within seconds of typing the address and hitting the "Enter" key, he saw what he wanted—"Hot Mom Contest—click here."

The first contestant to pop up was Kristen from Marrero. The beast imagined himself the photographer, looking through the camera, down at the posing blue-eyed beauty. Dark streaks accented her short, blonde hair. With a finely sculpted nose, thin lips, and narrow chin, she reminded the beast of Anne Heche. He could tell that she was wearing a hot-pink tube top and black bottoms of some kind, but for the most part, the angle of the overhead shot masked the clothing, accentuating her skin. The camera lens afforded a bird's eye view of floral tattoos in blue, pink, and a dash of yellow between each breast and on her collarbone. Although she was not overly endowed in the chest, nicely shaped thighs extended from the skimpy lower garment. With the exception of the tats, her skin was fair and unblemished, and the artwork was not at all distracting. Blue mascara and dark eyeliner magically brought everything together, while also presenting a contrast quite pleasing to the eye. Kristen from Marrero projected the image of a porcelain doll longing to be treated as anything else. "Your wish is my command," the beast muttered before going to the next photo.

He didn't give a whit about voting, but the menu denied progression to the next contestant until he did. Kristen from Marrero was a keeper, but not knowing what else he would find, the beast gave her an "8".

He did not linger long on the second entrant, but the third, Simone from New Orleans, was definitely in the running. The dark-eyed brunette, with long wavy tresses draping over the shoulders, was leaning back against a wall, clad only in a bra and panties. The lace-edged, half-cup bra revealed the upper portions of what had to be 36 or 38Ds. The beast's eyes tracked downward, along the tapering waist, to the thumbs invitingly hooked in the strings of the thong, pushing it to the point that her pubic area was barely concealed. The bright white lingerie against the tan body produced an exquisite contrast. "9" for Simone from New Orleans.

None of the next fourteen, in the beast's opinion, topped either Kristen or Simone, nevertheless he had to assign a rating to each, in order to proceed. Number 18, however, was a different story. The beast had enjoyed watching *Charlie's Angels*, the TV series of the '70s, and he thought Jaclyn Smith the sexiest of the three stars. Mandi from Mandeville could have been the actress's double. Long, full nut-brown locks cascaded down the shoulders of the seductive figure, positioned in the open doorway of what appeared to be an old delivery truck, with its steering wheel in the upper background. Donning a black, low-cut, chiffon dress with long sleeves, she was leaning back against the right side of the entrance. The sheer fabric became opaque where it was strategically gathered between elongated and well-contoured legs; the left dangling, the right hiked up. A high-topped, black boot rested against the left side of the open portal.

After these initial observations, the beast scrutinized her again and again, from top to bottom. Blue eyes gazed not at the cameraman, but off to her left, as if on the alert for anyone who might interrupt the naughtiness she was contemplating. Casting his eyes lower, the beast discerned pouty, full lips and a black choker. He instinctively brought his hand to the monitor and caressed the delicate neck. As he felt the pulse in her carotid quicken, a primal excitement stirred. With his index finger, the beast traced down the cleavage exhibited by the plunging "V" of the dress. He surmised she was a 36, but her size was not as easily estimated as Simone's had been. Yet, the beast had discovered years ago the power of imagination. In erotica, as with the culinary arts, presentation was everything. If done in the right manner, an area of the female body partially obscured could be more titillating than full nudity.

Without hesitation the beast clicked "10", and continued until he had seen the rest of the contestants—thirty-two in all—but none measured up to Kristen, Simone, and Mandi. Although he was fairly certain which of these three he considered most worthy of his attention, what would it hurt to take another gander?

In attempting to start anew, the beast somehow found himself back to the home page and, before again clicking the icon for the contest, spotted one that would enable him to listen to whatever was on the air. *Ah, some background music.* When he made the connection, a traffic report emanated from the speakers. Nevertheless, he kept it turned on and, by the time he once again navigated his way to Kristen from Marrero, Led Zeppelin's "Black Dog" was playing loud and clear. The song continued as the beast beheld the sight of curvaceous Simone from New Orleans in bra and panties, truly something to make burn and sting.

It was a close call, a damned close one, but the beast was mesmerized by the delicate, translucent material nestled between the splayed legs of Mandi from Mandeville, sensually veiling the sweetness beneath. This mom was hot to the nth degree, exuding a refined and cultured, yet mysterious and lusty, aura which the beast found irresistible.

As far as the beast was concerned, she was "it", but as he had expected, he could not find any further information about her on the site. Typing documents and searching the Internet were the extent of his computer skills. He wouldn't know where to begin in an effort to hack into the radio station's computer system. Although he knew someone who could, the beast was not one to take unnecessary risks. Oh, he supposed he could easily dispose of the hacker afterward, and there was also an outside chance that, with patient and meticulous use of a city directory, he could eventually track her down. But why bother with either of these time-consuming efforts when there were plenty of fish in the sea? It was now Carnival season in the Big Easy, and fitting prospects were pouring into the French Quarter by the thousands every day.

CHAPTER 39

There is a German proverb that goes something like this: "Virtue and vice divide the world, but vice has got the greater share". For visual proof of this observation, one need only witness Carnival season in New Orleans, when there are no commandments harder to live by than the first ten. It kicks off on the Twelfth Night, or Epiphany, twelve days after Christmas, the time many cultures celebrate the magi's presentation of gifts to the Christ child. Over the years, what began as simple masquerade balls evolved into a complex set of celebrations by the late 19th century, with private parties, public balls, and loosely organized street processions. Today, parades occur almost daily: from the elaborate ones on Canal and St. Charles in the city proper, and those of a similar ilk on Veterans in suburban Metairie, to the more crude (in every sense of the word) Krewe de Vieux, one of the few along the narrow streets of the Quarter, and the only one that tourism officials discourage parents from bringing young children.

It is difficult to ascertain the exact genesis of Carnival in New Orleans, but it was sufficiently established by 1781 to cause the Spanish authorities to forbid slaves and free persons of color from wearing masks during the celebration. "Mask," when used as a verb, means to conceal from view, but metaphorically it possesses a much deeper meaning: a metamorphosis which, if only for a while, allows the wearer to transcend his or her routine life and construct a new self, an altered psyche. It is this capability to escape the mundane and enter the realm of the taboo that bestows the enchantment and power of Carnival.

Relatively speaking, the Quarter was quiet Wednesday morning as Bo made his way to a beignet café on Royal Street. Although the hour was early, nightclub personnel were already hosing off the sidewalks and balconies of their establishments, washing away spilled brews and regurgitation—unappetizing evidence of the previous night's over-satiated appetites.

However, other than along Bourbon Street, there was no noxious stench carried on the morning zephyr, thanks to the beefed-up cleaning measures taken by the city since the storm. Each day street-sweepers came through once and garbage was picked up several times. Streets and sidewalks received a thorough cleaning once a week. But even these worthy efforts were no match for infamous Bourbon Street. Thus, as Bo approached its intersection with St. Ann, he held his breath until he made the crossing, and continued along St. Ann to Royal, just another block toward Jackson Square.

He turned right at the corner, walking behind St. Louis Cathedral and past the terminus of Orleans. He couldn't help thinking of the day Father Ambrose dropped him off there. The occasion marked the end of Bo's rehabilitation and the beginning of his resurrection.

Pausing only to fish three quarters from his pocket to get a *Times-Picayune* from the stand outside the neighborhood grocery at the corner of St. Peter, Bo continued along the next couple of blocks. He passed the sprawling steps of the State Supreme Court building where Filene, a talented clarinetist, was setting up in preparation of regaling soon-expected crowds with jazzy tunes. The scene reminded him of something Louis Armstrong once said when asked to explain what jazz actually was: "If you have to ask, you'll never understand".

After placing his order for beignets and bacon, Bo took his cup of coffee and found an empty table in the café's courtyard. He had no sooner opened his paper when he felt something alive brush against his leg, causing him to start, jarring the table and sloshing hot coffee. *A cat; a damned cat.* Bo hated them, for they were the only creatures he believed could see into one's soul, and that terrain was off limits. Bo had forgotten that several of these freaks of nature habituated the courtyard, and the other patrons there were aghast when he kicked the abomination away and walked off.

Now seated inside, Bo returned to his paper. Two stories took up the front page. "Burglars prey on officer's widow," read one. As word spread throughout the neighborhood of the death of a police sergeant, who was among the GIs to survive Hitler's guns in the D-Day invasion, and subsequently dedicated sixty-two years on the NOPD to serve and protect the people of New Orleans, two local men and a woman saw an opportunity. While the officer's widow was at a funeral home arranging his burial, the three degenerates broke into her house, stealing guns, money, jewelry, and medication. Bo reflected on the fact that there were some truly sick people in the world.

The other story, which he didn't start reading until after a kid with a zit-covered face brought him the beignets and bacon was, of course, about the "barbaric" slaying of Cindy Babineaux and the "macabre" display of her body "taunting" the investigating authorities. However, there was nothing in the article Bo did not already know. He would visit Lieutenant Winston Deschamps and see what the police knew thus far. They never released everything to the public, not even to the victim's family. Bo would wait until later in the day however, giving Chad Babineaux some time to grease the wheels. That was okay though, there were other matters Bo could tend to in the interim.

CHAPTER 40

By one o'clock, the French Quarter was teeming with specimens of every ilk and form. *Why do they call it tourist season,* the beast wondered, *if you can't shoot them?* He was taking his time, snaking through the growing throng on Royal Street. While everyone else was there for the parade scheduled to come through soon, the beast was on the prowl. Deciding there was no need to exert himself in his hunt—the prey would come to him—the beast sat on the curb across the street from a large, ritzy hotel. He watched the people pass by like contestants in a beauty pageant walking the runway for a close view by the judges. Ultimately, the beast decided they were all idiots.

A short, obese man, in Bermuda shorts and a T-shirt stretched to the bursting point, was puffing away on a cigar. The roll of flab flapping over his belt line prompted the beast to mull over how long it had probably been since the fat fuck had last seen his feet. One gray-haired woman was wearing a crown of orchids dyed purple, gold, and green. The beast knew these to be the colors of Mardi Gras, but if he ever knew what they symbolized, the knowledge escaped him now.

One possible candidate was a lithe blonde girl, probably a college coed. The hem of her yellow dress was so short that with every step she fretfully tried to hold it down against the wind. *What the hell did she expect?* The beast regretfully eliminated her from contention since anyone so stupid did not merit further consideration.

Aw, shit. There was another blonde, this one short and dumpy, lowering her black tube top at the beckoning of bead-armed assholes on the hotel balcony across the street. "Show us your tits!" they yelled. Unfortunately she obliged, jiggling a pair, of science-fiction proportions, much to their amusement, but to the beast's aversion. *Why was it always*

165

the ugly ones who did this?

The rumination was broken by the shout, in another direction, of one of the balcony revelers, "Hey, Tablecloth!" The beast turned and saw an approaching redhead donning a hideous red-and-white checkered dress. No boobs this time, though. She just kept on walking.

Pirates were evidently a popular masquerade as they were everywhere. The one walking by the beast now had on one of those puffy shirts, like the one the beast had seen in a *Seinfeld* episode, and skin-tight, black leather britches. Got to be a queer, the beast surmised.

Trailing behind the swashbuckler was a redneck wearing a red cap with the Playboy Bunny logo emblazoned on the front. "There going to be a parade or something here?" he asked the beast, who just glared at the sack of shit that housed such imbecility. Un-phased, Goober and his son, who appeared to be about ten, sat on the curb next to the beast. Within a few minutes though, they rose, crossed the street, and disappeared through the doors of the hotel. The beast didn't believe they were guests there—not exactly the type. Sure enough, they emerged in short order and resumed their places beside the beast, who guessed that the excursion had been one in search of a bathroom.

Relieving yourself outside was about the only thing that would get you arrested in the Quarter during Mardi Gras. Flaunting bared breasts or showing your ass, figuratively or literally, was kosher. Hell, one night, the beast happened upon a pair of revelers screwing their brains out right on the sidewalk just across from the cathedral at Jackson Square. As people, including two uniformed cops, walked by, around, and even over the copulating couple, they kept bumping and grinding away. Fornicating in public is one thing, but if you urinate, your ass is going to jail. The beast thought of George Carlin's astute observation: "Why do they call it *taking* a piss? You don't take it, you leave it." *Shit, this was getting boring.* Fuck this, the beast thought to himself, and stood to search elsewhere. He didn't go far.

As he stood and turned to leave, the beast noticed that the fickle finger of fate had guided him to Randy's Cabaret, which he knew from a billboard along I-10, to be a gentlemen's club. Never before having the need or desire to enter one, he wasn't sure what to expect. But what he did *not* expect to see posted in the front window of a strip joint was a sign warning: "Proper attire required." *Really? In a strip joint? How amusing?*

Stepping inside, the beast found a woman stationed behind the counter of what was apparently a gift shop, offering shirts of various styles, sizes, and colors, along with caps, visors, cups, and other miscellany, all bearing the Randy's logo. She explained there was a one-drink minimum, but no cover charge. The beast expressed his thanks, and reached inside the bowl on the countertop for a box of matches. Although he did not smoke, there were other ways that he could put them to use.

There was no problem locating an empty table, one right by the stage in fact, as there were only a dozen or so patrons. The beast found this odd, considering the plush red and black décor, and promptness with which a girl in a black cat suit approached and took his drink order. Perhaps, he thought, it was still too early in the day. However, while waiting for his rum and Coke, he saw why even the most lecherous ogler with a modicum of taste would find a parade more interesting.

While the surroundings and service were exceptional, *talent* was a misnomer. On stage, a topless dirty-blonde was crawling on hands and knees, steadily slapping her bare ass as if playing horsey, to the hoots and catcalls of only the five morons perched around the center-stage table. They looked to be college age, waving cowboy hats and enthusiastically slipping cash into the exotic dancer's thong each time she passed their way. The waitress soon brought the beast's cocktail.

While the beast did not find the performance the least bit arousing, he made it a point to give the performer more thorough attention on her next lap around the stage. However, what he saw on the return trip wasn't any better than the first. While beauty may very well be in the eye of the beholder, the beast didn't believe that even the masking, blurred vision afforded by alcohol could distort that face into anything appealing. As a matter of unalterable fact, she was just outright butt-ugly. If she had a bag over her head, the beast supposed her figure would suffice as far as his carnal purposes were concerned, but he wouldn't be able to see the fear. *So what would be the point?* Having already paid for his libation, the disillusioned beast made his exit.

Outside, the parade was in full swing. The crowd cheered passing majorettes gyrating to the loud and lively strain of an all-black, high-school band. Mamas and papas sporting T-shirts bearing the word *Security* walked along the curbs, protecting the flanks.

The beast turned left and elbowed his way past other strip clubs. Still disenchanted, he walked by with barely a glance. By the time he crossed Conti Street, however, his despondency began to wane, and even though he passed Baby Dolls and one of Larry Flint's clubs, he had regained enough resolve to give it another try at Hotties.

As at Randy's, there was no charge for going in, but the beast had to pop for another drink. Soon after a waitress set a rum and Coke on his table, a horse-faced girl in an abbreviated cheerleader outfit walked up and asked the beast if he wanted some company. She actually seemed offended when he unhesitatingly declined.

A voluptuous, chocolate-skinned dancer, with areolae as dark and large as the wafers of an Oreo cookie, was wrapped around the pole at the stage's center, seemingly making love to the silvery shaft. A movement which the beast detected out of the corner of his eye, to his right, drew his attention. Now *that* is more what I'm looking for, he thought.

A young girl with long black hair had walked from a back room to the bar. The G-string displayed a nicely shaped ass atop well-toned legs accentuated by high, stiletto heels. She looked in his direction, said something to the bartender, and sashayed toward the beast. As she approached, he saw that she had on a vest—Royal blue, matching her eyes and complementing her raven hair and tan flesh. Only the middle of the garment's three buttons was fastened, allowing an ample view of her upper assets. She was neither beautiful nor homely, but nonetheless rather exotic.

"Hi," she said, running a hand through a loose strand of long tresses. "Want some company?"

"Sure," the beast replied. And as he stood and pulled back a chair for her to join him, he heard a distinctive huff. Glancing behind him, he was amused to see the horse-faced cheerleader, stomping off in overt disgust.

"What's your name?" Blue Eyes asked, after taking the offered seat.

"John," the beast replied, and instantly rebuked himself for such a lack of imagination. "What's yours?"

"Destiny," she replied. Yeah right, the beast thought, but said nothing. "Your first time here?" she continued. After the beast indicated that it was, indeed, his first foray there, she asked what he did for a living.

This time, the beast was a little more creative in his response: "I'm a writer," he declared, "currently working on a thriller about a serial killer."

"Wow," she said, "a serial killer; how fascinating."

"You have no idea, Destiny."

By now, the black girl on stage had finished her mock masturbation against the metallic mast. Turning her back to the audience, she shimmied the bare cheeks of her derriere—first the left, then the right, then both—to the rhythm of the bass pulsating from the sound system. Some of the men flung cash onto the stage, in appreciation of this atypical talent.

"Sorry, but that's my cue," Blue Eyes informed the beast.

"So you dance too?"

"Sure. We all do," she explained. "Normally, we have to do three numbers in a set, but it's so slow today, we only have to do two. After that, I don't go back on for a few hours. So don't go away." Giving him a wink, she added, "That should give us time to *really* get to know each other—in the back, I mean." Looking in the direction of her nod, the beast saw a sign on another door: "VIP Room." Before he could say anything, Blue Eyes remarked, "I want to hear more about this psycho killer."

Smiling, the beast replied, "And I look forward to it. By the time we're done, you'll understand *everything*. It will be your *destiny*, Destiny." They shared a laugh at the pun before she went backstage.

It was with great expectation that the beast awaited Blue Eyes' performance. He was ready to be aroused. Thus, it came as a deflating blow when it became apparent that her routine was no different than that of Shimmy Cheeks—same thing, just delivered in a different package. The disappointment warranted reconsideration. Blue Eyes remained a possibility, but he would have to give the matter further thought. Since she had so kindly shared her schedule with him, the beast knew that she would be there for hours. He had plenty of time to contemplate and come back before she got away, if he decided that she was the one.

Before he could leave, however, Shimmy Cheeks came up and asked if he wanted some company. Jesus, he thought, what a racket. "No thanks," he curtly answered, and left the table. He pulled a $5 bill from his wallet to toss onto the stage for Blue Eyes, who was entwined around the pole. Almost as quickly as the thought occurred, he replaced the cash in his wallet. If Blues Eyes ended up being the one, he certainly couldn't afford to leave anything in her possession bearing his fingerprints.

The beast had seen as much as he cared in the strip joints. He had only been in two. Nevertheless, it was enough to convince him that there was little, if any, difference in what any of them offered. Midway down the block, after crossing St. Louis, the beast saw what was once Big Daddy's World Famous Sex Acts, now closed and boarded up in testament that an era had passed.

It was all so depressing. *Have I set my sights too high?* Remarkable as it was, the beast possessed photographic evidence that there were suburban mothers in Mandeville, Metairie, and New Orleans who were at least ten times more worthy than anyone he had happened upon on Bourbon Street. *Mothers, for crying out loud.* Speaking of which, the beast was somewhat puzzled at feeling the urge to hunt so soon after Sweet Cindy. It had only been a few days but the craving was to be quenched, never questioned.

At the next corner, the beast bid adieu to Bourbon Street, and headed for Jackson Square. He just wanted to sit and think. Somewhere in this metropolis was another young woman, of just the right ripeness. His patience had always been rewarded, but the urge and frustration were mere micro-degrees below the boiling point. Veering left at Royal, the message emblazoned on a T-shirt displayed in a corner shop caught the beast's eye: "Too Much Soul To Control". He couldn't have said it better, and five minutes later the beast exited the store with his purchase in hand.

As was usually the case that time of year, Jackson Square was teeming with humanity. All of the benches on the plaza in front of the cathedral were occupied. The beast turned right, wending his way between the artists' stands and shops of the upper Pontalba building. Stepping through the side gate and into the gardens, the beast spotted an empty bench tucked in a shaded corner to his left.

People of all shapes, sizes, and colors strolled by. A young Asian couple handed a camera to a grandmotherly Caucasian woman, coaxing her to photograph them in front of General Jackson's statue. The beast watched in amusement as the impromptu photographer couldn't decide whether a vertical or horizontal shot was better as she turned the unfamiliar apparatus one way and then the other, then back again. Finally, an impatient bald man, standing to the side, grumped, "Hurry up, Mabel. Just snap the dang picture, and let's go."

His urging only caused further delay. Grandma lowered the camera and echoed an adaptation of a local catchphrase painted on little signs for sale in some of the shops, "Be nice, Albert, or leave." Following the rebuke, she pointed the camera at the still-smiling and rigid couple, taking it through the same previous sequence of twists and turns.

"Aw dang, Mabel."

There was more to this exchange, but the beast had become more interested in a conversation behind him.

CHAPTER 41

Mandi Charbonnet and Beth Callahan were in the same sorority pledge class at Tulane. The bond of sisterhood extended well past anything of a Pan-Hellenic nature. It was due solely to this affinity and trust that Mandi had succumbed to her husband Adam's urging to pose in such a risqué way for Beth's camera. She was a CPA and a mother for chrissakes, and had no desire to enter a hot mom contest. Yet, she did. And much to her surprise received the call that morning that she had won.

There was no doubt that Beth possessed the gifted eye of an artist, putting it to use in selecting the location and wardrobe for Mandi's shoot, and putting her at ease during the erotic exhibition. Excited by Mandi's news, Beth was gung-ho in taking it a step further. A nude painting had formulated in Beth's mind, and Mandi would be the ideal model. It was, in fact, during the photo shoot that the idea had taken root. On the phone that morning, Mandi had summarily rejected the idea, but weakened somewhat at Beth's plea for assistance in expanding into a new artistic genre.

Beth's assurances that the painting would not show anything but her backside proved to be a further chink in Mandi's armor. And when Beth said that she would do the piece from a photograph, eliminating the need for hours of posing, Mandi agreed to at least meet with Beth and discuss it further. It was tax season, and Mandi prepared the returns for several of the businesses in the French Quarter. Since she had to pick up one such client's records that afternoon, Mandi told Beth that she would stop by Jackson Square afterward.

Beth stepped away from her stool and easel, and motioned Mandi over to the iron fence enclosing the Square, farther away from the ears of passing gawkers. There, she repeated her congratulations to Mandi for winning the contest, and went into more detail of what she now intended.

Beth wouldn't lie to her sorority sister; other artists and anyone else with a developed eye would know the painting was made from a photograph, thereby also knowing that the source was a model instead of the artist's imagination. Beth promised, however, that no one would ever know the identity of the model. Even with such a vow, Mandi would not have consented had the pledge come from the lips of anyone other than Beth. But it *was* Beth, and she agreed. What the hell, Mandi thought. She knew that Beth hoped to sell the painting. And she also suspected that once Beth was done with the photos, Adam would get a kick out of hanging them in their bedroom. It would be their secret as to whose rear end was digitally captured and memorialized.

"I knew you wouldn't let me down!" Beth replied excitedly. "That's why I went ahead and made arrangements after we talked on the phone. I know the perfect place."

"This *is* going to be inside, isn't it?" Mandi asked, cocking a doubtful brow.

"Yes Mandi. No worries, okay?" Beth pulled a slip of paper from her jeans and handed it to Mandi. "451 Burgundy, day after tomorrow at 9:00 p.m. That should give you enough time to tend to dinner and make the drive from Mandeville. I'll meet you out front."

"Whose place is this?"

"Sissy Waverly's."

"Sissy? Oh, my God! I lost track of her after graduation." Concern quickly pushed excitement aside. "Beth, I can't do this at Sissy's. I'd be too embarrassed."

"Honey, calm down. She and Walter are moving to Houston. They'll be there looking for a place and getting the kids enrolled in school. Sissy doesn't know you're involved in any way. When I talked with her, she gave me the combination for the front gate and told me where she hides a spare key for her unit. It's one of several condos around a central courtyard. Hers is number three." Seeing that Mandi was not entirely assuaged, Beth wrapped reassuring hands around her friend's. "Everything is handled. I promise."

Mandi let out a deep breath. "If you say so. Do I need to bring anything special to wear, or am I going to be totally butt-ass naked?"

"Only fishnet stockings and heels, love. And I'll have those for you. All you need to bring is your award-winning bod."

This elicited a laugh from both women. And as Mandi from Mandeville strode off, the beast smugly smiled. Good fortune comes to him who waits. Some cosmic force was inexplicably delivering to his altar the very sacrifice he had coveted, but believed beyond his reach. He really should have known better. He was, after all, omnipotent.

CHAPTER 42

That there is no love lost between local police agencies and the FBI is hardly a secret. Whether or not justified, it is practically a universal belief throughout the local rank-and-file that the Feds are *takers*; they expect—even demand—information while sharing little or nothing. This one-way avenue can create disastrous consequences.

Bo Landry recalled a murder case he had worked which began as a bank robbery. In making his escape, the perp took one of the tellers as a hostage. When the poor woman was no longer of any use to the bastard, she was summarily executed. Bo and the other investigators of the Jackson Police Department had exclusive jurisdiction over the murder charge, but shared concurrent jurisdiction of the robbery with the FBI. Logical minds would reason that murder trumps robbery. Even in the vast majority of pure bank robbery cases, the Feds are all too happy to dump everything in the lap of the local authorities. The exception, of course, is when: a) the case is a slam-dunk; and b) there is a lot of ink to be garnered.

Because of the extensive publicity surrounding the case, the Feds took control in this one. An arrest was made and the bureau acceded to the state taking its murder case to trial first, but the brief federal intervention was enough to gum up the works. Without bothering to tell Bo or any of the other veteran homicide investigators who were familiar with the ins and outs of state law, the FBI had hypnotized many of the eyewitnesses to assist in obtaining a description of the culprit and his vehicle. Mississippi law treats the testimonies of such witnesses as tainted and useless at trial. Whether the FBI was ignorant of that legal tidbit or didn't care could be debated, but the effect was the same. The defense attorneys quickly filed motions to toss all of the eyewitness testimony, and the judge was duty bound to grant the requests. The public was horrified, and Bo and his colleagues were outraged, but not surprised. A shit sandwich was not unusual fare doled out to the locals at an FBI picnic. Fortunately for Lady Justice, the son-of-a-bitch had confessed on live TV.

The memory of the near-fiasco flooded the thoughts of Bo Landry Wednesday afternoon as he made his way to the office of Lieutenant Winston Deschamps. In all likelihood it was probably triggered by Bo's acute awareness that if there was anyone who a homicide investigator distrusted and loathed more than an FBI agent, it was a private investigator. Thus, while the cool reception he soon received had not been entirely unexpected, Bo had hoped for some degree of cooperation from Deschamps out of respect for the wishes of the victim's husband. Not so.

Deschamps was unmoved, making it clear that not only would Bo receive no information beyond what was released for public dissemination, but also, in the future, Deschamps would be more circumspect in what he shared with Chad Babineaux.

Nevertheless, Bo held his temper. "Fine, Lieutenant. I've been there. I understand the one-way-street mentality; so I'll do all the talking." He related everything he knew about Todd Murphy, the Mississippi murders, and the apparent similarities in the mutilations of Serena Raven and Cindy Babineaux. When he was done, Deschamps stood and simply said, "Well, that's interesting. Have a nice day."

Bo was miffed at the summary dismissal. "At least get the JPD files," he urged. "And, once you see the connection, talk to Jack Parker; he's with the Marshal's Service in Jackson. He can tell you what's being done to find Murphy."

"Believe it or not," Deschamps responded, "the New Orleans Police Department is perfectly capable of conducting this investigation."

"Let's see," Bo snapped, "murder capital of the world—more casualties by gunfire here in the last three months than in fucking Afghanistan, and yet a rather dismal arrest and conviction rate. Excuse my doubts about the assurance, Lieutenant."

"You are indeed, excused—from my office," Deschamps declared without raising his voice. "Now, if will you be so kind as to get out, and stay the hell out."

Bo felt the heat rise in his neck and face. In the doorway, he turned to hurl a final barb, "I read about the patrol cars stolen off your *capable* department's lot. *Ouch*, how embarrassing."

Once the PI left, Deschamps sat back down behind his desk, and pulled out the files that were e-mailed to him earlier in the day, at his request, from the Jackson Police Department.

CHAPTER 43

Meticulous planning, tempered by flexibility in adapting to circumstances, serves a serial killer well. From the time the beast serendipitously overheard the women's conversation at Jackson Square, and learned the address of the photo shoot, the wheels and gears in his brain had been turning. With the precision of the most intricate Swiss timepiece, he assessed his options, settling on a nearby, yet secluded, lair in which he could leisurely and methodically prepare New Orleans' hottest mom for the sadistic pleasure of himself and his guests.

He was hopped up by this new twist. Killing could be so mundane. Any oaf can take a life; it requires no skill. Making one's mark in the process, however, is an entirely different matter. To accomplish that requires daring and a certain élan. The beast would bring these attributes to bear in entertaining his guests. And, as every good host knows, presentation is everything.

Since the centerpiece of the affair would be coming out of 451 Burgundy, some place nearby would be ideal but not necessarily mandatory, as the beast could abduct her and drive to a venue away from the hustle and bustle of the French Quarter. Standing at the gate of 451 Burgundy, the beast looked up and down the street, first toward Canal, then Esplanade. He was near the intersection of Conti. On one corner was a 24-hour tavern. The beast crossed Burgundy and took a left at the tavern. A little more than halfway down the block was a wax museum, and on the other side of the street was a parking lot somewhat hidden behind brick and stucco walls that warranted further inspection.

There was neither gate nor attendant. Forming the boundary on the right, or west side, was a building advertising the availability of apartments. The rear, or south side, was framed by the side of a structure that probably fronted Burgundy; and to the left, on the east side of the lot, were four boarded-up brick ruins, one behind the other and facing Conti. In all likelihood, they once served as slaves' quarters. The first three were two-stories high, and the fourth stood a story taller, consumed by brown dead vines hanging over the two wood-rail balconies and open arched doorways. If ever a building in the Vieux Carré epitomized a temple of doom, this was it.

It was out of sheer curiosity that, before going inside, the beast walked to the corner of Conti and Dauphine to take a look at the main building that had once required such an urban slave force as to warrant nine floors of living quarters. The front of this edifice was on Dauphine, next to a bistro, and like the rear structures, was boarded up. A faded paper sign proclaimed: "The shadow of the past holds the future hostage."

Returning to the parking lot, the beast walked to the left, along the inside of the wall, past the front of the first outbuilding. Through the shadows of the first three dilapidated structures, he made his way to the rearmost one. Inside, cypress planks were strewn atop rubble of broken brick and mortar. After examining the positions and soundness of the exposed joists on each floor, he was satisfied. It was perfect.

The beast made a brief stop at his place to alter his appearance with a cap, wig, and beard before striking out across the Quarter to an adult costume and novelty shop just off Decatur, on St. Philip. Arriving just before it closed, he made a cash purchase of four black leather hoods with openings for the eyes and mouth, the kind a medieval executioner might have worn at the chopping block. The beast handed the proprietor a $100 bill and explained that the hoods were for four guests for a party he was hosting, and that part of the "game" required that they come by the shop and pick up the hoods themselves. The C-note was intended for the man's assistance.

Fondling the crisp bill as he gave the matter some thought, the proprietor asked, "Why stop with the hoods when you can get the whole outfits?"

While the proprietor wrote out a list of the items and their costs on a pad, the beast browsed around the store to see what else might be fun to have on hand. Tossing a plastic bag containing a swing on the counter, he said, "Add that."

"Great. And to whom," the man asked, looking up, "shall I make out the receipt?"

"Henry," the beast answered. "Henry Tudor." After peeling off the necessary cash from his wad, the beast advised the man that he would contact him in two days to see how many guests had accepted their invitations by picking up their attire. Taking his receipt, the beast walked out the door absolutely elated. The new toy in the bag he clutched was no ordinary swing.

Back in his lair, the beast booted up the computer. After browsing several sites, he sought to place an "order" for four male escorts. He declined to pay online with a credit card, but advised in the message box that he would pay double the usual rate, in cash, if the escorts were into BDSM and willing to engage in unprotected, heterosexual sex. He explained that the party was a birthday surprise for his wife, who was very much into such orgies; in fact, the rougher the better.

If interested, a limo would pick up the four guests at a given rendezvous in two nights' time, at the stroke of midnight. The driver would hand them half their fee and drop them off at an undisclosed location in the French Quarter. The limo would return precisely one hour later to pick them up, and deliver the rest of their cash. The beast provided the name and address of the shop on St. Philip, and advised that the manner by which this invitation could be accepted was to go to the store in the next two days and retrieve the attire they were to wear to the gala. In nearly every other place on the planet, all of this may have sounded rather suspect or at least unusual, but this was the Big Easy. Walking along Decatur after his shopping trip, one of numerous T-shirts on display in a storefront had caught the beast's attention: "Keep New Orleans Weird" it urged. *And so I shall.*

Thursday, after tending to life's usual tedium, the beast called the shop and learned that all four "executioner" wardrobes had been retrieved. Exhilaration coursed through his veins as he drove to the nearest home improvement store to purchase some tools, steel chain, heavy-duty S hooks, Eye hooks, and a few other things. After all, what was a party without favors?

CHAPTER 44

Friday night had come, and Beth was waiting in her car for Mandi's arrival. She hated to give up her parking place in front of her apartment on Madison, especially during Carnival, but her equipment was too bulky to tote the distance to Burgundy, practically on the opposite side of the Quarter. Beth had caught a break, though. She made the block once, and stopped the second time around, to wait while a white SUV obligingly vacated a spot just past the corner tavern and almost directly across the street from the green, two-story building where Beth would do the shoot. The driver of the car that turned behind her was not as gracious. Motorists in the Crescent City are quick on the horn, and this one blared away at Beth, who rolled down her window and gave the usual Big Easy response—the prominent showing of a middle finger.

Since Beth was early, she considered going inside to begin getting her things set up. Mandi had the combination for the gate lock, so she could let herself in. However, since it would take Beth a couple of trips to get everything in, she opted to wait for Mandi to lend a hand.

While maintaining a close watch for her friend, Beth noticed an eye-patched pirate approaching on the opposite side of the street. The buccaneer had apparently gotten into the grog, wobbling along the sidewalk and slurring unintelligible lyrics. He listed to the right every few steps, bumping against the wall and causing his dangling cutlass to clank. He'd tip his bottle for a slug then brace himself for another few steps. By the time he made his way to the small yellow building at 453 Burgundy, his unsteady legs apparently could go no farther. After again propping himself against the wall and taking another pull, he slowly sank to a sitting position. Once he adjusted the red bandana tied about his head, he was motionless.

About that time, Beth spotted Mandi's canary-yellow Crossfire pass by, and as Beth exited her own vehicle, she saw Mandi disappear around the corner, taking a left at St. Louis. She was making the same circuit Beth had made, in search of a place to park, and Beth prayed she had the same good fortune. If Mandi had too much of a problem, it would give her an excuse to abandon the shoot and return home. Beth's concern grew when she saw the Crossfire continue down Conti, passing Burgundy. *Shit.*

Five minutes later however, Mandi strolled around the tavern on the corner. "Hey, girlfriend!" Beth beckoned. "Come give me a hand."

As they set the equipment on the sidewalk, Beth asked Mandi where she had parked. "On Conti, across from the wax museum."

"Good." Beth reached in one pocket, then another. "Shit. Please tell me you have that paper I gave you. I must have left mine at the apartment."

"I've got it, but bear with me. These jeans are so tight, it may take me a minute." After working a hand into her pocket, Mandi said, "Hold my keys. Now that they're out of the way, I can reach it."

Although it took some effort, Mandi produced the paper. "Call it out to me," Beth instructed.

A buzzer sounded as Beth punched in the last number, and she pushed the black, iron-barred gate. As Mandi held it open, Beth set her gear inside; then the two women carried it through a long dark, brick archway. The echoes of their chatter soon faded away in the corridor, and the soused swashbuckler outside rose effortlessly on strong, sturdy legs, and unerringly strode with purpose to the same gate, and entered the sequence of numbers he had just heard Mandi from Mandeville read off to her companion.

The beast glided through the dim corridor with impunity, on the trail of his prey. The same scent that he had gotten a whiff of on the sidewalk, while the women stood outside the gate, hung in the stagnant air. In the courtyard beyond, he inspected his surroundings.

The area was nestled among four connecting two-story townhouses, insulated from the raucous din of Bourbon Street, a mere two blocks away. The only sound in the night was the soothing, steady trickle of the fountain in the center of the courtyard. Lights were on in two of the four units, drapes drawn in both. Although the beast could not discern any numbers from his vantage point, he easily followed the now familiar perfumed fragrance to door number 3.

Stepping farther back for a wider view of the unit, he noticed that the bottom edge of a curtain had errantly hung on the interior sill of a large window. Someone had pulled the curtain aside to look out the window and afterwards carelessly let it fall out of proper position. Silently, the beast edged behind the flora of the perimeter garden and crouched at the window, peering through a triangular opening conveniently created by the drapery mishap.

Oriental rugs covered the hardwood floor of a spacious room. White fluted columns separated the great room from what, judging from the buffet and china cabinet, was the dining room beyond. The table however, had been moved to the far side of the main room, and Mandi from Mandeville was poised behind one of the pillars, donning only black heels and fishnet stockings.

Beth—that was the artist's name, the beast recalled. Unadorned as she was, there was a sensuousness about the petite, titian-haired damsel. With a touch of makeup here and there, in the right clothes and a few jeweled accessories, she would be as dazzling as her friend—even "beast-worthy." She definitely warranted further investigation, but that would have to wait.

Only one occupant at a time was allowed entry to the holy-of-holies of the beast's brainwork. While the legs, derriere, and lower back of the current object of his ruminations were boldly exhibited, she leaned behind the column far enough to cover her upper body. This posture, coupled with the pressure exerted by the stilettos, caused the magnificently contoured ass of New Orleans' hottest mom to cock up and out. Just above the right cheek was a small tattoo of some kind. All in all, it was one of the most inviting positions the beast could envision.

Turning the dimmer switch, and adjusting the shades atop her tripods, the artist experimented with the lighting. The beast leered in rapture as the room darkened and erupted by rhythmic flashes into a tableau of supreme eroticism.

The echo of hard heels striking brick, followed by laughter, snapped the beast out of his trance. Someone was approaching through the archway. He moved without a trace of panic, quietly and swiftly, away from the window, lurking in the darkness of a recess off the courtyard until the intruders ambled off in the direction of another unit. Returning to his voyeuristic station, the beast saw the artist bent over, packing up, and Mandi from Mandeville was out of sight, most likely getting dressed. It was time for the beast to also be on the move.

CHAPTER 45

Earlier that day, before the lingering last ocher rays from the western winter sky were extinguished, the beast, sporting the pirate outfit to which he had treated himself the previous day, had steered a rental car into the Conti Street parking lot. He was disappointed, but not concerned, that he had to settle for a space to the right, on the west side, farthest away from the abandoned abode that would serve as his dungeon for the night. The increased risk of being seen and forced to improvise only made the anticipation more titillating.

Unlike with Sweet Cindy, when he had desired a mobile dungeon, all that the beast now required of a vehicle was an anonymous means of transporting his tools, which he had stowed in a duffle bag and tossed into the backseat of the blue Chevy Aveo. Backing the compact into the space to hide the license plate, the pirate slung the bag over a shoulder, locked the doors via the remote on the key ring, and headed toward the slave quarters.

Halfway across the lot, a gray Dodge Neon wheeled past him, double-parking behind a car on the east side. By the time the beast drew near, the occupants—two young couples—had gotten out. As the pirate walked past them, he warned they would probably get towed, prompting the driver to tell him to get fucked. "I intend to," the pirate replied, never breaking his stride.

Stepping on broken brick and other debris at the entrance of the last vacant building, the beast heard one of the girls say to her companions, "Poor thing. He must be homeless."

He had arranged everything on the third floor. The most arduous task had been manhandling a discarded metal drum up the stairs. Although corroding, it proved sturdy enough to support his weight when he turned it on end, and stood upon it to set the hooks in an exposed overhead beam, and hang the chains. After sawing and hammering a few cypress planks in place, he was practically done.

Now that the photo session was over, the beast hurried to his car, poured out the water that was in his rum bottle, and filled it with the chloroform stashed under the seat. He quickly made his way around the corner at Dauphine, where he waited and watched.

Mandi Charbonnet soon emerged around the corner at the other end of the block. The same drunken pirate she and Beth had seen earlier was aimlessly stumbling his way in her direction, periodically pivoting in circles, oblivious to everything, certainly not paying any attention to her. In actuality, the beast was wheeling about in order to maintain a 360-degree lookout for witnesses. As he neared his prey, he paused to open the bottle. Slowly staggering, he retrieved a bandana tucked in his belt.

Ten yards from her, Mandi saw the drunken seaman with the eye-patch pouring his booze on a kerchief. *What the hell is he doing now? What is that odd smell?* Instinctively, she took an evasive step toward the street to give the oddball a wide berth, but before her other foot fell, the kerchief was pressed to her face.

The beast knew that he had approximately twenty minutes before she came to. Easily hefting her over a shoulder, he walked briskly into the parking lot, momentarily startled by several teenage boys standing by the first outbuilding. Some were zipping up, others still relieving themselves.

"Hey, Jack Sparrow!" one of them called out. "Looks like it's no nooky for you. She's wasted, man!"

CHAPTER 46

A hard slap by a gauntleted hand across Mandi's face stunned her back to consciousness. But it took a few seconds to see through the pain and bring her eyes into focus on the visage of the pirate just inches away. The beast had discarded the eye-patch, and Mandi's panic-stricken brain told her hands to strike out and claw at the evil-inhabited orbs peering into hers, but her limbs remained unresponsive.

Confused by this neurological incongruity and the throbbing ache in her shoulders, Mandi became aware that she was handcuffed, arms positioned above her head. Looking upward, she saw the small chain linking the two metal cuffs hoisted on a large hook at the end of a heavy chain suspended from a beam. However, the pressure of her full body weight was not channeled to her wrists since her toes were touching the floor.

"Who are you?" she screamed. The next words she intended to hurl were, "and what do you want?" However, her initial inquiry was swiftly met with another facial blow.

"Did I give you permission to talk?" the beast rhetorically asked. "No one knows that you are here. You are absolutely helpless. Whether you live or die is entirely up to me."

The captive's ensuing scream was stifled by a cloth gag. "I gave you more credit than that, love. Knowing that your life hangs in the balance, and that it is my finger on the scales, I assumed that you would see the wisdom of not distracting me. Oh well, you know what they say about assuming. So my dear, you can just suck on that rag while we get down to business."

Mandi's eyes bulged in terror as the beast drew his cutlass. "Ah, I see you're impressed. It's authentic you know. I found it in that antique weapons shop on Royal Street." He held the point of the blade to her throat for a lingering moment. After pulling it away, the beast touched the blood trickling from a corner of his captive's mouth. Placing the sharp tip of the weapon at the center of her chest, and with a quick flick of the wrist, he sliced away a button. "I've already seen you naked, Mandi. You have a beautiful body. Surely, you know that. But what you also need to understand is that it is here tonight for *my* pleasure. I will use it in any way that I choose."

The captive whimpered as he lopped off each of the remaining buttons. When the last one fell to the floor, he moved behind her and drew the blade vertically, cutting the blouse in half. Bit by bit, the top was shredded and flung away.

It was during this process, while the beast was behind her and no longer obstructed her line of vision, that Mandi saw that she was poised astride the narrow edge of a horizontal wood plank. It was anchored to the floor by diagonally positioned smaller boards. Almost comically, the head of a child's stick-horse was affixed to the front.

After stripping his captive of her blouse and bra, the beast likewise made short shrift of her jeans and panties. He leaned in close behind her, whispering in an ear, "You will have no secrets, no boundaries, nothing except maybe your life, when I am through with you." He reached around her with his gloved hands, cupping her bosom.

"To be sure, you will be ashamed for the rest of your days that total strangers will know the depth and tightness of every orifice; but it's not all about sex." He ran his hands along her curves, elucidating, "It will be much more than a carnal conquest. By the time I am done, I will take and own your soul, your thoughts. You will never be able to evict me from your dreams."

Mandi began to fidget and shift her weight. "I see you're getting acquainted with your pony," the beast noted, stepping around her and giving the stick-horse's head a pat. "Allow me to elaborate on the ride you are about to take." Pointing to her feet, which were stretched upward on tiptoes, he explained, "It's the inevitable fatigue of your leg muscles that will eventually force the torture. That's right my dear, torture.

"You will notice that your pony's back is at a height that, while you stand on your toes, as now, that tantalizing twat of yours clears this nasty, old, ragged, cypress edge by about an inch. Your arms are obviously of no use in relieving any pressure and before long, your calves and toes will cramp. Those exquisite legs will quiver, and when they desperately need a rest, you will have to settle onto your bareback pony. Your weight on the narrow, rough and splintered edge will dig into that sweet, tender, love nest, crushing its delicate flesh, and causing excruciating pain. It will be such agony that you will somehow summon the strength to force yourself back onto your toes. And guess what? It starts all over again! Up and down, up and down. Don't you see? That's the *ride!*"

The beast's prediction proved terribly accurate. His captive's leg muscles burned fiercely under the strain, their only relief coming at the expense of the promised crushing and laceration. Mandi repeatedly groaned, at times screaming into her gag, much to the glee of the beast. When it appeared she could take no more, he announced, "Let's get your mind on something else, shall we?"

Reaching into his duffle bag, the beast produced two "alligator" clamps. He squeezed them open, and dramatically held them at his captive's breasts. Eight "teeth" lined each spring-loaded device, and when the beast released them Mandi felt each tooth cruelly bite into the super-sensitive nerves concentrated in her nipples. Her muffled screams intensified.

Despite the horrific messages emitting from her brain, Mandi's nipples and clitoris responded as if they had a mind of their own; blood rushed to the stimulated sites, causing them to swell. "You're ashamed at your arousal," the beast informed her. She loathed her tormentor all the more because what he said was true.

At last, the incessant piercing drew tiny, crimson droplets, which the beast licked away with an undulating tongue. Mandi shuddered at his slimy touch, almost unbelievably preferring the wicked, unrelenting jaws of the clamps. With a finger, the beast confirmed the swollen state of his captive's womanhood the next time she raised on trembling legs. "Okay, that's enough," he said in a tone that almost seemed tender.

It was music to her ears, and hope soared yet higher when he removed the gag and clamps, heaved her over a shoulder, and off of the hook. She sucked in air, and could instantly feel the blood returning to her numb arms dangling down his back. He laid her on a blanket and removed the handcuffs. Rummaging in his sack, he tossed some clothing on top of her collapsed form. "Get dressed," he ordered, glancing at his watch. She only wished that she could comply with these welcome words.

Unable to move, Mandi could only watch as the pirate dressed her. Her heart sank into oblivion as he did so, for the attire was not her own. It was a woman's pirate costume. The miniskirt was actually in two pieces: the top portion was red, with a jagged hem, and cut at a diagonal; beneath it, and extending a few inches below the top portion, was a similarly cut black-and-white striped piece with hidden garters. The shirt was a white, midriff-cut, off-the-shoulder, peasant style, over which the beast placed a black satin lace-up corset. Next, he slid on black fishnet stockings, secured the garters, and added black high-top boots. As two final touches, he added an eye-patch and a red-cloth headband.

"Please," she sobbed.

"Shut the fuck up, or the headband goes around your slutty mouth." After looking again at his watch, he stooped to help her to her feet. "Upsy daisy," he said, once again slinging her over a shoulder.

The beast carried his captive to the adjoining room, and eased her down until her bottom settled on the nylon webbing of a swing of some sort. A swivel connected a conglomeration of nylon straps to a chain hung from an overhead beam. While Mandi was still trying to decipher the strange contraption, she felt the pinch of the handcuffs return to her wrists. One cuff of a second set was snapped shut around the small chain connecting the pair on her wrists. He ran the other open cuff of the second set through a slot in the swivel, and locked it. Thus, once again, Mandi's hands were held in place above her head, useless.

The beast gently pushed her backward until her shoulder blades rested on another strap, forcing her legs upward. Once her booted feet were inserted through stirrups at the ends of two other straps, Mandi was suspended in the swing; forced backward, legs up and spread eagle. Yes, the beast thought, presentation was everything.

Re-checking the time—ten minutes past midnight—the beast walked to a window on the north side of the room. As a black limousine pulled to a stop at the parking lot entrance, he pulled a hood over his head and said to Mandi, "Make yourself comfortable, dear. I must go downstairs and greet our guests."

The beast waved the four new arrivals over. When they joined him at the building's entrance, he simply jerked his head in the direction they were to follow him. On the way up he explained that they were not to speak while there. In the upper chamber where Mandi was helplessly cinched and trussed, the beast indicated with a circular motion of a hand that the four should gather around the captive. His further instructions to the guests were also intended as a warning to her.

"Lords of darkness, we have here, a traitor who has confessed her betrayal. Her sentence was two-fold. First was the element of retribution, physical punishment exacted solely to inflict such pain as to forever deter any recurrence of a deed so foul. That punishment has just been carried out by me, her husband.

"The second phase of her sentence is to test her claims of repentance. Taking the word of such a conniving wench will not suffice. She must prove, to our collective satisfaction, the assurance of her total submission to absolute male domination. This test is not one to be rightly judged solely by her mate. It requires complete objectivity. Why? you may ask.

Because if she proves herself believable, I am bound to let her live. If any among you are dissatisfied in her submission, there is but one penalty left, which I am equally bound to impose—death."

"This is bullshit," one of the hooded guests said. Yanking off his hood, he turned to leave; but before he took a second step, the beast pulled a small pistol from his belt, and put a pair of bullets into the back of the unsuspecting man's head.

"Anyone else care to disrupt the proceedings?" the beast asked the other three. "Good," he said when no one moved or spoke. "Follow my instructions, you not only live, you get his share," the beast added, nudging the lifeless body with a booted foot. Returning his attention to the captive, the beast held his cutlass to her neck. "My dear wife, do *you* understand?" When she merely nodded, the beast backhanded her, shouting, "Impudent bitch! Speak when I ask you a question. I repeat, Do you understand?"

"Yes," she mewled.

"You are completely open to us. You have never felt so naked in every respect," he said, slowly spinning her in the swing for the other three hooded men to get a good look. "You know that these executioners will see your most private, personal places. Any time they desire, they can reach out and touch those places, and they may do so with anything they choose. They are the strangers of whom I earlier spoke; who will know firsthand, the circumference of your mouth, the abyss of your cunt, and the snugness of your perky little derrière.

"As they twirl you around like a roulette wheel, you will wonder who, and in what orifice, it will be. They may be as rough as they wish, and there is nothing you can do to stop it. Do you understand?"

"Yes," she murmured.

"Yes, *Master*," he corrected, inches from her face.

Hesitating, she finally uttered, "Yes, Master."

"Oh, I understand your confusion. I told you earlier that it was not *all* about sex, but I never said that it had *nothing* to do with it. You really must listen more carefully, dear.

"Gentlemen, I see from your genital protuberances that you also fully understand. So...." The beast paused for dramatic effect as he slid his leather-covered hands under his captive's skirt and pushed it above her trimmed pubis. "Let's begin," he proclaimed, and gave her another spin.

For the next half hour, the beast watched as Mandi was brutally raped and sodomized. To her, of course, it was an eternity in hell. For him, however, time passed much too quickly. He was doubly delighted when, toward the end, while she was twirled and pushed from one to another, he could make out, from a nearby club, the clear beat and lyrics of Van

Halen's "Runnin' with the Devil".

Alas, he thought, all good things must come to an end. "Gentlemen, time to pack your gear and zip up." As the three remaining guests hitched their britches, the beast asked Mandi, "You enjoyed that, didn't you, dear?" She knew it was a statement more than a question, but she also had no doubt that her life depended on her response. In utter desperation and humiliation, she answered in the affirmative. "Well gentlemen, what do you say? Thumbs up, for life; down, for doom."

The three bewildered men weren't sure what to do. Had this madman meant it when he said that whether she lived or died was strictly up to them? If not, giving their thumbs up might very well result in a bullet to their heads. Thumbs down would render this woman's death a certainty. Nervously, they all gave the thumbs up and, along with Mandi, let out a breath of relief when the beast said, "So be it."

"Excuse me for a minute, dear," he said to her, "while I see our guests out. Then I'll release you."

A few minutes later, after the limo drove away, the beast emerged from the stairway and removed his hood. Why, Mandi wondered, had he worn it only in the presence of the others? As much as her body ached and her mind reeled, the answer was quick in coming to her. She was of no concern to him as a witness. He didn't care that she saw his face because, regardless of what he had led her to believe, he intended to kill her. As hard as her brain fought against this realization, there was no other logical explanation.

The beast grabbed her by a foot, still secured in a stirrup, and rotated her in the swing until he was between her outstretched feet. Maybe, she thought, he was only going to take his turn in raping her, but then he pulled the sword. With a flat side of the blade, he tapped the inside of her left thigh and with the tip, toyed with the dainty folds of her labia.

Cherishing whatever sliver of hope there might be that she was wrong, Mandi reminded her captor, "You said that you were going to release me."

"And I shall," the beast replied, plunging the blade with all his power. "I release you from your shame."

Then, leaving everything behind, including the gun, he calmly walked across the parking lot, down Conti, to the corner at Dauphine. Crossing the street, he waltzed into Déjà Vu Bar and Grill, and ordered breakfast.

*****

Meanwhile, nineteen-year-old Ricky Anderson had lagged behind his pals. They had just arrived in the Big Easy after a long drive from

Lebanon, Tennessee. Ricky had drawn one of the first shifts at the wheel, and had been drinking beer pretty much since relinquishing control to his successor. The closest parking space to the Quarter that they could find was on Rampart Street. By the time they crossed Burgundy, Ricky was desperately looking for a place where he could relieve his enlarged and aching bladder.

Noticing some empty ruins on the far side of a parking lot on Conti, Ricky told the others that he would meet them at Paradise Isle, and trotted away to the abandoned building at the end. He had heard rumors about how tough the cops were concerning such things, but even if any of the boys in blue came around in search of first-degree urinators, Ricky felt sure that he could be finished by the time they scoured the first three buildings.

He was contemplating the incomparable ecstasy of taking, as he was now, a much needed piss when he heard a continuous, steady creaking from above. Now that the frenzy of his emergency had passed, Ricky embarked on a mission of curiosity.

He found nothing notable on the first two floors; but when he ascended to the third level a shadow caught his eye. *The silhouette of a woman lying in a hammock?* The same early-morning gossamer that gently turned the suspended apparition also blew away the veil of clouds which had previously shrouded the moon. Ricky walked deeper into the pewter aura of the chamber until the sight of the sword protruding between the woman's legs froze him in his tracks. Retreating, he stumbled to the floor, and found himself staring into the unblinking opaque eyes of a dead man. For a moment, but only for a moment, Ricky Anderson was unable to force any sound from his vocal chords.

Around the corner, the beast was taking his first bite of scrambled eggs when he heard a man's hysterical shriek pierce the raucous din of the French Quarter. He dabbed a napkin to his mouth and smiled at the thought: *Mandi, you vixen. Even in death, you can make a man scream.*

PART III: Tribulation and Hope

CHAPTER 47

To hell with Deschamps, Bo thought, as he put in a call to Lenny Pitre. It was Thursday morning and there had been no word from Lieutenant Deschamps since Bo first dropped in on him a full week earlier. Bo had worked with Lenny at the Jackson Police Department years ago, before Lenny retired and took a job as an investigator with the Mississippi Gaming Commission. The new work necessitated a close relationship with all of the casinos' security forces, and doors had quickly opened for Lenny. First came a security position at a casino in the Mississippi Delta, a Phoenix of wealth dramatically rising from the cotton fields outside Tunica, Mississippi. It was in the same poverty-stricken area, known as Sugar Ditch, that Robert Kennedy had visited in the 1960s. The next career move for Lenny Pitre was a promotion to head up security at the same company's New Orleans facility on Canal Street, when it reopened after Katrina. Bo hoped that his former colleague could be of assistance in skirting the post-hurricane web of municipal red tape. If Bo couldn't get what he needed from Deschamps, he'd take a stab at going around him.

Bo briefly explained to Lenny what little he knew of the murders and his interest in them. "Yeah, I read about those in the paper," Pitre said, "but why the call to me?"

Pausing after relating Lieutenant Deschamps' stonewalling, Bo meekly continued on, "I was hoping…"

"Let me guess," Pitre interrupted, a flashbulb going off in his head. "You thought that since the mayor and police superintendent are black, and I'm of the same 'persuasion', I might have an in?"

"Well, do you?"

"I ought to be offended," Pitre said.

"Come on, Lenny. Get off your high horse. We're both realists, and it's just the way things are," Bo replied. "Can you help me or not?"

"I'll make a few calls, but don't make this a habit."

It was afternoon before Bo heard back from him, which worked out well since the wait had afforded Bo time to do something to justify his participation in the fire and boot-beating cases. Now he was holed up in Lenny's office, flipping through copies of the investigative reports. Lenny had pulled some serious strings to gain Bo a paltry hour of access, and there were conditions to boot. Lenny had to promise his undisclosed contact that none of the paperwork would leave his office. And, while note taking was permissible, nothing was to be photocopied. It wasn't a homerun, but at least Bo had managed to get on base.

Working rapidly, he began with the autopsy report of Cindy Babineaux, which listed two gunshot wounds to the back of the head as her cause of death. The report's description of the genital mutilation eerily resembled that which had been sadistically inflicted on Serena. The pathologist recovered both projectiles which, according to the ballistics report from the crime lab, were identified as .22 caliber "shorts." A foreign pubic hair, most likely Caucasian, was recovered from the body as well, but no semen.

The official cause of Mandi Charbonnet's death was exsanguination, secondary to a stab wound to the genital area, penetrating the uterus, both intestines, and stomach. There was also physical evidence of ante-mortem torture, rape, and sodomy. Semen was collected and determined to have come from more than one source. This was far different than in the murders of Cindy Babineaux and Serena, where no semen was found; but Bo soon saw that the police had nevertheless connected their homicides to Mandi Charbonnet's.

Bud Ritchie, whose body was found with Charbonnet's, was killed by two gunshots to the back of the head, just like Cindy Babineaux. Even more forensically significant were the projectiles themselves: not only were they .22 caliber "shorts," the lands and grooves perfectly matched the two rounds that killed Cindy Babineaux. All four projectiles were conclusively determined to have been fired from the firearm recovered at the Charbonnet/Ritchie crime scene: a stainless-steel, five-shot, snub-nose, mini-revolver or derringer. No fingerprints of value were found on the gun, or on an antique sword removed from Charbonnet's body, and there was not yet any information in the file concerning a registration trace of the gun.

Finishing with the autopsy and crime lab reports, Bo turned to the investigative notes and summaries, reading that one Beth Callahan was believed to be the last person to have seen Mandi Charbonnet alive.

Callahan, a Jackson Square artist residing at a Madison Street apartment, advised authorities that she had met Charbonnet at 451 Burgundy, Apartment 3, at 2100 hours on the evening in question, for the purpose of taking photographs of Charbonnet for Callahan's use in a painting. According to Callahan, they left the residence together between 2215 and 2230 hours. Callahan last saw Charbonnet walk left, around the corner of Burgundy and Conti. It was noted that, upon Charbonnet's arrival earlier, she told Callahan that she had parked on Conti. Indeed, the police found Charbonnet's 2010 Chrysler Crossfire parked on the 900 block of the street. After being processed for possible evidence, the vehicle was released to Adam Charbonnet, the victim's husband. Callahan reported that she did not see anything unusual, or any person of a suspicious nature, and she could not imagine anyone having any reason to harm Mrs. Charbonnet.

There were more pages, but Bo's hour was up. Lenny had gone out on a limb, and Bo wasn't about to lop it off and let his friend take a fall. After thanking Lenny and returning the papers, Bo left. Exiting the casino on the Canal Street side, he walked the short distance to the Aquarium of the Americas and caught a trolley car to Jackson Square.

Madison is a one-block, one-way bystreet just north of the Square, running from Chartres to Decatur. Despite its position in the heart of the French Quarter, few locals—even the pizza delivery guys—know of its existence. Hurrying across ever-busy Decatur Street before the red light changed, Bo stopped momentarily to catch his breath at the corner of Madison Street. He was in front of Tujague's, a bar built in the early-to-mid 19th century on the site of an old Spanish armory. It was where writer William Sydney Porter, better known as O. Henry, became a fixture during the year he had made the Big Easy home, and where Bo had sated his thirst his first night in the city over a year ago.

Looking down the byway, Bo spotted the building that had to be the address he was looking for. Counting only three floors, he wondered whether he had made a mistake in recalling the artist's apartment number as 4A. Midway along the block, Bo found the address numbers encased in blue tiles above a black gate of scrolled ironwork that guarded a dim, brick passage to a courtyard. From the sidewalk, Bo could see a statue of St. Francis of Assisi nestled in a corner among ferns and palmetto. He ran a finger down the buttons, on a panel mounted to the left of the gate, until he came to one labeled: "Callahan 4A." He had remembered correctly, but was at a loss where the fourth floor was located.

Whatever. It's New Orleans, isn't it? He pushed the intercom button, and just when it seemed by the ensuing silence that Beth Callahan was not home, a female voice emanated from the speaker, "Who is it?"

CHAPTER 48

The line separating insanity and normality is not always one drawn with a sharpened pencil. Oft times, the demarcation is actually no line at all, only blurred gradations of gray. This is especially so when it comes to dealing with those possessed with artistic leanings. They are blessed, yet cursed; gifted, yet afflicted. They run the gamut from being upbeat, outgoing, and creative "movers and shakers", to withdrawn and sullen invalids. Their mood fluctuations are similar to those suffered by bipolars, only not as extreme. And more often than not, the change in the artist's temperament is triggered by something internal rather than any circumstance imposed by the outside world. The artist is, therefore, unpredictable and despises routine, preferring impulse and new experiences infused with feeling and meaning.

For as long as Beth Callahan could remember she had been motivated by the need to understand and to be understood. Yet lately she felt neither, and her attempts at self-analysis were no more productive than trying to solve the riddle of the Sphinx. Nevertheless, Beth's consciousness took a stroll across the terrain of her past; and everyone's past begins with their parents.

Beth's father, Robert Callahan Sr., had recently retired after many years of teaching philosophy. Family aside, his great loves were Tulane University, books, and fishing. Since he came from a family of means, he was able to enjoy these pleasures as he wished. His retirement was not a complete severance of the scholastic umbilical cord. Green and blue had run in Beth's father's veins for so long that totally shutting off the Green Wave lifeline would have proven as fatal as a blood clot. Unable to grasp the thought of never again waxing eloquent and challenging young minds in a Tulane classroom, he was now teaching a class on

Tuesdays and Thursdays under the title of professor emeritus.

The professor was a perennial favorite among the students, especially a co-ed by the name of Rachel, Beth's mother. For obvious reasons, they had kept their dating secret, but married just as soon as Rachel graduated; out of love, of course, plus the fact that she was pregnant with Robert junior. Beth came along four years later, and her younger brother Jake arrived, kicking and screaming his way into their world, in another couple of years. While Beth's father presided in an ivy-shrouded, stone hall of academia, her mother oversaw the rearing of the three children in the stately Callahan ancestral house on St. Charles Avenue, in the Garden District. When the nest had emptied, Rachel opened a bookstore on Prytania Street, where the professor now kept her company, at least until he started to wear on her nerves. On those occasions, Rachel merely made some off-handed comment about the weather, opining what it might bode as far as the fish biting. Invariably, he was soon out of her hair.

Brought up as free thinkers, and encouraged to fully tap their individual proclivities, Beth and her brothers gravitated to different avocations, but ones sharing a common denominator: some form of artistic talent. Jake was in school at the CIA—not at Langley, learning to be a spy; rather, he was at the Culinary Institute of America, in Hyde Park, New York. Beth didn't know whether Jake would return to New Orleans or seek his fortune elsewhere, but it was hard to imagine a good chef not doing well in a city as addicted to fine cuisine as the Big Easy.

Bobby, too, was imaginative; but, being somewhat more obsessed with perfection than Beth and Jake, his artistry was more appropriately channeled through a career as an architect. He was working at a firm in Destin, now a booming resort on the Emerald Coast of Florida's panhandle. The family had vacationed there many times while Beth and the boys were growing up, when it was still a sleepy, little fishing village. While Bobby saw economic opportunity in the sprawling growth, his father longed for the old days, never seeing the irony in ceasing the vacations in Destin because of the influx of tourists. He insisted he had never been one of them; he was a part-time local. If it could somehow be accomplished without loss of life, the professor wished that a hurricane would level everything, returning the land to its natural state.

"The world, as God made it, is truly magnificent," he once told Bobby. "No architect will ever design anything of such majestic beauty. We are entrusted with it during the brief time we are here. It is a special stewardship; for if not our responsibility, then whose?" Beth had overheard the remarks, and they made an indelible impression on her, prompting her to capture the world's beauty, majesty, and allure on film, beginning with a disposable Kodak that her father purchased for her at K & B Drugs.

After abandoning Florida, the saltwater bays, lakes, bayous, and marshes southeast of New Orleans became Robert Callahan's wildlife and fishing Mecca, always taking the entire family along with him. While some, if not most girls, would have considered this a form of parental torture, Beth found that she had an instinctive longing for the natural, the pastoral, the bucolic. Whether fishing, paddling around in a pirogue, or wandering the Spanish moss-shrouded trails, she was quite at home in the wild, and nature seemed to welcome her. She was as enamored by the natural world's anomalies and flaws, as by its symmetry and beauty. She was just as apt to drop everything and grab her camera to memorialize an oddity, as she was to capture some amazing array of colors.

The progression from photography to drawing, and ultimately to painting, was a natural one for Beth. She felt an insatiable longing to convey beauty not only as it is, but also as it could be; beyond the realm of film, into those of imagination and interpretation. But it was a gift that was occasionally unsettling. On more than one occasion, Beth had been told that some scene she painted from a panorama in her mind's eye actually depicted a real event in the life of someone who was theretofore a total stranger to her.

Now Beth felt that everything was shutting down. Whatever the cause or explanation of the artist's vacillations in temperament, one thing is certain: when the emotional pendulum swings downward, it is difficult, if not impossible, to do any creative work. Fortunately, the artist's talent, their gift,-is not lost. But even though the gas in the tank has not evaporated, the creative engine that drives the artist goes into vapor lock, resulting in a complete stall.

In Beth Callahan's case, added to these usual artistic quirks, were the emotional effects of Mandi Charbonnet's brutal demise. Beth just couldn't get her mind wrapped around it. Even though she knew Mandi was gone, the past four days Beth kept expecting to hear her friend's voice each time she answered the phone. Beth was in the uncharted waters of utter numbness, and it scared her. She was unaware that this was a normal defense mechanism of the mind, allowing her to absorb Mandi's death as she was able, thereby protecting her from being completely overwhelmed.

Beth was actually questioning her sanity. At times, she didn't feel like moving. "I'm just too sad to do anything," she had told her concerned, inquiring mother. Then inexplicably, she became fidgety and restless.

However, if she got up and about, she soon lost focus of her task. Her emotions were constantly changing, leaving her exhausted at the end of the day.

As one might expect, there was the sadness—the crushing sensation that it would never release its grip and that the tears would never cease; but the weight of the melancholy was made more onerous by self-blame. Beth's whim to paint something new, coupled with her manic insistence to involve Mandi as the anonymous, enticing vessel, had resulted in Mandi's death; or at least Beth so believed. She had been doomed to a life of curiosity, and one need only ask the proverbial cat where that trait leads. Even worse, Beth's guilt was a two-headed monster: not only did she blame herself for putting Mandi in harm's way, she also stood convicted at the bar of her own conscience for certain feelings and desires. How could she ever again engage in the pleasures of life when her dearest friend had been cruelly robbed of life altogether?

Mandi was the first person with whom Beth was close to, to die, at least since Beth reached adulthood. Thus, when it came to grief, she was a virgin. She had only imagined what the experience would be like, based upon her observations of others when she was a child. She recalled from the archives of her memory, dour, black-clad people who observed a strict period of mourning, conveying the stern conviction that any self-indulgence before the lapse of the expected time of bereavement would be blasphemous to the memory of the departed loved one.

Beth's very nature was at odds with her preconception, for she took an artistic approach to every aspect of her life. She knew herself to be gifted, intuitive, original, and unique. She had focused on her individuality and on carving her own distinct image. At twenty-eight, Beth was still an attractive woman with a 32-24-34 figure, which was not too damned bad, in her opinion. She longed for the art of love, as much as she relished the love of art. However, self-absorption, tempera mentality, and unpredictability, while going with the territory of being an artist, are not exactly ingredients of a recipe for any kind of lasting, meaningful relationship. She had resolved to pair her stubbornness with her keen eye for what is truly unique, special, and rare, searching for such a man—one who could see, beneath the shell, the person she knew herself deep down, to be. The passion for which she hungered was rooted in quality, not quantity.

Above all however, Beth desired to be passionate and true to her feelings, which ran deep. She had never before been afraid to go emotionally where others feared to tread. Yet she now feared that remaining true to her love and passion for life would be disrespectful of Mandi's loss. And without that passion, Beth knew that her art would be as dead as her friend.

This was the conundrum in which Beth was entangled; two terrains of the same heart were in conflict. Beth had been one to take pride in her inner strength and self-sufficiency, but now she felt insecure, suspicious, irritable, and even angry. Only the night before, while taking a shower, she was suddenly overcome by a white-hot rage, screaming at the top of her lungs before sliding to the bottom of the tub, washed by chlorinated water and pure tears.

Although Beth had faith that she would eventually get through this awful experience, she was equally certain that she would never be the same again; and if she were not the same, nor would her art. She had turned to yoga and meditation techniques to try to clear her head of this emotional morass, and was doing so again when the doorbell rang.

CHAPTER 49

Beth Callahan believed that, as Americans, the most basic right we enjoy is that of simply being left alone, particularly in the asylum of one's home. Wishing at the moment to exercise that privilege, Beth's frustration in trying to cope with Mandi Charbonnet's death quickly evolved into irritation that anyone would be so insistent in invading her personal space and contemplation. Still creeped out by what had happened to Mandi, Beth was acutely mindful of the counteracting forces that seemed to be in perpetual motion among the denizens of the Big Easy: the carefree, live-and-let-live attitude of the gentler souls, and the dark nature of those who preyed upon them. One never knew which of the two sorts the winds of fate might blow to one's door. *Should she answer or not?* For the first time in a long while, Beth Callahan felt indecisive and vulnerable, and she didn't like the incapacitating feeling enveloping her. Okay Beth, an inner voice told her, get yourself together; you will *not* be a victim in your own home. Steeling herself, she pressed the intercom button and asked, "Who is it?"

"Ms. Callahan? Beth Callahan?" a male voice asked.

"I know who *I* am," Beth snapped. "Who are *you?*" *Jesus, Beth. What are you doing? If he's a potential customer, you're pushing him away. Calm down.*

"Ma'am, my name is Bo Landry. I'm a private investigator."

Okay, he's not a customer, Beth immediately thought. There was no reason to make nice. The image of Jim Rockford, the character portrayed by James Garner in *The Rockford Files,* a television series her father used to watch religiously, popped into her head. "What do you want?" she asked, and sarcastically added, "I'm not in the middle of a divorce, I work for myself, so there's no reason for you to be doing a background check on me, and I've witnessed no car accident."

She heard the man softly chuckle. "Yes, ma'am, I understand. I just want to talk to you for a few minutes about Mandi Charbonnet."

"Look, I don't know what kind of dirt you're trying to dig up on Mandi or why, but she was a good, decent person, and was just buried, so...." Beth had to pause, choked with emotion.

"I know, Ms. Callahan. It isn't what you think. I'm trying to help, and I know what it's like for you. I lost someone to the same killer."

"What do you mean?"

Bo waited for two pedestrians to pass. "Ma'am, do you really want to have this discussion overheard by everyone who walks by down here? Just ten minutes, that's all I'm asking."

After an ensuing silence, Beth advised, "Okay, ten minutes."

"Thank you, ma'am."

"On one condition."

"What's that?"

"You stop calling me ma'am.

Again, Beth heard the good-natured laugh, then, "Deal."

The next thing Bo heard was the electronic click of the gate unlocking, and he pushed it open.

Beth quickly found her cell phone and called Dr. Marsalis, the persnickety but kind, elderly widower who lived in the apartment below. She informed him that a man identifying himself as Bo Landry, a private investigator, was on his way up to see her, and that she had agreed to speak with him for ten minutes. She asked Marsalis to call the police if she did not call him back by that time. He agreed, but of course was still prying for more information when the knock on the door came.

"I'm sorry, Dr. Marsalis, I have to go. Thanks a million."

Bo took his time climbing the stairs to 4A. Although he had seen an elevator, he wanted to give Callahan time to think about things before his arrival. Wondering what he might ask usually caused interviewees to run all kinds of possibilities through their curious minds. Besides, taking the stairs afforded him the opportunity to get a better view of the layout. You never knew what might be important, and he, too, suffered a streak of curiosity. He had to find out how a building with three floors had an apartment numbered 4A. As it turned out, her place was a loft apartment perched atop the third story, set back from the front of the main block of the structure, completely out of view from the street.

After he knocked on the door, Bo knew that Callahan would be watching him through the glass peephole. He said nothing, but in an effort to put her at some ease, he held his credentials to the tiny round glass. Shortly afterward, he heard the sliding of a chain and turning of a deadbolt.

Whether or not it's a conscious act, we all make visual assessments of the people with whom we have face-to-face conversations. With Bo, it was a cognitive process, and one that he began with Beth Callahan as soon as she opened the door. As he stepped inside and passed within a foot of her, Bo estimated that she was five-foot-three, maybe five-four. Silky, straight, strawberry-blonde hair hung loose, just to the tops of her shoulders. The lips—the upper one only slightly thinner than the invitingly-full bottom one. Other than a smidgen of freckles, her complexion was slightly tanned to a soft, golden shade which he deduced was from the many hours she must spend each day in Jackson Square. The tone gave her prominent, high-set cheeks a pleasing, warm glow.

But what Bo found to be the most interesting of Beth Callahan's facial features were her eyes. They were the color of sapphires, a hue he had rarely seen other than in a mirror. They were as deep in blueness as Serena's had been in green. It was evident however, that Beth Callahan had been crying, and in the milliseconds that ticked away as he walked past her, he wondered if they sparkled like Serena's when her mood was less morose.

Bo allowed Beth to lead him to wherever she would feel the most comfortable talking. The apartment was as one might expect for an artist's single-room studio, but bigger than, and not as cluttered, as Bo had envisioned. A small bathroom was to the left of the entrance, formed by an eight-foot-high partition of painted sheetrock. Bo had time to only sneak a glance, but saw that the floor was laid with small black-and-white octagonal tiles, and a large claw-foot tub sat at the far end. The color-scheme seemed to be mostly black and white, modernly accented with some chrome and a light plum color. To the right, beneath a platform supported by six-by-six square posts, was an area where the artist apparently wore her photographer's hat. Photos of every size, in black and white as well as color, lined the brick wall at the opposite end. Various tripods, shades, and lights stood neatly arranged on the floor, ready for use. A closet, which most likely contained her cameras and other supplies, extended halfway along the brick wall flush with the front door. And beyond that, in the corner, sat a computer.

Following his host into the main quarters, Bo noticed a small staircase at the corner of the photography section spiraling up to the platform which he surmised was her bedroom. Glancing upward, he saw that the boudoir "walls" consisted of numerous alternating strands of small mirrors and crystal prisms, each string separated by one of large black beads. The reflection and refraction of the sunlight, pouring in from skylights high above, and the tall windows of the long wall at the far side of the studio, cast the entire place in a dancing array of every color in the solar spectrum.

Stepping past the staircase, into the great room, Bo saw several easels to his right; some held canvases of what looked to be finished pieces, while others were obviously works in progress. In the corner was a deep laundry-style sink where he supposed she washed the brushes, which were now projecting out of various-shaped and sized jars on shelves above. To the right of the sink were a stacked washer and dryer.

A sitting area occupied the center section of the large chamber, and Beth gestured for him to take a seat on a semi-circular, white sofa, of the 1950s retro ilk. As Bo obliged, he noticed a rolled-up yoga mat propped against the nearby wall. "Would you like some cucumber water?" Beth offered, walking toward the kitchen area.

"Some *what?*" Bo asked.

The tone of the question, which caused Beth to turn and look at him as she reached for the refrigerator handle, as well as Bo's perplexed expression, amused her and somehow eased her anxiety a bit. Not sure that he had heard correctly, and curious as to what he thought he had heard, Bo had arisen from the sofa and was almost to Beth when he saw that even the slightest hint of smile, as fleeting as it was, did indeed cause her eyes to dance—glitter in a deep-blue, ocular sea. Bo was well acquainted with grief, he had suffered it and he had dealt it, and thus had some appreciation of what Beth Callahan was going through. But he could tell that, even amid her turmoil, this lady was not immune to mischief.

"It's just water with a few thin slices of cucumber," she explained with a soft laugh. It was the first time in days she had done so, and it felt as good as it did wrong. "It's calorie-free, but quite refreshing," she added in a matter-of-fact tone.

"Thanks, but I'll pass. I know I'm on the clock."

"Well, have a seat while I make some for me. Your time won't start until I sit down. How's that?"

"Fine by me," Bo replied, ambling back in the direction of the sofa. "But what about your senior-citizen sentry?"

Beth ceased her slicing and turned, standing in amazement between the refrigerator and the bar separating her and her visitor. How did he know? she mused. Seemingly reading her mind and returning to his seat, Bo explained, "If I were you, it's what I would've done. Plus, the old guy who just happened to come out of his apartment on the third floor and linger at the stairs, just as I happened to get there, and then just happened to go back to his apartment as I got halfway up the stairs and he thought I wasn't looking, seemed a little too coincidental. Plus, he didn't exactly have a poker face."

As Bo talked, Beth dropped the cucumber slices into a glass pitcher. "But how could he know you would choose the stairs and not the elevator as most people do?" she asked while stirring.

"Easily enough; he didn't hear the motor."

"Hmmm," was all Beth could come up with, pouring the mixture into a glass of ice. "I have lemonade, if you'd rather have that," she offered.

After declining that as well, Bo told Beth, "I'm serious, what about the old guy? He's going to have the police barreling in here any minute."

As she moved across the room to join him, the sound of her flip-flops drew Bo's attention to a pair of relatively small moving feet, and he thought of his grandmother who warned him long ago when he began to really notice girls, to stay away from those with big feet; that they were mean as hell. He guessed that Beth Callahan weighed about 100 pounds, 110 max. But it was difficult to tell much more about her size or her figure, due to the baggy sweat suit she wore.

Beth took a seat on a modern-styled armless chair of black leather and chrome with an adjustable back, one of two positioned opposite the sofa where Bo sat. Between them was a rather unique coffee table. The top was fashioned from a large, irregularly-shaped piece of cypress, planed smooth and lacquered with a clear sealant, resting on two decorative urns. After considering Bo's question about her neighbor for a moment, Beth flipped open her phone. "Everything is okay, Dr. Marsalis.... Yes, he's still here.... No, it's fine.... I don't think it's necessary.... All right, Dr. Marsalis, I'll be expecting your call in thirty minutes.... Yes, I understand, thirty minutes. Thank you."

Snapping the phone shut, Beth advised Bo, "There, you have a reprieve."

"More like a stay of execution," Bo replied. "I'm betting the old codger is pretty trigger-happy with a double-barrel shotgun that was made at the turn of the century, and I don't mean the twenty-first century."

"Dr. Marsalis?" she asked incredulously. "He's just a harmless old PhD."

"Yeah, *magnum cum loaded.*"

This was not the first occasion that Beth had seen this imposing man with the broad shoulders. She rarely forgot a face, and had almost immediately recognized him, yet he was distinctively different. He had unnerved her that morning on the Square, but there was nothing disconcerting about him now. In fact, he exuded an assuring calmness which she found contagious, and despite her best efforts not to do so, when he chuckled, she couldn't help but do the same.

Instead of rumpled clothes that looked like they had been slept in for a month, the man now wore crisply-ironed tight jeans and a navy-blue sport coat over an open-collared, buttoned shirt. He was clean-shaven, and while his sandy-brown hair remained thick, it was no longer the frenetic mane of a madman. It was now cut in short natural waves of the length and style that doesn't require combing or brushing.

Bo had just begun to explain his interest in, and his connection to, Mandi Charbonnet's case when Beth absently reached for the pencil and sketchpad on the cypress table. Many of the questions Bo asked were the ones the police had posed. And as Beth recited the same answers, her drawing hand took on a life of its own. It was odd how she could see more than a person's image in her drawings. Their emotions, personalities, difficulties, and loves seemed to reveal themselves to Beth more readily through the medium of her art than her mere retinas. "You know I've seen you before," she announced, roughing out an ovate outline on her pad. She had not looked up when she spoke, yet she sensed him tense.

"Where was that?" he asked, hoping she didn't detect his uneasiness.

"Last year, on the Square. You were...er...*asleep* on one of the benches, and I woke you before the police came by." She glanced up for another look at his forehead, and saw that he was blushing.

"I vaguely remember—not many details, I'm afraid. I was going through a bad time, but I recall being pretty ungrateful. I apologize."

"Rude," Beth replied while fine-tuning the wide forehead of her subject, supposedly indicative, as she recalled from her astrological readings, of someone who executes duties diligently.

"Pardon?"

"You weren't just ungrateful, you were downright rude," she explained.

"I said, I'm sorry."

"I know. Apology accepted." With the diligence-in-duty trait still on her mind, Beth asked, "How did you get into private detective work?"

Bo began to wonder which of them was really conducting the interview. But he relaxed, finding that he liked her un-intimidated, yet subtle, matter-of-fact mien. "I used to be a cop; seemed like a natural segue."

Beth was now working on the chin, which relates to a person's stamina: the more square it is, the greater degree of endurance. The one she sketched was slightly rounded, not quite square, and flowed with a gentle fullness of the head and face, which meant that, for this man, life in his sixties or seventies would be very satisfying. She couldn't recall what the dimple signified, but anything that resembled Omar Sharif or

Kirk Douglas couldn't be bad.

Although hair concealed the tops of Bo's ears, Beth could see that they were set close to the head, meaning that he plans ahead, not liking to leave much to chance. "I'm guessing that a cop or a PI has to be tenacious and systematic," she declared.

"Yeah, I guess that's right. Why?"

"I also see that you're good at what you do, and life is going to be good to you later on."

Bo laughed. "Well, at least you got the first half of that right."

"Time will tell; you'll see."

The thickness of her subject's hair was an indication of his physical prowess and resilience. She understood now what he had meant when he expressed doubt about a good life awaiting him. So far, life had repeatedly inflicted hard blows against this man. Nevertheless, the great recuperative powers he possessed enabled him to persevere and bounce back after each adversity. Despite the trials and tribulations, life's challenges proved irresistible.

"When you were outside," she said, "you mentioned that you had lost someone to this same killer; care to elaborate?"

"No," Bo tersely snapped, and Beth thought it best not to push the issue, concentrating instead on his nose. It was a good-sized one, indicating wealth, with a straight, full, and fleshy tip. The nostrils were gently flared, but well concealed; a sign of cordiality, a warm personality, and empathy with others. He sets high standards for himself and is well mannered, Beth silently noted. Bo's straight and even lips conveyed to the artist that he was very self-assured, and self-controlled. The philtrum, the groove between the upper lip and nose, was well defined, deep and long, an omen of strong energy levels and vitality.

"Have you always enjoyed wealth, or is that something new? Kind of unusual for a cop, isn't it?"

It was now Bo who was the one at a loss for words, and the silence caused Beth to look up from her work, noticing his eyes. They were not slanted, which was good: upward indicative of an opportunistic personality; downward, a submissive one. Since there was at least one eye-width between both eyes, Beth believed Bo was possessed with a clear view of the world and well-balanced judgment.

"Unlike you, it's kind of new for me," Bo finally said.

Beth's pencil stopped. "Unlike me?"

"This is not the loft of a starving artist. Look around this place, it screams money. So you either come from a lot of it, or you are good at what *you* do. But not so good that you still don't tromp off to Jackson Square each day to sell what you can." Hurt and anger flooded her eyes, and Bo couldn't tell which predominated. Either way, he apologized for his bluntness.

"No, no, go on," she urged.

"Well, I mean, take the painting you said that you wanted to do of Ms. Charbonnet for example. That doesn't seem to be the usual tourist fodder. They want to take back scenes of what they see in New Orleans, hang it on their walls for their friends to see, or to remind themselves of their visit here. You've probably done so many of the same ones that you can churn them out like an assembly-line worker. No, that piece was meant to go in a gallery, and I doubt that you have one of your own or you wouldn't be out on the Square. So you intended for Ms. Charbonnet's painting to be displayed in someone else's gallery.

"I suspect that you're in a transition period. You crave doing the art you *want* to do, not the run-of-the-mill stuff you *need* to do to pay the rent. And, regardless of your family's wealth, you're independent, so you don't want to be dependent on that. It's against your nature *not* to pay your own way. It's part of the way you want to leave your stamp on the world."

Beth slid off her flip-flops and curled her legs under her, instinctively drawing herself into a cocoon on the chair. While she longed to be understood as an artist and as an individual, it was nevertheless disturbing to a degree that this stranger was seeing a little too much too soon.

His eyes were deep-set, like those of Val Kilmer, bespeaking an intense, possessive, observant nature, and romantic to the core. Beth felt herself redden at her recollection that such a deep blue color, much like her own, meant that she was in the company of a highly sexed, yet gentle and sensitive, being. But there was also something even more striking about this man's eyes which she had not noticed during their earlier encounter at Jackson Square; the iris of his right eye also had a section of brown. The condition, known as heterochroma, is usually the result of an imbalance in the melanin content of the iris. Although it is not that unusual in the animal kingdom, it is rather rare in humans. Her pencil again jumped to life.

His eyes were not beady, squinty or shifty, which would reveal a secretive, nefarious nature. Instead, they were large and remained firmly set, looking at her steadily, reflecting yet another sign of a solid and persevering nature, and a person of stability. The assessment was shattered, however, at his next words, "May I see the photographs?"

"What photographs?"

"The ones you took of Ms. Charbonnet. The ones you were going to use for the painting."

The word pervert raced through Beth's head. What use would they be, other than to satisfy some prurient interest? she wondered. But before she could convert the thought to words, Bo added, "It's not what you think. I want to take a look at the *scene*. See, I know who did this, and he doesn't just pick out victims at random on the spur of the moment. He's very calculating."

"What do you mean, you know who did it? Why don't you go to the police?"

"I have, but they're not convinced."

"Then…"

"Just bear with me, okay?" Seeing her nod, Bo continued, "This guy, Todd Murphy, didn't just grab your friend…"

"Mandi."

"Yeah, Mandi. We know she didn't make it to her car, and I'm telling you Murphy didn't just grab her off the street on a whim. He stalked her, which means that he knew where y'all would be, and when you would be there. He got her during the few minutes after she was away from you, but before she reached her car. So he was there, or close by, the entire time, watching and waiting for that chance. "So think back, Beth…"

It was the first time he had said her first name, and she found it soothing, causing her to uncoil.

"Did you see anyone hanging around the place?" Bo asked. "He would not have made himself obvious. Anyone at all?"

"No, no one, other than a guy in a pirate suit, and he was so wasted he didn't know what world he was in."

"What did he look like? Think hard."

"I don't know—just a pirate! What difference does it make, if you know who did this? What does this Murphy look like?"

"Beth, calm down. I told you the police don't believe me. I'm looking for more proof. But if I tell you what Murphy looks like, any description you give will be tainted, useless. So please concentrate. You're an artist, you subconsciously study faces. You probably never forget one. Hell, you remembered me from a chance encounter a year ago. You can do it."

"But it's not the same. My mind was on Mandi, not him. You know how it is around here during Carnival. He didn't look out of place. I had no reason to pay him any attention. The only thing I remember is the eye-patch."

"Bullshit. You remembered me, and I sure don't look the same." Bo mistakenly took her silence as contemplation, but it was embarrassment. "Beth?" he prodded.

"I told you, it's not the same."

"What's the damned difference?" he asked in frustration.

"Because that morning on the Square I *was* paying close attention to you. I can't explain it; maybe I'm crazy, but there was just something about you. Despite the soiled clothes, facial growth, wild hair, and—excuse me for saying it—smell, you didn't fit. You were out of place, out of sync with everything. To most eyes, I guess you blended in with the other riffraff, but to mine, you stuck out like a sore thumb. Why did you think I woke you, and you alone? You think I take care of all the bums on Jackson Square?"

Her responses were coming in such rapid-fire fashion, all Bo could do was listen until she finished. And when she was done, it was hard to tell which of the two was more abashed. Finally, convinced that Beth could not provide any descriptive details of the "pirate" Bo broke the silent stalemate. "I believe you. It's okay. But I would still like to see those photos."

Regaining her voice, Beth answered, "And I still don't understand why. What do you hope to see?"

"I don't know, but they're part of the scene and he was there. You never can tell what might be found. Even if there is no evidence there, being at the scene used to help me reconstruct everything in my mind, putting myself in the place of the killer, and seeing everything through his eyes."

"So it's the scene that's important, and not Mandi?"

"Yes, Beth. That's what I've been saying all along."

"Then I'll take you there for a firsthand view. The Waverlys are still out of town and I can get us in. It's the last thing I want to do, but you can get your look, and Mandi's privacy can be protected."

It was more than Bo could have hoped for. Instead of informing Beth that he had already seen the autopsy photos, rendering the dead woman's privacy a moot issue, he readily took her up on the offer. Looking at his watch, he said, "Tell you what, I'm famished. If you promise to do that, I'll pop for dinner at Coop's—I love their rabbit and sausage jambalaya—that is, unless you're a vegetarian or something."

"Thanks, but I haven't had much of an appetite."

"Look, I know how it is. I've been there. But you've got to work through this, and part of that is keeping something in your system."

There was earnestness in his words and face. "You're right. And now that you mention it, I do feel a little hungry." Already feeling a bit more cheerful, she added, "Now, Mr. Investigator, why would you think I'm a vegetarian 'or something'?"

"You offered me cucumber water, for chrissakes," Bo reasoned, laughing.

"Well, I'll have you know that I'm quite partial to the duck quesadillas," she advised, joining in the laughter. "Give me a minute to change?"

"Sure. Take your time, but first call the old guy."

After assuring Dr. Marsalis that all was well, Beth ascended the spiral staircase to her sleeping area. She kept the sweatshirt on, and as she discarded the sweatpants and pulled on some jeans, her mind remained fixed on the visitor below. Her only personal experience with a cop was the one who responded to her cry for help the time that some creep flashed her while she was selling paintings in the Square. Actually, Beth couldn't decide who had been the biggest jerk—the flasher or the cop who asked her if she really wanted to press charges against a man for exposing himself to art. The asshole really thought that was funny. Moreover, whenever Beth had previously thought of detectives, it was of super cops like the characters portrayed by Clint Eastwood in the old *Dirty Harry* movies that periodically ran on TMC (his name was Callahan, too) and by Mel Gibson, in the *Lethal Weapon* series. Bo Landry, however, was different. While projecting an aura of self-assurance, he also exhibited social poise, sensitivity, and empathy.

Peeking through the dangling mirrors and prisms, Beth saw Bo standing at an easel. Damn, she thought. It was the one holding the large blank canvas on which Beth had intended to paint Mandi's form. The one on which Beth had taped the photograph that she had intended to use, and Landry was now ogling. Damn him. She hoped she had not been wrong in her favorable interpretations.

By the time Beth laced up her tennis shoes and started for the stairs however, Bo had moved away from the photo and was closely inspecting one of the oils hanging on the brick wall. It was one of Beth's favorites, a self-portrait of sorts; not painted from a photograph, but one she had envisioned from countless experiences. Beth was in jeans and a white blouse tied at the midriff, stretched out in a pirogue with her bare feet lazily draped over the low freeboards. The craft floated listlessly on the still bayou water, sporadically illuminated by the moonlight filtering through a canopy of Spanish moss and cypress giants. Portions of the water's surface were as dark as the night while others shifted from dark gray to pewter, and on to brilliant silver. Beth recalled how metaphoric she found such occasions: whether the currents of life took her into dark, misunderstood waters or those of illumination, there was beauty to be found if she only looked, relishing life by the moment, taking a chance.

For Beth, art was not merely metaphorical or magical—it was sacred. This belief was one of the reasons she never touched a piece—whether it hung in a museum, gallery, or someone's home—and she was fascinated when she saw Bo Landry stretch out his fingers, almost touching her figure in the pirogue, in apparent reverence; but then he stopped and drew his hand away.

Bo had only been able to look at the paintings a moment before Beth descended the stairs, and they were out the door. He had wanted to check out the photos hanging on the wall as well; if had he done so, he would have seen several of Professor Robert Callahan taken at the retirement party thrown by some of his favorite former students. Among the group, and posing with the professor along with three of her philosophy classmates, was a smiling Serena Raven.

CHAPTER 50

Coop's Place is the funky dive described by Zagat as a place where the "not-so-elite" meet to eat. A gigantic chalkboard menu graced one of the old brick walls, listing a broad range of Cajun food, but Beth and Bo already knew what they wanted. While standing and waiting for an empty table, a boy who barely looked the legal age to enter, came up behind Beth and Bo, followed almost immediately by a hot-looking co-ed about the same age. Until both of them simultaneously moved toward the lone empty stool at the bar, Beth and Bo assumed that they were together. "You take it," the boy offered, smirking. "I know your feet have got to be hurting, because you've been running through my mind all day."

Beth let out a groan, and Bo guffawed along with the girl, who between giggles, asked the lounge-lizard wannabe if such a corny line had ever actually worked. Nevertheless, she didn't hesitate in taking the seat.

Resuming his place in line behind Beth and Bo, the boy gave a shrug, a tacit "no-pain-no-gain" message. Bo laughed again, this time at Beth rolling her eyes. "Why do y'all do such stupid stuff?" she whispered. Before Bo could come up with something to say, however, he spotted a couple leaving a small table to the left, by the front window, and quickly ushered Beth in that direction.

A waitress came by and took their orders. Beth placed hers first, and was ambivalent about indulging in anything with alcohol, concerned that it would seem like partying so soon after Mandi's funeral. But then she looked around and thought, I'm in New Orleans, for crying out loud; people have parades, wakes, and drink all the time here when folks die. While ruing the loss, they celebrate the life that was, and the memory that would live on. Convincing herself, at least momentarily, that's the way Mandi would want it too, Beth ordered a glass of wine, but immediately regretted it when Bo ordered a Diet Coke. "I'm sorry," she told Bo after the waitress left. "I wouldn't have ordered that if I had known you had something against drinking."

"Don't be silly. I don't have a thing in the world *against* it; I just can't *do* it." Extending a hand, he added with a smile, "Hello, my name is Bo, and I'm an alcoholic."

She shook his hand, and replied, "Hello, I'm Beth, and I'm so, so embarrassed."

"Don't be. It's just a fact, and my own fault, at that. I tried to drown my sorrows, but the damned little critters kept crawling back."

When the waitress brought them their beverages, Bo poured his over ice and held up the glass. "To Mandi," he offered as a toast.

"To Mandi," Beth agreed, clinking her goblet against Bo's tumbler.

After they drank, Bo asked, "So what's the worst line anyone pitched to *you*, Ms. Callahan?"

"Good grief, Landry, they're all bad."

"Come on, what's the worst?" Reflecting on the matter brought a smile to Beth's face and a twinkle to her eyes. "I can see you've thought of something," Bo observed. "Give it up."

"Back in college, at my first sorority pledge-swap; the guy was real cute, but a total jackass. Anyway, I saw him walking toward me, holding a cup of beer in each hand. After he handed one to me and I thanked him, he eyed me up and down, and said, 'You must have cleaned those pants with Windex, because I can definitely see myself in them.' Then he winked; the son-of-a-bitch actually winked!"

Bo's roar further loosened Beth up. "All right, hotshot," she countered. "Let's turn this around. What do you consider the *best* that *you* have ever used? I'm telling you, they're all bad. There is no good so-called 'line.' They never work."

"Oh, I wouldn't go that far," he replied.

"Oh yeah? Then tell me; what do you consider your personal best?" Before he could answer, she added, "And more importantly, did it honestly work?"

"Yes, it worked," Bo declared.

"Well, what was it?"

"Ten minutes. It'll just take ten minutes," he said with a broad grin.

"Ten minutes?" Beth asked. "You are such a liar."

"Why do you say that?"

Beth leaned across the table, and lowered her voice, "Well, first of all, notwithstanding all the bravado, I've never met a guy who could go ten minutes."

"I see," Bo chortled.

But Beth didn't understand what he found so humorous. "Seriously," she said, "you're telling me that actually worked on somebody?"

"Yep," Bo assured her. "On *you.*" As she tried to make sense of the remark, he explained, "Got me in your apartment just like that," snapping his fingers.

Beth buried her face in her hands, which only caused Bo to guffaw louder. She was grateful to hear a female voice say, "Here you go, enjoy."

Bo waited for Beth to finish a sip of her merlot before broaching what might be a touchy subject. "I'm curious about something," he began. "Don't get mad—I'm just trying to understand—but isn't it kind of cheating for an artist to paint from a photograph?"

"That's a fair question," she replied, to Bo's relief, "and one that's still debated in the art community. Some think that it is. But others, like me, don't think it's really as much a matter of cheating as it is a matter of whether the resulting artwork maintains integrity."

"Meaning what, exactly?" Bo quizzed.

"A good artist can still *interpret* a photograph. Plus, photography itself can be an art form. Since I'm the photographer who took Mandi's photo... That is the one you're specifically asking about, isn't it?"

Awkwardly caught with a mouthful of jambalaya, Bo nodded and, with a hand, encouraged Beth to continue.

"So, in this instance, I would have been creating art in one form, by interpreting another form of my own art. How's that cheating?" Bo held up both hands in surrender. "And in my opinion," she continued, "it would not necessarily be artistically dishonest if I did a painting from a photograph taken by another person. It's all about learning how to process rather complicated, visual information and making editing choices, depending on the artist's ultimate goal. A photograph has flattened out three-dimensional space, and broken its subject down into discreet forms of light, lines, and mass. Good artists...."

"Aw shit!" Bo exclaimed, eliciting stares from some of the other patrons. A huge gray cat had leapt from the floor onto the windowsill. Only then did Bo notice the small bed where the cat now curled up and lay. "Sorry," he said, amid the laughter of Beth and other diners. "You were saying something about good artists," he prodded.

"Right," Beth snickered, finding it difficult to stop laughing altogether. Composing herself, she took another sip of her wine. "Okay, now that you've met Stella, I'll continue.

"Good artists can draw, and they can paint. They know what to do with color values and the nuances of shadows to re-inject the dimension taken away by the camera. And don't forget, the artist is free to interpret and edit along the way as he or she pleases. The painting doesn't have to be an enlarged clone of the photograph. The resurrection, the breathing of new life, is not merely what is shown in the photo, but rather the interpretation given to the image by the artist, and their ability to project that to the viewing eye. Understand?"

"Actually, I think I do."

Bo paid the check and they made their exit. Retracing their steps past the front window, Bo saw the source of his abashment slumbering without a care in the world, and he couldn't resist the urge to bang on the glass. Stella, however, didn't move a muscle. "Damned cat," Bo mumbled, and Beth howled in delight.

Turning right at the first corner, they ambled up Ursulines, and Bo asked about the gargantuan French Colonial-looking building to the right. Beth explained that it was the Old Ursuline Convent, and related what she recalled of its history. The building, she explained, was the oldest in the entire Mississippi Valley, and the only one of the original French Colony still standing, built for the Ursulines, or Sisters of Ursula, an order of nuns who came to the colony in 1727. There, Beth informed Bo, the nuns founded an orphanage, asylum, and school for girls, the Baroness de Pontalba being one of the most notable of the school's alumnae.

In 1788, gigantic flames swept through the French Quarter, carried on a southerly wind, destroying hundreds of homes and other buildings in the fire's deadly path north. When it became evident that the convent would be the conflagration's next victim, one of the old nuns, Sister St. Anthony, climbed the hand-crafted cypress staircase, carrying a small statue of Our Lady of Prompt Succor, another name given to the Virgin Mother, the principal patroness of the city. As the Mother Superior stood by, Sister St. Anthony placed the statue on the sill of a window facing the approaching, roaring fire. According to the legend, as the two nuns knelt and prayed, the wind suddenly changed direction, blowing the flames backward and saving the convent.

"There's another destructive power sweeping through this city," Bo solemnly declared, "and it's pure evil."

"Then we'll just have to do like Sister St. Anthony, and pray," Beth replied in all sincerity.

"So you believe in God?" Bo asked.

Beth started to say, "Oh course I do, don't you?" But, for all her curiosity and open-mindedness, she found herself not wanting to hear his answer. Wishing to be honest, but choosing her words carefully, she thought it over before saying, "I believe that there is an order to the universe, originally perfectly balanced. The natural world is so amazing I look at it in awe. What was created could not have been through some accident. So yes, I believe it was created by a supreme, divine being, and do not understand how anyone can take a close look at the marvels of nature and think otherwise.

"So I do believe in God, Author of Life, and Creator of Heaven and Earth. If those miracles are due to some big bang, He caused it, but no, we're not here by some freak, spontaneous accident. He gave us a perfectly balanced world, entrusting us to maintain it. The human race however, abused that trust. To the extent the world is out of kilter, I'm afraid we're the ones at fault, not God."

"Interesting," Bo said. "Have you asked yourself where God was when your friend was being raped and murdered?"

"I know where you're going with this," Beth said. "If He exists and is omnipotent, why did He let this happen?" At Bo's nod, she continued. "I don't claim to have all the answers. Hell, I don't have *any* answers. I can only tell you how *I* feel, what *I* believe."

"Go ahead," he coaxed.

"I'm outraged at the animal that killed Mandi. I'm mad as hell at myself for putting her in his path, but I don't blame God. I believe He is a loving God—the creator of such beauty and wonder, couldn't be anything else—and He wants to be loved. But no love is genuine if it is forced, so He gave us free will. We can think as we wish, love as we wish, hate as we wish, and do as we wish.

"You mentioned that there was an evil power at work here, and I agree with that. But if you believe in evil, you must also believe in good. God allows us to choose between the two paths, and they are not infinitely parallel. They bend and snake, often crossing one another. So just because a person sets out on the path of goodness, and stays on that trail, doesn't mean there will never come a time that he runs into someone following a path of evil."

"You're quite the philosopher, aren't you?"

"Sorry, I don't mean to sound that way. Like I said, I don't claim to have answers."

"I'm the one who asked."

"I guess what I'm trying to say is that sometimes bad things, even horrendous things, happen to good people because of the free will God has given us. And I like to think when that happens, God grieves with us for the choice that was made and the resulting tragic consequences. But the only way to completely ensure that the good never fall prey to the bad, would be for God to revoke free will so no one could ever again choose a path of evil. Would you want anyone, even God, dictating to you what to think, believe, and do? I know I wouldn't."

Bo just shook his head, and Beth wasn't sure if it was a silent, negative response to her last question or an indication of disbelief in everything she had said. They were now at the Chartres intersection. Wanting to steer the conversation to surer, more neutral ground, Beth pointed to their left. "That's Stella."

"The cat?" Bo asked.

"No silly, the restaurant where my brother Jake interned last summer. He's going to be a chef."

"Can he make cucumber water?" Bo teased.

"Watch it, Landry," she replied.

A car zooming from the left came close to hitting Bo, who had stepped onto the pavement while staring off to the right. He had been trying to read a bronze plaque outside a building, but could only make out the words: "Beauregard House." "Son-of-a-bitch!" he yelled. He bent over slightly, resting his palms on his thighs while attempting to regain his wits. "Did you see that?"

It was a rhetorical question which Beth nevertheless answered, "I told you to watch it."

"Aw, jeez. How about injecting a little of that artist passion in your voice next time. I thought you were talking about my cucumber water comment."

"What were you looking at?"

"That house, the Beauregard House. PGT Beauregard?"

"Yes, he moved here sometime after the war." Bo did not require any clarification. In conversation between any two Southerners, there is never a need to be any more specific than saying "the war" unless one is referring to some armed conflict other than the American Civil War. Beth, however, was curious about his interest. "Why do you ask?"

"He lost Shiloh, you know. Snatched defeat right out of the jaws of victory."

"So you're a history buff too?" Beth inquired.

"Not really. But a man who was like a father to me was, especially concerning the Civil War. I guess some of his knowledge rubbed off."

"You used the past tense, what happened to him?"

"He was murdered."

"By the same man who killed Mandi?"

"No."

"Would it help to talk about it?"

"No."

The sparkle had vacated Bo's eyes. What Beth saw in them frightened her, and she wondered how much violent death surrounded this man. A tense silence ensued between them, one that Beth attempted to fill as they strolled past Croissant d'Or Patisserie, and she took the opportunity to mention what a pleasant place it was to pass peaceful, leisurely mornings with a newspaper, Café au lait, and amazing pastry.

Continuing on Ursulines, they crossed Royal and Bourbon, and swung left on Dauphine. Halfway down the block, a house on the right was set farther back from the street than the adjoining buildings. The sidewalk widened, reaching into the resulting recess, creating a small concrete "yard." There, two young girls manned a makeshift lemonade stand, and an even younger one was dancing to a tune from a boombox on the front porch.

Several adults sat in rockers on the porch, and beamed when they saw Beth draw her companion to a halt with a light touch on his arm, saying, "Oh, how cute!" Their smiles broadened even more when Bo walked over and dropped a dollar bill in a small bucket by the go-go tot. So as not to be the cause of hurt feelings, he also purchased a couple of cups of lemonade from the two young entrepreneurs. Receiving hers, Beth asked, "What was wrong with the lemonade *I* offered you?"

"Nothing, I'm sure," he replied, "but a world of difference in salesmanship."

"Oh yeah?" she inquired, arching a brow.

"Yeah, big difference. *You* didn't wink at me. I'm a sucker for that every time."

They were still laughing as they rounded the corner at St. Philip, in front of Matassa's, the little neighborhood market where Bo walked most mornings to buy a newspaper. Reaching Burgundy at the end of the block, they veered left and, a half-dozen blocks farther, arrived at 451.

Beth didn't know whether the spirits of those who were violently snuffed out, irrevocably erased from the face of the earth by the hand of evil, lingered at the venue of their unexpected and inexorable departure, either in benign confusion at the suddenness or on a malicious mission of retribution. Even if departed souls did occasionally loiter about, Beth didn't know whether Mandi's ghost would have chosen the ruins where she was slain or here, where she had come under the stalking eye of her murderer. If phantoms existed, there were probably few neighborhoods in America as haunted as New Orleans' Vieux Carré. Beth Callahan had never seen or sensed any such phenomenon, but she knew beyond all question, walking through the darkened corridor from the front gate to the courtyard, that malevolence still lurked there.

Thankfully, they were not long inside the Waverly residence. Bo briefly looked around, asking Beth to show him exactly where Mandi had posed and where Beth had positioned her camera. Before returning outside, he inquired whether Beth had, for any reason, adjusted the drapes or pulled them back to look out the window. When she said that she had not, he only nodded and replied that he was finished inside, but wanted to take a closer look in the courtyard. After closing the door and testing it to make sure it was locked, Beth found Bo examining the plants outside the Waverly window. "I don't see any footprints," he said, "but he was here."

Beth wasn't sure if he was speaking to her, or to himself. In either event, she asked, "If there are no footprints, how do you know?"

"These ferns are trampled down," he replied, as he squatted level to the bottom of the window. "And he watched y'all through this space left in the drapes. When he saw you packing up, he left." Now standing, Bo appeared to Beth to be in a trance. "You said you heard nothing, saw nothing, from the time you came out until you drove off. Yet, he grabbed her before she reached her car. So he didn't follow her, he already knew where she had parked and waited."

For the most part, the decisions Beth made in life were mood-driven, and the systematic, logical approach, such as Bo was utilizing, intrigued her. As engaging as she found the process, however, it was trumped by her neck hairs standing on end. "Please tell me that we don't have to try to locate the spot where she was abducted…" Even though Bo was shaking his head, Beth continued on, "And, oh God, there's no way I can go to where she was…where he…where he did all of that to her."

"No," Bo replied, "you don't. I've already been there."

Beth was relieved. And as the two of them stepped out onto Burgundy and walked north, in the opposite direction of the grisly scene Beth imagined, Bo considered how trusting she was to be alone with him in this relatively quiet portion of the French Quarter.

CHAPTER 51

This time, as Beth and Bo neared the intersection of Burgundy and Toulouse, they dropped in at McCormick's. Although Bo knew he needed to remain focused on his mission, he saw no harm in a brief diversion, and suggested they stop for a drink. Beth had demurred, but Bo insisted. That he was enjoying her company came as a surprise, a rediscovered pleasure he wished to prolong.

Lauryn was minding the bar, and Ben, one of Sam's other bartenders, although off the clock, was nevertheless on hand. In his booming basso voice, he was holding forth about something obviously stuck in his craw, periodically pausing only long enough to keep his vocal cords lubricated with a mug of dark draft.

"What's he going on about?" Bo inquired, edging his way into an opening at the bar. Lauryn merely rolled her eyes, and turned for a can of Diet Coke. Bo asked Beth what she would like, and relayed her order to Lauryn while she poured his cola over a glass of ice. Grabbing their drinks, they looked for a place to sit, and Bo spotted LB, in a far corner, waving. "Come on," he told Beth. "You'll like these folks."

While Bo commandeered a couple of unoccupied chairs from another table, LB and Robin did some shifting to make room. Ben was still ranting, and after introductions were exchanged with Beth, Bo asked the same question he had posed to Lauryn. "Ben? He's on a tear about his alma mater's mascot," LB explained.

"Knox College, in Galesburg, Illinois," Robin added.

"Okey dokey," Bo replied.

With a mischievous gleam in his eyes, LB hollered out, "Hey Ben! What's the nickname of that football team again?"

"The Prairie Fire!" Ben roared. "Now I ask you: what kind of fucking name is that!"

Bo had not paid much attention to Sam while he went about his customary ritual of making the rounds, glad-handing his customers, but Bo took notice when Sam strode across the floor and disappeared into a storage room. He re-emerged a few seconds later, carrying an empty plastic milk-crate. Without fanfare, Sam walked up to Ben and set the crate on the floor at the orator's feet. "I don't have a soapbox," Sam advised, "but maybe this will do."

As the place erupted in amusement, Ben obligingly stepped onto the crate, resuming his diatribe. "The mere mention of a football team of big bruisers from the Midwest is supposed to strike fear in an opponent, dammit!" Then, in a somewhat lower, mocking tone, "Oooh, I'm so scared. We're going up against some burning grass."

After the laughter waned, Homer yelled, from the table next to LB's group, "Ben, I don't mean to stoke the fire, no—whadda ya call it—pun intended, but what name you suggest?"

"The Sodbusters!" Ben shouted. Irked by the crowd's ridiculing response, he insisted, "That's a mean, tough name fit for Midwesterners!"

"This is quite an interesting group," Beth said to Bo.

"Oh, honey," Robin cautioned, "you don't know the half of it."

"That's okay. I'll be happy to teach you the other half of what you need to know," LB volunteered, earning a slap on the arm by Robin.

"Y'all see what a rough life I have?" LB quipped, just before Mike called from one of the pool tables, "LB! You're up!" LB stood and grabbed a cue, and Bo excused himself for a trip to the men's room.

"You look familiar," Robin said to Beth. "The Square; you're one of the artists on Jackson Square, aren't you?" Beth confirmed that she was, flattered when Robin surprisingly mentioned several pieces that had caught her attention.

After Bo rejoined them, Robin asked Beth, "So what's a girl like you doing with a guy like this?"

"I'm helping him with a case."

"Her best friend was that woman whose body was found off Conti," Bo partially explained.

"Oh shit," Robin replied, "I'm really sorry. I didn't mean to throw a turd in the punchbowl."

"You didn't know," Beth said, wiping away the moisture welling in her eyes. "It's just so hard to process."

"You won't believe this now, honey, and I realize it's a cliché; but time has a way of healing. Just hang in there and give it time. You'll be all right. It worked for Bo here, and it'll work for you."

Bo and Beth soon said their "goodnights," stopping at the bar on their way out for Bo to settle the tab, and drop some cash in one of the jars Sam had agreed to put out. Bo felt reasonably certain that, while LB would politely decline a cruise as an anniversary present if it came from any one person, he might accept the gift if it were from a group of anonymous McCormick's regulars. So Sam had labeled the jars for that purpose and encouraged everyone to pitch in what they could. Since Bo had already purchased the gift certificate, Sam would turn over to him whatever was collected, as reimbursement. If it didn't cover the entire amount, that was okay with Bo. He wanted to pay for the whole thing anyway. Sure enough, Sam told Bo that even the alternate plan had made LB a little self-conscious, but he finally relented when Sam called his attention to the hurt feelings that would be suffered if LB declined.

Bo and Beth exited the doors on the Toulouse Street side. Doglegging their way, they turned left on Dauphine, then right on St. Peter. Bo was thankful, especially considering his present company, not to see Sea Urchin anywhere around. Well before getting to Bourbon Street, an awful rendition of Abba's "Dancing Queen" could be heard. The source was soon determined to be three co-eds belting out the tune in a nearby karaoke club. As they passed, Bo shot a thumb toward the open doors, and asked, almost screaming to be heard above the racket, "How about it?"

"No way!" Beth proclaimed, not slowing an iota, crossing Bourbon Street.

They continued in silence down the next block and, by the time they crossed Royal, the cacophony had dissipated by enough decibels that Bo thought he could be heard without shouting. "So what's been the wildest or most embarrassing thing you've ever done?"

"Oh no; you don't know me nearly well enough for me to share something like that."

We'll see about that, Bo thought, but instead said, "I bet it has something to do with karaoke." When she reddened, he thought he might have hit on something. "I'm right, aren't I? What was the song?"

"You're way off, Landry," Beth insisted, remembering the tune well. The protestation was belied by her face flushing again, but this time she didn't say anything further, and was grateful that Bo appeared equally satisfied to let the matter drop. There was no way Beth was going to tell him that the song was Oates and Hall's "Private Eyes", lest he try to read something into it that wasn't there. Or was it? she considered, her emotions still running amok.

Passing in front of the cathedral, Bo asked Beth if she was sleeping okay. "Not at first," she said. "And even when I slept, I had these weird dreams about Mandi."

"Yeah, it was the same with me. You said 'not at first'. Are you taking anything now?"

"No prescription drugs, if that's what you mean," she said. "It's just some tea I make with a dash of Valerian Root."

Bo didn't want to show his ignorance by asking what that was, and walked the rest of the way in silence. At the gate to her building, he thanked her for her time and assistance.

"I needed to get out," she replied. "I enjoyed it."

"Yeah, I had a good time too."

They bade each other goodnight and, as Beth entered the corridor, Bo turned up the sidewalk. Going only a few indecisive steps, he briskly returned to the gate, and saw that Beth had not yet made it to the courtyard. "Hey!" he called out, and she turned around. "Would you consider having dinner with me some night?"

"I had dinner with you tonight."

"No, I mean…like…, well…." he stammered. He felt like a bashful adolescent.

"You mean like a date?"

"Yeah, I guess you could call it that. Nothing fancy, maybe a pizza at Turtle Bay?"

"Sure."

"Damn," Bo said. "That does work better than the Windex line."

"I can teach you some stuff, Landry," she said, before rounding the corner. Once out of his sight, she leaned against a brick wall and closed her eyes, wondering where the hell those words had come from.

CHAPTER 52

The beast was now alone, relaxing and reflecting. If there was anything he savored more than killing, it was toying with people, keeping them off balance. That his plans were falling nicely into place was not at all astonishing; they always did.

The robe which he wore was much too small for his frame, but well suited for its purpose nonetheless. He nuzzled against its collar, relishing the pleasing scent which still lingered after these many months. This had become a private, nightly ritual, never failing to jumpstart exquisite memories. The beast repeatedly drew the ends of the sash through his fingers, recalling the way it felt when he had used it to vanquish the goddess to whom it once belonged. "Well Serena, what do you think of her?" he asked aloud.

CHAPTER 53

Bo had not been able to get anywhere with Lieutenant Winston Deschamps. Even the urgings of Chad Babineaux, the husband of one of the victims, had fallen on deaf ears. Consequently, while Bo didn't invest any real hope that his solicitation of Beth Callahan to accompany him to Deschamps' office the next morning would loosen the detective's lips, there remained the slight chance that forcing him to face the pain behind Beth's startling blue eyes would move the proverbial mountain. At worst, the effort would afford Bo more time with the artist. As far as he was concerned, it was a no-lose proposition.

"Mademoiselle, it is good to see you again," Deschamps said. After gracefully offering them chairs, he advised Bo, "There have been some developments, Monsieur, and I am anxious to get your take on them." Bo's internal bullshit antenna was picking up some strange vibes. Previously, Deschamps had been anything but friendly and solicitous. *And what was up with the French?*

"Should I wait outside?" Beth asked. Bo believed the change in Deschamps' mien had to be due to Beth's presence so he viewed her intended voluntary departure as his "golden goose" committing suicide. Bo shot her a look unmistakably conveying the message, "Don't you dare."

Thankfully, Deschamps intervened, "No, no. Please stay," he urged Beth. Once that issue was settled, the detective continued, "As I said, there have been developments. But I must confess that I am not sure what to make of them. Perhaps a fresh set of eyes would be helpful."

"Sure, Lieutenant," Bo replied. "Anything I can do to help."

"It seems you were right about this Murphy fellow."

While Bo wanted to gloat, in the worst way, he suppressed the urge and simply asked, "What did you find?"

"The gun. Madame Babineaux and Monsieur Ritchie were killed by the same firearm." With a nonchalant wave of the hand, he added, "But of course, you already knew as much." Realizing from the comment that Deschamps knew that he had reviewed the police files, Bo shifted uneasily in his chair. "But what we learned only this morning," the detective continued, "is that the weapon was last registered to Monsieur Murphy."

"Well there you have it, Lieutenant. Surely you have enough for a warrant. Have you found him?"

"Oui, Monsieur, I do have a warrant. But according to the Marshal's Service, there is still no sign of Monsieur Murphy. Their last verifiable intelligence places him in Cuba."

"Goddammit, I saw him with my own eyes, here in New Orleans, just this past week!"

"It is as you say, Monsieur, 'with your own eyes,'" Deschamps responded. "I find it interesting that your unverifiable claim is the only indication that Monsieur Murphy is not where the paper trail, the real evidence, places him."

"Only indication my ass, Deschamps. You said yourself, the gun came back to the son-of-a-bitch."

"Oui, oui. But I also said that it *seemed* that you were correct, Monsieur. There is another interesting thing about the gun. I took your suggestion and requested the files from Mississippi, but not just the one regarding the murder of Mademoiselle Raven. In running Monsieur Murphy's criminal history, I saw that shortly before that murder, he was arrested on a narcotics charge."

"I know that, Deschamps; I made the bust."

"Quite so, Monsieur. Which means you had the opportunity to confiscate any weapon in his possession at the time; no?"

"I don't remember him having a gun on him."

"Come now, Monsieur," Deschamps scoffed. "A .22 derringer could have easily been concealed from your fellow officers, and its seizure just as easily and conveniently omitted from your report."

"You've lost your fucking mind," Bo declared.

"I don't think so, Monsieur. You see, I have also been in contact with the agents at Quantico. Did you know that serial killers gravitate toward positions of power and authority?"

"So?"

"So you were in law enforcement for many years, were you not?"

"Deschamps, you and a host of others fit that profile. Do *you* have an alibi?"

The detective ignored the question, asking another of his own, "Were you aware that a hallmark of many serial killers is a fascination with fire? It is true, Monsieur. Another commonality is that they like to inject themselves into investigations concerning their crimes. So what am I to think, Monsieur, when I learn that you wormed your way, shall we say, into an arson investigation when you have no experience, whatever, in that sort of thing?"

"Goddammit, I was hired by...."

"And then, Monsieur, you attempt to nose around in *my* investigations—first, the Babineaux murder; and now, obviously, the Charbonnet/Ritchie murders. You even went over my head in the process." Deschamps turned his attention to Beth, "So this is where you can help me, Mademoiselle. Did you seek out Monsieur Landry's assistance, or was it the other way around?"

Beth's silence and subconscious closing of her eyes spoke louder than any possible words. "Beth?" Bo said, "You can't possibly believe...."

"No, Mademoiselle," Deschamps sarcastically interjected. "How could you possibly believe what you are thinking when Monsieur Landry's business card was found in Madame Babineaux's purse? Quite a coincidental connection, wouldn't you say?"

"Goddammit, Deschamps...."

"Indignation, Monsieur? Surely you do not deny pumping Monsieur Babineaux for details of his wife's murder, the specific evidence that I possess or lack."

"He asked for my help!" Bo declared.

"No, Monsieur. You volunteered your services, and at no charge." Redirecting his attention to Beth, Deschamps asked, in a tone dripping with cynicism, "So Mademoiselle, how could you suspect Monsieur Landry when, on top of everything else, none of this misfortune befell us until after his arrival in our city, and shortly after his release from rehabilitation?"

"Deschamps, you don't even believe your own bullshit," Bo accused, rising to his feet. "You already said that you have a warrant for Murphy."

"Oui, I do have a warrant, Monsieur; but it is for *you*, not Monsieur Murphy. Your visit has spared me the effort of finding you. Now, please have the dignity not to make a scene. Sit." As Bo did so, Deschamps pulled the papers from a drawer in his desk. "You will see, Monsieur, it is not for your arrest. As you have noted, there is only coincidence at this time, but enough of it to get a sympathetic judge to sign off on a warrant for some samples of your blood and hair."

The detective was not sure of the nature or extent of any relationship between Landry and Beth Callahan, and the last thing Deschamps needed or desired was another woman's dead body. To make sure that Beth understood the possible danger any association with Bo posed, the detective advised her of the physical evidence recovered from the bodies of the two women, and the significance of forensic comparisons with those from a known source. In this instance, that known source would be Bo Landry.

"Mademoiselle," Deschamps said, after finishing the explanation, "it will take some time for this to be done properly. There is no reason for you to wait. I'll have a car drive you home." The offer was more than a courtesy; the subliminal message that, unless and until the comparison scientifically excluded Bo Landry as the killer, it would be best for Beth Callahan to sever any and all contact with him, came through loud and clear.

After Beth left, and while awaiting the forensics team Deschamps summoned, Bo told the detective, "You're not only wasting your time, you're ignoring another case. Surely, you see the maiming in the Babineaux and Charbonnet murders as a common denominator."

"I do," Deschamps agreed. There was no "oui" this time, Bo noted. Deschamps had scuttled the French.

"And Serena Raven?" Bo inquired.

"Yes, her too. I believe that all three were killed by the same hand."

"Then your theory concerning me is blown to hell. There's no physical way that I could have been at Serena's house the night she was killed. I was with a judge, at his house, surrounded by deputies."

"That troubled me too," Deschamps confessed, "until I learned of the tunnel."

"What fucking tunnel?"

"The one under Judge Davis's house. I told you before, we are very thorough."

"I didn't know about any tunnel, dammit."

"Sure," Deschamps replied, smiling.

"You're crazy. I was with Tom Davis."

"Whom I understand was killed that same night, and *you* were the only person known to be inside the house with him, acting rather bizarre."

"So you also think I killed Tom?" Bo asked incredulously.

"His death *was* a rather large financial boon for you, was it not?"

CHAPTER 54

A hair. Because of a solitary biological filament, the hunter had become the hunted, and Bo Landry could not believe it. He had been detained for hours in an interrogation room while lab technicians performed their analyses. At last, a uniformed officer escorted him back to Deschamps' office, where the detective promptly announced that, at least for the time being, no charges were being brought regarding the murders of Mandi Charbonnet and Bud Ritchie. The DNA isolated in the blood drawn from Bo did not match any found in the semen recovered from Charbonnet's body.

"You'll be hearing from my lawyer," Bo curtly replied, and turned to leave.

"It would be wise, indeed, for you to get a lawyer, Mr. Landry. The pubic hair recovered from Cynthia Babineaux *is* yours; a perfect match."

No trace evidence of any kind was found on Serena, and nothing recovered from Mandi Charbonnet linked Bo to her murder. Furthermore, all Deschamps had, with respect to Ritchie's death, was the gun registered to Todd Murphy, and Deschamps evidently considered Bo's link to the weapon rather tenuous. Otherwise, Bo thought, he would surely be charged with the Conti Street double-murder. But that one hair found on Cindy Babineaux posed a problem, and a big one.

Bo had been pacing, processing Deschamps' words, and as the gravity of facing the death penalty gripped him, Bo walked to a window and peered through the warped metal slats of venetian blinds that had to be at least a half-century old. The colors of Mardi Gras were everywhere; purple, green, and gold—representing justice, faith, and power. As far as Bo was concerned, the symbolism was meaningless. There was no justice in the world, and he had lost all faith. True, Bo's parents had been missionaries, but it seemed to him that their faith, as everything rooted in formal religion, had been nothing more than a legacy of guilt which he had long ago shirked. After all is said and done, of the three ideals commemorated during Mardi Gras, the only one that truly mattered in this world was power; and Bo sensed his strength oozing out of his pores in a cold sweat.

He was lost in his thoughts when he heard Deschamps calling his name. As he turned from the window, the detective handed him a document. "As you see," he formally advised Bo, "that is a warrant—one for your arrest for the murder of Cynthia Babineaux. Now that you have been served, you will need to be booked. Because this is a capital offense, there will be no bail, at least at this stage."

"My phone call?" Bo inquired.

"Technically, Article 230 of the Code of Criminal Procedure states that, from the moment of your arrest, you have the right to procure and confer with counsel, as well as the right to use a telephone or send a messenger for the purpose of communicating with your friends or with counsel. But, as a practical matter, that right is customarily afforded *after* booking. However, in your case, Mr. Landry, I am not taking any chances. I will not provide whatever slick lawyer you hire any loopholes or technicalities. The code says 'from the moment of arrest,' and that is what you will have."

Bo pulled out his cell phone. "Is it okay to use my own?"

"By all means," Deschamps replied. "Come with me." After leading Bo back to the interrogation room, the detective told him, "This will provide some privacy. Knock on the door when you are finished."

Bo had spent countless hours over his career in similar chambers. There was the stereotypical large mirror, which he was sure was two-way, and behind which Deschamps and any number of other detectives would be watching and listening, and a security camera mounted from the ceiling in a corner. He was not in any position, however, to debate the meaning of privacy.

Bo's initial thought was to call Philip Moreau, the lawyer who had hired him in the Paradise Isle fire case, but Moreau's practice was exclusively civil in nature. Bo was confident the attorney could nevertheless steer him to a heavy-hitter in criminal defense, but he didn't want to put the lawyer in an uncomfortable position. Bo knew in his gut, once learning of the accusations, Moreau would feel both compelled to share the information with his Paradise Isle clients, and to refrain from doing so due to the privileged nature of the communication in which he learned that information.

Bo thought that LB might know who to call, but was greeted by his friend's voice mail when he tried to reach him. After a brief urgent message, Bo next tried Monsignor Ambrose. The priest said that he would be there as quickly as possible. To Bo's dismay, however, Deschamps did not tarry any longer in having him booked. This, of course, meant that the arrest was now public fodder and the media frenzy would soon begin. It also meant that all of Bo's belongings, including his phone and clothes, would be confiscated. However, instead of being taken to the parish jail afterward, Bo was returned, in a prison jumpsuit, to the interrogation room where he found Monsignor Ambrose waiting, a courtesy extended for some unknown reason, by Lieutenant Deschamps. As Bo walked in, Ambrose stood and warmly grasped the prisoner's hands. "Thank you for coming, Father. I don't know how much time we have. I need your help, but I don't know where to start."

"Slow down, my son. We have as much time as you wish." Noticing Bo's doubtful expression, the priest explained with a mischievous smile, "The lieutenant is a parishioner, and a rather devout one at that. So relax."

After taking a seat at a metal table opposite Monsignor Ambrose, Bo said again, "I don't know where to begin."

"I do," the clergyman announced. "You don't mind if I say a prayer, do you?"

During his years as a cop, Bo had callously listened to thousands of arrested people say, "I know this looks bad, but...." The excuses were endless. Now, after Ambrose finished his supplication, Bo heard the same words; this time, however, it was from his lips they emanated.

"You needn't persuade me," the priest said.

Bo shook his head in disbelief. "I don't have an explanation anyway, Father. Because I don't know anything."

"Answers will come in due time," Ambrose assured. "Meanwhile, heed the advice and take heart in the assurance of Isaiah: *wait on the Lord; trust in Him and He will act; He will make the justice of your cause shine as the noonday sun.* I'm paraphrasing, of course, but you get the drift."

"I'm sorry, Father, but if God was interested in justice, I wouldn't be here. For heaven's sake, if I waited on Him, I could get the death penalty! I've got to get out of here and handle this myself."

"Did it occur to you, Bo, that God means for you to be exactly where you are? "

"Well that's just great. How fucking reassuring. Sorry, Father."

"Bo, just because neither you nor I know the reason does not mean that there is not one. If we are where He chooses, what better place is there? How do you think the Israelites felt when they found themselves trapped between the sea and pharaoh's army? Have faith and wait, Bo. He will provide a way out."

"Father, I don't want to waste time arguing with you. Regardless of what you believe or I don't believe, the bottom line is that I'm charged with murder, and could end up a resident on death row. I need to get a lawyer who knows what the hell he's doing. I was hoping you might know of someone?"

"Possibly. I know of a few, but only by reputation. Considering the gravity of the situation, I would feel more comfortable soliciting the opinion of some trusted friends."

"That would be great, Father; the sooner the better."

"I'm afraid that the lieutenant relieved me of my phone, so I'll have to leave you long enough to make some calls."

Alone in the room and left to his thoughts, specters from Bo's present and past went to and fro in his mind. Although he never doubted that his sins would one day catch up with him, he never dreamed that it would be in this manner. Becoming restless, he stood and paced some more. In the mirror, he could see the earlier versions which he had shed, and wondered whether this was the way in which it would really end for him.

The epiphany came while scrutinizing the reflection. From the time Beth had taken him to the Waverly residence on Burgundy, something had nagged at Bo in his reconstruction. Until now, it had remained elusive. Beth Callahan could very well hold the key to his freedom. Thanks to Deschamps, however, Bo feared that he was the last person she would be willing to help. In all probability, she wouldn't even speak to him.

"I spoke with...," Ambrose began, returning to the interrogation room; but Bo cut him off, "Pen and paper, Father. Will you find a pen and some paper?"

Before the priest could answer or act, an elegant man in a tailored suit behind Ambrose announced, "I can help you with that."

Ambrose moved aside, and the new arrival confidently strode into the room. After setting down an alligator-skin briefcase, which appeared to match his belt and shoes, he extended a hand holding a business card. "Mr. Landry, my name is Michael Coulon. I'm an attorney with a fair amount of experience in criminal law. An intermediary asked that I visit with you. But, of course, whether you desire my services is entirely your decision."

"I appreciate that, Mr. Coulon," Bo said. "But Father Ambrose, here, has already...."

"Bo," Ambrose broke in, "Mr. Coulon is being modest. He has more than a 'fair amount' of the experience your case requires."

"I understand," Bo replied. "But I want to give this careful thought." Turning from the priest to the lawyer, Bo added, "I'm sure you understand how important it is."

"Absolutely," Coulon responded.

"Father, you were about to give me some names when you came in?"

"*A* name, Bo; and it's on that card you're holding."

Coulon was smiling, possibly at the dialog, or maybe at the confusion evident on Bo's face, or both.

"But you only started making calls a little while ago," Bo noted to Ambrose.

"Your benefactor is not the good monsignor," Coulon explained.

Bo could see, by the uneasy glance the lawyer gave Ambrose, that he was not sure how much he should divulge. "Whatever you can tell me, you may say in the presence of Monsignor Ambrose. It will remain confidential."

"Very well," Coulon said. "Let's just say that you have a good friend in Judge Alex Stillwell."

"Alex?" Bo asked, in surprise. "I mean, I know he's a good friend, but how did he...."

"As I understand it, Judge Stillwell received a call from a mutual friend. Someone by the name of LB?"

Bo was still connecting the dots, recalling the voice mail he had left for LB, when he heard Coulon say, "Mr. Landry, Mr. Landry?"

"I'm sorry," Bo said. "What were you saying?"

"I said that you and I can discuss my fee in a moment. First, however, I want to remove some anxiety so you can consider that matter of business with a clearer head because I don't come cheap. You might even consider my news as an indication of my worth."

"What news?"

"You are not entitled to bail until there is a hearing...."

"And that's supposed to ease my mind?"

"No, but the fact that I have already secured for you something to which you have no entitlement should be of some relief."

"You've arranged for bail?"

"Yes, but it will be costly. Bail is set at $1 million. Since you do not own any property in Louisiana, you cannot post a property bond. That leaves two options: a corporate surety bond or a cash deposit. If you go the surety bond route, you pay a bail bonding company ten percent, and an insurance company stands good on the bond. The upside is that you only have to come up with $100,000 instead of the full amount. The downside is that you don't ever get that back; it's the premium the insurance company charges. The cash deposit would have to be the entire million, but if you make all court appearances, and don't violate the conditions of your release, you eventually get that back.

Bo didn't hesitate. "I'm not about to piss away a hundred grand," he declared. Remembering the priest's presence, he added, "Sorry, Father."

"That's quite all right, my son. I wouldn't piss it away either."

Bo was chuckling, but Coulon remained dead serious. "Very well," he said. "Father, would you excuse us? I need to discuss my fee with Mr. Landry."

"Certainly." Reaching the door, Ambrose turned and said, "Blessed is he who waits for the Lord." Without waiting for a reply or comment, he went on his way.

"What was that?" Coulon asked.

Breath reeking of dead scripture, Bo was thinking; but he simply replied, "It's a long story."

CHAPTER 55

Nineteenth-century French journalist Alphonse Kerr once wrote, "Every man has three characters: that which he shows, that which he has, and that which he thinks he has." Alone in her apartment, Beth Callahan was pondering the extent of the chasms separating these three with respect to Bo Landry. Could she have been so terribly wrong in her assessment? she wondered. Beth thought back to her teenage years, when her father tried to convey to her the importance of choosing the right people with whom to hang out. "However people seem at first," he advised, "sooner or later, their true character will surface. It may be temporarily masked, but never intrinsically altered." Recognizing that adolescents considered their parents morons, Professor Callahan had resorted to Ralph Waldo Emerson as independent, corroborative authority, reading to Beth the great philosopher's observation that, "No change of circumstance can repair a defect of character."

On the other hand, Beth Callahan also remembered something by Dr. Willard Gaylin that she had read in her Psych 101 course: "We are what we seem to be." Bullshit, Beth thought; what Bo Landry had earlier seemed was not anything close to what the evidence now suggested. A hair from his genitals empirically connected him to that other young wife and mother, cruelly raped, murdered, and mutilated. And the same gun which ended her life had killed the man found with the maimed remains of Beth's best friend. It appeared to Beth that the concept of a Dr. Jekyll and Mr. Hyde was not merely a figment of Robert Louis Stevenson's imagination.

Beth considered herself a good Catholic. But even if the monster who committed these mortal sins eventually secured divine absolution, Beth found it inconceivable that her heart would ever yield any measure of forgiveness. She was aghast at the realization that she had spent a pleasurable evening with the man the police said was responsible for these atrocities. What, she wondered, did that say about her? She was still fretting over it when her doorbell rang.

"Yes?" she asked, rather grumpily, into the intercom.

"Beth, I need to talk to you," a familiar voice said.

"Go away."

"I know you don't believe me," Bo acknowledged. "I wish you would, but I can appreciate that you can't—at least right now."

"I said, Go away!"

"Okay, I will; but I need your help."

"My help?" Beth asked incredulously. "Go fuck yourself."

"It seems that I've already somehow done that. I'm leaving a note for you down here. Please read it; you're my only hope."

"Then you're screwed."

"I just pushed it through the gate, and I'm leaving. You don't have to talk to me or see me. But please, for the love of God, come down here and get it before someone else picks it up."

"You don't believe in God. Do you think I'm a fool? I don't want you near me."

"There's no way I can get in, even if I hung around. But I'm going now."

"Good!" This time there was no reply, no further plea.

Beth spent the next fifteen minutes or so fidgeting about. She thought some herbal tea might calm her, but it was to no avail. Exasperated, she went downstairs and saw a white envelope on the brick pavement of the passageway, a few feet inside the security gate. As Beth drew closer, she expected Bo to step into sight at any moment; but even as she picked up the envelope, no one appeared.

Back in her apartment, curled up in a chair, Beth opened the envelope and unfolded the paper. It was no mere note. Knowing that his life depended on the words he chose, Bo had written a detailed request in the interrogation room:

Beth, look at the photo of Mandi that you had on the easel—the background is blackened out. But when we were at the scene, there was a large mirror on the dining-room wall which would have been behind Mandi. I assume you intentionally eliminated the background for artistic purposes. Get on your computer and pull up the original photos. The mirror should be in the background.

He was correct about Beth's editing the photo, but she could not imagine how that could be of any help to Bo. Nevertheless, she read on. *Standing where you said you were positioned, and looking in the direction where you said Mandi was posed, I saw myself in the mirror. I also saw the reflection of the window behind me, including the corner of open space in the drapes.* Beth could now see the significance, anticipating what came next. *If I am correct in my theory that the killer watched you through that hole, one of your shots may have captured his reflection in the dining room mirror! Look at every photo that includes the mirror, zero in on the hole in the curtain, and enlarge it as much as possible.* Bo had asked that she e-mail anything she found to him.

CHAPTER 56

The sun was well in its descent in the overcast, winter sky as Bo, dejected and frustrated, walked away from Beth's apartment building. At least for the time being he was free, and needed to make the most of it. Although he knew that what he *should* do was get right to work, what he *wanted* was some companionship, and what he *craved* was a good, stiff drink. Even though Bo realized that, in his current state, he would be tempting fate, he ambled through the French Quarter to McCormick's. He quickly motioned Sam to the side, and before the proprietor could offer any solace or encouragement about the charges and arrest, Bo shoved a small card into the man's hand. "This is my AA sponsor, Milan Fortunato," he explained. "If you see me take a drink, give him a call right away. I don't trust myself tonight."

"We'll just head this off at the pass," Sam replied. He turned to Ben, who was working the bar, "Bo's cut off, from the get-go." The directive was all for show, however, since Sam had instructed all of his help, after Bo's first visit to the pub upon finishing rehab, that they would be fired on the spot if they ever served alcohol to him.

Knowing his boss had made the statement solely for Bo's benefit, Ben feigned his understanding with a nod and poured a Diet Coke into a tumbler of ice. "Thanks," Bo said to him. The bartender scanned the drinks of other customers, seeing if any needed to be refilled, and Bo told Sam, "I still want you to hang onto that card. The urge hasn't been this strong in a while."

"Okay," Sam said, slipping the card in his shirt pocket. "Look," he continued, "I want you to know...."

"I do know, Sam," Bo interrupted. He gave the man a soft pat on the shoulder, and turned to see if LB was around. Homer was edging by him, en route to the men's room. "Hey, Homer, how's it going?" Bo asked.

"Glad it's fucking Friday," Homer tersely replied, not stopping.

When the door to the can closed, Bo shot Sam a quizzical look. "I guess that's the Cajun version of TGIF," Sam offered, shrugging his shoulders.

"That would be GIFF," Bo corrected.

"Like I said," Sam responded, "it's the Cajun version."

"Bo!" someone called out, causing Robin Harper to turn her attention from a video-poker machine. Glancing around, Bo saw LB Harper waving from a corner bistro table and with him was Judge Alex Stillwell. As Bo made his way over to join them, he was intercepted by Robin who had abandoned her game, and gave him a hug.

"Hello, Bo," Stillwell said, rising and shaking Bo's hand. "Good to see you."

"Good to be able to see you," Bo replied. "I sure appreciate the call to Coulon." Stillwell waved it off as if it were no big deal. "No, I mean it," Bo persisted, "I don't know much about judges, but I imagine it could spell trouble for you, sticking your neck out like that."

"Bo," the jurist replied, "we both considered Tom Davis a father. So doesn't that make us brothers of a sort?"

"Yeah, but...."

"But, for the record, you don't *know* from your personal knowledge that I did anything, right?" When Bo, somewhat confused, didn't immediately respond, Stillwell continued, "So, as far as everyone at this table is concerned, I didn't do a damned thing, right?"

"I don't know shit," LB declared, prompting his wife to push a cocktail napkin toward him, saying, "I want to see that in writing."

Catching Stillwell's drift, Bo raised his glass and, in a mock toast said, "So thanks for nothing." The four of them sat and talked; Bo relating the events of the day, and the others extending assurances of support, and predicting a favorable outcome. "By the way, Alex," Bo eventually asked, "what brings you to the Big Easy? I hope it wasn't just on my account."

"Just a conference." Stillwell assured him.

"Where's your girlfriend?" Robin asked Bo.

"Beth?"

"Yes, dumbass," Robin said, lightly bumping Bo's forehead with the heel of a palm.

"What's this about a girlfriend?" Stillwell inquired.

"She's not my girlfriend," Bo said. "We only met yesterday."

"Okay, then friend-girl," Robin said in exasperation. "The point is you don't need to be alone tonight."

"Let's just say she's a little stressed," Bo replied.

"You know what's good for that, don't you?" LB asked.

"Shit, LB," Robin chided, "you think *that's* good for every damned thing."

"And your point is?" he asked. Undeterred by the laughter, LB continued to make his own point, "It's true. Hell, I saw on the TV the other night that something about stress gets female hormones raging."

Robin, still laughing, disagreed, "Bullshit. If that was the case, living with you would have me in perpetual heat."

"You got me, there," LB conceded, and Robin nodded in agreement. But LB didn't—couldn't—let it drop, "Perpetual raging? No doubt about it... but in heat?" He was giving his head a "no way" shake, and while Robin's glare would have withered the stoutest of men. LB, however, was always one to push the envelope as far to the edge as possible, "Well, like I said, when you're right, you're right." Leaning to put an arm around his wife, he said to Bo, "Forget that theory; Exhibit 'A' here blows it to hell and back."

"It's not the theory that's going to get blown," Robin laughed.

LB slid the napkin back to her. "I want *that* in writing."

"Okey dokey," Bo said, "moving right along...."

"Absolutely," Robin concurred. "Anyway, Bo, let me talk to Beth. We kind of hit it off last night. Speaking to her girl-to-girl may help."

In any other circumstance, Bo would have nixed such an idea. He had made an effort, and now it would be up to Beth to make the next move, but he needed her help, and quickly. "Knock yourself out," he told Robin. "I think she has the key to my freedom in her computer if she will just look."

"What do you think is in there?" LB asked.

"A picture of Todd Murphy spying on Beth and the Charbonnet woman taken not long before Charbonnet was murdered."

Seeing the expected astonished expressions on his friends' faces, Bo nodded in affirmation. "It's just a hunch, but I'd bet my ass that I'm right."

"Jesus," Stillwell said.

"You got that right," Robin agreed, and asked Bo for Beth's phone number. It had been in the police report that Bo had perused, but he couldn't recall what it was. "I don't remember it, but I have it in my notes at home."

"Don't worry about it," Robin said, "I'll catch her on the Square tomorrow."

"I don't think so," Bo replied. "She hasn't been working." He was soon relating to the others everything he knew about Beth Callahan, including the eerie link to his past: the photo on Beth's wall of Professor Robert Callahan with several coeds, including Serena Raven. Robin ultimately asked where Beth lived so she could pay her a visit. As Bo was giving the address, Homer hollered from the video-poker game that Robin had abandoned, "Hot damn! I just won $475 without putting anything in it!"

Robin was on her feet in a flash. "Goddammit, Homer; that was my game!"

"Shit," Bo said to LB and Stillwell, "I'm the one who interrupted her." He told his buddies that he thought it was a prudent time to make his exit, and they agreed.

CHAPTER 57

Beth Callahan sat on her sofa, knees tucked under her, and wrapped in a soft, cozy blanket. It wasn't so much the temperature, as it was the desire to recede into the protection of a cocoon. The letter lay opened before her, on the cypress table. She had read it several times, and now just stared blankly at it.

Beth had been sure of herself her entire life, questioning her judgment only at the news of Mandi's death. Since then, she had been on an emotional roller coaster that had sapped all vitality, and laid to waste her confidence in everything and everyone, especially in herself. It was just yesterday that she had begun to sense a resurrection from the ashes of despondency. But today, the rising Phoenix had been shot down and, by all appearances, the man who had pulled the trigger was Bo Landry. The same man who had just left the threshold of her sanctuary, asking her to trust him. Trust him? Beth didn't even trust herself.

So, it was out of curiosity, rather than trust, that Beth shed her covering, picked up the letter, and walked across the room to her computer. It took a few minutes to boot up and for all of the icons to appear on the monitor. After clicking the one for the Photoshop program, she scanned through the files, locating the one for Mandi.

Tears welled in Beth's eyes, her gut wrenching, as she proceeded through the photos. This wasn't such a good idea after all, she thought. She had the cursor on the "x" and was ready to click the mouse, but something compelled her to reconsider and forge ahead, possibly some notion that, by escaping, she would be abandoning her friend whose images were the only tangible things Beth retained of her. Memories would be treasured, but they were ephemeral, eventually fading unless periodically refreshed by some scent, sight, or physical object. Believing that she had horribly and irrevocably failed Mandi once, Beth was determined not to do so again, no matter how painful. She would not abandon her best friend with the click of a mouse. One does not log off from loyalty, ever.

Passing through the edited versions, Beth found the raw one in which she had zoomed the closest to Mandi. Bo was right. Captured in the dining-room mirror, beyond Mandi, was the space left by the errant curtain. An eerie pall enveloped Beth as she went about the editing work Bo requested, focusing on that space, clicking it larger and larger. With each touch to the mouse, a face gradually took form, but too much clarity was lost in the enlargement process to be of any benefit. Nevertheless, Beth printed a copy and returned to the sofa.

Bo had told Beth that he was sure Todd Murphy was the killer, but she had never seen Murphy, not even in a picture. Even if she had, it would be no use since the photo enlargement was too blurry and grainy to compare with her memory. Because it could be almost any male face Beth was looking at, she believed sending it to Bo would be useless in spite of his familiarity with Murphy's appearance. Moreover, Lieutenant Deschamps warned Beth, for her own safety, to break off all contact with Bo. Thus, she wasn't of a mind to send anything to him, or otherwise communicate with him, unless and until she became convinced that he was not involved in any way, in the murders.

Although she considered it impossible for anyone to say whose face was in the photograph, Beth hoped that she could at least satisfy herself whose it *wasn't*. She carefully scrutinized the image, comparing what could be gleaned from it with the image she held of Bo Landry in her mind's eye. However, no matter how hard she tried, it was a futile effort. While it could be a hundred others, she couldn't, in all honesty, say it wasn't Bo.

Disappointed and anxious, Beth had to find some way to relax and exorcise the demons tormenting her mind. She didn't trust herself in her current state, but her true self had yet to fail her whenever she had been able to find it. Consequently, Beth unrolled her yoga mat and popped in a Sri Chinmoy CD into the Bose.

One of the principles of traditional yoga meditation Beth had learned, was that she should not believe anything she is told. On the other hand, however, she should not reject anything either. She was to follow a systematic path of insight attained by thinning the soul or spirit of extraneous clutter. In trying to explain the process to Mandi, Beth had used the metaphor of a painting. "Our true self is just behind the canvas on which we paint or allow others to paint, countless layers of suggestions, teachings, or other concepts," she began. "We can't get *behind* the canvas to our true self, however, until we first get *to* the canvas; and the only way to do that is by removing each layer of paint."

Utilizing a meditation method of focusing on an object, Beth now directed all of her concentration on the image she had seen in the photograph, allowing all thoughts of what she had been told by everyone else to subside. Sometime later—how long, she couldn't say—Beth rose to her feet, retrieved a pencil and sketchpad, and re-settled on the sofa.

After turning the photograph upside-down on the table, she allowed her drawing hand to move as it willed. At times, as the soothing, enchanting music continued, her eyes would close; even when open, her gaze was fixed, trance-like, straight ahead, and focused on nothing. The pencil was at rest when the spell broke, and in the minutest, clearest detail was the face of the man Beth Callahan was certain was Mandi's killer.

CHAPTER 58

Bo Landry laid on his bed atop the covers, shoes still on. The lights were out, his eyes closed, and the rhythmic drone of the ceiling fan was intermittently drowned out by the roar of the revelers at a nearby corner bar. Arriving home from McCormick's, Bo had locked up, detoured into the bathroom to empty his bladder, and proceeded to his bedroom where he collapsed.

Everything was unraveling; the very essence of whom and what he was turned inside out. Life, as he knew it, had been tossed on its head. Being on the receiving end of the criminal justice system was unnerving, and as exhausted as the realization of his circumstances left him, he knew sleep would be impossible. So he would simply lie there and exist, content in an inert state, until either a brilliant idea or further catastrophe struck.

"Who you calling a prostitute?" Bo heard someone shout from the sidewalk. "Aw, jeez," he mumbled, opening his eyes.

"I ain't no prostitute!" The voice of the indignant, accused, street strumpet, worked at sounding feminine, but Bo could tell without investigating the protest emanated from a male. "Hey, where you going? I ain't near 'bout tru wid you!" He, she, or whatever called out, "I'm calling da po-lice!" Yeah, Bo thought, that's just what you need to do. "Hello, 911?... Yes, my name is Bliss Knight, that's spelled wid a 'K'; and I want to report... Hello? Hello? Hell-o-o? Shit." After evidently re-dialing, he heard the voice again, "Yes, 911?... Hello? Hello? Hell-o-o? I said, 'Hell-o-o.' Hello, hello, hello..."

"Damn," Bo said, rising from the bed. Enough was enough. He was in the hall, on the way to his front door, when he heard the whiney voice of Ray Romano announce from the computer in the home office, "Check your mail, already!" Bo was surprised to see that it was an e-mail from Beth. He had not expected to hear from her, at least not until after Robin Harper interceded on his behalf. The message was brief: "I don't have any idea who this is, but maybe it will help. Sorry I doubted you."

There were two attachments; the first was labeled "Photo," and the other "Drawing." *Drawing? What the hell?*

Bo had requested the photo, and was confident in what it would prove. Anxious to see that proof, which he intended putting in Deschamps' hands, he opened the photograph and his heart sank. Yes, someone was peering through the window, and it could be Todd Murphy, but Bo knew the features were so distorted Deschamps would never be convinced. "Shit," he sighed. He took a deep breath, let it out, and was about to send a reply, thanking Beth for the effort, when he remembered the other attachment, and opened it instead. *What the...*

It was a professional-grade portrait of sorts, complete in every detail, the face of a man gazing through a window. Beth had obviously drawn the window and drapery from the photo, but the face was not that of Todd Murphy; nor was it of some stranger. *What the hell* was *this?*

Bo walked to the living room, where he had tossed his notepad on the coffee table, and flipped through the pages to the notes he had jotted down while perusing the police files in Lenny Pitre's office. Finding Beth's number, he gave her a call.

"No," she told him; it was no joke. Just as she had written in her e-mail, she did not know who the man was.

"Beth, the photo is the best evidence. Hell, it's the *only* evidence, and the guy shown in it could be anybody."

"I know, I know," Beth replied. "That's why I sent the drawing. I don't know who it is, but I know what I saw."

"What you saw?" Bo asked in exasperation. "What the hell are you talking about?" Hearing Beth's explanation, he erupted, "Great! That's just fucking great! All I have to do is hand the photo to Deschamps and say, 'Don't worry that you can't tell who's in the picture, Lieutenant, because I have this drawing. No, it's not from an eyewitness. A Jackson Square artist saw it in a vision.'"

"It was not a vis...."

"Wait, wait! The good thing about doing that would be that I wouldn't have to stand trial for murder because I'd be declared fucking insane!"

"Bo...."

"But the downside is that they'd lock me up forever in the loony bin when they took a look at the drawing—a damned sitting, well respected judge! Really, Beth?"

"A judge?"

"Yes, Beth, a trial judge back home in Mississippi. *The* judge who's like a brother to me, and is doing everything he can to save my ass. Judge Alex Stillwell."

"I'm confused."

"No shit, Sherlock. So let me *un-confuse* you with some facts. Aside from knowing him practically my entire adult life, and the kind of man he is, he can't possibly be the murderer. Not only..."

"How can you be so sure of that, Bo?" Beth interrupted.

"Because not only are all of the murders down here tied in forensically, they're also connected to Serena's murder up in Mississippi. The same guy did it, and the blade, with Serena's blood on it, was found in Todd Murphy's house. *He's* the damned killer, not Alex Stillwell. Jeez, Beth, what the hell were you thinking?"

"I was *thinking* that you asked me to trust you. That it was hard to do, but I took a step in faith. I was *thinking* that it's time for *you* to do the same for *me.*"

Bo's head was spinning. He wanted to trust her, to exhibit some reciprocity of faith, but doing so seemed totally illogical. How could he possibly put everything on the line, based on an artist's drawing?

He recalled seeing another painting by that same artist, however; the one that had captured his attention the first morning he awoke in New Orleans on a Jackson Square bench. The piece was an eerie depiction of his encounter by the river with that creep who called himself Warlock. The event occurred only the night before he saw the painting, which meant Beth had seen the event before it happened And Bo was an eyewitness to the event; he knew it was real. Now, that same artist had seen something else which she drew, and was asking Bo to have faith that it, too, was real.

Out of the blue a biblical passage resurfaced from Bo's childhood, a time when he had been a believer: *Your sons and daughters shall prophesy, your old men shall dream dreams, and your young men shall see visions.* What Beth was asking of Bo defied all reason and logic, yet he knew that, at least once before, she had been right in what she had "seen." *But jeez, this?*

"Bo, are you there?"

"Yeah, sorry. I was just thinking."

"And?"

Knock yourself out; she may hold the key. That's what Bo had said, in giving Robin Harper his blessing to speak with Beth on his behalf. Alex was there and heard. He had heard Bo talk about Beth's assistance and that the "key" was a photo, on Beth's computer, of the killer spying on

Mandi and Beth. Actually, Bo had said the photo was of Todd Murphy, but what if it was Alex, as Beth had drawn? He'd do everything possible to destroy the evidence and the person who possessed it. Christ, Bo recalled, the last thing he had mentioned before leaving the pub was Beth's address!

"Okay, Bo, I'm hanging up now," Beth announced after what seemed an eternity of silence.

"Get out!" Bo barked.

"I said, I'm hanging up."

"No, no, that's not what I mean. You need to get out, you're in danger. He knows you have the picture and where you live!"

"What? How would he...."

"There's no time to explain, Beth. Just get out, now!"

"Okay, okay, I'll go to my parents' house."

"Good. No, not there."

"I'll be safe," she assured.

"I don't think so," Bo sheepishly replied. "I ran into LB, Robin and Alex a few hours ago at McCormick's. Robin asked where my girlfriend was, and Alex wanted details. I told them everything, including your father's name and about one of the photos of him I noticed in your apartment."

"Why would you mention a photo of my dad?"

"Now's not the time, Beth. If it's Alex, he can easily go online now and find your parents' address. Don't go there."

"If it's Alex," Beth echoed. "You don't really believe me, do you?"

"I don't know what the hell to believe. But I'm not taking any chances with your life while I sort out this shit."

"Is that what I am to you, Bo—your girlfriend?"

"Dear God, Beth. This is not the time." After a pause, "Is there any place out of the city you can go?"

"Yeah, but what about you? What are you going to do?"

"Try to get some hard-core proof that will either confirm or disprove this damned drawing, and I've got to hurry, but not until I know you're safe. I've got your number, and now you've got mine stored in your phone. I need to know where you'll be and...."

"It's my father's fishing lodge, southeast...."

"Don't tell me now. There's no time. As soon as you hang up, call that old geezer in your building."

"Dr. Marsalis?"

"Yeah. Get him to come to your apartment and see you to your car. Just tell him you're kind of weirded out by everything, but don't tell him what's going on. I don't want him shooting the first person he sees. Can you send e-mails on your phone?'

"Sure."

"As soon as you're safely on the road, e-mail me the directions where you'll be. E-mail, don't text. That way, I can print it out. Where are you parked?"

"Right in front of the building."

"Good." After getting the make, model, and color of her vehicle, he said, "I'm headed your way to make sure you're off safely. Don't forget to e-mail those directions." Ending the call, he sent a text message to LB. *Please, dear God, let him still be there.*

CHAPTER 59

The eight ball could not have been in any better position: right on the lip of a corner pocket, no other ball in the path between it, and the cue ball only two feet away. It was a shot everyone in McCormick's knew LB Harper could make blindfolded—game over. But for LB, with age came the hard-learned lesson that nothing in life was to be taken for granted, and especially so in an endeavor as important as pool.

Left arm extended, index finger and thumb held like a rifle sight, LB crouched low, chin barely above the stick drawn back by his right arm, cocked and ready to fire; except this particular shot wouldn't require much firepower, a "gimme" if there ever was one. In fact, LB was a little miffed that Dan, the bona fide '60s hippie whose long ponytail had long ago turned gray, was actually requiring him to go through the motion, missing the irony in getting perturbed at someone who also took nothing for granted.

However, LB's state of pique was nothing compared to his irritation when, just as he pulled the trigger, the phone in his pocket vibrated and beeped. The tip of the stick lurched forward, but missed the cue ball's center, striking it instead on the right, and causing it to bump into one of Dan's solids.

"Wrong ball," his wife Robin deadpanned.

Scowling, LB slowly raised his head and noticed Dan holding a cell phone to an ear. "This better not be you," LB snarled, reaching into his pocket. Luckily for the perplexed flower child, who had taken a call from his sister, the text message for LB was from Bo: "Alex still there?"

Having lost, LB stood aside, making way for Dan's awaiting challenger to rack the balls for a game that LB knew he should be playing, and sent a rather harsh reply to Bo: "No mf. Btw, u o me. Cost me game." After putting the phone back in his pocket, he told Robin, "Come on, let's go."

"Oh no, not until you play again. You'll be in a snit the rest of the night."

Before LB could say anything further, he received another text. He read it twice, shook his head in confusion and, without saying anything to Robin, walked to the bar. Although she couldn't hear what was said, Robin saw him speaking to Sam and assumed he was settling their tab. So she was somewhat bewildered when LB walked past her to the vacant, un-bussed table they had earlier occupied with Bo Landry and Alex Stillwell, carrying a paper bag.

Life with LB was full of surprises and odd moments; curious as to what her husband was up to now, Robin trailed behind, only to witness him pick up one of the empty tumblers with a napkin, and place it in the bag. LB turned back around and, still without an utterance, proceeded past his wife, and out the door. Catching up with him on the sidewalk, she said, laughing, "Okay, I've got to ask: What the hell are you going to do with that glass?"

"Shove it up Bo Landry's ass," LB responded. Despite Robin's further exhortations for clarification, that was all he said the entire walk to Bo's place. And judging by the purpose evident in his face and gait, Robin believed he meant it.

CHAPTER 60

Bo Landry had serpentined his way through the Carnival carousers, down St. Ann, and as far as Jackson Square when he received LB's text message that Alex Stillwell was no longer at the pub. Driven by a heightened sense of urgency, Bo sped up his pace on Chartres, pushing and shoving his way along the short block to Madison Street.

Beth had said that her SUV, a white Outback, was parked in front of her building, and Bo exhaled in relief when he didn't see any such car there. Just to be sure, he trotted the rest of the block to Decatur and back again to Chartres in case he had overlooked it the first time. No white Outback. Wanting to make damned sure Beth had not encountered a problem, Bo fished out his cell phone. While pulling up the received-calls menu, he received a text from Beth: "Am ok. On rd. Directions sent." He fired off a quick reply, stating that he would stay in touch and asking that she do likewise. Now if he could only get some good news from LB.

Bo could not fathom Alex Stillwell as a sexually sadistic, serial killer. Nor was there was any real evidence indicating that he was anything of the sort; not a scintilla. Yet Bo had sent Beth skedaddling off to God-knows-where, in the middle of the night. It was crazy. He had acted on nothing but faith, and that trust was in someone he barely knew. Bo felt rather foolish, and returned to more familiar territory—that of logic and deduction. He was determined to find proof which would either eliminate Alex, in which case Bo would never mention any of this to a soul, or confirm Beth's suspicions, vision, intuition, or whatever the hell it was; which was why he grew increasingly anxious, receiving no further message from LB. *Did he get Alex's glass in time, or was it already in Sam's dishwasher?*

There was no way Bo could present Beth's drawing to Lieutenant Deschamps without something corroborative. Furthermore, even if the detective believed that it was Alex in the photo, it would only prove that the judge was a voyeur, a peeping-tom. While that might get him removed from office, it was hardly the basis for a murder rap. Something conclusive would be required, and Bo hoped that Deschamps could be persuaded to have Alex's DNA, extracted from his drinking glass at McCormick's, compared with the DNA from the semen found in and on Mandi Charbonnet's body.

Bo certainly couldn't be the one to approach Deschamps with such a notion, but he knew someone who could. No doubt, there was plenty more that would have to be explained: the pubic hair found on the body of Cindy Babineaux and identified as Bo's; the gun, registered to Todd Murphy, used to kill Babineaux and Bud Ritchie; the surgical blade that had mutilated Serena, found in Murphy's house. All of that, however, would just have to wait. *One step at a time.*

Such were the thoughts tumbling in Bo's head as he hoofed it, the best he could, back up St. Ann. As he neared Dauphine, LB's apartment came into view. The lights were off and shutter-doors closed, sure signs that neither of the Harpers were yet home, causing Bo to ponder whether his friend had totally disregarded the last text request. Actually, Bo wouldn't have blamed LB if he had ignored it. Bo knew he was not making any sense.

He ascended the steps of his own stoop, and was in the process of unlocking the doors when he heard, from his left, the familiar, deep voice that belied LB's slight frame, "Hey, you want this or not?" Bo followed the direction of the voice. People were still steadily descending upon the Quarter from the parking area around Louis Armstrong Park, but Bo didn't see LB or Robin among the procession. Squinting for a few seconds, he spotted them halfway up the block, emerging from the shadows of an awning and into the soft luminescence of the streetlights. LB was lifting up a paper bag for Bo to see. Opening the glass-paneled door beyond the louvered ones, Bo motioned for them to follow.

However, rather than waiting to see them in, he left the door ajar and phoned Father Ambrose, apologizing for disturbing him at such a late hour. Multitasking at the computer, Bo asked a huge favor of the priest, while simultaneously pulling up Beth's e-mail. Just as it appeared on the screen, however, he heard LB and Robin coming up the steps, and clicked "Print." *No time to read it now.* "Hey!" LB called out.

Lowering the phone, Bo yelled back, "I'll be right there!" "I'm on my way, Father," he said into the phone, "and many, many thanks." Snatching the printout, Bo proceeded to the front room.

Robin Harper was looking around, taking in the décor; and Bo embarrassingly realized she had not seen the inside of his home since the rainy day the three of them had hurriedly jammed it with furniture and boxes. "Alex said you did a good job fixing up the place," she commented, still scanning the room." Bo briefly regretted not having invited his best friends over at least once.

The fleeting thought was gone when LB growled, "You want to tell me what the hell is going on?" shoving the bag at Bo. It was so abrupt that Bo, in accepting the container, reflexively let the printout drop from his hand.

"I think Beth's in danger," Bo replied. Although the thought was uttered, Bo found it nearly impossible.

LB's gruffness evaporated. "But what does Alex's glass have to do with any...."

Only then had Robin's off-hand comment registered with Bo. "What did you say about Alex?" he quizzed her.

"I said he complimented you about the way you fixed up the place."

"I haven't had Alex over. Hell, today was the first time I've seen him since I left Mississippi," Bo snapped.

"Don't get huffy," LB replied. "It was the day you became a rich man. You weren't home, and he found me at McCormick's. Had a large brown envelope and told me what it was—a fucking cashier's check for over a million bucks. Said he didn't want to leave it sticking out of your door or mailbox. Made sense to me. So he asked if I'd see that you got it. Hell, I sure didn't want the damned thing lying around the bar. So I told Alex I could do better than that; that I had a key to your place."

"I knew from the note you left with the package that *you* had come over. But why didn't you say anything about Alex being with you?"

"I didn't leave the envelope or any note."

"Goddammit, LB, what the fuck are you saying? You're talking in circles!"

"You gave me a key, but I haven't been in here since the day you moved in."

"So you gave Alex your key? He came in by himself?"

"Made sense to me. What's the big deal?"

"Goddammit, LB. Why?"

"Why what? I was in the middle of a pool game, and Alex brought the key right back."

"Goddammit, LB," Bo repeated.

"Like I said, made sense to me. You got the check. What's the damned problem?"

Bo didn't know the answer to that question, but the note from LB that wasn't from LB sure raised a red flag, in addition to Beth Callahan's odd warning. And Bo recalled the note had been typed. Alex Stillwell could have easily manufactured it on Bo's computer while inside the apartment. "Why was Alex really in New Orleans?" Bo asked LB. "Surely he didn't make a three-hour drive just to deliver a check. It's also hard to believe he made the same drive to meet with Michael Coulon about my case. Why not just pick up the phone?"

"Hell, Bo," LB replied, "Alex makes frequent trips down here; whenever his panel hears oral arguments."

A Mississippi judge hearing cases in New Orleans? Bo needed answers, but trying to pull them from LB was akin to Batman interrogating the Riddler. "You're talking in circles again, LB."

"Alex is on the Fifth Circuit," LB explained. "He spends most of his time in his Jackson office, but since the court is based in New Orleans he's down here a lot. Hell, he even has a condo in the Quarter; on Iberville I think."

Bo's mind was reeling. "When did this happen?"

"I don't remember exactly. Sometime just before you got out of rehab and showed up at McCormick's to see Sam."

"And you're just now telling me?"

"You're just now asking me," LB glibly replied. "I'm retired, you know. The last people on my discussion list are lawyers and judges. And you still haven't said why Alex, or his damned glass you had me bring over, is so important."

"Jesus, LB, Alex may be the killer."

"Have you lost your damned mind?"

"I only suspected Beth might be in danger, and now I'm even more concerned. I told her to get the hell out of Dodge until I sorted things out. She's on her way to a fishing camp somewhere."

"You *have* lost your mind," LB replied, as Bo placed the bag on the table, pulled out his cell phone, and called Beth's number. It went straight to her voice mail. *Fuck.* "Beth, this is Bo. Call me ASAP. Alex is...." A call was coming in. Hoping it was Beth, he answered, but was mistaken as to the identity of the caller. "Yes, Father, I understand. I'm on the way too." To LB, "I know it sounds crazy; that's why I needed this," picking up the bag. "It *was* a favor, LB, and I *do* appreciate it. But I'll have to give you the details later. I've got to hurry."

Bo had moved past LB and Robin, who had been standing there, mouth agape, during the astounding dialog, and was out the door and on the stoop by the time LB asked, "Go where? Have you talked to the police?"

"That's where I'm heading. But I don't know how long it will take to convince Deschamps to get a test on this glass. Then I've got to locate Beth. Shit, I don't know how I'm going to do everything, LB. I'm just winging it here. I really need to go. Lock up for me, will you?"

The Harpers looked at each other in total shock. "I don't like that she didn't answer her phone," Robin said. "I have a bad feeling, LB; a real bad feeling."

While his wife was fretting, LB bent down and picked up a piece of paper off the floor. He studied it, and said to her, "Then come on."

CHAPTER 61

Beth Callahan had hurriedly crossed the street, and unlocked her car. Before getting behind the wheel, she forced a reassuring smile, and waved at the kind, grandfatherly-looking gentleman standing on the sidewalk outside their gate. If the circumstances had not been so dire, she would have found the sight of Dr. Joseph Marsalis quite amusing. Clad in blue flannel pajamas, matching slippers, and a black wool overcoat, the geriatric sentry was peering up and down Madison Street.

With his left hand, the old man grasped a lapel and pressed the unfastened overcoat against his body, fighting the nippy gust from the nearby river, funneling between the buildings along the street. Had it been any other time when the coat served its usual purpose, Dr. Marsalis would have put the buttons to good use. Now, however, they would be a hindrance, for Marsalis's primary objective was not warmth, but concealment—of the sawed-off, double-barrel shotgun held by his age-blotched hidden right hand. Regardless what the State of Louisiana might have to say about the illegal weapon, Beth was grateful that Dr. Marsalis had it now, a sentiment she expressed with a quick peck on the old man's pink, wind-chilled cheek before scampering to her car.

It was only after Beth turned left on Decatur that her bodyguard's huddled image vanished from her rearview mirror. As soon as Beth made the turn, she stalled in traffic and thought she'd make the most of the pause by sending Bo the directions she had promised. "Shit!" she exclaimed, pounding the steering wheel. In her hasty exodus, she had left her phone inside her apartment. Par for the course, she mused. Leaving home once seemed impossible for Beth Callahan; it was usually more like leaving-returning-leaving home.

Inching bumper-to-bumper along Decatur, Beth eventually reached

Dumaine, the first cross-street, and turned left. She couldn't continue her circle home, however, with a left at Chartres, as it was one-way in the opposite direction. Even though the SUV's windows were closed, while Beth waited for a herd of frolicking humanity to cross the intersection, she heard laughter and music booming from a corner bar popular with the locals as well as tourists. Beth thought of the Bloody Marys served there, and believed it sported the best jukebox in the city. "My Baby Don't Wear No Panties" was a perennial favorite selection. Only true blues junkies like Beth Callahan knew of Mean Gene Kelton, a Mississippi-born musician with a knack of picking a mean guitar to bad lyrics—"bad" as in "naughty."

At last, the intersection cleared and Beth continued up Dumaine for another block, then took a left on Royal. She passed several art galleries, including one on her left where she had several pieces displayed on consignment. Coming to the intersection at St. Ann, she turned left, around the city's first "skyscraper," a three-story structure erected in 1801 known as the Languille Building.

Down St. Ann, left on Chartres, and right on Madison, Beth was back where she had started almost a half-hour ago, but with no available parking in sight. She pulled the SUV halfway onto the sidewalk, directly in front of her gate, killed the engine and lights, and activated the emergency blinkers. As long as she allowed enough room on the street for cars to squeeze through, it shouldn't be a problem.

It didn't take any time for Beth to spot the phone. After calling Dr. Marsalis earlier, she had set it on the table in the sitting area, while pulling on a jacket, before dashing out the door. Beth opted not to bother her good-natured neighbor a second time. After all, her car was only a foot or two from the gate, and explaining her absentmindedness would be embarrassing.

Nearing the gate through the cavernous passageway, Beth heard a horn blaring. Drawing closer, she saw that a delivery truck was unable to get around her car. Through the gate, she waved in acknowledgement to the driver. *I'm coming!* In the hands of Big Easy motorists, however, horns are not mere accessories, they are weapons. Even though this particular driver clearly saw Beth raise her hands in surrender, he continued to lay down an unmerciful barrage. Beth jumped into the Outback and bolted off the curb. Once fully on the pavement, she lowered her window and aimed another popular road armament at the obnoxious honker—a middle finger.

Rather than fighting the Decatur Street traffic all the way to Esplanade, Beth again escaped the congestion at the first opportunity by turning left on Dumaine. She made a right on Chartres and proceeded to

Esplanade. After turns at St. Claude, St. Bernard, and North Claiborne, the Outback was soon crossing Elysian Fields, the Industrial Canal, and continued on Judge Perez Drive in the area north of the Chalmette National Historical Park, site of the Battle of New Orleans. Staying on Judge Perez, Beth continued through Chalmette, the governmental seat of St. Bernard Parish.

Driving through an expanse of pastures between the towns of Mereaux and Violet, Beth set the cruise control. She e-mailed the directions to Bo, followed by a text message that she had done so, and that she was safely on the road. The route soon carried her southeast, parallel to the Mississippi River, on her right. Just east of a point where the river forms a drastic bend southwest, Judge Perez crosses Highway 300; there, Beth turned left, heading east, parallel to Bayou Terre aux Boeufs and then southeast toward the town of Reggio.

Snuggled between the Mississippi River, to the south, and the Mississippi River Gulf Outlet waterway, to the north, is Delacroix Island. The name is misleading, for the "island" is actually one of the largest estuaries in the world, flanked by bayous to the west and marshes to the east. This area, referenced by Bob Dylan in *"Tangled Up In Blue,"* was first settled in the 1780s by Islenos, or Spanish Cajuns, from the Spanish Canary Islands. By the 1820s, Delacroix Island was firmly established as a fishing Mecca, supplying the restaurants of New Orleans, decades before the Civil War, with a seemingly inexhaustible supply of shrimp, fish, and crabs. Beth recalled the first time she had made the trip with her family. Although only a forty-five-minute or so drive from the city, Beth thought they were traveling to the end of the world, a suspicion confirmed in her mind by a sign that read: "End of the World Marina."

Coming up on Reggio, Beth retrieved her phone from the passenger seat, thinking it a good time to let Bo know she was okay and not too far from her destination. The digital display, however, read "Battery Low." She fumbled through the glove box and console, searching for her charger, but couldn't find it in either one. It might be under a seat, but she didn't want to stop and look. For whatever reason, sometimes when she couldn't make calls, she could still text. Utilizing the glow of the town's lights, Beth thought it would be a rather easy task to perform; even more helpful were the more direct beams leveled by an oncoming vehicle.

Beth continued to drive with her left hand, holding her phone at eye level with her right. *Yes, the lighting is great.* She started pressing buttons with her thumb: "Almost there. No prob...." But that was as far as she had gotten before her attention was diverted by flashing blue lights behind her. The car she had just passed was making a U-turn. Checking the speedometer and seeing that she was well under the speed limit, Beth was certain that the "Smokey," as her father would say, was after someone ahead of her. Thus, as any good citizen should, she pulled aside on the shoulder to let him pass.

When Beth insisted to Deputy Sheriff Jason Wells that she had not been speeding, the skinny, towheaded lawman, appearing to be little more than a dewy-eyed kid still fighting—and losing—a war with acne, replied, "Yes, ma'am; license and registration, please." After perusing them, and comparing the photo with Beth's countenance, he asked her to step out of the vehicle.

"Are you arresting me?" she asked indignantly.

"No, ma'am, just procedure—for officer safety. I need you to stand behind your vehicle while I get in mine and run this information through."

"For what?"

"To see if there are any outstanding warrants or wants, ma'am."

"You've got to be kidding."

"No, ma'am."

Beth was growing increasingly agitated while the deputy followed his protocol. She had made it safely out of New Orleans and reasonably sure she had not been followed. But what if she was wrong? What if that deranged judge had come to her apartment, only to see her leave, and tried to follow? She imagined that the driver of every passing car was him. Even if he had lost her along the way, that snafu was now rectified. *Hey, no worries; there she is, standing on the side of the road. I'll just pull off a little farther down, wait for her to pass me, then I'll follow right behind. Thanks, deputy.* Beth instinctively turned her head at each passing vehicle to see if it stopped anywhere in sight.

"All clear, ma'am," Deputy Wells announced, exiting his car and walking toward her. "Except this," he added, holding out a piece of paper.

"A ticket? For what?" Beth demanded.

"Your phone, ma'am."

"My phone? Are you telling me it's against the law to use a cell phone!"

"No, ma'am; not to make calls, anyway. That is, not for someone your age."

"I beg your pardon?"

That he had committed a grave faux pas against all womanhood totally escaped the youthful deputy. He had only meant that Beth did not appear to be what the state statute termed a "novice" driver, banned from any cell phone use behind the wheel. "But texting while driving *is* a violation, ma'am," he continued.

"What makes you think I wasn't calling someone?" Beth argued.

"Your phone was on the console when I came to the window, ma'am. I couldn't read the words, but I saw some still lit up on the display."

But you couldn't have seen that when you pulled me over, you moron! Beth wanted to scream. She had seen enough episodes of *Law and Order* to suspect he had no probable cause to make the stop; that any evidence he acquired after that illegality was tainted, inadmissible. However, more than straightening out this yahoo, Beth wanted to get in her car and leave, to be on the move to safety. *Be smart, Beth. Don't let your Irish temper get the best of you.*

Beth's anxiety had been apparent to the deputy while he had watched her from his cruiser, and it continued throughout their ensuing dialog. Her manner seemed to be out of proportion to merely receiving a ticket. Looking beyond her, through the rear window of the SUV, Wells could see that whatever was in the storage area was concealed by a retractable, opaque screen pulled from a bar attached across the backseat.

"Ma'am, do you mind if I ask what you've got back there?" he asked, pointing at the Outback.

"A few canvases," she snapped. "I'm an artist."

"Mind if I take a look?"

"Be my guest," she replied in disgust, and stepped aside.

Instead of reaching for the handle, however, the officer studied her for a moment, then inexplicably said, "Aw, that won't be necessary, ma'am. Have a safe trip." He returned her credentials; and once he climbed into his cruiser, Beth got behind the wheel of her car. She picked up the phone, finished her message, and sent it to Bo's number. Deputy Wells remained behind her until she pulled off, then made another U-turn and went on his way, in the opposite direction.

CHAPTER 62

"I waive all that bullshit," Bo Landry scoffed at Lieutenant Winston Deschamps when the detective mentioned the irregularity of an accused leaving his attorney out of the loop. "Nothing about these cases has been *regular,*" Bo observed, "and there's no time to waste going through a mouthpiece."

"Understood," Deschamps replied. "So what do you have for me warranting such urgency?"

They were in the office of Monsignor Ambrose, who had aroused the lieutenant from his slumber at Bo's request. It was the first time Bo had seen the priest without his cleric's collar and Deschamps in anything but a coat and tie. The detective was visibly irritated, the priest puzzled; for Bo had not offered a reason in asking Ambrose to pick up the phone and summon Deschamps beyond the assertion that Beth Callahan's life could be in danger. Now that the three were gathered, Bo would have to explain, and it didn't take a genius to predict Deschamps's reaction. Well, here it goes, Bo thought, sucking in a resolute breath.

Surprisingly, neither of the other men interrupted, only staring in silent disbelief. However, when Bo finished, Deschamps asked, "Are you mad?"

"Very mad," Bo replied, "but that's beside the point. What have you got to lose by having the test run?"

"On a federal judge? No evidence? Just for the hell of it?" the lieutenant barked in staccato cadence. "What do I have to lose? Well, let's see: esteem among colleagues, self-respect, my job—*everything,* you idiot!"

"Then don't use his name," Bo calmly suggested. "Just submit the glass as some numbered exhibit, possibly containing DNA from an unknown source. If it matches with any of the Charbonnet semen samples, then you can connect the dots in the paperwork by taking statements from LB Harper, a retired judge from Mississippi who lives here now, and me. We're your chain of custody, and can testify that we personally witnessed Alex drink from the glass."

Deschamps looked at Ambrose to gauge his reaction to this nonsense, but the priest failed to meet his gaze, staring at the night sky through a window. "No," Deschamps declared, returning his attention to Bo. "You, Mr. Landry, are the one charged because the *evidence,* not *conjecture,* points to *you.* Merely requesting such a comparison—even of an unknown—would undermine those charges. I will have no part in that."

"Well, we certainly couldn't risk *that,* could we?" Bo rhetorically replied. "Deschamps, you enjoy the reputation of having a steel-trap mind; but it's more like concrete—all mixed up and permanently set."

"Let me tell you one damned thing, you…."

"Save it. I'm done here," Bo interrupted, rising from his chair. "Thanks anyway, Father."

"Bo, wait," Ambrose beckoned.

"No, Father, I can't. I wouldn't be able to sleep tonight without knowing I did everything in my power to protect the next possible victim, and that means being with Beth." At the door, he paused and turned, "What about you, Deschamps? You going to be able to sleep, satisfied that *you* did everything possible? Good luck with that. Because if I'm right, you're going to be spending a long-ass time in one of the rector's confessionals. Maybe you should make your reservations while you're here. I've got to get on the road, but you think about that."

"You would be well-advised, Mr. Landry, to let the police handle this. I'm sure your attorney would agree."

"Deschamps, the only thing you've become adept at handling is notifying victims' families on the ass end that their loved ones have become a statistic. Thank you, but I'll handle this myself on the front end since you won't."

"Remember the terms of your bail, Mr. Landry; carrying a firearm is grounds to revoke your freedom."

"Who said I need a fucking gun?"

The door closed and the room fell into a disconcerting quietness. "He's misguided, still finding his way," Ambrose remarked, breaking the silence, and the detective nodded in agreement. "But he's neither crazy nor an idiot, Winston. I believe in him."

"Forgive me, Father, but you're *too* trusting."

The priest shrugged his shoulders, "Perhaps. Some people are too trusting; others, not enough."

"You mean me."

"I wouldn't accuse you of being too trusting, Winston," Ambrose stated. His lips slightly twisted into a teasing smirk, and his eyes twinkled as brightly as the stars at which he had moments earlier been gazing. "All I ask," he continued, "is that you keep an open mind."

"I always do," the detective protested.

"Yes, well, let me put it another way," Ambrose said. "When someone says, Lieutenant Deschamps is on the trail of a killer, it's taken as a metaphor, correct?"

"True."

"But let's look at it literally. Suppose you and your officers are in hot pursuit of a fleeing murderer in the French Quarter. Some of the bystanders—witnesses, if you will—point and exclaim, 'He went that way!' Yet, others are just as insistent in pointing in a different direction. The man can't be heading in opposite directions, so what do you do?"

"Divide my men, of course; dispatch them in both directions, searching every street in the area."

"Quite so," Ambrose affirmed, "and, if I know you as well as I believe I do, every alley, too."

"No question."

"So, Winston, since you *are* on the trail of a killer now, why would you deviate, and *not* check each street and alley in the figurative, as well as the literal, sense? You'll never know what you might find unless you do."

As the lieutenant listened, he had been rehashing the strange events of the case while fixated on the crucifix hanging on the wall behind Ambrose's desk. Winston Leblanc Deschamps dared not equate any human with the Son of God, but it occurred to him, as Ambrose talked, that Pontius Pilate had considered Christ a mere mortal when he doomed the Son of Man to the cross by washing his hands of the matter presented to him. Bo Landry had asked Deschamps to check out an "alley," authorizing a forensic test, and he had refused to even look, responding that he wanted nothing to do with it. *Can I really wash my hands in such a flippant, peremptory manner when a person's life might be hanging in the balance? Am I no better than Pilate?* These silent questions were disconcerting.

The DNA test could be justified, Deschamps reasoned, on the grounds of thoroughness. After all, it had already been determined that the semen recovered from Amanda Charbonnet's body came from more than one source, and Bo Landry was not one. Moreover, as Landry said, there was not yet any necessity of even mentioning Judge Stillwell's name.

264

The judge, the detective recalled, was the one who volunteered—perhaps a little too eagerly, now that Deschamps thought about it—the information about Landry's inheritance, and the availability of a tunnel as a means for him to surreptitiously exit the house in Mississippi in order to kill the Raven woman. The information had been important in punching a hole in Landry's alibi for that murder since that victim's killer had to be the one leaving corpses in Deschamps's jurisdiction. Landry had been arrested for one of those murders, but the case would fall apart if he were excluded in the Mississippi case. If innocent of one, Landry would necessarily be innocent of all. True, the lieutenant noted to himself, the murders had not started in New Orleans until Landry got out of rehab here; but likewise, the killings had not begun until after Stillwell's own arrival in the city.

On the other hand, New Orleans does not keep its secrets well, and the lieutenant was aware that Alex Stillwell, although he had tried to keep it "hush-hush", was responsible for Landry's unusual release on bail. Surely, if the judge had any culpability in the murder for which Landry was charged, he would not have interjected himself. He would have let Landry rot in prison. *Many serial killers attempt to interject themselves in investigations.* Those were the words Deschamps had hurled at Bo Landry, and now the detective realized they could be just as applicable to Judge Alex Stillwell. But the judge's behind-the-scenes orchestration of Landry's release didn't make any sense to Deschamps, unless..., unless Stillwell *needed* Landry on the streets for some purpose. *To deprive him of the most ironclad alibi in the world—being in jail.* If that were the case, there could be but one explanation: Stillwell intended to kill at least one more person, and needed Landry roaming free at the time, so he might be blamed for it too. It made perfect sense.

Winston Deschamps did not have any idea how long it took a crime-lab analyst to actually perform DNA testing, but he was well aware that the average turnaround time for his office to get the results was forty-five days. He hoped the time-lag was due to the backload of cases, instead of the test itself. If so, Deschamps could cut to the head of the line, day or night, with a well-placed phone call. He knew someone in the lab who owed him, big-time, but it was not a call he wished to show up on the records of his department-issued cell phone.

"Father, you mind if I use your phone?" he asked.

CHAPTER 63

Bo Landry hustled home from his fruitless face-to-face with Lieutenant Deschamps to retrieve the directions he had evidently left there in his haste to put the glass in the detective's hands. Thinking back, the last time Bo recalled holding the printout was on his way to the front room to see LB and Robin Harper, but it was nowhere to be found. *Damn, what could I have done with it?*

Bo sat at his computer, trying to remain calm. He had hurried from this very spot, knowing the Harpers were on their way inside with the glass. He couldn't imagine that he had taken the time to delete Beth's e-mail, yet it was neither in his inbox nor old mail. Still, Bo didn't panic. Surely, he would find it at the top of the deleted messages, for it was only once in a blue moon that he bothered to empty them. No dice, however; it was gone. Of all the e-mails, including a ton of spam, jokes, cartoons, and inane observations, it was Bo's rotten luck to have somehow permanently deleted the most important one.

He tried to call Beth, but was again immediately directed to her voice mail. After leaving another message, he sent her a text: "Resend directions!" However, it did little to alleviate his angst. If Beth's calls were not getting through, there was little hope that her text messages were not also being relegated into some stratospheric black hole. Bo was at a loss as to what else he could do. He briefly considered calling Beth's parents, but they didn't know him from Adam. The chances of them coughing up their daughter's whereabouts to a complete stranger calling in the dead of night seemed pretty slim. And if they had seen the story of his arrest on the local evening news, getting her location from them would be nothing short of ludicrous. Tilting his head back in exasperation, then letting it hang in defeat, one other possibility came to mind.

Ten minutes later, Bo was repeatedly pushing the buzzer labeled: "Dr. J. Marsalis." "Who's there?" an irritated voice eventually asked through the speaker.

"Bo Landry, Doctor. I'm a friend of Beth Callahan, a private investigator. You saw me visiting with her in her apartment a day or so back. You remember?"

"Yes, I remember," Marsalis snapped. "She wasn't too sure about you. Wanted me to look in on her. What do you want?"

"I need to find her, Doctor. She's in danger and I have to make sure she's okay."

"Wait a minute, aren't you the one I saw on the news?"

Shit. "Yes, but...."

"I'm calling the police."

"Wait, please!"

"She's not home anyway. Go away or I'm calling...."

"I know she's away! A fishing camp! She's on her way to her family's fishing camp, and I'm the one who told her to go!" Bo was talking as fast as he could, desperately trying to keep Marsalis engaged. "She sent me the directions, but I've lost them. I've tried calling her, but everything is going to her voice mail. I can't reach her, and that worries the hell out of me. Please, Doctor, for Beth!"

"What do you want from *me*? Why don't *you* call the police?"

"There's no time for that. A key. Beth obviously trusts you. You look out for her, don't you? I'm guessing that at some point she gave you a key to her place, to check on things when she's away or in the event of an emergency. Am I right?" Silence. "Doctor?"

"Hold on." Less than a minute elapsed. "You're right. My call went straight to her voice mail and, yes, I do have a key. What do you want it for?"

"To take a quick look on her computer. She e-mailed the directions to me from her phone, and I mistakenly deleted the message. I'm hoping *she* didn't."

"I see," was all Marsalis said, obviously still hesitant.

"I won't be but a minute Doctor, and you can watch everything I do." Bo took the ensuing silence as a deafening rejection of his plea, but then he heard the electronic lock on the gate click, and he hurried through before Marsalis entertained second thoughts.

The screensaver was a welcome sight, signaling that Beth had left the computer on. With any luck, Bo wouldn't have to worry about a password. The old man stood beyond Bo's reach, leveling the sawed-off shotgun at him. Although unnerving, Bo ignored him as best he could, and pressed the spacebar on the keyboard. The screensaver was replaced by the Yahoo! home page; and, much to Bo's relief, Beth had checked the box for the ISP to remember her user name and password. *Finally, something is going right.* Accessing the mail was a snap, and the message to Bo, with the attached directions, topped the list of the "Sent" items.

Bo opened the attachment and stepped away from the monitor. "Take a look, Doctor," he invited. Marsalis warily approached, looked, and nodded. "Satisfied?" Bo asked. "She would never have sent them if she didn't trust me."

"I suppose that is true," Marsalis agreed.

"So how about pointing that thing in another direction?" Bo urged, pointing at the shotgun. Once Marsalis obliged, Bo resumed his place at the monitor to print the directions.

CHAPTER 64

Beth Callahan slowed to make the turn off Highway 300, the Delacroix Highway, onto the oyster-shell drive which led eastward to the modest cabin her father simply called, "the camp". She had been fighting sleep since passing through the hamlet of Wood Lake, exhaustion overcoming her ire at being ticketed in Reggio. "Thank God, I'm here," she murmured.

To Robert Callahan, it was more than a place to sleep at day's end after fishing the bayous or marshes; it was a retreat, a sanctuary. Valuing the bliss of privacy over convention, and extra land over convenience, he had eschewed the smaller and more expensive lots of Delacroix proper, and purchased a larger, more remote tract farther north, opposite the fork of Bayou Terre aux Boeufs and Bayou Lery. Moreover, the site the professor selected on which to erect his lodge was farther off the road than those of his neighbors. There was no mailbox, address placard, or any other marker on the highway offering any indication that this was the turnoff for the Callahan place. Whenever giving directions to newcomers who Beth knew would be arriving after sundown, she suggested they drive the few extra miles to the Sweetwater Marina, where her father berthed his thirty-one-foot Lafitte Skiff, turn around, and backtrack to the first driveway they came to on the right that seemingly had no house to go along with it.

It wasn't that the acreage was a vast expanse of real estate; in fact, the Callahan hermitage was on a long, narrow finger of land, three feet above sea level, separating the bayous to the west, and the marshes to the east. Rather, Beth's father had taken advantage of the natural vegetation, backing the cabin nearer the marshes, and shielding its front from the highway behind acres of black mangrove shrubbery and several of the few cypress trees of significant size that had defied the tempests of Katrina.

A soupy, gray fog was drifting in from the marshes, casting everything in a ghostly veil, and forcing Beth to continue at a snail's pace, grateful it had not rolled in any sooner. Her father had taught her that one cause of the phenomena was the drastic cooling of warm, humid air from the gulf. Sure enough, when Beth glanced at the digital display on the air conditioner/heater she saw that the outside temperature was much cooler than when she had set out. Thankfully, Beth had at least grabbed a coat on her way out of her apartment. She had not taken time to pack anything, and did not have any idea how long she would be here. That's okay, she thought; there was nothing for her to unload and unpack. She could go straight to bed. It seemed the sluggish crunch of shell under the tires would never end. Then, abruptly the cabin, perched atop ten-foot-tall creosote poles, emerged from a fleeting break in the vapors. As relieved as Beth was to be here, the sight was downright spooky and sent a shiver down her spine.

Although the concrete slab beneath the elevated structure was originally used as a carport, it was soon littered with a disarray of tools, ice chests, oars, gaffs, nets, and other fishing accoutrements. Eventually Beth's father installed a counter, housing a deep sink, on which he could clean the catch-of-the-day, and a freezer to store it in. No one had been able to park there in years; so Beth nosed the Outback as close as possible to the clutter. After shutting off the motor, she picked up her phone and slipped it into her coat pocket as she proceeded up the stairs.

Unlocking the door and stepping inside, Beth was surprised by the musty, cool environs, a sign that her father had not been there in a while. Mom must be keeping him pretty damn busy, she thought, smiling. Robert Callahan was a creature of habit as well as a penny-pincher, always turning off the thermostat before returning home, and it seemed to Beth that it was colder inside the house than outdoors.

Emotionally and physically spent, Beth paused only to turn on the heat en route to the guest bedroom, the one on the "highway" side. Her parents' room was the one to the rear, opening onto a balcony overlooking the marshes. When Beth and her brothers were children, their sleeping accommodations consisted of bunk beds along opposite walls, the extra mattress available for any friend who tagged along. Now the headboard of a queen-size bed was positioned at the center of a wall that was once covered with rock-and-roll posters. They had been replaced, however, with a few of Beth's photos and smaller paintings.

Too tired to bother hanging her jacket in the closet, Beth laid it on the dresser and pulled open drawers in search of something to sleep in. She normally preferred the freedom of her "birthday suit," a phrase Beth picked up from her mother; but as cold as it was inside the cabin, it would take some time to warm up. However, even as Beth opened each drawer, she already knew it would be a futile effort. Dr. and Mrs. Callahan had three adult children and a myriad of friends who required the availability of the single small dresser, and it was decreed that no one was permitted to store items there indefinitely. Still Beth looked, hoping something she could use had been accidentally left behind. Finding nothing, she walked to her parents' room and helped herself to one of her father's T-shirts. Back in her chamber, Beth stripped and pulled it over her head. The soft cotton and Old Spice scent were as comforting as chicken soup on a wintry day. Sliding between the percale cotton sheets, Beth pulled the patchwork quilt her great-grandmother had stitched together a quarter-century earlier, over her shoulders from where it lay, folded at the foot of the bed. Beth let out a sigh. *Everything will be all right.*

She had thought sleep would come easily, but the stale-smelling air inside the house became bothersome. Once her body heat warmed the linens, she emerged from her cocoon and padded to a window, raising it a few inches for some fresh air. Rebuilding her nest for the night, or at least whatever remained of the night, Beth remembered that she was supposed to call Bo. *Crap. The phone is in my coat, across the room on the dresser. I don't want to get up again.* Reasoning that the text message she had sent in Reggio would suffice, she closed her eyes.

Slumber still remained elusive as once again, specters of self-doubt and second-guessing crept out of dark crevices of Beth's mind and into glowing consciousness. *Could I be wrong? The police wouldn't lie. The man physical evidence linked to these horrible crimes was the man who urged me to come to this remote locale and discouraged me from calling my parents or the police, stating that he would handle everything. My God, he's the* only *one who knows where I am! No, it can't be. Get a hold of yourself, Beth Callahan. Even if you're not sure of your trust in him, you can't lose trust in* yourself. *You can't abandon your instinct, your gift, your true self.*

Beth's eyes flew open. She had no idea of the hour and was unsure if she had finally dozed off and woke up, or had been lying there in perpetual fitfulness. But whatever her previous state, she was now fully alert, and the sound of grinding tires was unmistakable. *Someone is here.* Her initial thought was that it had to be Bo, since he was the only person who knew she was there. But she was torn whether she should consider his arrival as heralding security, or something more ominous.

Cautiously, Beth approached the window and was shocked to see, not one, but two figures meandering through the billowing shroud, and one of them was carrying a long-barreled gun. Fear shot through her veins, but almost instantaneously it mutated to befuddlement at her recognition of LB and Robin Harper. Beth was wondering what the hell could have brought them there at this hour—LB armed, no less—when the light came on. Not a metaphoric light, symbolic of an answer arising in her brain, but rather one that literally lit up the interior of her car.

CHAPTER 65

The beast guessed that it had been a couple of hours, maybe a little more, that he had been coiled in his transitory lair, patiently waiting. It had been risky going to Beth Callahan's apartment, but eradicating both her and her computer was a necessary mission. As he turned the corner onto her street, he had seen her wave to a gray-haired man, get behind the wheel of a white Outback, and drive away. The old man and the beast briefly faced each other on the sidewalk as the man turned to disappear through a gate. A gust of wind caught a bottom corner of the old man's trench coat, affording the beast a glimpse of a firearm barrel. *How quaint.*

The beast had lurked in the shadows on the street, considering his options. *Should I wait for the bitch to resurface, or take care of the damning evidence while I'm here?* He decided upon the latter course of action, and was weighing various means of gaining entry to the apartment when his concentration was pierced by the sight of his prey driving by. *Returning so soon? She must have forgotten something.* He moved at once, hoping to take her as she entered the gate, but his timing was thrown off when he stumbled on an uneven paver in the sidewalk. By the time he regained his balance, Beth had disappeared into the bowels of her building. However, considering where she had parked, the beast was certain she would return momentarily; so he stepped to the side of the gate, opting to strike as soon as he heard it open. *But what if there was an encore performance by the same buffoon who escorted the bitch earlier? Even armed, the old man wouldn't pose much of a physical threat, but the few seconds it would take to neutralize him might provide the bitch an opportunity to bolt, screaming her head off. She was obviously in a rush, so just maybe...* A smile crept across his face when he tested the hatchback door of her vehicle and it opened.

I was not the only one who caught a lucky break tonight. That hick deputy will never know how close his nosiness came to costing him his life. Perfectly still throughout the journey, the beast had endured aches, followed by numbness, curled atop canvases in the storage area of the Outback, diverting his consciousness from the discomfort with the anticipation of pleasures to come.

"Thank God, I'm here," the woman had uttered, snapping the beast out of his self-administered trance. But where was "here"? he wondered. Until he knew, he couldn't exactly pop out and slit her throat, they could be anywhere with witnesses around. Thus, after the beast heard the car door open and shut, he remained motionless for a few more minutes before easing back the retractable cover, just enough to take a peek. Total darkness, no sound except the steady hum of insects. Gradually sitting up, the beast liked what he saw. *We're in the middle of no-fucking-where.*

Since lights were aglow in the house, he dared not yet open a door. There was no hurry now, none at all. In fact, he decided to make his appearance much in the same way as he had with Serena—*after the bitch is asleep.* She wouldn't be able to get to her phone, and it would afford him time to knead the circulation back into his blood-deprived muscles. Well after the house was thrown into darkness the beast was still massaging them—that, and fantasizing. The thrill of being able to take his sweet time with Beth Callahan caused his pants to swell. But, just as it was time for relief, twin beams of light suffused the fog. A car was coming up the drive.

The beast quickly crouched and pulled the cover back over him. He momentarily heard two doors open and close. He neither knew nor cared who the two arrivals were, only *what* they were—interlopers. Enraged that his planned gala was in jeopardy, the beast waited for the footsteps to pass by. He slowly slid the covering open and rose. *Yes, they are in front of me now. I have to get them before they reach the steps or call out to the bitch.*

As silently as possible, he pulled on the latch and froze, ascertaining whether the sound was as loud to the intruders as it had been to him. *No, they're still walking toward the house.* The beast slid out as the door raised open, and was behind the two figures in a split second. It was a man and a woman, and the beast could see that the man carried a rifle or shotgun in one hand, and that the other arm was grasped tightly by the woman. How convenient that they are so close together, he thought. Before they could turn fully around, sensing that something was swiftly coming at them, the beast spread his powerful hands, and slammed the pair of heads against each other, dropping the meddlers on the spot.

He looked up, pleased to see that no lights had come on inside the cabin. But between floating tendrils of fog, he saw Beth Callahan's face peering down at him through a window. The beast glanced at the bodies at his feet, surprised to see LB and Robin Harper. They were still breathing, but he would have to delay finishing them off until he had the bitch inside under control. That was imperative before she got to a phone. The beast stooped to pick up LB's gun, which appeared to be a .22 automatic, and slung it into the darkness. Reaching into one of his pants pockets, he felt the familiar shape and texture of the aluminum wrapper. Knowing that the surgical blade it housed would soon be put to use, the beast bounded up the stairs.

CHAPTER 66

Beth Callahan had stood at the window, paralyzed with terror, witnessing the figure slink from her car, and realizing that the monster had been with her throughout the drive. *I was hurrying so to get my phone I must have forgotten to lock the car. Dear God, is there no end to my absentmindedness?* The speed and ease with which the killer had leveled LB and Robin was bone chilling. But what finally ignited the synapses in Beth's brain, jumpstarting her muscles, was the face. Her drawing had accurately depicted the features of the stranger Bo identified as Judge Alex Stillwell, but no human hand could have captured the unadulterated evil emanating from the face and eyes now directed up at her. Beth Callahan experienced the misfortune of apparent doom that the lone, helpless yearling, separated from the flock, must see in the eyes of the wolf closing in to sink its fangs just before spraying blood and ripping flesh.

No, I will not be helpless. Propelled by the most primordial instinct of all creatures—survival—Beth dashed out of the room, not delaying to dress, clenching only her coat. She could hear the echo of feet falling apace on the stairs as she sprinted across the hall, and into her parents' room. In the nanosecond it took her to reach the sliding-glass door, the monster was hurling his body against the wood door at the top of the stairs.

Fully aware that every second was crucial, Beth did not hesitate on the balcony. There were no stairs; nonetheless, pausing only momentarily to pull on her coat, she hoisted herself onto the railing, straddling it as she would a horse. Leaning forward, and gripping the banister, Beth shifted her weight until her right foot found purchase on the decking, and brought her left leg over. In a single fluid motion, she released her grip on the rail and pushed backward with her legs, letting herself drop. Ten feet below, Beth tumbled in pain over the ground. It was anything but a manicured lawn of soft grass. Momentarily dazed, she forced a quick inventory of body parts:—cuts and scrapes on her naked forearms, thighs, and hips. Although they stung like a son-of-a-bitch, they appeared to be superficial. Nothing felt broken, but she wasn't sure if she had sprained an ankle. As she got to her feet, her head was pounding, but her legs held her weight.

No, by God, I will not be a victim. I am a survivor, and I will *survive.* The splintering of wood, as the front door crashed open, sent Beth darting under the house. While she listened, hunkered behind the nearest creosote pole, she spotted a gaff hanging on a nail. Determining from the footsteps above that Stillwell was still hunting for her in the house, she yanked down the gaff and scurried toward the marsh.

It was nearly impossible to see in the pea soup, but there was a path, through a stand of Marsh-hay cordgrass, that led to the boats. Beth's knowledge of its location was one advantage she possessed over her pursuer. She knew, or at least prayed, he would have a difficult time finding the narrow pathway in the haze. Even for Beth however, taking advantage of the escape route was not easily done, for it was not a walkway of fine, pristine, soft, white sand; instead, it was a foot-worn trail of coarse black sand and dirt, infused with burs and small, sharp rocks, which sliced into Beth's bare feet.

Two boats were beached right where she hoped they would be, turned upside down and covered with tarps. One was an aluminum john-boat, and the other was the fourteen-foot fiberglass pirogue Beth's father had given her years ago. She hadn't had time to hunt for the kayak paddles under the house, and the handle of the gaff she had snatched was much too short to pole herself across the water, so sailing away was not an option. But Stillwell didn't know that.

Beth jerked the tarp off the pirogue, the lighter of the two craft, and rolled it up. Next, she raised the pirogue on its side until it teetered and dropped on its bottom. Because of the low freeboards, it didn't require much effort for Beth to heave the rolled-up tarp into the boat. Standing at the rear, she tugged at the roll until the top half was elevated at a forty-five degree angle and resting against the stern, and the other half was laying flat on the inside bottom.

The marsh was shallow, which was the very reason flat-bottomed pirogues still maintained their popularity with many Southeast Louisiana fishermen. And after shoving hers into the water, Beth walked it farther and farther away from shore, until she detected rustling in the cordgrass. Wading back to shore as expeditiously as possible, yet careful not to splash, Beth retrieved the gaff from the ground and turned to see that the ruse just might work. In the foggy night, the son-of-a-bitch may very well mistake the shape of the rolled tarp as her silhouette. If convinced she had escaped, he might leave. Still hearing movement, Beth hid in the tall grass. She selected a spot near the trail, afraid that if she ventured too far into the vegetation, she would spook any deer that might be bedded down and give away her position.

Crouching low, Beth strained her ears to differentiate the sound of her pursuer from nature's symphony of insects and other creatures of the marsh; relieved that what she was listening for, was now fading. The monster was moving away from her, but he could reverse course at any moment. Beth used the respite to ease her phone from her jacket. It might very well be her lifeline, and she had been careful not to walk the boat so far out as to risk getting the phone wet. As Beth shivered in the cold, goose bumps rising on her wet skin, causing it to take on the appearance of a plucked chicken, she typed her message and pushed the "Send" button. *God Bo, wherever you are, please come for me.*

CHAPTER 67

Rapidly spinning tires kicked up shell macadam on the Sweetwater Marina parking lot, as Bo Landry jerked the Pathfinder's steering wheel hard to the left, and stomped the accelerator to the floorboard, summonsing all the power the V8 possessed. He had followed Beth Callahan's directions in going there, intending to turn around in a less conspicuous fashion, and meandering back up the highway in search of the Callahan turnoff. Bo had stopped, and with the engine idling, was re-reading Beth's instructions for finding it when her text message came through: "He's here, call 911 4 me!"

The Pathfinder fishtailed away from the marina, straightened on the highway, and zoomed past houses and trailers on the right, not slowing until past the last residential outline Bo could make out. His headlight beams, diffused by the fog, soon spread over oyster shells abutting concrete. Bo quickly shut off his car lights, eased down driveway, and killed the engine. Nictating lights filtered through the dark abyss, flickering like candles in the wake of shifting vapors, but far beyond the neighboring structures. This has to be it, Bo reasoned. And with that determination, his training and instincts as a Navy Seal took over.

The primary objective of his mission was of course, to save Beth - and by whatever means were necessary. That she had been able to send a message did not mean that she had not since fallen into Stillwell's clutches. Bo knew his adversary's modus operandi was to take his leisure, prolonging the thrill methodically and deliberately. Although seemingly callous to allow a second of such diabolical perversity, Bo feared that charging onto such a scene, like a knight mounted on a white steed, would prompt the sick bastard to hasten the kill. Convinced that was exactly what the police would do, Bo quietly said aloud to no one,

"Fuck 911. You're mine, asshole."

Bo reached under his seat for the military-issued, black sheath-knife he kept there. Before coming to New Orleans, he had mended some wiring under the hood, and hoped the roll of electrical tape he used was still in the glove box. It was, and Bo laid it on the passenger seat with the knife, replacing it with his watch and ring. *Expose nothing which glitters.* As an afterthought, he tossed his cell phone in the glove box with the jewelry; the last thing he needed was for it to sound off or vibrate.

Bo pulled the keys from the ignition, and scooped up the knife and tape. With a slight creak, he eased the door ajar, just enough to press a finger on the button controlling the interior lights. Keeping the finger in place and the lights off, he stepped outside and listened, picking up the rhythm of the undulating cacophony of insects and frogs. Utilizing the next crescendo to mute the noise, Bo gently pushed the door shut. *Take advantage of natural sounds to cover your movements.*

After securing the straps of the knife sheath around his right calf, Bo soundlessly cut off several small pieces of the black tape and wrapped them around his belt buckle to keep it from reflecting any light. With plenty of tape left, he wound the roll around the sheath and his leg a few times for good measure. Slicing off the spool, he stuffed it inside a back pocket of his jeans. Taking in the immediate surroundings, Bo noted the mangroves, up to three feet in height, blanketing both sides of the driveway. They would provide adequate cover for his approach, and also prevent Stillwell from escaping by driving around the Pathfinder.

Under the cover of fog and shrubs, Bo crept along the drive, praying he was not too late, and dreading what horror might lie ahead. Of the possible scenarios playing out in his head, he was not expecting the confounding sight of two people crawling in circles, on hands and knees. Visibility was poor in the haze, and Bo couldn't make out their faces; but the hatchback door of Beth's Outback was raised up, and the vehicle's interior lights, coupled with the floodlights on the house, emitted sufficient illumination for Bo to identify the second vehicle—LB Harper's BMW.

Bo wormed along the ground until he was behind the first creeping figure. Robin Harper didn't hear a thing until a hand firmly covered her mouth. In spasmodic terror, she clawed at the hand until she heard murmuring in her ear, "It's Bo, Robin. Don't move or say anything. Nod if you understand and I'll drop my hand." Once her head bobbed, Bo gently twisted her head so she could see his face. When he saw the fear ebb from her eyes, he too, nodded and removed his hand, letting a finger linger on her lips as a sign for her to maintain silence. Leaning to her ear, he whispered that he wanted her to lie face down on the ground until he returned with LB.

By the time Bo got to him, LB had located his rifle. With Bo leading the way, the two men bellied their way to Robin, and onto the driveway. There, the three rose to stooping positions. Crouching below the tops of the mangroves, they made their way to Bo's vehicle. Through whispers and gestures, Bo learned that Stillwell was somewhere behind the house. Hearing him thrashing about in the tall grass, LB and Robin had groped around, hoping to find the rifle. Bo unlocked his car and handed the keys to LB, who vehemently shook his head, conveying the clear message that he and his wife were not going anywhere.

"Then lock yourselves in here," Bo instructed. "If he runs down the road, take him out immediately. If a car comes down the road, it will be Beth's, but you won't be able to see who's driving because of the headlights in your eyes. I'm not leaving without Beth. So if those lights don't flash three times, shoot like hell." Once LB nodded his acquiescence, Bo hurried off.

Hidden beneath the house, Bo saw what LB had heard—Stillwell was flailing away at a stand of tall marsh grass beyond the backyard with what looked to be a boat oar, periodically stopping to look back toward the house. It was evident that he believed Beth was in the vicinity, but had not yet found her. There was no guarantee, however, that Stillwell wouldn't stumble upon her by the time Bo rushed at him from the house. If that happened, the son-of-a-bitch could cut her throat, or take her hostage before Bo could get to him. Besides, Stillwell appeared to be on the alert for someone—probably LB—to make a move on him from the house.

No, Bo determined, it would be better to take out Stillwell from the other side of the grass he was searching. Bo might even be able, with some luck, to find Beth first and whisk her away; or at least, put himself between her and the killer.

Among the clutter that Bo carefully tiptoed around in his retreat, was a small anchor. Bo knelt to examine the texture and diameter of the attached rope. *Three-quarter-inch nylon.* It would be too cumbersome to carry the entire length. So after freeing the end tied to the anchor, Bo held his arms wide, measuring off a wingspan's worth. After severing the section, he tied it around his waist, covering the bright-yellow cordage with his sweater, and disappeared into the mangroves. Creeping and crawling, frequently stopping to listen, he could still hear movement in the grass coming from his distant right.

Among the legions of creatures habituating the marshes and swamps of Louisiana is the black-crowned night heron. As its name implies, it is a nocturnal hunter, and one that had been stalking some frog or crawfish, expressed its irritation at the unwelcome creature invading its territory with a harsh, barking *quawk!* Stillwell, however, did not seem to be alarmed. His search neither halted nor became more frenzied. Although the bird's call was brusque, there was a certain tempo to the barking, and Bo used it to time his movements through the vegetation.

Eventually the mangroves yielded to chest-high grass, and farther on to an expanse of water. Moving apace up the shore, Bo happened upon the charred dregs of a fire-site. At a glance, Bo could make out blackened tin cans, glass bottles, and other noncombustible debris. Looking to his right, away from the water, he saw the shadowy outline of a darkened structure. Determining that he had worked his way directly behind the property adjoining the illuminated Callahan lodge, and that he had come upon the place where the neighbors apparently burned their trash, Bo took a knee. *One man's trash...*

Drawing his knife, Bo poked the blade into the ashes, stirring and probing for anything useful. Lying on the perimeter was the remnant of an inner tube. Bringing it to his hand with the point of the knife, he rolled the rubber between his fingers. Although it had escaped total consumption by the flames, Bo could feel rough squares, cracked by the heat. Nonetheless, when Bo pulled on it, he discovered that it still maintained some elasticity and should provide the five bands he needed if reinforced with the black tape in his pocket. *Make use of all available cover, and attempt to blend with the background as much as possible.*

Bo untied the rope from his waist, and hastily went to work. Just as the last of the grass he cut was in place, the mock-mollifying tone of a man's voice pierced the heavy, cold air, "Olly olly oxen free!"

Bo raked his fingers through the ashes, and smeared them over his face, ears, neck, and hands. He also toned down the rope's hue by drawing it through a fistful of cinders. Once fashioning it in the desired configuration, he was ready. *Whenever taking down a sentry, get as close as possible before attacking, ideally within six feet. Then kill swiftly and silently.*

CHAPTER 68

Clothed only in a T-shirt and jacket, Beth Callahan laid in the grass, curled in a fetal ball, waiting for God-knows-what. The mangled soles of her bare feet stung, and the soreness in her hips and legs were aching seeds of the ugly crop of black and blue fruit that would surely spring forth. The rough, spindly grass bit into a plethora of scratches, and she trembled in the cold darkness—in fear, despair, and soaking wet.

Under such circumstances, Beth thought it odd that something she had read in school by a 17th century French author, would pop into her head: "There are men of whom we can never believe evil without having seen it; yet there are few in whom we should be surprised to see it." *Francois de La Rochefoucauld; that was the guy's name. Funny how the mind works. Focus, Beth, focus; for the face of evil is approaching, its tongue beckoning.*

"Come on out, Beth. It's playtime!"

Peeking from her hiding place, Beth saw Stillwell's form, backlit by the cabin's lights which he must have turned on while looking for her. He had discovered the trail, and was swinging a boat paddle from side to side, whipping the grassy flanks as he advanced. Jumping up and running would unquestionably disclose her presence. And in her condition, Beth doubted she would get very far. However, she couldn't just lie there. It would only be a matter of seconds before the predator was on her. There was no escape. Beth's fingers instinctively constricted around the gaff's handle, gripping it tighter in tactile remembrance that all any cornered prey could do was to turn and fight.

Near and nearer the beast drew. But when he was only a foot or so away, and Beth was about to leap in a desperate, last-ditch counterattack, the arm wielding the oar lowered. His gaze was no longer fixed downward into the vegetation, but instead directly ahead. Beth dared not breathe, much less move, seeing that the bottoms of his legs were within her arms' reach. The hunter and the hunted were both at the trail's end, and the beast was staring over the marsh. *The pirogue! Maybe he sees it and thinks I got away. If I just stay still, maybe he'll leave.*

The seconds that ticked away seemed like eons, yet Alex Stillwell remained in a rigid stance. *Why doesn't he go away?* Shattering Beth's puzzlement like a battering ram was the scratching sound of the pirogue bottom striking shore. *Oh no, the wind shifted!*

Suddenly Stillwell pivoted, and yelled toward the house, "Bitch, you dare toy with me!" *He thinks I doubled back to the cabin. When he gets there, I'll move down the shore and wake up one of the neighbors.* That hope, however, was dashed almost as soon as it arose. As the beast took a few steps past Beth, a shrill beep resonated from her jacket pocket.

Little did Beth know that all of her messages from Bo that night, from the time she started her car, had been grossly delayed, indefinitely suspended somewhere between relay towers, satellites or wherever the hell they traveled; and she was just now receiving the one he had sent after leaving the Harpers at his apartment. The very instrument Beth had counted on as her lifeline had betrayed her - but the offending device also swept away any indecision.

Stillwell was quick, but Beth was quicker. He had barely begun to turn when Beth, fueled by high-octane adrenaline blended with outrage, enmity, and fury, vaulted from her refuge, raising the gaff aloft in a high arc, and viciously buried its barb into the back of his right shoulder. It struck at the confluence of the trapezius and deltoid; the ensuing blood and feral bellow confirmation that the hook hung from meat, not mere fabric.

As her pursuer contorted, Beth lurched past him toward the cabin. Even in the throes of agony, however, Stillwell had not dropped the oar, which he ferociously swung with his left arm, clipping the back of Beth's head. Although a glancing blow, the force was sufficient to knock Beth to the ground, momentarily stunned. Before she could scramble to her feet, she heard him roar again, and felt fingers entangle her hair, unmercifully jerking backward.

The gaff hovered above, dripping blood, his foul fluid, onto Beth's face. Stillwell leaned in so close that she could feel his breath as he spoke, "So you want to play hooky, huh?"

CHAPTER 69

He needed him alive—at least until he got some answers. *Come on, you bastard, only a few more feet.* Alex Stillwell was standing straight ahead of him, on the shore at the edge of the cordgrass. Each time Bo Landry inched forward the irate heron kicked up a ruckus. An unmanned boat drifted to shore and, for some reason, it pissed Stillwell off - he let out a yell, and disappeared into the grass. Focused with laser intensity on the man, Bo was oblivious that Beth Callahan lie huddled in the vegetation. That is, until the stillness was shattered by the blaring of an electronic peal, instantaneously followed by a howl of fury.

Rushing in the direction of the uproar, Bo found a trail, and in the wake of the commotion, was able to scamper across larger distances before pausing. His blood was already boiling, and it taxed his willpower to refrain from launching into an all-out sprint when Stillwell grabbed Beth by her hair. But the bastard was right where Bo wanted him—back turned and concentrating on his captive. *Hold on a few more seconds, Beth.*

Each time Beth tried to get to her feet, the son-of-a-bitch shoved her head back down and pulled, forcing her to crawl behind him like a dog. They were almost at the end of the path, about to come out of the grass and enter the open backyard, when a glint under the house caught Bo's trained eye. *Shit!*

Stillwell noticed it too, yanking Beth up and whipping an arm around her throat. "Drop it, LB! Or I'll snap her neck like a chicken's!"

Bo estimated that he was still eight feet away, but he couldn't wait any longer. *Now!* The instant the noose went over Stillwell's head, Bo gave him a hard kick behind a knee, knocking him off balance. With his left hand pressed firmly against the back of Stillwell's head and his arm stiff, Bo yanked the loose end of the rope, tightening the noose under the chin. Unconsciousness would come in seconds, death soon thereafter. Only when Beth tumbled out of her captor's grip, and onto the ground, did the relentless constriction abate.

The Harpers were running up as Bo lowered Stillwell's body; LB armed with his rifle, Robin with her phone. When she started punching in numbers, Bo told her to abort the call. "I'm calling 911," she replied.

"I know who you're calling. Hang up."

"Are you fucking cr...."

"Not until I get some answers from this bastard," Bo explained. "He's not dead and once in custody, he's likely to lawyer-up."

Hesitating, Robin looked at her husband for guidance. When LB nodded she stowed the phone, and took Bo's suggestion that she help Beth inside where she could get cleaned up, dressed, and warm. Once the women were gone, Bo gave an appraising look at his friend who had not yet spoken. "You okay, LB?" Again the man only nodded. "Then say something, for crying out loud."

"That was the second shot of mine you fucked up tonight," LB replied, his face devoid of any expression, and referring to his earlier interrupted game of pool.

"Yeah, I'd say you're okay."

"What about him?" LB asked, pointing his rifle at Stillwell.

"Like I said, he's not dead, just out. He should be coming to anytime now."

"It's colder than a well-digger's ass out here. Can't you get your answers inside?"

"If you can get his legs."

LB laid his gun down, and grabbed Stillwell by the ankles. Bo bent to slide his arms under the armpits, and the man's eyes flickered. As Stillwell's vision slowly defogged, he took in the blurred, upside-down visage looking down at him. Al Jolson in blackface was his first thought, but then the vertical grass stems encircling the head, swaying in the breeze, seemed out of place. *No vaudeville act I've ever seen.* The countenance briefly vanished, only to appear, right-side-up, with the rest of the body. The same type of grass as around the head was fastened about the upper arms and knees. *I must be having a helluva dream.* However, at his first attempt to push himself up, he heard a familiar voice, "Get up, asshole—slowly."

Judge Alex Stillwell raised his upper body, sitting for a moment, before trying to stand, and erupted in laughter when he recognized Bo Landry as the tribal chieftain of his hallucinations. "Well, just call me Bwana!" he said to Bo; and to LB, "Dr. Livingston, I presume?"

CHAPTER 70

Any notion of Bo's that Alex Stillwell would clam up was quickly dispelled. Bound with rope and duct tape to a straight-back chair in the den of the Callahan fishing lodge, the beast relished telling all to Bo and LB. Beth and Robin were holed up in the master bedroom.

Bo's questions selfishly zeroed in on the evidence that had put him on the hook for Cindy Babineaux's murder, beginning with his pubic hair. "You really should clean your toilet more often, Bo," Stillwell advised.

"My toilet?"

"LB graciously offered me the key to your apartment to leave the closing papers for the house."

"Yeah, but...."

"While I was there I had to go to the bathroom. When I looked down, there it was on the rim. Well, I couldn't pass up such a gift, now could I? So I helped myself to a sandwich bag I found in the cabinet under the kitchen sink. I thought it might come in handy. When I was done with Sweet Cindy, I placed the hair on her. As your calling card, so to speak."

"Jeez, Alex," LB said.

"What about the gun you killed her with?" Bo wanted to know.

"And the wuss on Conti - don't forget about him," Stillwell pointed out.

"How'd you get Murphy's gun, Alex?" Bo persisted.

"After my, uh, *rendezvous* with Serena, I went to his place to plant the blade. It was a nice touch, if I say so myself, slipping it into that Shakespeare book. 'Unsex me now!' That was pure genius. That's what I did to her, you know."

"Is he talking about Sam's daughter?" LB asked, shifting his attention from Stillwell to Bo, noticing him tense.

287

Bo Landry had killed—in the military and on the police force. That it was necessary and in the line of duty, offered little solace. He vividly remembered every one because their restless spirits wouldn't allow him to forget. Now however, looking at Alex Stillwell's smug face and listening to his mocking words, Bo was consumed with a lust that he didn't believe could be sated by anything less than the beast being drawn and quartered.

"Easy, big guy," LB urged, a firm hand on Bo's shoulder. "We're trying to get you off a murder rap, not pick up another one."

Bo nodded, and in a few seconds his muscles began unknotting. Only then did LB remove his hand. "You still haven't told me about the gun," Bo continued.

"I found it in the drawer of Murphy's bedside table. The one the Bible was on."

"Where the switchblade was stashed?"

"Right."

Officer Melvin Spann was doomed only because he was in the wrong place at the wrong time. Alex Stillwell had carefully avoided getting any of Serena's blood on himself, but Spann's was all over the judge's coat. Inside Todd Murphy's house, Stillwell appropriated a sweatshirt he found in a bureau. Although a snug fit on Stillwell's muscular frame, it sufficed. He put his bloody coat in a garbage bag, burning it later.

"But why kill any of them, Alex?" LB asked. "My God, you had everything."

"For the same reason federal judges do anything—because I can." Without further prompting, he proudly related, in detail, the slayings of Mandi Charbonnet and Bud Ritchie.

"Well, you slipped up when you used the same M.O. on Cindy Babineaux and Serena," Bo pointed out.

"Do you think my little surgery on those two was the result of some brain fart?" Stillwell scoffed. "Give me more credit than that. I was always careful to vary the M.O. as well as the means. It was a game, a challenge. Do you believe I picked Murphy's Bible at random to stow the knife? Such bourgeois thinking. It is the glory of whom, Bo, to conceal things? Come on, think; Proverbs 25:2."

"What the hell is he talking about?" LB asked.

"God. It is the glory of God to conceal." Bo answered.

"Bravo! I would give you a round of applause, but you have only yourself to blame for the deprivation of that accolade," Stillwell said, looking at his bindings. "LB, kings seek out what God conceals. I am God, and I threw down the challenge for would-be kings to find what I chose to conceal. But they're not kings, only mere pretenders."

"He's insane," LB told Bo.

"Yeah, I think we're done here," Bo agreed.

"Done?" Stillwell asked. "You haven't asked me about Tom."

"Tom?" Bo was puzzled. Jim Blackwell had killed Tom Davis while Bo slept. Blackwell had even killed himself after being indicted. "You killed Tom?"

"It's not *always* about poontang, Bo. He pissed me off."

Bo and LB listened as Alex Stillwell recounted how he had approached George Bishop, Mississippi's junior United States Senator, to snag the federal district court appointment. Bishop informed Stillwell that Bob Devereaux, the senior senator, had already decided to submit Tom Davis's name to the President for the open judgeship. Craving a higher position of power, the protégé set his sights on eliminating the mentor.

Stillwell first attempted to do so by staging a fatal accident. When Davis asked Stillwell to join him for cocktails at the Walthall lounge, Stillwell went prepared. After Tom announced that the Chivas Regal just delivered to their table would be his last for the evening, he had excused himself to the restroom, and Stillwell seized the opportunity to spike the drink with a touch of a hallucinogen. Stillwell didn't know if Davis could taste anything amiss. In any event though, Davis drank very little after returning to the table. As a result, rather than dying in a traffic accident on his way home, as Stillwell had hoped, Davis didn't start hallucinating until after arriving at the Raymond courthouse, ultimately tumbling down the stairs.

"I was so, so pissed to hear his voice on the phone the next morning," Stillwell said. He told Bo and LB about Tom Davis asking him to bring Tom's laptop to the house. While there, considering some other way to kill Tom and make it appear accidental, Jim Blackwell had stormed inside, irate over losing his job. He had even threatened Tom. Little did Blackwell know, as he complied with Tom's request, handing him the letter opener, that he was sealing his fate as well as Tom's. Stillwell considered his problem solved: he need not make Tom's murder look like an accident, he'd simply manipulate it in such a way that Jim Blackwell took the fall for it.

"But the place was surrounded by deputies," Bo observed. "How'd you get past them?"

Stillwell smirked. "Serena helped me with that," he said. "She came to the courthouse in Jackson, looking for Tom. His administrator had told Serena he was working at home, but that I would be going to see him. She had a package she wanted to get to him ASAP, and asked if I'd take it with me. Of course, as soon as she left my chambers, I opened it to see what was so urgent. It was only a letter from her father, and an article from the New Orleans newspaper, with excerpts from the diary of an ex-slave - one of Tom's ancestor's Uncle Toms, as it were.

"Anyway, the old darkie went on and on about Tom's forebear—also a judge by the way—entrusting him to whisk away the family jewels: the silver and the judge's granddaughter. Emma, I believe was her name. Word had come that federal marauders were close by."

"Dammit, Alex, I asked how you got by the deputies and into the house." Bo reminded him.

"The same way Uncle Remus got *out* past the Yankees: the tunnel."

"What tunnel? Deschamps mentioned one too."

"Yeah," Stillwell said, chuckling, "I planted that little seed. At any rate, there's a large, brick-lined shaft from Tom's house—correct that; *my* house—to the woods. It comes out near the Natchez Trace. You access it through a spring-activated door built into the back wall of the pantry." Wanting to twist the knife in Bo's heart a little more, Stillwell added, "If you had taken a little more interest in Tom, I'm sure he would have showed it to you. It didn't take much of an effort for me to get him to tell *me* all about it."

"You son-of-a-bitch."

"Easy, big guy," LB coaxed Bo.

"Yes, LB, it was rather easy," Stillwell said. "Tom gave me the grand tour; showed me how to enter both ends of the tunnel. After Bo arrived and I left, I pulled off the Trace and hiked into the woods to make sure I could find it. Some bald freakazoid, wearing a skintight onesie, was lurking around. You'll find his grave nearby."

Bo and LB exchanged glances, both wondering just how high the death toll had run, nauseated at the flippant manner their friend narrated executions.

"Of course, I didn't take time then to bury him. It wasn't until after I bought the property from you, Bo. I guess you see now the real reason I so willingly took it off your hands. All that wealth you have now. How does it feel to know it's blood money? You realize, don't you, that's why I had to do Serena? She was the only one who would know about the tunnel and might put two and two together. I wonder how her father is going to take the news that the package he sent her was her death warrant."

"Easy, big guy," LB urged again, anticipating Bo's reaction. "He's baiting you."

"That's right, Bo. You're very much like me. Give in to those primal urges." Bo glared, but said nothing and Stillwell continued. "So after I took care of Serena—*wow*, she really was a good piece, Bo. So good I just had to take a piece with me."

Determined not to give Stillwell the satisfaction of seeing any evidence of the hurt, Bo turned his back to his tormentor, and walked into the kitchen, seeing if there was anything to drink in the fridge to cool him off.

"Am I boring you, Bo?" Stillwell called out.

"Keep going, asshole!" Bo yelled back.

The bedroom door cracked open. "What's going on?" Robin asked.

"It's okay," her husband assured, gesturing for her to close the door.

"Where was I?" Stillwell asked. "Ah yes—Tom. After Serena and the cop, I drove back to take care of Judge Tom. I walked through the tunnel, into the pantry, and waited there until you were alone," he said to Bo, who was back in the den, holding a glass of water. "You opened a Diet Coke, set it on the kitchen counter, and went upstairs; I assumed to check on Tom. While you were away, I put a little GHB in your pop."

"What's that?" LB asked Bo.

"A date-rape drug," Bo answered; "which explains my weird behavior and lack of some memory the next morning."

"And completely tasteless and odorless," Stillwell added. "I slipped back inside the pantry to give it time to take effect. When it did, I put on some gloves, found the letter opener that I was sure had that clod Blackwell's prints on it, and went upstairs. You know the rest."

"Thank God, he at least went in his sleep," LB muttered.

"Oh, no," Stillwell said. "Once I had the point of the opener at his throat, I kept whispering his name until he opened his eyes. I asked him the same thing I asked Serena, 'How does it feel to know you are going to die?' Before he could move or say anything, though, I gave it a good plunge. Very messy."

"Well, you're done for now, you sick motherfucker," Bo declared.

"That's right, it's over," LB agreed, "and we saved Beth."

"And Robin," Stillwell added. "Don't forget your wife, LB."

"Robin?" LB asked.

"Sure. She was next on my list."

"Why Robin? She didn't know anything."

"True, but it's not what she knows; it's what she *has*; what lies between her thighs. What can I say? I am what I am. Tell me though, LB, is that auburn hair natural? I was so looking forward to making that thing *shout!* You know, gashing the gash."

Before Bo could blink, the sound of bone crunching filled the room, as LB rammed the butt of his rifle into Stillwell's face. Bo looked at his friend, still standing over Stillwell, shaking in rage, contemplating whether to strike again. "What happened to all that 'Easy, big guy' shit?"

Bo asked him.

"I just can't abide a fucking filthy mouth," LB replied.

"It's time to call Deschamps," Bo told LB. "His number is in my phone. Why don't you take a walk to my car and get it?"

Although relieved of several teeth and spitting blood, Judge Alex Stillwell continued to ramble on while LB was gone. When LB returned and handed Bo the phone, Bo saw that he had a text message. It was from Lieutenant Deschamps: "Test run. Confirmed what I already knew. A.S. is not killer."

Bo shoved it at LB, saying, "You call him, I'm going in there to see about the girls."

"Girls?" Stillwell said. "Let me tell you about the entire suite of sweet-sixteens I once enjoyed."

As the bedroom door was closing behind Bo, he again heard the whack of the rifle butt, while LB mumbled, "Dirty-mouthed bastard."

EPILOGUE
SUNDAY, AUGUST 29, 2010

While a cliché, there's a lot of truth in saying the darkest hour is that before the dawn. Bo Landry, Beth Callahan, and all of New Orleans had weathered the storm of evil that struck six months earlier. Except from a distance, Bo had not seen Beth during that time of emotional recuperation. Like grief, the aftermath of near-death experiences is processed and dealt with in innumerable, diverse ways and steps.

Bo lost himself in work. Satisfied that no one associated with Paradise Isle was involved in any kind of foul play with respect to the fire, the insurance company had confirmed coverage and the renovation was well underway. Knowing Gary Borden to be an avid duck hunter, Bo presented him with a top-of-the-line Browning over-and-under in appreciation for the crash course Gary had given Bo on arson, and the substantial fee that came with the favorable outcome.

Thus far, Jamie Applewhite had not sued The Box Score, nor was there any indication that doing so had even crossed his—or her—mind for the pummeling suffered by the lamé footwear wielded by Frank Johnson. As long as Applewhite continued to grace the place in chiffon, satin, and taffeta, it was Bo's belief, which he shared with Dimitri Dixon, the manager, that broaching the subject with Applewhite might only give him ideas of taking a chance in a lawsuit lottery.

Beth, however, had withdrawn. Not from life, but specifically from Bo. She initially made excuses whenever he called or pushed the intercom button at her gate. Eventually though, she ran out of alibis, and told him she needed time and space. Bo took it as a nice way of saying that she associated him with the horrible slaying of her best friend, and her own near similar fate. Nevertheless, Bo still called periodically, asking how she was faring, and if she had resumed painting. For the longest time, such communications were brief and tepid. Beth would say she was okay and painting again, but never elaborating, and Bo did not press her. Over the past couple of weeks however, their calls lasted longer, and seemed to him like actual conversations.

This day marked the fifth anniversary of Katrina, one of the five deadliest hurricanes in the annals of the United States, and the costliest in Louisiana history. The disaster, revisited by the media and politicians, was even the cornerstone of Monsignor Ambrose's sermon that morning. The priest had phoned Beth, beseeching her attendance; he would have a place near the front reserved for her. Beth was a member of the congregation, and felt the special attention unnecessary; but how did one decline an invitation from a man as kind and caring as Monsignor Ambrose? After Beth acquiesced, Ambrose made a similar call to Bo. Separately ushered to their assigned seats, and finding that they were beside each other, all they could do was smile at the wily ruse.

When church let out, Bo was pleased Beth had accepted an invitation to accompany him to the wharf where LB and Robin Harper were scheduled to disembark from their cruise ship. LB's anecdotes of the excursion kept them in stitches during the drive to the Harper home. Although Bo and Beth made several attempts to leave the voyagers to their unpacking and getting resettled, the Harpers would not hear of it.

The afternoon lapsed with stories swapped over cheese and crackers, wine and Diet Coke. Ultimately, inevitably, the pool tables beckoned, and LB urged everyone to reconvene at McCormick's. Bo and Beth politely declined, and strolled down St. Ann toward the river.

They were on The Moonwalk, ambling along the river, the descending sun shooting streaks of red through the strata of clouds, and purple across the dark water. It had been a good day for both of them, and now communication succumbed to introspection.

"God comes at last when we think He is farthest off," Bo recalled their priest-friend say during his homily earlier. Something Beth had said a half-year ago also came to mind. It was during their walk from Coop's Place to the apartment on Burgundy, as they passed the old convent on Ursulines: just because we don't understand God's plan for us does not mean that He doesn't have one. As Bo's father once told him, "God is no botcher." Maybe his dad and Beth had been right; that there is a certain divine balance to the world. Bo didn't need to be convinced that it was full of evil, which logically meant that it was also endowed with goodness. And no man better recognizes goodness than he who has endured evil.

Bo's thoughts rewound to Alex Stillwell, incarcerated and awaiting trial for multiple murders; to the killer's braggadocio which only Bo heard while LB walked to the car for Bo's phone. It was hardly over, Stillwell had told Bo; his legacy, his progeny, would live on. "There are many others just like me," Stillwell said. "They will know of me, read of me, and learn from me, as I did from the masters who preceded me. Why do you think I told you everything, and intend to tell all to Deschamps? You can't stop us. We're at every socio-economic level. When you luck out and snare one, his story, his fame, gives birth to legions. So it is you, the self-righteous, who are actually caught in a classic catch-22. Do you let us roam at will, or nab one and exponentially increase our number?"

That those pronouncements were probably true was a sobering thought. Monsignor Ambrose had reminded the worshippers of King Solomon's observation that there is nothing new under the sun; that Katrina was not the first natural disaster, yet the human race endured, life went on. Bo thought the same could also be said of evil and murder: they've afflicted mankind since the age of Genesis, and would continue on ad infinitum, just as Alex Stillwell said.

But reading from Song of Solomon, Ambrose had assured everyone that love is as strong as death; its passion as fierce as the grave; its flames no flood can drown. It bears all things, believes all things, and endures all things. "Therefore," the priest exhorted from a passage in Hosea, "hold fast to love and justice, and wait continually for God." No one knows when anything will end, as all things inevitably must. Thus we are to live one day at a time, wringing for ourselves and bringing to others, all the joy we can as if it were our last.

Bo remembered the first time he had made this same walk along the river, contemplating how times change, and us with them. It had been less than two years, but he felt a very different person than the confused, lonely, heartbroken drunk he was then. Bo wanted to believe everything Beth and Monsignor Ambrose said. "A man without religion is like a horse without a bridle," his father once admonished. Perhaps Bo had, deep down, always believed, but allowed life's repeated miseries to clog the pipeline. While Oliver Cromwell's troops crossed a river in preparation for battle, he was reputed to have advised them, "Put your trust in God, but keep your powder dry." Bo had always been pragmatic, down-to-earth; and he was beginning to understand that putting faith in God doesn't prevent one from being practical. Maybe it was time to dissolve the clog with a little trust. What could it hurt as long as he remained vigilant and kept his powder dry?

Bo still had regrets, and supposed he always would. As far as he was concerned, he had failed Serena and Tom. It was too late, however, to call back yesterday. The game we call life is unlike tennis where we get a second serve when we hit the net. That's what had scared him about nurturing another relationship; he didn't wish to screw up yet another person's life, if not see them buried. It seemed that everyone and everything he held dear prematurely died. An aura of death had encircled him.

But when Bo had gone to McCormick's the previous November to make amends with Sam Raven, Sam told him that Serena didn't blame him; that life was for the living, and she wanted him to have a life, not a mere existence. To have a life means strife, and Bo had come to believe it better to endure strife than solitude. He couldn't quite put his finger on his emotions regarding the remarkable woman at his side. It was too early in their friendship for him to use the "L" word; but there was something about her that stirred a feeling that had lain dormant. Beth Callahan made him care, believe, and hope; and Bo liked how that felt. Whether it was or ever would be mutual, he didn't know; but he was anxious to see where things might go. Bo might have his heart broken yet again, but he was determined to live. And where there's life there's hope. Were it not for hope, all of us would be doomed to heartbreak.

Resolving to take a chance, Bo remained quiet, but took Beth's hand in his as they continued on, encouraged by her gentle, brief squeeze as if she were saying, "Me, too." He was not aware that, unlike him, she already knew where their relationship would lead; that it was vividly portrayed in her last painting, which she kept hidden away at home. In a way, it was comforting, but it also scared her. It had taken time to sort through her emotions and consider the appropriate response. Beth was afraid to let Bo know, lest he bolt. Besides, she knew only the destination, and was anxiously anticipating the thrill of the journey. Beth, however, could not conceal the letter written upon her heart, for such a missive is read in the eyes. And as Bo dared to look into Beth's sapphire orbs, he was moved by what he saw in them. "You know what, Landry?" Beth asked. "You still owe me a Turtle Bay pizza."

It was, indeed, a pleasurable time in the French Quarter. Spring had come and gone; summer too, was drawing to a close, autumn around the corner. But, as it's been said, in the land of hope there is never any winter.

ACKNOWLEDGEMENTS

Heartfelt thanks to my friends in Jackson and Raymond, Mississippi—there are none better anywhere—for their steadfast support during some tough times; also to my colleagues, friends, and other characters of New Orleans' French Quarter who make it such a unique place, particularly my buddies at Fahy's Irish Pub. If you are ever in the Big Easy, stop by there for a quaff, and tell them who sent you.

Book publishing is indeed a team effort, and I am very fortunate to have on my side the editing skills of Kate Stewart and her staff at ebookeditingservices.com, as well as the formatting services of ironhorseformatting.com. Much appreciation also to Brandi Doane McCann, ebook-coverdesigns.com for such an awesome cover.

As with everything else I've done, which might be considered worthwhile from the time I had the good sense to ask her to marry me, I owe the lion's share of thank-yous to my wife Peggy, to whom this, my first novel, is dedicated. Without her unwavering support, encouragement, and input, not to mention a wealth of forbearance, this endeavor would have never left the ground.

I own up to all errors. They are entirely mine.

Made in the USA
Coppell, TX
05 February 2022

72975876R00167